About the Author

Tricia Stringer is a bestselling and multiple award-winning author. Her books include *Table for Eight* and *The Family Inheritance*, and the rural romances *Queen of the Road*, *Right as Rain*, *Riverboat Point*, *Between the Vines*, *A Chance of Stormy Weather*, *Come Rain or Shine* and *Something in the Wine*. She has also published a historical saga; *Heart of the Country*, *Dust on the Horizon* and *Jewel in the North* are set in the unforgiving landscape of nineteenth-century Flinders Ranges. Tricia grew up on a farm in country South Australia and has spent most of her life in rural communities, as owner of a post office and bookshop, as a teacher and librarian, and now as a full-time writer. She lives in the beautiful Copper Coast region with her husband Daryl, travelling and exploring Australia's diverse communities and landscapes, and sharing her passion for the country and its people through her authentic stories and their vivid characters.

For further information go to triciastringer.com or connect with Tricia on Facebook, Instagram @triciastringerauthor or Twitter @tricia_stringer

Also by Tricia Stringer

Queen of the Road
Right as Rain
Riverboat Point
Between the Vines
A Chance of Stormy Weather
Come Rain or Shine
Something in the Wine

The Flinders Ranges Series
Heart of the Country
Dust on the Horizon
Jewel in the North

Table for Eight
The Family Inheritance

The Model Wife

TRICIA STRINGER

First Published 2019
Second Australian Paperback Edition 2021
ISBN 9781867207962

THE MODEL WIFE
© 2019 by Tricia Stringer
Australian Copyright 2019
New Zealand Copyright 2019

This is a work of fiction. Names, characters, places, and incidents are either the product of the author's imagination or are used fictitiously, and any resemblance to actual persons, living or dead, business establishments, events, or locales is entirely coincidental.

Published by
HQ Fiction
An imprint of Harlequin Enterprises (Australia) Pty Limited (ABN 47 001 180 918), a subsidiary of HarperCollins Publishers Australia Pty Limited (ABN 36 009 913 517)
Level 13, 201 Elizabeth St
SYDNEY NSW 2000
AUSTRALIA

® and TM (apart from those relating to FSC®) are trademarks of Harlequin Enterprises (Australia) Pty Limited or its corporate affiliates. Trademarks indicated with ® are registered in Australia, New Zealand and in other countries.

A catalogue record for this book is available from the National Library of Australia
www.librariesaustralia.nla.gov.au

Printed and bound in Australia by McPherson's Printing Group

For Alexandra

The Model Wife

by

Mrs Gladys Norman

London 1928

In my role as a surgeon's wife I have managed a busy household, raised three children and maintained a healthy happy marriage. I feel it my bounden duty to offer the benefit of my wisdom and experience for new brides here in the pages of this book.

One

Natalie King put her shoulder against the wooden door and shoved it open, then cringed at the shuddering bang it made against the solid wall. Another dent in the hundred-year-old plaster. Milt kept promising he'd install a new stopper, just like he'd promised to replace the window runners in the bedrooms and the warped kitchen door.

The warmer air inside was a relief from the chilly wind gusting across the dry paddocks. It was already late May but so far there'd been no rain of any significance. She kicked the door shut behind her and made her way along the scuffed wooden floor of the passage to the kitchen. In one hand she clutched a basket filled with exercise books and in the other a bag of shopping and her handbag. Both loads threatened to pull her arms from their sockets.

In the kitchen the old black-and-white cat rose from its position in front of the vestiges of a fire in the slow-combustion stove.

"What are you doing still inside, Bubbles?"

The cat stretched and blinked sleepy eyes at her.

Natalie's mobile began to ring. She dumped her basket and the bag of groceries on the big wooden table, clear except for a small vase of gerberas in the centre with a scrap of paper beside it, and dug in her bag for the phone.

"Hello."

"Mum, are you free to talk?"

Natalie held her breath. She knew the waver in her youngest daughter's voice well. "What's up, Laura?" She kept her own voice light.

"Nothing." The response was a little too happy; the pause too brief. "I just wanted to know if you were home over the weekend. I thought I'd come up."

"Of course. Your dad and I will be. I'm not sure what Bree's plans are. It'd be lovely to see you." Natalie allowed herself to relax. Perhaps no crisis after all. "Bringing anyone with you?" Laura's visits usually involved one, often two girlfriends; girls from the city who played at being farm girls as they fed animals and rode motorbikes.

"No, just me."

Natalie picked up the scrap of paper lying beside the flowers and realised it was a piece of an old envelope and on it was a scribbled list. *Landmark* was written in Milt's bold hand at the top. No doubt another job to add to her string of after-school duties tomorrow.

"Shall I cook lasagne?" she asked.

"Only if you want. I'll see you Thursday. Bye, Mum."

"Bye, darling." Natalie stared at the screen a moment. Laura's phone calls were usually half an hour long at least, full of the minutest details of her day. Perhaps she was tired. That might explain the off-note in her voice and her indifference to the offer of her favourite meal. Although now that she thought about it, Laura's phone calls had been fewer and shorter for a while and... Natalie tapped her finger against her lips trying to remember the last time her youngest had been home to the farm for a visit…her granny's birthday. That had been nearly two months ago.

Natalie flicked on the kettle and rolled up the blind. The late-afternoon sunlight streamed in from the side verandah, highlighting the golden honey glow of the solid pine cupboards as well as the crumbs and smudges on the worn laminex bench, left by whatever Milt and Bree had eaten for lunch. She turned away from the mess and back to the window, and looked out over her patch of brightly coloured gerberas and the hedge of rosemary, beyond the rusting wire fence and the barren outer yard towards the sheds. There'd been no dogs to greet her and Milt's ute wasn't anywhere to be seen as she'd driven in. He and Bree must still be off in a paddock somewhere.

Behind her the house phone rang. She strode across the kitchen to the desk in the corner and plucked the handset from the cradle.

"Hello, Natalie speaking."

"Terry Porter here from Landmark Agricultural Services. Is Milt available?"

Natalie took a breath. She'd known Terry for ten years and what Landmark was at least twice as long but he was always so formal on the phone. "Hello, Terry. Milt's not in yet. Can I help?"

"When will he be home?"

Natalie gritted her teeth and glanced at the clock. "Not for a few more hours, I expect."

"I've left a message on his mobile."

"He'll get it when he's back in range then. Do you want to leave a message with me?"

"Just get him to call me back. Thanks, Natalie." The line went dead.

Natalie shook her head as she replaced the handset. Terry always insisted on speaking to Milt and the two of them would play phone chasey for days. If only he trusted the woman of the house with a simple message it would save a lot of trouble. She wrote a note on the whiteboard on the wall beside the desk and busied herself putting away the groceries, turning her thoughts to what she might cook. Laura hadn't been home for such a long time. Natalie wanted to make some of her favourites.

Part way through wiping down the bench she paused. Laura had said *see you Thursday*. That was a day earlier than usual. She had a full-time job at a city hairdresser. Her long hours earned her the odd Friday afternoon and weekend off. The wavering note in Laura's voice replayed in her head but she pushed it away. If there was something wrong Natalie would find out all about it on Thursday. She fed the cat and stacked the small pile of mail, all envelopes with windows, between the vase and Milt's list. Then, with a cup of tea in hand, she settled at the kitchen table, her basket on the floor and the stack of exercise books in a pile beside her.

The table was a big one and yet they'd filled it. She glanced around, picturing her three girls sitting at the solid pine top doing their homework or playing cards, talking about their day, squabbling and laughing; Milt's mum, Olive, presiding over them as if she was mistress of the manor, while Natalie cooked dinner for them all and her father-in-law, Clem, with his slow nod and twinkling smile sat at the head of the table taking it all in.

Dear Clem. Perhaps that was why she was feeling a little melancholy. She'd realised when she'd looked at the calendar this morning that a year had gone by since he'd died. They'd had a special bond, not father and daughter but very good friends. She wondered if Milt remembered the date. Neither of them had said anything.

A year ago today Milt had been the one to find his father sitting on the side verandah in his old wicker chair, just resting his eyes, as he liked to say when he dozed off. Only this time his eyes were permanently closed, never to rest his kindly gaze on any of them again. Milt had been a rock for his mother, for all of them, but when they were in bed after the long days of dealing with the sorrow and the quagmire of paperwork, Natalie would hold him close while his silent tears washed his cheeks. They didn't talk about it, it wasn't Milt's way to talk openly about his feelings, but she knew he'd been hurting badly. She wondered if he still had the unexpected stabs of memory, the surge of loss that she did from time to time.

She pushed back from her chair, the exercise books unopened, and looked around her neat kitchen. She had a sudden urge to bake; even though her freezer was full of food ready for the extra mouths to be fed during lamb tailing she knew Laura would appreciate some fresh home-baked goodies.

Natalie went to the little desk in the corner of the kitchen and rummaged through her shelf of cookbooks. She had a mind to make a caramel shortbread slice. The recipe, a favourite of Laura's, was in a church ladies guild compilation crammed with old favourites.

When it wasn't among the cookbooks on the shelf above, she pulled open the drawer below. It came part way out then jammed. She tugged, to no avail, then reached in and felt something stuck at the back. Wiggling out one item at a time, she soon had a pile of well-thumbed school fundraisers and CWA cookbooks. At last the book at the back came free. Her heart skipped a beat as she stared at the little red book in her hand. How on earth had that got in this drawer?

She stared down at its faded cover, more maroon now than its former vibrant red. The title had been embossed into the leather and was almost rubbed off but Natalie knew what it said. *The*

Model Wife. The book had originally belonged to Milt's grand-mother who had passed it on to Olive as a young bride. Natalie remembered the first time she'd seen it. Olive had given it to her when she was pregnant with Kate. Natalie was still at the feeling nauseous stage and not full of the joy of expectant motherhood she'd observed in her friends. She had laughed when Olive had handed the book to her, thinking it was a joke to cheer her up – until she'd seen the serious look on her mother-in-law's face.

Now she sunk to the chair. One hand clutched the book and the other hovered over the cover. She felt the gnaw of anxiety in the pit of her stomach. Finding the book again was a bad omen, surely, if she believed in those things. She drew a breath, whipped it open and immediately she was back to the night she'd shown it to Milt.

They'd just hopped into bed. She'd hidden the book under the sheet and swept it out to show Milt as if she was letting a genie out of a bottle. Little did she know she was letting something out, but it wasn't a kind genie. She could still hear the laughter that had been in her voice.

"Look what your mother gave me today."

"An old book." Milt's tone was sceptical.

"It was your grandmother's."

He took it from her. "*The Model Wife.*" Then he looked at her with that rakish gleam in his eye that turned her insides to mush. "I've got one of those already."

"Look inside," she urged then rested her chin on his shoulder and cuddled against his naked back as they both read the writing on the flyleaf.

The top inscription was in fading brown ink. *For my daughter Charlotte on the occasion of her marriage to Thomas King with all my love Mother. October 1935.* Olive had told her Charlotte was Olive's mother-in-law who had come from England to marry Thomas

King, a man she hardly knew. Underneath was another neatly written message, in blue ink this time. *To Olive my new daughter-in-law with best wishes for a happy marriage from Charlotte. April 1957.* And then in black biro written in Olive's tidy cursive: *To Natalie, welcome to the family from Olive. July 1985.*

"I didn't know Mum had this." Milt traced his finger gently down the page. "I don't think I've ever seen it."

"It's meant for the women in the family."

"Why didn't she give it to Connie then?"

"She said it should go to the eldest and if the eldest was a boy then to his wife." Olive had explained that when Natalie had asked the same question. Natalie thought it was more about Olive thinking Connie already had all the makings of a model wife, qualities Natalie apparently lacked.

Milt turned to the contents page, glanced down then turned to the first chapter and roared with laughter.

"A Husband is Master."

"Yes, my lord," she said in a subservient voice and laughed too. She snuggled closer, enjoying the intimacy they only had alone at night. The quarters where they slept had originally been fully separate, but years earlier when the house roof had been replaced it had been extended to include the old quarters, which now connected via a door to the main passage. Even though it was basic Natalie had thought of it as her haven.

Milt and his father worked long hours on their property and she'd found it hard to get used to. Teaching filled her week but she was often home before Milt, even with the hour drive from town. When she got home she did her prep for the next day and then helped Olive prepare the evening meal. Not that she had to do much. It was usually meat and three veg followed by some kind of dessert, often fruit and ice cream.

"*The model wife loves her husband truly,*" Milt read on, "*and does not highlight his faults. She accepts her husband's demands and never criticises, argues or speaks disparagingly. The master of the house has the right to expect good health, good habits, and a sound knowledge of house-keeping in all of its phases from his wife who must provide for his every desire.*" He wriggled his eyebrows up and down then went on again. "*She shows affection, but never in public and is always attentive. If she is frigid she should not be in a hurry to inform her husband. To him it makes no difference in the pleasurableness of the act. Heed this advice. It has saved many women from trouble.*" He frowned at her. "Is this for real?"

"I guess it was in your grandmother's day."

"I think I'll like this book if chapter one is anything to go by." Milt's voice was low, his words rumbling through her thin nightie and to her skin.

She snuggled closer. "I thought you would." She truly did love Milt, truly, truly, more now than when they'd married three years earlier, and she thought she was doing a good job of providing for his every desire – up to a point. "I'm the model wife already," she chirped.

"I know." He kissed her cheek.

"But I'm not sure about every desire," she said, noting the spar-kle in his eye had turned roguish again.

He reached for a pen from the bedside table.

"What are you doing?" Natalie hissed as he underlined the heading. She glanced around, expecting Olive to appear through the door and reprimand them. "It's a family heirloom," she gasped as he wrote *YES* with lots of exclamation marks next to the head-ing for Chapter One.

"I'm giving it my endorsement." He laughed again then gently pulled her round in front of him, resting his hand on her belly.

"You weren't honestly planning on passing this on to our children, I hope."

"No, but…well, it's an antique."

"One that stops with us," he said and started to nibble at her neck.

She responded and they were soon fully entangled in each other's arms, his lips leaving a sensuous trail down her neck. Natalie only gave a vague thought to Olive's reason for giving the book to her as it slid from the bed and hit the floor with a thud.

The next morning when she was making the bed she kicked it with her foot then, with a pang of remorse, she picked it up and opened it to the first chapter. Milt's pen was still on the bedside table. She took it and glanced towards the door, once again expecting to be sprung by Olive, then drew a funny face with goggle eyes and a tongue poking out beside his *YES*.

A lump of wood shifted in the pot belly with a thud, bringing her back to the present. She glanced down at the book in her hands. So much had happened since those heady days of early marriage. Some wonderful, some not so, but they'd made a decent life together in spite of the hiccups. She flicked through the chapters with their demanding headings written for women of a past era, and caught glimpses of her own writing scribbled around the edges and on the blank pages between chapters. On some pages she'd stuck photos, family snaps from special celebrations, and others had clippings, a favourite cheesecake recipe, Clem's death notice which included their personal words of love for him. If Olive knew Natalie had turned the precious book into a crazy form of scrapbook she'd be horrified even now.

The pages flopped open at the last chapter, 'Family before all else'. Immediately she thought of the dark days after Bree was born when she'd believed she'd failed as a mother and a wife. Snatches of words from the page jumped out at her, *children are a blessing* — she'd even underlined it — *keep poorly feelings to herself, not bother her husband with too much baby talk*. It had been such a low time in her life. There was a name for it now, post-natal depression, but back then she had simply thought she was going mad and the insidious words had mocked her. That's why she'd underlined *children are a blessing*. It had been the first time she'd written in the book since the night she'd shown it to Milt and it had felt good.

Several pieces of notepaper and magazine clippings poked from the pages. She flicked to the page on family, opened out a piece of notepaper that had been stuck there and smiled. Written in Laura's primary school hand was the title 'Giraffe Soup', then a list of ingredients and the method. As a little girl Laura would never eat pumpkin. It was the only vegetable grown on the property and they had it in abundance. Natalie had cooked up a big pot of it one day and added other vegetables. Laura had been about four and had eyed the bowl of soup, speckled with the green of zucchini and the brighter orange of carrot, with suspicion. Olive had appeared in the kitchen behind her granddaughter and had announced it was giraffe. Laura had eaten the lot and asked for more. Natalie had been grateful for Olive's intervention and from then on pumpkin and vegetable soup was giraffe soup in the King household.

Natalie could have thrown the recipe out, she knew it by heart, but she'd written Olive's name in brackets after the title. That was a reminder of how helpful her mother-in-law could be and a counter for the other times when Natalie got so frustrated by Olive's interference.

And that was one of the reasons why she didn't simply toss the old book away. Between its moralising pages were the mementos, mostly happy, of a different life to the one the book prescribed. Natalie's life. Her family's own real life. If anyone else saw Olive's name next to the soup title they wouldn't realise the significance but Natalie did, just like she knew the family photo she'd glued inside the front cover held special memories.

She'd insisted on having the portrait taken before her eldest, Kate, had left home for uni. It was an informal photo. Milt was seated in the middle, Natalie leaning into him, his arm around her waist and their three daughters cuddled in behind and to his other side. The girls had hated the photo when it had arrived from the photographer. Laura had braces back then, Bree had very short hair and said her ears looked too big for her head, and Kate always said she had a silly look on her face. But to Natalie it was a precious moment in time and even though the large framed copy was banished to a hall cupboard, she'd kept this small copy for herself.

She folded the recipe carefully back inside the pages. It was a silly book, full of rational and irrational messages and she knew her family would think her crazy for keeping it. She'd found Laura with it once, just before she left home to start her hairdresser training. Laura hadn't got any further than groaning over the hated photo before Natalie had snatched it away. Not able to destroy the book she'd banished it to the back of her underwear drawer. She must have put it in the desk drawer after she'd stuck in Clem's death notice.

She dropped it back to the desk now and turned her thoughts to food. Perhaps Laura would enjoy some soup as well as lasagne. Natalie went to the fridge, dug out some pumpkin and zucchini and lost herself in the comfort of chopping and slicing.

The soup was simmering gently by the time she glanced at the clock. Time to get some marking done before she had to start the real dinner. Soup alone wouldn't be enough for Milt. She'd bought Atlantic salmon at the supermarket and it wouldn't take long to cook it and throw together a salad. She got out her stickers and her favourite purple marking pen and opened the first book.

By the time she heard a vehicle and dogs barking she'd become absorbed in the creative writing produced by her year three class and was laughing out loud at Matty's comedic storyline. Trust him to come up with a talking tractor that saved a singing horse from a flood. She packed up the books at the sound of boots thumping on the verandah. The familiar shuddering bang of the door echoed along the passage.

"Go easy!" Milt sounded tetchy.

"Weren't you supposed to fix that?" Bree's voice was equally strained.

"I was going to do it yesterday but I didn't have a replacement stopper in the shed. I've put it on the list for your mum..." Milt stepped through the kitchen door as Natalie stood up. He was a tall man but his shoulders slumped at the sight of her and he had the grace to look sheepish. He knew she hated his lists of jobs for her to do but as he so often said, no point in them both driving into town and wasting good fuel when she went in three days a week for school. "Hello, love. Good day?" he said.

"More what I'd call challenging. Young Leo Tanner fell and broke his arm. Thank goodness Tom was on duty and realised there was something major wrong straight away." Natalie counted off her fingertips as she spoke. "Clancy's mum took the corner too close and clipped the end of the school bus and Billy from my class threw up in the doorway just as we came back in from lunch." She wrinkled her nose. At least the vomit was the only extra thing she'd had to deal with personally. It really had been a strange day. She chuckled as she recalled the new young principal, hopping from foot to foot. "Poor Paul nearly had a fit when he saw the damage to the bus."

"Nothing out of the ordinary then." Milt gave her a weary smile. She wrapped him in a quick hug. Over his shoulder Bree's smile didn't reach her eyes. Irritation smouldered there, as it often seemed to these days.

"What about you two?" Natalie glanced from one to the other.

"We only had a blocked water pipe," Bree said. "Took a bit to fix it though."

On closer inspection, Natalie could see the splatters of mud on their clothes.

"It needn't have," Milt muttered as he poured himself a long glass of water.

"I'm going to have a shower." Bree ducked away. Clumps of mud splattered her thick brown ponytail.

"I'll have dinner ready soon," Natalie called after her.

Bree tipped her head back through the door. "Thanks, Mum, but I've got a basketball meeting in town. I'll have dinner at the pub." She disappeared back into the passage.

"Say hello to Owen."

There was no response. Either her daughter hadn't heard her or she was being ignored. Owen had only recently been brought out to meet them. They'd had dinner and both Natalie and Milt had been impressed with the good-looking young man with the larrikinish sense of humour who Bree was obviously smitten with.

Natalie looked from the empty doorway to her husband. "Everything all right?"

Milt was sitting at the table opening the first of the envelopes.

"Milt?"

"Hmm?" He glanced up. "Yes, it's fine." He grimaced. "We might have had a few terse words."

Natalie swallowed her sigh. Milt had trouble remembering he was his daughter's employer out in the paddocks, not her father. Unlike her older and younger sisters, Bree had been born with the farming genes. Her return to the family property several years earlier, after university and a stint on a farm in the south-east, had coincided with Clem slowing down and their need for an extra worker. Bree had shadowed her grandfather then, and she'd embraced it. Clem was easier on her than he'd been on his son, enjoying being a mentor.

"You know what Bree's like," Milt grumbled. "She won't listen. Thinks she knows how to do it quicker, better."

Natalie buried her head in the fridge. She did know. Trouble was, often Bree's ideas were good ones and it was Milt who wasn't prepared to listen. There was regular tension between father and daughter when it came to work, like there had been between Milt and his father. She tried to keep out of it, but lately she'd noticed a restlessness in Bree.

"Have you seen this bill?" Milt said.

She turned to look at the paper he was waving at her. It was apparent none of the envelopes had been opened before he got to them. "No."

"Fuel's gone up."

"Put it in the tray. I'll catch up with the paperwork over the weekend."

"Isn't Bree meant to be doing that now?"

"She is…will be. There's a lot to get your head around."

"Did you pay the bill for the sheep?"

Natalie turned to the calendar. "No. Has it been a week already?"

"Yes." Milt's brow creased. "You're usually on top of all that."

"I'll do it after dinner."

He nodded and looked down again at the papers in front of him.

Natalie set out the vegetables beside the chopping board and picked up the knife. The damned account-keeping got more and more complicated every year. Once upon a time all bills came due at the end of the month, but these days it was any time; the fuel bill one day, phone bill another and for sheep, accounts were due within seven days from purchase. She thought about the early night she'd planned. That wouldn't be happening. Farm paperwork was one of the jobs that had been handballed to Natalie once it became computerised. Olive had been happy to hand it over and Natalie had tackled it alone for years. Milt pretended to know little about computers and Bree wasn't showing a lot of interest. Not that Natalie blamed her. She had enough to do without paperwork as well.

"What's that message on the whiteboard?" Milt asked.

"Terry from Landmark rang."

"What did he want?"

"He wouldn't say."

Natalie looked around as Milt took out his mobile. *The Model Wife* lay on the desk beside the open drawer. She strode over, slid the book into the drawer and pushed it shut a little too forcefully. Milt glanced up, a puzzled expression on his face, which changed to a frown. He jabbed at his phone. "It's gone straight to voicemail. Surely he could tell you what he wanted."

"No." Natalie shook her head. They'd had this conversation a dozen times before.

"I'm off," Bree called from the passage and the back door shut.

Natalie went back to the vegetables.

"Bree's been on about restoring the tennis court again." Milt's statement sounded more like a question.

Natalie turned and his steady gaze met hers. Bree had been on about redoing the overgrown tennis court ever since she'd met Owen and had taken up tennis. Natalie felt a chill at the thought of it. "It'd be a waste of time and money now." The tennis court had been left unloved since the two older girls were babies and that's how it would stay. That decision had been made before Laura had been born.

"I said I'd think about it."

She took a deep breath. "But you won't." There weren't many things Natalie stood her ground over but this was one of them.

Milt's brow was furrowed, his look determined as he watched her. "I said I'd think about it," he repeated.

Natalie pursed her lips, turned back to the vegetables and began to chop. Tennis had nearly ruined her life once; she wasn't about to let that happen again.

Two

An hour later Bree King parked her ute on a side road in town, halfway between the sports club and the pub. She would be late for the meeting if she ate first but she was starving. Hunger churned in her belly along with the annoyance she still felt with her father and his pig-headedness. They would have got the job done in half the time today if he hadn't been so insistent on doing it his way. She loved her dad but she was doubting her ability to work with him even more. She knew he'd felt that way about Pa but somehow they'd managed. Pa had been a different personality. Still determined but more mellow in nature. She and her dad were too much alike, according to her mother. They struck sparks off each other.

She got out of her ute, hunched her shoulders against the cold and strode to the end of the quiet street. She passed old Mrs Bell's place with its arches of roses and wind chimes tinkling softly in the breeze and then two original cottages with a skip bin piled high with rubbish out the front. She'd heard someone from Adelaide had bought them to do up for holiday accommodation. They'd been empty and run-down for years so a new lease of life for them had to be a positive for the town. Across the corner, the front door of the pub burst open, and a couple of out-of-towners stepped out into the chilly autumn night accompanied by voices and laughter. Sounded like a crowd inside. Unusual for a Tuesday night. She shoved her hands into the pockets of her clean jeans and crossed the road.

"Hey, Bree." Luke Thomas was the first to notice her. "Lucky you came here first. We've just decided to hold the meeting over a meal."

She took in the rest of the faces turned her way, smiling and waving drinks. They were all from the basketball club.

"Bree!"

She looked over to the other pub door and her grumpy mood faded. Here was the other reason she'd come to town. Owen Ferguson's smile was wide as he strode towards her and took her in his arms. She gasped as he pressed his lips to hers right there in the front bar of the hotel. They'd been what her mother called an item for a few months now but mostly they were very private about their relationship. She'd only recently taken him home to meet her parents. Around them there were hoots and whistles and he let her go.

Bree swept some loose hair back into place and tugged at the hem of her shirt. "That was some welcome," she said, relieved that her quick glance showed the rest of the bar focused back on whatever they'd been doing before Owen had made his big entrance.

He took her hand and leaned close again. "Let's go outside. There's no-one out there and I've got news."

Happy to get away from the crowd, she followed him as he led the way to the outdoor area. Bert, the owner, called it a beer garden but everyone else called the simple paved area, with its scattered wine barrels, stools and plants, the smoking den. Even though it was outside and the air fresh and cold, the smell of stale cigarettes lingered.

Two beers sat on one of the barrels used as tables. Owen passed one to her.

"You were expecting me then." She raised it to her lips. "After my day I could use this."

His cheeky grin turned serious. "Wait." He put a hand out and she lowered the glass. "I said I've got news."

She studied his face, trying to guess what he was going to say. He'd only been in town a year, working as a mechanic at the local machinery firm. It was a small town and newcomers not that frequent so she'd been aware of his arrival but she hadn't actually met him until she'd taken a truck in to be serviced. She'd been impressed by the way he'd been able to get their old farm work-horse to purr along like a real truck again. She'd offered to buy him a drink and their friendship had been sealed.

"Mick's going to sell me the business."

Bree's heart leaped. When Owen had first arrived in town he hadn't been planning to stay. By the time they'd consummated their relationship she knew she loved him and she was pretty sure the feeling was mutual but there was always the question of how long his job would last. Mick had gone through a series of mechanics in recent years.

"That's fantastic." She raised her glass again, excited at the prospect of him putting down roots nearby.

"Wait." He was still studying her closely. He reached for her hand. "Before I take over Mick wants me to do a job for him."

Bree nodded and glanced at the beer she'd put back on the barrel. Her stomach was grumbling from lack of food and her throat was parched.

He gave her hand a squeeze. "It's in Marla."

"Marla! As in the dot on the map nearly to the Northern Territory border?"

"It's a nine-hour drive."

"You've checked?"

"Of course. Mick owes the guy at the servo a favour. His mechanic wants to take some extended leave and he needs a replacement. Mick had promised to help him out but he's not up to it any more. His shoulder has had it. He said if I went he'd make the deal sweeter for me to take over his business."

"How long will you be there?" Bree was practical. He'd be gone a while but he'd be coming back.

"Six months."

"Six months!"

"The offer Mick's making me is a valuable one. I wouldn't be in a position to take over his business for years otherwise but—"

"I guess it's not that long." Bree tried to hide her disappointment in the face of his enthusiasm.

"Here's the thing." He took her other hand in his and for a brief moment she thought he was going to get down on one knee. She was never one for the mushy love stories both her sisters wept over so she was surprised to feel her heart skip.

"I wondered if…I hope you might come with me."

"To Marla?" She let out a sigh, not sure if she was relieved or sorry he hadn't said something else. "What about the farm?"

"You were only saying the other day how you think your dad would be better off with someone who wasn't his daughter working for him."

"What would I do in Marla?"

"There's waitressing work at the servo."

She opened her mouth but he pressed his fingers to her lips. "It's only short term and you said you waitressed when you were at uni."

Bree had worked in a cafe for two years part-time while she'd been a student. "It's not the waitressing. I can't just up and leave the property. We've got tailing coming up and—"

"The farm will be here when you get back. This is a chance for us. We can live together. See how compatible we really are."

"In Marla?"

"Won't be anywhere else to go." His eyes crinkled and he gave her that look, the one that made her toes curl inside her boots. "We'd have to make our own fun."

"I don't know, Owen. I'll have to think about it."

He picked up the glasses, handed one to her again and tapped his against hers. "Here's to a new venture for the two of us."

"I said I had to think about it."

They both sipped. The slightly bitter taste reached her tongue first and then the bubbles of the sparkling ale slid a refreshing trail down her throat.

"You haven't got long. I'm leaving next week."

Bree took another sip and this time the fizz was from the excitement building in her stomach. Could she do this? She wouldn't be able to go when Owen did but maybe after tailing. Her dad could employ someone and she could take a break, try life with Owen, test their relationship in a different space.

"It'd only be for six months, Bree, nine at the most."

"Nine!" She almost choked on the beer.

★

A few hundred kilometres away in Adelaide, Laura King sat in the middle of the little flat she shared with her friend Spritzi and looked at all her worldly goods stacked up around her in boxes and bags. Not a lot to show for six years of flatting but enough to cause some concern. Her car was a Hyundai hatch and while the boot was spacious for a small car, she wasn't sure it would be spacious enough for the piles she was planning to pack into it.

"Here you are, girlfriend." Spritzi came out of the shoebox they called a kitchen and handed Laura a coffee. "Are you sure you don't want to take the coffee machine with you?"

"Mum and Dad have one."

"What about your bed?"

"Mum and Dad have them too."

Spritzi gave an eye roll. "It's your bed."

"It won't fit in the car. With any luck your new flatmate will need it."

Spritzi shifted Laura's stack of pillows and quilt along the battered couch they'd picked up from kerbside rubbish when they'd first got the flat and plonked herself down.

"I'm sorry I can't hold the space for you but you know I can't afford the rent on my own. Bella's coming Thursday to check the place out and with any luck she'll move straight in."

"Of course. And I'm not sure when or if I'll be back so you have to get someone else."

Laura wasn't sad to be leaving the hairdressing job she'd grown to hate, nor did it bother her to leave Adelaide but she'd miss Spritzi. It wasn't her real name. Laura had met Sally Pritzker when they'd both been taken on as new apprentices with a large hairdressing business in the city and they'd become instant friends. Gareth the salon owner liked his staff to have quirky names. He'd insisted on calling her Laurita, much to her irritation. But Sally had embraced the idea and made up the name Spritzi, instantly winning Gareth's adoration. The name had stuck, even in her personal life.

Spritzi frowned at her now. "But it's only temporary, staying with them, isn't it? Till you find something else? Please tell me you're not going home to bury yourself in the country never to be seen again."

"Don't be so dramatic. You love coming with me to the farm."

"For weekend visits, yes, but I don't want to live there."

"I can't wait," Laura said, a tad forcefully. She wasn't sure how she was going to adapt to life at home again either but it was her only option at the moment.

"And you're not running because of that dickhead Kyle?"

Laura's stomach did a lurch at the mention of her old boyfriend's name. "I'm not running from anyone, least of all Kyle."

"Good. 'Cause you know he's not worth a second thought right?"

"Yes."

Spritzi eyed her closely. "He hasn't been back here again, has he?"

"No." Laura gave an emphatic shake of her head. Kyle had swept her off her feet six months ago on a night out at one of their favourite bars in the city. He was like no other guy she'd ever dated. He was a man. Seven years older than her, he'd made her feel like a princess. She'd been in love with Kyle, thought he'd loved her, until she'd caught him out with another girl in a little bar off Hindley Street a few weeks ago. She'd already had a few drinks under her belt, told him what she thought of him and gone on with her friends to another couple of bars. The next day had been the worst of her life, with both a hangover and a broken heart, and Kyle had come to the flat, saying it was all a big mistake. Thankfully Spritzi had been well enough to send him packing, threatening to call the police if he showed his face there again.

Laura had blocked his number and unfriended him from her social media but he'd kept trying to contact her. He hadn't come back to the flat but the next day he'd appeared outside her work. By then Laura had had the strength to send him on his way but yesterday he'd been waiting for her when she came out of the gym. He'd been angry, a side of him she'd never seen before, and it had frightened her. She'd firmly told him to stop harassing her, made it to her car, locked the doors and driven away. She hadn't seen him since but it had shaken her up. Spritzi hadn't been home when Laura had arrived so she'd rung her mum. She hadn't mentioned Kyle of course. It had been enough to hear her mother's reassuring voice and tell her she was coming home; she just hadn't let on for how long.

"What on earth will you do with yourself?" Spritzi's question startled her back to the present. Since she'd quit at the salon almost a week ago, Laura had asked herself that same question several times.

If working in the city for the last six years had taught her anything it was that she didn't want to live there permanently. Trouble was, she wasn't sure where she did want to live, or how she was going to earn an income for that matter.

She stretched her arms above her head, drawing in a deep breath. "Sleep in, for starters. Let Mum spoil me. When I get sick of that I'll think about the future."

Spritizi's phone let out its crazy ringtone. She picked it up. "That's Jazz wondering where I am." She unfurled herself from the couch and gently hooked her fingers around one of Laura's rainbow locks. "Are you sure you won't come out with us? You know Jazz was only trying to help when she coloured your hair."

Laura shook her head. "I don't care about the hair. And we were out together on the weekend. I've got a bit more sorting to do before I head off on Thursday."

"I'll see you in the morning?"

"I'll be here."

"Good. We'll have breakfast together." Spritzi bent down and air kissed Laura's cheeks, stepped around the boxes and let herself out.

Laura sat perfectly still and let the whirlwind her friend's presence always created settle. Spritzi's suggestion of breakfast together wouldn't happen, of course. She'd sleep through her alarm as she always did after a night out. And when she eventually did get up she'd fly around the flat like a maniac getting ready and dash out the door with a piece of toast in one hand and a coffee in the other, as she always did. They often ran out of mugs because they would all end up rolling around in Spritzi's car until she'd clean them out and the whole cycle started all over again. Laura was going to miss her.

Outside, the car revved to life and burbled away, blending with the sounds of nearby traffic. That was something Laura was looking forward to, the absence of traffic noise and the blare of sirens and horns that were a regular occurrence outside their busy main road flat. There'd be nothing more than the odd roar of a motorbike, the caw of a crow or bleat of a sheep at home.

She chewed her lip at the thought of home. Spritzi made her feel much braver than she was. After years of hairdressing Laura had settled on a style that tamed her blonde curls to straight. It had meant constant work with straighteners but she liked it and she'd add deeper honey or bronze highlights depending on her mood. Gareth had been on at her to update her look. He liked his staff to reflect current styles and the more out there the better. It had been Jazz who'd suggested something more vibrant for her hair. Trust me, she'd said, and after a few drinks and with Spritzi's encouragement Laura had let Jazz loose.

Now, she dragged herself to the tiny bathroom, took a breath and looked in the mirror. There was no avoiding the vibrant stripes of colour. Jazz and Gareth had loved it, even Spritzi had expressed enthusiasm, but Laura hated it and it had been the last straw. Gareth had gone on about her not embracing the ethos of his salon. The day after Jazz's hair dying experiment a week ago, he'd raved on longer than usual, told her she needed to get with it or get out. Normally she'd remain silent in the face of his demands, swallow her annoyance and get on with her work, but not that time. Emboldened by anger, she'd given Gareth her notice and he hadn't fought her on it. In fact, he'd said she could leave at the end of the week and she had. Spritzi had begged her not to and had offered to cut her hair short or dye it black, but it wouldn't hide all the colour. It would wash out over the next few weeks but until then…

Laura's parents had been shocked when she'd gone gothic a few years ago. It had been another of Gareth's ideas to have his staff dye their hair black, each with a splash of single colour. Hers had been purple and Spritzi's green. They'd worn heavy make-up and black shirts and skirts to work, and she was sure they'd lost customers over it. Not that her mum had said much about her hair at the time but her dad had kept going on about how poorly it made her look. Deep down she'd agreed with him but she hadn't let on.

She sucked in a breath and turned away from the mirror. By this hour in two nights' time they would have seen the rainbow look. That would be one hurdle down but it was far more than the colour of her hair that troubled her. For the last year she'd been dragging herself to work. She'd lost her passion for it. Gareth was always coming up with the latest, often outrageous styles and colours. She detested them but was expected to sell them to clients. She was fed-up with his over-the-top expectations, which were more about her appearance or upselling rather than the quality of her cutting and styling. She'd done a lot of extra courses in her own time and at her own expense and received excellent feedback from her tutors, but somehow her heart wasn't in it any more and the ending of her relationship with Kyle had sealed it. She needed to make changes to her life.

She just wasn't sure how to tell her parents she'd quit her job. They'd probably be glad. She knew they'd wanted her to do something different to hairdressing after she left school. Her mum had been hoping the last of her daughters might be a teacher but her parents had supported her choice. Now they'd want to know what she was going to do next, which was something Laura herself didn't know.

She slumped into the space on the couch Spritzi had vacated. She was in need of some sisterly advice. Not Bree. Her older sister would say Laura was making a mountain out of a molehill and just to get on with it. Kate was the oldest of the three and the one who'd be a reliable listening ear, take her side. Laura took up her mobile and selected the number.

The phone was about to go to voicemail when Kate answered.

"Hi, baby sis."

"Hi. How's your day been?"

"Busy." Kate sighed. "I've been at the office since six this morning and every morning for the last week. Sean has been on the road."

Laura had always envied her sister, marrying the gorgeous, rock-solid Sean Brock and moving to country Eyre Peninsula with him, but right now Kate sounded as jaded as Laura felt.

"What have you been up to?" Kate's question was the perfect opening for Laura to pour her heart out but she held back.

"I'm heading home for the weekend."

"Mum and Dad will be glad to see you."

"Maybe not at first."

"What have you done now?"

Laura had always tested anything she wanted to run by her parents on her oldest sister first but Kate's tone had been sharp. Perhaps she'd start with the easiest thing first.

"I let one of the girls at work have free rein on my hair."

"Oh no, Laura, what have you done? Please don't tell me you've chopped off your beautiful hair again."

"No, it's still way past my shoulders."

"That's good. A bit of colour's okay."

"It's more than a bit." Laura winced. "Think My Little Pony."

"Cack. Dad will have a pink fit."

"More like a rainbow-coloured one."

"Really?" Kate started to laugh. "I wish I could be there to see his reaction."

Normally Laura bristled when her sisters laughed at her expense but this time she was pleased to hear the sparkle in Kate's voice.

"I wish you were going to be there too," she said. "Dad won't see the funny side."

"Maybe not at first but it's only colour. It'll wash out eventually."

"Mmm."

"Perhaps you could put it up and wear a hat."

Laura groaned.

"Sorry, Laura. I've gotta go. I can hear the ute. We've had a long day here. I said I'd put something on for dinner and I haven't started yet."

There was a pause. Laura pressed the phone to her ear. "Kate?"

"The folks will get over it." Her sister laughed again. "Wish I was a fly on the wall though. Ring me and tell me how it goes. Love you."

"Say hi to Sean." Laura sagged back onto the couch. Her sister hadn't helped her to feel better at all.

★

Kate stared at the phone in her hand. Talking to Laura was like taking a breath of fresh air. If only life's problems were as simple as a change to your hair colour.

She jumped as two strong arms came around her neck and the bristles on her husband's chin brushed her cheek.

"I didn't hear you come in."

"You were on the phone."

His lips skimmed hers and she tasted lanolin and dust. Her truck driver husband had just unloaded a mob of sheep at a nearby farm. She'd called in to see him on her way to their small acreage on the outskirts of town.

"Done for the day?" she asked.

"Yep." His face was drawn and his eyes weary. He'd made three trips interstate this week. "I didn't get back to the office with the paperwork."

"I'll drop it in tomorrow."

Sean's family owned a stock transport business and Kate worked a few days a week in the office and ran errands, which this week had been constant with Sean, his two brothers and their dad all on the road. Local farmers were worried about feed and in the last two weeks stock runs had doubled.

Kate put down her phone. "I haven't started on dinner yet."

"Who were you talking to?" Sean poured himself a long drink of cold water from the fridge and tipped it down. Drips dribbled from the stubble on his chin and rolled down his neck.

"Laura."

"What's happened this time?"

"Nothing. Well, I don't think there's anything, other than her new hair colour's a bit too bright by the sound of it."

"There's always something with Laura."

"She's going home for a few days."

He studied her. "Is that why you look so sad? You want to go too?"

"No."

"What then?"

Kate swept up a pile of mail that had been scattered on the table since yesterday. Sean had always been able to read her. She tried to swallow the big lump of…she wasn't sure what…disappointment, perhaps sorrow, even unease that had been burning in the pit of her stomach since lunchtime. Laura's call had been a distraction.

"Come on, Katie-Q, what's up?" His big brown eyes opened wide as he raised his eyebrows.

"I had lunch with Sarah today."

"Usually that's a good thing." He tipped his head to one side, his eyes still locked on hers. "Isn't it?"

What could she say? She couldn't explain the terrible resentment to herself let alone to Sean. "We argued."

He straightened. "What about?"

Kate turned away and pretended to look through the envelopes in her hands. She couldn't tell him what Sarah had actually said. "It was silly stuff but it blew out of proportion. I shouldn't have let it get to me."

Sean huffed behind her. "You know Sarah. She can shoot her mouth off before she's thought it through. I'm sure she'll be on the phone apologising before the night's out."

"Mmm." Kate still couldn't look him in the eye.

He kissed the back of her neck. "She'll have forgotten about it by the next time you see her."

"Probably."

"I'm starving." Sean moved away and opened the fridge again. "What will we eat?"

"There're still some chops. I'll toss a salad."

"I'll cook the meat on the barbecue."

"It's my turn to cook."

He came back to her and put a hand on each of her arms. Even though she was tall, Sean was a good head taller than her. "We're both done in. I'll cook the chops, you make the salad." He kissed her forehead. "Let me have a shower first."

"Okay."

"And don't worry about Sarah. It'll blow over," he called over his shoulder as he left and she continued to stare at the space where he'd been.

She hadn't argued with Sarah, in fact she'd hardly said a word once they'd settled in their favourite cafe. No sooner had the waiter taken their order than her friend had burst forth with news that had cut Kate much deeper than any squabble. Sarah had announced she was pregnant. Kate knew shock must have registered on her face before she'd made the obligatory congratulatory noises. Evidently Sarah and her husband Rick had been going through IVF. Kate had been stunned by that. She and Sean couldn't have children and neither could Sarah and Rick, until now.

Her best friend had supposedly decided against IVF as had Kate and Sean. Aside from the cost and the intrusion, it hadn't been such a hard choice for Kate. She'd never felt the maternal tugs at her heartstrings that many of her friends talked about. When she nursed their babies she was always relieved if she managed to last five minutes without making the often-squirming bundles cry and then she happily handed them back.

But still, it had sent Kate's world spinning to see her close friend, the one she'd thought understood and even shared her lack of interest in having a child, bursting with excitement with the news that she was well on her way to producing a baby and after only one round of IVF. A procedure she hadn't even mentioned she was having. Kate had been stunned, shocked and, if she was honest, hurt. Now she and Sean would be the only childless couple in their circle of friends.

She knew Sean would say it didn't matter. He had enough nieces and nephews he adored but Kate was already an outsider. She'd only moved to the district six years ago to live with Sean. It was a small community, not unlike the one she'd left: conservative, not always tolerant of newcomers and differences. Some of the older members of the community had been asking them for years when they were going to have a baby and there were others who thought it; she could tell by the way they skirted around the topic when it was raised.

She and Sean had had tests early in their marriage. He'd been keen to start a family then and she'd gone along with it without thinking it through. He'd been worried when no babies came; she'd been secretly relieved. The results showed his sperm had low motility and her womb was tilted. Not a total disaster, the doctor said couples had overcome those odds before, but conceiving a child would be more difficult. As Sean joked, put his slow swimmers in her lopsided pool and there was trouble making babies.

The doctor had said nature could still take its course or they could be candidates for IVF, but Kate knew, after all the tests they'd already been through, that IVF wasn't for her, just like she felt sure motherhood wasn't right for her. She and Sean had talked of nothing else for weeks. He wasn't keen on IVF either. They'd agreed they could live with being childless although Kate thought he secretly hoped the doctor was right in saying they could still conceive. He'd suggested they not use contraception and she'd agreed and nothing had happened. Kate hadn't given babies a thought for years but Sarah's excitement had thrown her. Not only was Kate's womb tilted but her emotions were too. What if she one day regretted not having tried harder? What if Sean did?

She dragged herself to the fridge. The simple task of making a salad seemed all too hard. Between her friend's exuberant revelling in motherhood and the long hours she'd been working, Kate felt tired to her core. Sean's phone rang in the distance, propelling her from her lethargy. Surely she could make a simple salad.

They were both quiet over dinner. Kate couldn't bring herself to tell her husband Sarah and Nick's happy news. The television played to itself in the lounge behind them.

"What's on the agenda for you tomorrow?" She tried to rustle up some enthusiasm as she reached for his empty plate.

Sean stopped her and collected the plates himself. "Cleaning trucks and paperwork."

She groaned.

"After that I've got a few days off." He stood beside her, the plates in his hands. "How about a break to the beach?"

Her spirits lifted at the thought. His parents owned a shack about two hours' drive away. It was isolated and fronted a white sandy beach washed by aquamarine water that could outdo any Queensland holiday brochure, except for the lack of year-round warmth. "Just us? That would be lovely."

Sean took the plates to the sink. "It won't be just us."

Kate studied his back, waiting for him to turn around. He was the youngest of Mary and Tom Brock's three sons. His parents and his two married brothers all lived in town. When his dad had sold the farm all those years ago he'd also bought the small beach shack. Perhaps one of the other families were going. She got on well with her in-laws. The thought of a few days relaxing at the beach lifted her spirits. Sean clattered the plates in the sink and turned on the water. She got up and took a tea towel from its hook. "Who else is going?"

His shoulders were hunched over the sink. Froth bubbled up past his wrists; he always used too much dishwashing liquid. He turned to her, his brow wrinkled and his face twisted as if he was in pain.

"Oh, no." She backed away from the sink.

"It's just a weekend."

"Not Damo?"

Sean's face screwed up tighter. "And Shortie."

Kate shook her head. "No way."

"Damo rang as I was getting out of the shower. Shortie's had a bust-up with his girlfriend."

"Why am I not surprised? If they spent less time with each other and more time with their women maybe they'd keep a girl-friend for longer than five minutes."

"They want to get away for a few days."

"Shortie's a loose cannon, Sean. You know we don't get on."

"I know." He raised his hands in the air and water dripped down his arms and onto the floor. "But he's Damo's mate and Damo's my mate."

"He's not always the most reliable either." Kate had never really forgiven Damo for the spray tan he'd organised for Sean at his bucks night before their wedding. It was almost five years ago but Kate was reminded of it every time she looked at their wedding photos.

"Just a few days fishing and drowning our sorrows." He was watching her intently.

"And you really thought I'd like to be included in this...this..." She waved the tea towel in the air. "Bonding weekend."

"It's been a tough couple of months. We could do with a break."

The fight slipped out of her in a long sigh. "I know, Sean." She swallowed her disappointment that he was spending their first free weekend in months with Damo instead of her.

"You need a break too." He pulled her in close, the wet from his hands soaking through her thin shirt. She nestled closer, not caring, then suddenly found herself at arms' length with Sean smiling like a Cheshire cat.

"Why don't you go home?" he said.

"I am home."

"To your parents. Didn't you say Laura was heading there this weekend?"

"Yes, but it's a five-hour drive for me."

"Stay the week. I'll only be gone for the weekend and my runs next week are to Victoria again." Sean's look was eager. No doubt it would appease his conscience if she didn't simply stay home alone while he went off with his mates. "You could leave tomorrow, come back when you're ready next week."

He was warming to his idea and so was she.

"I don't know about tomorrow."

"Might as well."

Kate thought about the mountain of grotty work clothes in the laundry and their sheets and towels that she hadn't changed in over a week. His mum hadn't been well and Kate had worked almost as long hours in the office as Sean had on the road these last two weeks. They shared a lot of household jobs but washing clothes wasn't often on his agenda.

She nestled against his chest again, her ear pressed to his shirt, listening to the comforting thud of his heart. Sean was a good man. If only his warmth could shake the heavy weight that dragged at her shoulders. Going home to her family might be just what she needed. Kate longed to sit at the big table in her mother's kitchen and talk. Laura would be there to make her laugh, and she found herself even keen to see Bree, who could be so prickly, and her parents. Her dependable father and her mum, who was always reassuring with her words of wisdom. It was Natalie who held everything together. She'd never really told her mother too much about the fertility issues and their lack of desire in that department. Her mother had never said anything about wanting grandchildren but maybe it was a topic that needed to be discussed before she did.

"I think I will go home," Kate mumbled into his shoulder. "Surprise them."

Three

Natalie was aware of the tall young man who slipped through the classroom door and propped his butt on the overflowing games cupboard, arms folded over his thin chest trapping the navy-and-red striped tie against the white of his shirt. She didn't make eye contact with him, conscious only of his stiff presence in her classroom. She glanced around the class, glad to note all faces were still locked on the boy at the front of the room.

Joel Fanning had the floor and every one of his year three cohort was hanging on his words. Since he'd first entered her classroom at the start of the year he'd found it difficult to settle. This was the first time she'd seen him still and focused for longer than five minutes and it was halfway through term two.

"So the difference for my grandpa was…" His voice faltered, the bravado that had enabled him to speak out ebbing away. Natalie held her breath. Perhaps she shouldn't have let them go down this path of comparing floods to bushfires, what was the same, what was different, but it was the first time the whole class had been engaged in a topic this year and so she'd run with it. It had developed from NAPLAN practice, not the topic that Paul

Brown, the new principal now observing her class, had instructed her to do but the object of the exercise was the same. The annual test was done for this year, only a couple of weeks ago, and her class deserved the chance to explore topics they were interested in.

She studied Joel as he took a deep breath and then another. The young boy had just poured out how his family had been trapped on their property by a bushfire just before last Christmas. They'd lost everything, including his grandfather, and now he seemed to have lost his voice.

His thin shoulders lifted and his dark eyes searched out Natalie and held her gaze, and she saw his strength return. "Maybe if it had been a flood he could have got away, Mrs King." His voice was steady, his tone low.

She wavered a moment, disquieted by the principal's presence, then she gave her brave young student a reassuring smile. His mother had told her he never spoke of the fire or his grandpa. "That certainly may have made a difference, Joel. He was a fine man, your grandpa, I'm sure he would have done his best." The whole community had been devastated when the experienced CFS volunteer had become trapped by the fire and lost his life.

A soft rustle rolled around the room, a subtle shifting in seats, a rub of a cheek. The sharing of their experiences of bushfires had been an intense forty minutes. From the corner of her eye she saw Paul unfold his arms, straighten as if he was going to say something then sag against the cupboard again.

The sharp tones of Annalisa Drummond cut the silence. "Floods can be bad too."

Natalie stood up and gave the little girl a reassuring smile. "Yes, Annalisa, your family's loss was also very sad and had many similarities." It had been three years since the flood in their district, which had been another local tragedy. Several other children began to talk. "We're going to hear from those people with flood stories next week. Would you be happy to wait and share your story then?"

Annalisa's face softened and she gave a nod of her head.

Natalie glanced at her watch. It was nearly home time. They needed to end the day on a bright note and some more Roald Dahl would do the trick. "The room is already packed up. How about you all find a comfy spot and I will read one more chapter of *The Twits*." The calls of delight were immediate, along with the crash and bang of chairs against tables as they each found a space on the floor with one of the many colourful cushions she provided for this kind of activity. She sat in her chair with them all gathered at her feet and opened the book, only realising then that Paul had slipped out of the room as quietly as he'd slipped in, leaving behind a judgemental air.

The final siren of the day sounded and the classroom had no sooner emptied of children when Eloise, the new young teacher from the class next door, burst into her room, a stricken look on her face.

"He came in again. He's like the phantom; he appears out of nowhere, watches for a while and leaves."

Natalie knew she was referring to Paul.

"It's his way of keeping in touch with what's happening in the classroom." She tried to sound reassuring.

"I'm sick of his spying. He can take over altogether if he wants." Eloise's lip wobbled and then a giant sob burst forth followed by tears.

Natalie sat her on one of the student chairs, poured her some water and put a gentle arm around her shoulders.

"You're doing such a good job," she said soothingly. "Paul's learning to be a principal just like you're learning to be a teacher."

Eloise sniffed and took a tissue from her sleeve. "No-one watches over his shoulder."

"Principals have their line managers too."

"Do they pop in unannounced every five minutes?"

Natalie patted the young woman's shoulder. She had a point and it was what Natalie had tried to talk to Paul about the last time Eloise had come crying to her after one of his visits. Eloise lacked confidence. She'd had to take over in terrible circumstances when her predecessor, Penny, had died suddenly. Penny had been a dedicated teacher, fair but firm, whose students had adored her and it was hard enough for Eloise to pick up the pieces, take over a class and find her way in her first job in a totally new community, without feeling the principal was scrutinising her every move.

Eloise blew her nose hard and stood up. "I'm sorry, Natalie. I always seem to be crying on your shoulder. It was tricky with Emile today. His lack of English makes some lessons harder than others, and Tabitha wet her pants again. The other kids noticed before I did and a few of the boys teased her and it took me ages to get everyone back on track then Paul came in." She took a deep breath.

"Try not to think of him as judging you. He understands how difficult teaching can be some days." Natalie spoke with an authority she didn't feel. She wasn't sure Paul did understand but she didn't want to undermine him or Eloise.

It was after four and Eloise had dried her tears and gone back to pack up her own room when Natalie's mobile phone rang from the bottom of her basket. She turned back in surprise from the whiteboard she'd been cleaning. She usually kept the phone on silent. Thank goodness it hadn't rung during class time.

"Terry was only ringing to say the damned rolls of pipe and wire had arrived." Milt's voice bellowed from the speaker before she'd even said hello.

"Hello, Milt. How was your day?" she said gently.

"One stuff-up after another," he grumbled but at least his tone had dropped a few decibels. "What about you?"

"Yes, all good here." Her day in the classroom had gone particularly well until Paul's visit and then Eloise's tears.

"Do you think you could collect the pipe and wire when you get the other stuff on the list?"

"Yes."

Her phone beeped softly. She glanced at the screen. There was another call but an unknown number. "I'll see you tonight," she said and accepted the next call.

"Mrs Natalie King?"

"Yes."

"Mrs King, I'm ringing from the breast care centre. Last week you had a mammogram at one of our mobile clinics."

Natalie's mouth went dry. "Yes."

"An anomaly has been found and we would like you to come to Adelaide for further investigation."

"An anomaly?" What did that mean? Was it a lump? She put a hand to one breast and then the other. Which one was it? She'd fronted up to the travelling bus for her two-yearly mammogram last week feeling confident there was nothing to find. She knew the drill; she checked herself regularly, her breasts weren't dense, she hadn't felt any lumps, there was no family history, she'd breast-fed her three daughters, each for longer than a year. How could there be anything left in there when they squeezed her breasts so flat? She felt sick in her stomach and fear gripped her heart.

"I realise you live in the country, Mrs King, but can you be here by tomorrow afternoon?"

"Tomorrow?"

"We like to call people back quickly...so they don't worry."

Natalie wanted to ask how she was supposed to not worry but instead she scribbled the details into her diary. The call finished, the phone lay beside her diary on the desk as a million thoughts whirled in her head. Her knees were jelly and she lowered herself to her chair. She stared at the phone. She should have asked more questions. What did further investigation mean? Perhaps a biopsy? The woman's parting words had been *try not to worry* and she'd disconnected before Natalie could gather her thoughts. What kind of help was that? Natalie looked down at her shirt, crumpled now from the day. Beneath it she felt the constriction of her bra encasing her breasts. They'd found an anomaly. She pressed her fingers to her lips. She had cancer.

"Natalie?"

She looked up in surprise, not sure how long she'd been sitting there.

Paul stepped into her classroom. "I'd like to have a chat."

She stood up and began tidying her desk. She worked part-time. Thank God her week was over. Her colleague, Claire, taught the class Thursdays and Fridays.

"Natalie?"

She stopped, looked at Paul. He must have said something.

"Pardon?"

"I'm concerned about letting the children talk about the fires in such detail."

She stared at him, trying to focus on what he was saying.

"It's not part of the curriculum we mapped out at the start of the year," he said.

"It's reinforcing the skills they learned for NAPLAN testing." Her voice was a croak.

He frowned. "Bushfires were not one of the examples we discussed for year three."

It was as if he was chastising her. Personal worry mixed with professional. "The similarities and differences between frogs and toads didn't hold their interest."

"You're uncovering issues better dealt with by a counsellor."

He was only voicing the very concern she'd had when the children had first suggested the topic. She lifted her basket, placed it on her desk and began scooping papers and pens into it. "I talked to Pat about it and we discussed possible scenarios and strategies. She thought it would be beneficial. Life doesn't always fit easily into compartments. Anyway, it was one of the children who initially raised the topic of floods and fires and I let the parents know via our weekly class newsletter." She was rambling, the words burbling from her mouth. She took a breath and stopped, her gaze meeting his. He looked back at her through large dark-rimmed glasses that gave him a scholarly appearance. In reality he was young enough to be her son and in spite of her earlier reassurances to Eloise, she wondered how much actual classroom experience he'd had.

"I don't remember okaying that letter."

Once more Natalie felt rebuked. "I send one home in their communication books each week to let parents know what we've been doing and what's coming up."

"Notes home to parents should be approved by me."

Natalie gaped at him. "Even the notes in their communication books?"

He shifted his feet and tugged at the knot of his tie. "Not every one but any that might be considered…controversial."

"Climate isn't controversial…unless you're a politician. Nearly all of the children in the class have been affected by fire or flood or both. It made more sense to go with a topic they were interested in." She waved a hand towards the large map of their district pinned on the wall. "It's become part of our maths, mapping affected areas. The children have written poetry, painted and even used the topics in creative writing. They're all engaged and learning. Surely that's the most important thing."

He stood straighter, his cheeks infused with pink. "I am asking you to follow the plan we agreed on."

Natalie felt as if her head was going to roll off her shoulders. She had a bloody anomaly in her breast and he was talking curriculum. She wanted to tell him where to shove his plan. Only she never would. A lump formed hard and tight in her throat. Penny would have told him in no uncertain terms what she thought of his plan and where he could put it.

Penny had taught the class beside hers. They hadn't been the closest of friends but they'd worked well together. She'd been so gung-ho and full of life and planning a great birthday bash in February to celebrate her sixtieth but the week before it she'd dropped dead from an aneurism. Instead of a birthday bash they'd had a funeral. The shock of it had swept the whole community. How could someone so vibrant be there one day and gone the next?

"Natalie? Are you okay?"

She turned away from Paul's concerned look to pick up her basket and give herself a moment. Her mind was in turmoil and it frightened her to be reminded of Penny's sudden loss and her own medical appointment. Would tomorrow see her facing a fight for her own survival? Paul watched her closely from the other side of her desk.

"Something's come up...a family matter." She stumbled over her words. "You may need to organise a temporary teacher for me next week...I'll let you know."

By the time she got into her car her hands were trembling so hard she struggled to insert the key in the ignition. She pressed her shaking fingers to her lips. Paul probably thought her past her prime and now he'd be thinking she was crazy after her dash from the classroom.

She drained the last of the water from her bottle then remembered it was Wednesday. She always called in on her mother-in-law on Wednesday. She glanced at the clock as she started the car. If she didn't go, Olive would wonder why. Best to call in quickly.

Natalie turned into the unit driveway and was barely out of the car before the screen door opened and Olive waved to her from the doorway.

"I can't come out. I'm in my slippers," she called as Natalie approached. "I thought you were lost."

"I had to do a tidy up at school." Natalie bent to kiss her cheek. "How are you?"

"A bit weary."

"Oh?" She swept a quick look over her mother-in-law. Olive wasn't usually one to complain about her health. She'd been stoic since her husband's death but it was only a year since he'd died, after all.

Olive stepped back to let Natalie through the door of the new unit she'd moved into only a few months after the funeral. It had an open-plan living area and two bedrooms and was spotless as always. Once a fortnight Natalie vacuumed, mopped the small kitchen and cleaned the bathroom. Apart from that Olive managed the rest herself. The kitchen bench was clear, no sign of the kettle and the two cups she would usually have ready for Natalie's arrival.

"I haven't put the kettle on," Olive said. "I hope you don't mind but I'm feeling a bit too tired to do the shopping. Would you pop down the street for me? I only need a few things."

"Of course." Natalie smiled while inside she was churning with a sudden desire to say no, but it wasn't Olive's fault Natalie was walking around with an anomaly in her breast. In some ways it was a relief. She wouldn't have to make small talk for half an hour. She could drop back with the shopping and go home.

In the supermarket she couldn't move fast enough; every aisle was stacked with boxes or crammed with other shoppers. She knew most of them but apart from stiff smiles she didn't acknowledge them. She was almost finished when she spied Nancy Phelps ahead of her. Nancy was one of those women who made up the backbone of the community. Only a couple of years older than Natalie, she was on nearly every committee and it was joked in the district that if Nancy didn't know about it, it didn't happen. She brought her trolley to a stop in front of Natalie's. No-one avoided Nancy.

"Hello, Natalie. Good to see you."

Natalie smiled with one eye on the packet of washing powder she'd been about to lift down before Nancy had blocked her way.

"I haven't seen you since the dawn service on Anzac Day."

"School's busy and we've had lots happening on the property."

"Of course. You haven't forgotten about the netball meeting next week, have you?"

Natalie shook her head. She had but she wouldn't admit it.

"I've put your name down to organise the catering for the carnival. We need a level head in charge. Some of those new younger players—"

"I'm sorry, Nancy…I'm not sure if I can be there." Natalie couldn't think past tomorrow.

Nancy's eyebrows shot up. "Surely you won't miss it. You've been a stalwart ever since Kate started playing. How is Kate, by the way? Any babies yet?"

"No." She shook her head, and from the look on Nancy's face it was another failure on Natalie's part that her daughter hadn't produced a grandchild.

"Grandies are such a delight but I've told my girls they can't rely on me for constant babysitting. I love having the children sometimes but I won't be a dogsbody. I'm far too busy myself. Next week there's the community garden meeting as well. That's something you'd enjoy—"

"I have to get on, Nancy. Excuse me." Natalie reached forward and tugged the box of powder from the shelf. "If I'm not there please don't put me down for anything." Nancy's look of surprise was comical, though Natalie felt every emotion but humour. "Bye, Nancy." She backed up her trolley and swerved away, almost running to the checkout.

Back at Olive's she put three bags of shopping on the kitchen bench. The list had run to more than a few things.

"You'll unpack it for me, won't you?" Olive's voice wavered from the lounge where she sat in a chair watching the end of a pre-news game show.

Natalie bit back her sigh and set to work. The news was on by the time she'd finished. She bent down to kiss Olive on the cheek. It was a robotic kiss forged from years of polite greetings and farewells. "What will you have for dinner?"

"I'm not that hungry." Olive dragged her gaze from the screen and stood up. "A sandwich will do now that I have fresh bread. Thanks, Natalie. I'm feeling much better."

There was a beautiful arrangement of roses on Olive's buffet. They were too perfect to be from someone's garden.

"What lovely roses."

Olive glanced around. "Constance called in. She knew I'd be specially missing her father this week." She forced a smile. "So thoughtful of her to bring me roses. They were Clem's favourite."

Natalie pressed her lips tightly together and swallowed a lump of guilt. She and Milt had done nothing to mark the occasion.

Trust Connie to turn up bearing gifts. Milt's only sibling was married to a farmer and they lived just over an hour away to the south, and to Natalie's knowledge this was probably only the third visit she'd made to her mother since she'd moved in to the unit.

"We went out for lunch at the hotel."

"Today?" Natalie couldn't help the sharpness of her response.

"It was good of her to spend time with me when she's so busy. We had a lovely afternoon."

"Sorry I missed her." Natalie gritted her teeth. Why hadn't Connie done the damn shopping?

"She had to get back by four," Olive said as if reading her thoughts. "They've got something happening on the property next week, some kind of farm day out, and their place is on the list. She was in the middle of cooking for it." Olive looked Natalie up and down as if for the first time. "You're looking tired. Perhaps it's time you gave up the teaching."

Natalie sucked her lips tightly over her teeth. How often had she heard that over the years? Olive had not been happy that Natalie had kept teaching after she'd married Milt nor when she'd returned to it once Laura had started school. Of course, Connie hadn't worked outside the property. She'd had three sons and was on hand to help on the farm at all times.

"I'm fine." Apart from some kind of breast anomaly, but Olive was the last person she'd tell about that. Natalie's head hurt from trying to contain the whirl of thoughts going round and round. Perhaps it would spin right off her shoulders. Then Olive would have a definite reason to tell her to stop teaching.

Olive studied her closely. "You haven't forgotten the church trading table on Friday morning? I told them you'd make a couple of your orange cakes."

Natalie pressed her fingers to the side of her head. Who knew where she'd be on Friday or what would be happening? Would they start treatment on her straight away?

"When did I agree to that?"

Olive's head jerked back, her forehead creasing in a frown. "You always make cake for the trading table. The families come in a couple of weeks. Surely you haven't forgotten."

"I'm sure it's in my diary," Natalie squeaked. Their church raised money each year to give several city families who were doing it tough a country holiday. "But it's not till the holidays, is it?"

"No, but there's an extra group. I'm sure I told you about them. Several young mothers coming overnight without the children. They'll be here before the holidays. It's only one night but I haven't put us down for home hosting this time." Olive was still eyeing her closely. "A picnic day at the creek will be our contribution."

Natalie grabbed her car keys from the counter. "Not this time, Olive. I'm sorry. I'll see you…" Her voice dwindled away as she rushed to her car without looking back. She wasn't sure when she'd see her mother-in-law next and what state she'd be in when she did and she certainly wasn't up to hosting a barbecue out on one of their creeks.

On the long drive home Natalie's thoughts leaped from one scenario to another. The anomaly could turn out to be nothing, or an early detection requiring minimal intervention, or one of those aggressive cancers that she'd heard about that would need radical treatment. God, she could lose her breast, or both breasts. How would she deal with that? How would Milt? By the time she pulled the car into the garage her hands were trembling again.

She struggled out of the car with her basket and followed the cracked cement path to the verandah, where she paused. The back light was on, casting a pool of dull light which in turn gave the stone walls a grey appearance. It matched her mood.

Their cat mewed, rose from its position on an old chair and jumped to the ground.

Only Milt's boots sat on the rack against the back wall. Beyond the screen, the internal door was open and Natalie could hear sounds from the kitchen. The cat nudged her legs and mewed again.

"Hasn't anyone fed you?"

Milt turned to her from the drawer he'd been rummaging in when she entered the kitchen. She stopped, remembering she'd shoved *The Model Wife* in the other drawer. She'd be embarrassed if Milt saw it now. With its photos and clippings it had become almost like a diary, highlighting the highs and lows of her life, and so personal. Sometimes she wished she'd thrown it away the moment Olive had given it to her.

"What are you looking for?" she asked.

"A new notebook."

"Second drawer."

She set her basket down while he took out one of the small spiral-bound pads that fitted his pocket. Her knees trembled at the thought of explaining.

"Are you all right?" He moved towards her.

The anticipation of his big strong arms wrapping her in a hug brought tears to her eyes. She blinked them back as he came to a stop in front of her.

"Did you pick up the stuff from Landmark?"

"Oh, no, I forgot all about it."

"Damn it, Nat, I needed the wire first thing tomorrow."

Her hand went to her head. Was she losing her mind as well as her breast? She gasped. Why had she even thought that?

"Mum rang and said you were short with her." Milt was frowning at her still. "I know she can be a bit demanding but she's still pretty fragile."

Natalie spun away from him and put her basket on the floor in the corner. It was the unexpected shopping trip for Olive that had made her forget Milt's list.

"Then I had an odd call from Paul," Milt said. "He was checking to see if you were okay."

Natalie sucked in a breath. Normally no-one cared what she did but now they were all studying her as if she was a specimen under a microscope.

"Nat?"

She took another breath and glanced around. "Where's Bree?"

"Shutting up the chooks."

"I have to go to Adelaide tomorrow and I need you to come with me."

"Hell's teeth, Nat, we're about to start mustering. I haven't got time to—"

"I've got an anomaly," she blurted.

He shook his head. "A what?"

"The breast cancer clinic rang today. There was an anomaly with my mammogram. I have to go down tomorrow for further investigation."

"When did you have a mammogram?"

"Last week." She'd told him. Perhaps she hadn't. She couldn't remember. Every time she tried to concentrate on something the thought slipped away out of her reach. He took a step towards her but she busied herself at the fridge, taking out the food she'd cook for dinner. When she'd first walked in, the strength of his embrace was what she'd yearned for but now she knew if he took her in his arms she'd fall into an abyss she mightn't get out of. Bree would return at any minute and this was something she didn't want to burden her daughter with. Not yet. She sensed Milt standing close behind her.

"I don't want to go alone but I don't want anyone else to know about it." She fumbled the lid of the carrot crisper. "At least not till we know what we're dealing with."

Bree's voice carried from the back door, talking to Bubbles.

Nat glanced back at her husband. "We're going to Adelaide to do paperwork for Clem's estate," she whispered. "We might even need to stay overnight." She didn't like lying to her daughter but it was the first thing she could think of and in reality a job they did have to do soon.

Milt nodded his head. "You'll be fine, Nat. I bet they're just being cautious. It'll be nothing. Don't worry."

She turned back to the bench and this time managed to wrench the lid off the wretched container. The ever-practical Milt had determined all would be well. How could he know that? The words bubbled inside her, wanting to come out, but she swallowed them as Bree arrived in the kitchen.

Later, in bed, staring up at the ornate rose in the centre of the ceiling, all she could think of was the bloody anomaly and Milt's assurance it would be nothing. An assurance he had no authority to give, but she accepted now that he was trying to be positive and she appreciated the sentiment. Tonight he didn't read as he usually did before sleep. He flicked out the light, slid his hand into hers and gripped it tight. They lay side by side, enveloped in silence, thinking about tomorrow.

Four

Natalie's knees were like jelly as she put her feet to the floor. The room that housed the ultrasound was warm and airless. The sonographer had apologised. Their aircon wasn't working properly and the day outside unusually warm for late May. Natalie had been lying on the vinyl bed for so long that perspiration had soaked the back of the gown they'd provided. In the small cubicle her skin was clammy and her fingers were useless trying to do up her bra. She gave up, stuffed it in her handbag and pulled on her loose-fitting shirt. All she wanted to do was get out of this place as fast as she could.

She made her way along the corridor, past closed doors to other cubicles, other rooms with diagnostic machines, serious-faced technicians and specialists handing out life-changing diagnoses. She moved faster.

Her anomaly had been a cyst, nothing sinister the specialist had assured her once the sonographer had called him to check her ultrasound results. A needle biopsy had also been done but he said he was confident the result would be the same. It wasn't cancer. She felt lightheaded with relief. During the long drive to

Adelaide, the wait for the appointment after they'd arrived far too early, the tests and the serious faces peering at screens, Natalie had lived her life over and over again, thinking about all the highlights: her childhood, her marriage to Milt – not all of it great but it had given her their three beautiful daughters – her teaching career, the work she did on the property and in her community. She halted and shot a hand to the wall to steady herself. She'd been lucky, with few major catastrophes, but lying on that vinyl table waiting for the specialist to come and give his deliberation, she'd been hit by a ghastly thought: was this all there was to life?

She took a deep breath and straightened. She'd had a reprieve. The strength was returning to her limbs. She wanted to run along the corridor; to grab Milt's hand and drag him out of this place before someone changed their mind.

Natalie came to the waiting room entrance and paused at the pane of glass in the wall that allowed a view into the room. She froze, her few seconds of elation sucked away. In the far corner of the waiting area stood a man with his arms around a woman whose head was pressed to his chest. The man was Milt, her husband of thirty-three years, and the woman he held was Veronica Halbot, the creature he'd had an affair with twenty-seven years ago.

*

Bree shut up the dogs and headed back to the house. It was only mid-afternoon but today's mustering had been finished in good time. Graeme and the other two guys her dad had employed had been easy to work with, except for their regular breaks to have a smoke, and she'd sent them home, ready for an early start tomorrow.

In the kitchen she paused to look around. The chairs they'd sat in that morning were pushed out, askew from the table, which was still scattered with the milk and butter, Vegemite and jam and the brightly coloured placemats Nat always set out for breakfast. Even the mugs and plates they'd used were stacked in the sink instead of the dishwasher. Normally her mother wouldn't leave the house unless the kitchen was spotless, but she'd only made it as far as the sink when Milt had pushed his clean town hat onto his head and moved to the doorway, keys jangling in his hand. It was odd that they would go to Adelaide on the day mustering was supposed to start.

Her phone pinged with a message. It was from her dad saying they were staying the night and would be home first thing tomorrow. She stopped thinking about her parents and selected Owen's number.

"What are you up to?" he asked. They rarely rang each other at this hour on a work day.

"I thought I'd cook you dinner tonight, at the farm."

"Sounds good."

"It'll just be you and me…you could stay the night."

"Sounds even better."

"Great! See you when you get here."

She pocketed her phone and dug in the freezer for something to take out for dinner, humming at the thought of having Owen here and the place to herself. She put a lasagne on the sink to defrost and checked the fridge for salad ingredients, tidied up the breakfast things then set the end of the kitchen table for two and glanced at the clock. She had time to finish a couple of quick jobs before she'd need to be back to shower and put the lasagne in the oven.

★

Laura pulled up near the back gate and knew from the empty garage that her mum wasn't home. The dogs weren't there to greet her either so Bree and their dad must be off somewhere as well. It was a good chance to unload all her stuff and put it in her bedroom. She'd be able to pick her own time to let her family know she'd be home for a while.

With her arms full of the first load she was met by Bubbles at the back door.

"Hello, pussycat," she crooned. The cat gave her a sideways look then stalked inside, tail straight up in the air like a one-fingered salute. Laura propped the door open and followed.

She set down the box and bag in the bedroom she could now call her own. Bree had moved into the quarters and Kate rarely came home these days, and if she did it would be with Sean and they took the spare room with the queen bed.

On her way back to the door she wandered into the kitchen. The table was set already and only for two. She looked at the casserole dish defrosting on the sink with lasagne printed in black texta across the plastic cover. Obviously some of the family were going to be out tonight. Once again she felt relief. She hoped her mum was the one staying in. It would be easier to talk with her on her own.

Laura emptied her car and moved it out of the way to the old shed behind the house. She parked beside Bree's ute. Wind ruffled the leaves at the top of the stand of gum trees that stretched along the yard boundary. The sliding door of the shed rattled and the canvas on a nearby trailer flapped. Laura hurried back to the house, the keenness of her isolation intensifying.

An image of Kyle's scowling face popped into her head. She banished it. Thankfully their relationship hadn't gone on long enough for her to bring him home for a visit. Now that she thought about it, he'd never asked much about her family, certainly not where they lived. He would have thought their property the end of the earth, he was such a city guy.

Bubbles miaowed at her as she approached the back door.

"Thank goodness for you, Bubbles." She scooped the old cat into her arms and he reluctantly stayed as she carried him with her to her bedroom where she sat him on the bed and flipped open the large case that held most of her clothes. There was also a garbage bag stuffed with coats and jackets, another two full of shoes, and a box of scarves, belts, t-shirts and assorted caps.

Bubbles recovered from his burst of annoyance and made himself comfortable on her bed. Laura had a sudden urge to join him. She'd been tense over the whole Kyle break-up and hadn't slept well since she'd quit her job, even though she knew she was doing the right thing. Once she'd told her parents and her dad got over the shock of her hair, life would settle and she'd have time to ponder what next.

She stretched out on the bed, one hand behind her head and the other scratching the cat under the chin. Lined up on either side of hers were two more beds, Kate's on the fireplace side and Bree's on the other. Laura had been in the middle between her two older sisters, and not just with her bed. She was always the mediator between Kate and Bree, who could easily rub each other up the wrong way. This room had seen many things, fun and fights, laughter and tears, the pandemonium of three sisters sharing its huge space, and yet even with other bedrooms available none of them had ever moved out, not permanently. They'd said they would, of course, threatened to on several occasions after one falling-out or another, a few times one of them had actually gone through with it, but when it came to the crunch they'd always come back and stayed, sharing the room.

Laura's eyes felt heavy. The drive was a long one and tiring if you hadn't slept well the night before. She rolled over and cuddled Bubbles in closer. The reassuring sound of the cat's purrs and the soft comfort of her childhood bed soon had her drifting towards sleep.

★

Natalie put a hand to her mouth. The sight of Veronica in her husband's arms took her back to that terrible time, and the events that had rocked her very being. The cancer scare and her relief were forgotten in an instant. Milt eased Veronica away from him but the image of his arms around her was burned into Natalie's brain.

Milt saw her over Veronica's shoulder. She blinked, forced herself to move. His look changed from sad to questioning.

Veronica must have sensed her approach. She turned, her eyes red, her face pale, and Natalie knew immediately what she was going to say.

"I've got breast cancer." Veronica's words were studded with sobs as she reached for Natalie. "Don't tell me that's why you're here. Not you too?" She pushed her face into Natalie's shoulder and clung to her. Natalie stood stiffly, arms at her sides.

Over Veronica's head Milt watched her closely.

"I'm okay," she mouthed.

They both looked at Veronica. Natalie gave her two crisp pats on the back. "I'm here for a check-up, that's all. I'm fine." There was no joy in saying the words now.

"Veronica's here alone," Milt said. "She's rung Bob but it'll be late by the time he gets here. I said we could stay with her...so she's not on her own."

Veronica pulled away from Natalie, blew her nose on a soggy tissue and swept her hair from her eyes. She was doing her best to pull herself together. She drew a deep breath and looked steadily at Natalie. Her eyes, which had once been a sparkling blue, were cloudy.

"The staff have been so kind. They've made an appointment for me to see a specialist in the morning and then a breast care nurse."

"That's good." Natalie knew the words were wrong but what did you say in these circumstances? It would have been hard enough with a friend but with a woman she abhorred the right words were lost altogether. Even though they lived in the same community, they'd managed to avoid each other as much as possible for twenty-seven years. Natalie couldn't remember the last time she'd been this close to Veronica. Deep lines creased the other woman's temple and eye area and her neck skin was creping. Natalie had seen the same signs of ageing in her own reflection but not as pronounced. She felt a flash of pride instantly followed by contrition at having vain thoughts at such a time.

"I appreciate your support." Veronica's tone was firm now. She turned to Milt. "I'm assuming you've other business or need to head home." Her shoulders began to shake and Milt reached out his arms and drew her into a hug again. Natalie bit back a 'For God's sake' and resisted the urge to wrench the woman from her husband's arms. She was ashamed of herself for the strength of her dislike for Veronica when she was so vulnerable but Natalie couldn't stop her barraging emotions.

"We're staying with you, Vee," Milt murmured over Veronica's head, looking straight at Natalie. "We couldn't leave you alone at a time like this."

"Of course not." Natalie managed to squeeze out the words but the air had left her lungs at his use of the endearing nickname everyone else in the district used for Veronica. Not that her name was ever mentioned much in the King household but she was strictly Veronica if it was.

"Is your car nearby?" Milt asked.

Veronica nodded and dug in her bag for another tissue. "I'd planned to stay at the unit for a few days. I didn't truly think there was anything to worry about. I was going to go shopping, see a movie..." Her words trailed off as more silent tears rolled down her cheeks.

How weird life was, Natalie thought. She'd been beside herself with worry and her lump had been benign and Veronica had obviously been relaxed enough about her recall to plan some free time in the city.

"Give me your keys." Milt held out his hand to Veronica. "I'll drive you and Nat can follow in our car."

Natalie did as he'd asked. It was the last thing she wanted to do but how could she refuse? She wanted to be celebrating her good fortune with her husband but none of that would happen tonight even if they did have time to themselves. Veronica had stolen that moment just like she'd almost stolen Natalie's husband all those years ago.

They left the building together. Outside the sky was grey, the temperature had dropped and a gust of wind stirred the left-over autumn leaves in the carpark. Veronica gave her the address and Natalie put the directions into Google maps in case she lost sight of the other car but the traffic was heavy and they remained locked in tandem. They arrived in a quiet leafy street and Natalie pulled her car in behind Veronica's at the Halbots' Toorak Gardens unit. They'd bought it when their children had been moving to Adelaide for university and now it was kept as a family overnighter when needed – a luxury Natalie had often wished her own family had but Milt had never thought necessary.

Natalie shivered as she followed Veronica inside. The warm day hadn't penetrated the brick walls shaded by leafy trees and a breeze had sprung up that made her drag a cardigan over her long-sleeved shirt. Veronica went into another room. Milt took a step towards Natalie but they had no time to talk before Veronica was back. She'd thrown a camel-coloured jacket over her navy-and-white-spotted shirt and navy pants, and swapped her heels for flats. Her face and hair might be dishevelled but her clothes were stylish.

She looked around as if not sure what to do. "There're a few things in the fridge but I'd planned to eat out. I could make us a cup of tea."

Milt strode forward and gently guided her to a chair. "Sit down."

Veronica did. Milt waved Natalie to another chair. Once again she wondered what she would have done if she'd been on her own and met Veronica. Offered sympathy and left the other woman to her despair or stepped in and taken over like Milt?

It was Milt who found his way around the little kitchen and made them a cup of tea. It was Milt who spoke again to Bob, gently taking the mobile from Veronica's shaking hands, to let him know they'd stay with her until he got there, and it was Milt who rang up for takeaway. He put the heater on low when he noticed Veronica shiver. The unit felt chilly and not just because of the weather.

Natalie watched him find his way around the sparsely furnished rooms. Perhaps intentionally devoid of clutter, it was probably deemed minimalist. She thought *impersonal* a better description but even so Milt's big frame seemed to crowd the space. He brought them both a glass of the wine he'd found in the fridge. It was moscato. Natalie shuddered at the sweetness of it but took another sip all the same.

"Can I do anything else?"

They both looked up at him and shook their heads, mute, or in Veronica's case numb perhaps.

The food came. They moved to the table. Natalie was surprised to see it was only six o'clock but she was ravenous. She'd not eaten anything since breakfast and then she'd only picked at some toast. Milt tucked in to the gourmet pizza as well but Veronica barely touched hers. Natalie could only imagine what must be going through her head.

The other woman punctuated their all-but-silent meal with short bursts of what the doctor had said. An aggressive cancer but found early. Several treatment options to be discussed. Possible mastectomy. Natalie had found it hard not to look at Veronica's breasts then. They filled Veronica's t-shirt to full stretch, at least double the cup size of Natalie's bra.

She glanced down, remembering she'd stuffed hers in her bag, and made an excuse to use the bathroom and got herself re-dressed. She left her cardigan off, gripped the handbasin with both hands and pressed her forehead to the mirror. The cold was a relief from the living room, which was way too warm now but she didn't dare ask to turn the heater off.

Cancer was a blow Natalie wouldn't wish on anyone, not even the person she felt she disliked more than any other person in the world. Veronica may be a bitch but she didn't deserve this. Her son, Jack, was only three years older than Laura. Natalie hadn't seen him for years. She wondered if there were photos of him in the unit, then pushed the thought away. She couldn't face that old worry now. She thought instead of Veronica's two daughters who were younger. Back then she and Veronica had nearly ended up in the local hospital together when the Halbots' first daughter was born only a few days after Laura.

Natalie lifted her head and stared at her reflection. Bloody hell, Laura! She'd forgotten her youngest daughter was coming home today.

Five

Bree pulled a brush through her tousled hair, studying herself in the mirror at the same time. There was a glow in her cheeks and a sparkle in her eyes, and the reason for that was now taking a shower. Owen had got away early from work and arrived at the farm by six o'clock. She'd been going to give him a guided tour of the house, but they hadn't made it further than her bedroom in the quarters.

All that activity had reminded her she was hungry and then she remembered the lasagne she'd popped in the oven when she'd heard Owen's ute pull up. She hurried out along the narrow quarters' passage, smiling as she passed her bathroom and the happy sound of Owen singing, and into the main house and the kitchen.

She was greeted by the delicious smell of food cooking, not burning as she'd feared. Peering through the glass she could see the top layer of cheese bubbling to a nice golden brown. She removed the lasagne from the oven, put the radio on and immediately the kitchen was filled with the sounds of Ed Sheeran singing 'Shape of You'. She moved her body in time to the music as she put together a green salad.

A pair of strong arms slid around her waist drawing her backward. She rested against Owen's bare chest, savouring this rare time alone.

"I forgot to bring a clean shirt," he murmured.

She twisted in his arms and kissed him. "I'm not bothered about eating my dinner sitting beside that body…" She trailed a finger down his torso and shivered. "Perhaps I should find you something though. I'd hate you to drop some lasagne and burn yourself."

He grinned as she slid from his arms.

"Help yourself to a beer," she called and almost skipped from the kitchen, thankful for whatever meetings had kept her parents in Adelaide.

★

Laura's eyelids sprang open. She blinked, trying to focus on the room, her brain not registering where she was, then the soft fur pressing up against her neck reminded her. She was home. She sat up. Bubbles stretched, opened one eye and curled into a ball.

Laura lowered her legs to the ground. A sound had woken her. Now she realised it was the thump of music drifting through the open door that had disturbed her. She glanced in the old dressing-table mirror, the outer edges covered with stickers from every fad the girls had been through, tugged her hair back into a ponytail and pulled on the cap that hung over one of the posts suspending the tilting mirror. She decided a cap and a splash of bright lipstick might distract from the brilliant-coloured stripes through her hair.

In the passage she relaxed a little. It must be Bree at home. The music was loud and not the ABC, which would normally be on at this hour. The smell of cooking, warm and delicious, wafted from the kitchen. Bree must have heated the lasagne as well.

"Hello," Laura called as she rounded the door then stopped in her tracks. A hunky-looking guy stood side on, shirtless, his head tipped back, swallowing from a beer bottle.

An expletive was lost in the splutter of beer that came from his mouth. He slapped at the liquid splashing down his bare chest. Eyes wide, she stepped into the kitchen.

He grinned. "You scared the crap out of me."

"Who are you?" They both spoke at once.

"I'm Laura King and I live here." Laura got in first as she moved further into the room.

"Here you are." The shirt in Bree's hands slipped from her fingers as she caught sight of Laura. "Bloody hell."

The bloke by the fridge raised his bottle, a grin on his face. "Not quite what I said but we're on the same page."

"Laura!" Bree's face changed from surprise to something else, disbelief perhaps. "What are you doing here?"

"I told Mum I was coming." Laura looked from the two of them to the table with its two place-settings. "Obviously you weren't expecting me."

"No." Bree frowned. "Mum didn't say anything."

"Where is she?"

They all startled as the back door banged against the wall and another curse echoed along the passage.

"Kate?" Laura looked at Bree and they both turned to the door as their sister walked through, a backpack over her shoulder and bags in both hands.

"Hello." She looked weary but her smile was warm, then her eyes opened wide as her gaze reached the bloke still standing between the table and the fridge, his beer mid-air. "And hello to you," she said.

Bree snatched up the shirt she'd dropped and made her way round the table to where the bloke was standing, the grin still wide on his face. She passed him the shirt then turned to her sisters as he pulled it on, her hands on her hips.

"What are you two doing here?"

"It's our home." Kate was the first to respond, her chin jutted forward. She stacked her pile of bags against the wall.

"You must be Kate." Hunky guy had finished pulling on an old oversized t-shirt of Bree's with *Real country girl* emblazoned in large letters across his chest. He walked the length of the table and held out his hand. "Bree's told me about her sisters." He shook Kate's hand and then reached for Laura's. His grip was warm and firm. "I'm Owen."

"Sorry to mess up your dinner for two." Kate had obviously taken in the setting at the other end of the table too.

"No problem." Owen looked back at Bree who was standing where he'd left her, hands on hips. "That lasagne's big enough for four, isn't it, Bree?"

Laura assumed he'd turned his charming smile on her sister because Bree's rigid jaw softened. "Of course. It was just a surprise to see you both." She went to the drawer and took out more cutlery. "Mum didn't mention you were coming home."

"I definitely told her." Laura sat at one of the fresh settings Bree put out. "She said she'd cook lasagne for me."

"Sorry, baby sis, but I took this one from the freezer this afternoon, long after Mum and Dad left." Bree set the lasagne she'd taken from the oven on a mat on the table.

"Maybe she thought I was coming tomorrow." Laura removed her cap.

"What have you done to your hair?" Bree frowned.

Kate laughed. "You're right, Laura. No-one could miss that."

Bree turned her appalled look on Kate. "You knew she'd done this to herself?"

"It's only hair dye. She hasn't got a tattoo or slashed her wrists."

Laura swallowed and ducked her head. There was no hiding the hair but the other…well, best if she didn't mention that.

"I like it." They all looked at Owen who'd taken a seat at the head of the table. Once more his smile was wide. "All the women in the local hairdressers have their hair done in the same boring way."

Laura stared at him and knew her sisters were doing the same.

"It's a point of difference." He shrugged and took a swig from his beer. "In business you need that."

Laura decided she liked him.

Bree ignored him and focused on Laura. "When did you get here anyway? I didn't see your car."

"It was late afternoon. I unpacked and put the car in the back shed." She did her best not to falter under her sister's piercing look. "I did tell Mum I was coming."

"I, on the other hand, didn't tell anyone I was coming." Kate sat between Laura and Owen. "Glad I didn't interrupt anything more than dinner." She grinned.

Bree plonked a tossed salad on the table in front of her. "You could have rocked up to an empty house if I'd gone in to Owen's place instead of him coming here."

"Where are Mum and Dad anyway?" Kate looked around as if they might suddenly appear.

"In Adelaide. They weren't sure if they'd stop overnight when they left this morning. Dad sent me a text earlier to let me know they were staying."

"Leaving the house empty for you two." Once more Kate's eyebrows arched.

"I've heard about you, Owen," Laura intervened, knowing Kate's teasing would stir Bree's temper further. "It's nice to finally meet you."

"Likewise."

"Well, you're a complete surprise to me," Kate said. "I thought my little sister was celibate but that's obviously not the case."

Owen grinned. Bree opened her mouth but was distracted by her mobile ringing. She got up and went to retrieve it from the bench. Granny didn't allow phones at the table but it was agreed they could be excused to answer them. It was an ingrained habit they followed even when she wasn't there.

"Mum." Bree looked back at them with a slight shake of her head. "Yes, Laura's here."

Kate waved her hands frantically. "Don't tell her I'm here," she hissed.

"It's okay, Mum." Bree looked away. "I took a lasagne out so Laura's happy. Everything go all right with your meeting?"

There was a pause while Bree listened. Laura dished herself some lasagne and offered it to Kate. Anyone would think it was the only food she ate, the way they all went on about it. She'd been a bit fussier as a kid and lasagne had been one of her favourite meals but her tastes had broadened since then.

"Okay," Bree said into the phone. "Yes, I'll tell her. You don't have to hurry home. Laura and—" She glanced at Kate who was waving her hands frantically sideways again. "Laura can help with the mustering until Dad gets here. We'll see you tomorrow."

Laura reached for the salad. She hated mustering. She didn't have the natural instincts for sheep work that Bree and Kate seemed to, but Kate could go with them. Laura would volunteer for food and drink duties.

Bree dropped the phone on the bench, came back to her chair and frowned at Kate. "Why didn't you want me to tell Mum you were here?"

Kate shrugged. "I wanted to surprise her. If I get half the reaction I did from you it'll be worth the trip." She turned to Owen. "Now let's hear all about you."

Laura glanced at Bree's thunder-like face and helped herself to salad. She felt sorry for Bree but Kate was only doing what they'd put her boyfriends through. Laura and Bree had delighted in giving anyone she brought home the third degree. Just as well Dad wasn't here. He was always full of questions. Living in the city had meant she'd never had to go through the family interrogations. She understood why Bree would want to keep Owen to herself.

*

Natalie's arm dropped to her side, the mobile phone, silent now, clutched tightly in her hand. How could she have forgotten Laura was coming home? She moved further along the footpath outside Veronica's place where she'd come to make her call as soon as she'd remembered. Now she couldn't face going back inside the over-heated unit, the TV playing but no-one watching, Milt trying to make small talk and fussing over Veronica. Natalie had wanted to get away to a motel but Veronica had offered them the spare room and Milt had agreed immediately.

"What are you doing out here?" Milt strode along the path towards her. He looked down at the phone. "Did you ring home? Everything all right?"

"Yes. Laura's there."

"What's she doing home? I was going to suggest we have a coffee with her before we left in the morning."

"She rang me...yesterday..." Natalie dragged her fingers through her short hair trying to remember. "No, the day before. Said she was coming home for the weekend. I forgot."

"At least Bree will have help till I can get home."

"Yes." Natalie thought about her younger daughter and her notorious dislike of sheep.

Milt glanced at his watch. "I hope Bob gets here soon. I've run out of things to say."

"Perhaps it's best not to say anything." Natalie couldn't imagine what Veronica was feeling but she thought she had a small idea after her own turmoil.

"Ready to go back?" Milt put an arm around her shoulders.

It was dark but not like at home. The streetlights were on and a nippy wind blew now but Natalie didn't want to return to the cloying heat of the unit.

She leaned against his shoulder. How good it felt. Tears of relief welled in her eyes. She wanted a moment with her husband to celebrate her reprieve. "Can't we stay out here a little longer? It's so hot in there."

Milt pulled away. "Veronica needs us. Maybe you more than me. I'm surprised you've hardly spoken to her."

Natalie's tears dried up. He'd been making enough fuss for the both of them. "I don't know what to say. We're not at all close."

"What does that matter? You're a woman. I'm sure Veronica would have been supporting you if today's results had been reversed."

His words were like a slap. Would he have preferred she was the one with the cancer? "I'm doing my best. Veronica needs someone she's close to. Bob should be here soon."

His look softened. She could see he was out of his depth but she couldn't help him. She didn't want to help Veronica either. What kind of person did that make her?

"I'm going back in." He started to walk away then stopped and held his hand out. "I'll turn the heating down."

Natalie wanted to take his hand, hold him close, but she couldn't face going back inside. Not yet. "I'm going for a quick walk first."

She turned away from the disappointment on his face, clutched her cardigan tight across her chest and started to walk. She had no idea where she was going but she had to walk or she'd scream. The last twenty-four hours had turned her life on its head and now that it was righted she still felt out of kilter, as if things hadn't fallen back in all the right places. She walked faster and faster until she was almost running but she couldn't escape her thoughts and the fear that her life was rolling away from her like a skittering cotton reel unravelling just beyond her reach.

Six

The sun was lightening the sky and colouring the strips of cloud over the eastern horizon with soft pinks as the sound of Owen's ute faded and disappeared, masked by the closer sound of the dogs barking. Bree took them some food, since it was usually her father's job, and on the way back inside she fed the cat, which was part of her mother's morning routine.

In the kitchen she soaked the frypan she'd used to cook eggs and bacon. She was glad neither of her sisters had appeared, allowing her time alone with Owen over breakfast, but now she needed them to get moving. Especially Kate, who had agreed to come mustering this morning. Bree glanced at the clock and stacked the breakfast plates and mugs in the dishwasher among last night's dinner dishes. Part way through wiping down the sink she paused to stare out the window at the new day.

Last night hadn't been the disaster she'd been expecting when both her sisters had materialised in the family kitchen. After they got past their initial teasing, they'd enjoyed their meal together and Kate had even offered to clean up, sending Bree and Owen off to the quarters early. They'd made the most of their night and this morning they'd both been in a deep love-sated sleep when Owen's alarm had roused them. Bree smiled and pressed her arms to her body. She was tired but happy. They'd discussed Marla again and she'd all but decided she'd go. After the last twelve hours the thought of living with Owen on a daily basis was irresistible.

Once more she glanced at the clock. The rest of the mustering team would be here soon. She strode up the wide passage to the guest bedroom Kate had said she'd use. Bree rapped on the door and stuck her head in. "Time to get going."

The room was dark. The early-morning light hadn't reached the edges of the closed blind in this room, which was sheltered by a wide verandah. The lump in the bed didn't move. She went closer.

"Kate?"

The lump stirred and a groan came from under the covers. "Go away."

Bree swallowed a flutter of irritation. "You haven't got long if you want—" She ducked as a pillow flew through the air, fell short and lobbed at her feet.

"I'm not well."

Bree thought about the stash of empty beer bottles in the kitchen. Kate and Laura must have partied on last night. "You know Dad's rule: you play up, you front up."

Kate let out a guttural groan and sat up. "I didn't play up." She blinked bleary eyes from a pale face and sported a bird's nest of hair.

"Talk about the living dead."

"Go away." Kate moaned and lay her head back on the pillow. "I feel sick."

"Bad luck. There's work needs doing." Bree picked up the pillow at her feet and slung it on the end of the bed.

"Get Laura to help. I'm staying in bed." Kate curled into a ball and pulled the covers back over her head.

"Lazy sod," Bree muttered. She strode on to the next bedroom, the one all three sisters had shared and the one Laura claimed as hers when she was home.

The door was open and Bree stopped, taking in the bombsite that was her sister's bedroom. The middle bed was empty with the quilt and sheets rumpled and draped to the floor. Bubbles was curled up asleep on the end, a paw over one ear. The two beds either side were covered in bags and boxes, some open with clothes hanging out. The floor at the end of the bed was scattered with shoes spilling from a large garbage bag, every kind from strappy high heels to neat ankle boots. Bree shook her head. "Bloody Imelda Marcos has moved in." Who needed that many pairs of shoes? Laura's mess was everywhere but there was no sign of Laura.

Bree went back through the house. Perhaps she'd gone to the bathroom but there was no sign of her there either.

From outside she heard a vehicle rumble over the stock grid from the track that led to the road. "Damn!" That was probably Graeme and she wasn't organised. Bree gave up on her useless sisters, grabbed her cap and strode outside. Halfway across the yard to let the dogs out she saw Laura coming back from the direction of the creek paddock.

Bree stopped, hands on hips, and waited for Laura to get closer. "Where have you been?"

"Out walking. I wanted to clear my head."

"You're looking a lot brighter than Kate. What did you two get up to last night?"

"Nothing much." Laura grinned. "We weren't the ones with a red-hot fella in our bed."

Bree wasn't in the mood for teasing this morning. "Get your work gear on," she snapped. "Kate says she's sick—"

"What's wrong with her?"

"Hungover I guess."

Laura frowned and looked towards the house.

Graeme's ute came to a stop over by the machinery shed and the dogs barked madly, turning circles in their enclosure.

"Are you going to give us a hand this morning or not?" Bree said.

"Not."

Bree's mouth fell open.

Laura gave Graeme a wave as he climbed out of his ute. "It's not as if you're on your own and you weren't expecting Kate or me anyway. I'll bring you out some morning tea, though. Which paddock are you mustering?"

Laura looked boldly at Bree. The rays of early-morning sun highlighted the rainbow of hair flowing out from under her green cap that had a round-eyed frog and the words *Hop to it* embroidered on the front. Her hot-pink Lorna Jane t-shirt and platinum-coloured gym tights outlined every one of her perfect curves and even from the distance of a metre Bree could smell the sickly floral perfume she preferred. Bree glared at her sister. It was hard to imagine her helping out anyway; she might break one of her brightly painted fingernails.

She shrugged. "Fine. We'll be somewhere in the tank paddock. And take it easy when you come. Don't want you frightening the sheep and messing up our hard work."

"I'll be there at ten." Laura spun on her heel and headed back towards the house.

Bree stared after her. She hadn't been expecting help but it would have been nice if one of her sisters had stepped up, at least until her dad got back, around lunchtime according to the text she'd had from her mum earlier. Bree strode on to let the dogs out. Her sisters had always been useless when it came to working on the property. She didn't know why she'd hoped that had changed.

★

Laura could feel Bree's look boring into her back as she walked away. She hated sheep work. She was always in the wrong place at the wrong time and they never went where she wanted them to. Behind her a motorbike roared to life and the sound of its revving engine was joined by another vehicle. She didn't look back.

The previous night, Kate had said she'd help with the mustering, much to Laura's relief. After Bree and Owen had left for their little love nest, Laura had poured two glasses from a bottle of red and told her older sister all about her decision to leave the city. Kate had nodded and murmured in all the right places but she hadn't said a lot. Laura had thought she looked tired but had put it down to the drive. Now she said she was sick, according to Bree.

Inside the house she could hear the shower. She knocked on the bathroom door. The shower stopped and a string of invective exploded back at her.

"It's me, Laura. Just checking you're—"

The door flew open and Kate stood in a whirl of steam, a towel clutched to her torso. "Sorry. I thought you were Bree."

"She's gone."

"Damn. Did she say where?"

"Tank paddock, but don't worry about it, she'll manage till Dad gets back."

"Have we heard from him?"

Laura shrugged. "I haven't. I'll take morning tea out later." She peered at Kate. "Bree said you were sick."

"Not sick exactly. Just feeling tired and a bit off. We've had a full-on couple of months. I think I just hit the wall. I'd kill for a tea though, and some toast."

"I'll get on it. I haven't eaten yet."

"Thanks." Kate flicked her a grateful smile and shut the door.

In the kitchen Laura stopped and looked around. This room was the hub of their home. The wooden furniture gave off a soft golden glow and all the family photos gave the large room a welcoming feel. The working space was vast and filled with every cooking gadget known to the gourmet chef. She felt inspired and had an overwhelming urge to cook. The basic kitchen in her city flat, with only two functioning hot plates and a small oven-come-grill with a door that didn't close properly, wasn't conducive to cooking anything but the simplest of meals. And when she came home for the odd weekend, cooking was the last thing she felt like doing, especially because her mother always had it all organised.

Laura was thinking cornflake crumb biscuits because they were her favourites, little cakes with the tops cut out and filled with cream, and maybe even some savoury pinwheels if she could find all the right ingredients. Something that would brighten Bree's face when she took it out for morning tea. It would also be a help to her mother if Laura had an assortment of freshly baked food ready for mustering. She forgot all about breakfast and threw herself into her task with enthusiasm.

"What the hell are you doing?"

Twenty minutes had passed when Kate's voice startled her from her work. She dropped the spatula dripping with cake batter onto the floor and snatched it up again. She'd wipe the cupboard and floor later. "I'm making morning tea to take out to the paddock."

"You do know Mum would have the freezer full already." Kate cast her gaze around the kitchen. "What happened to breakfast?"

Laura looked back at the bench. She'd spread out a bit but she was trying to get the cake and biscuits ready to go in the oven at the same time then she'd put the pinwheels in when she took the sweet stuff out. "I forgot. I've boiled the kettle."

Kate felt the side of the kettle, flicked it on again and took out a travel mug. "I'll take a ute out and help with the mustering."

"Okay." Laura was a little disappointed. She'd hoped Kate would stay and help with the cooking or at least the washing up.

"You'd better have this lot cleaned up before Mum gets home."

"Yoo-hoo."

Kate and Laura looked at each other. "Granny?"

"You are home. I was beginning to wonder—" Olive arrived in the doorway and stopped, her words petering out as she looked from Kate to Laura. "What's happened?"

"Hello, Granny." Kate was the first to move. "Nothing's happened. Laura and I are home for a visit." She wrapped her grandmother in a hug and kissed her cheek.

"Nobody told me you were coming. Are you here for mustering? I'm meant to be at a trading table but they seemed to have enough helpers and I thought..." Over Kate's shoulder Olive eyed the kitchen. "Where's your mother?"

"Mum and Dad are on their way back from Adelaide." Laura stepped up to embrace her grandmother. She smelled of violets and was her usual mix of old and new. Her clothes were always neat if a little old-fashioned but she bought a new pair of glasses each year with trendy frames. Her current pair were round in a tortoiseshell pattern of pinks and reds and her straight grey chin-length hair was parted to one side and held back with a bright pink clip that reminded Laura of a child's hair.

"What on earth are they doing in Adelaide? What about mustering? Who's doing the food?" Olive barely paused for breath before she took a lock of Laura's hair and gave it a gentle tug. "I do hope that's not a permanent aberration, Laura dear."

"It'll wash out...eventually."

"Oh well, every lining has a silver cloud, I suppose."

Laura swallowed a grin. Granny was fond of idioms but often muddled them up.

"Bree's started the mustering with Graeme from next door and the other two fellas Dad hired." Kate plucked an apple from the fruit bowl. "I was about to head out to help."

Olive's sharp gaze flicked from one to the other. "What did you say they went to Adelaide for? Your mother told me she wouldn't help with the church trading table but she didn't mention Adelaide."

Laura shrugged. One of the things she'd enjoyed about living away from home was that she didn't have to constantly inform everyone of her movements. "It was a last-minute thing, I think. Something about farm paperwork."

Olive frowned. "What paper—"

Her words were lost in the distant tooting of a car horn.

Laura led the way outside to the sight of Graeme's ute pulling in beyond her grandmother's car at the back gate, with the dogs barking excitedly from the tray. The ute had barely stopped when Graeme leaped from the front seat. "Bree's come off her bike. She's hurt."

Through his open door they could see Bree propped in the passenger seat. Laura and Kate gave a collective gasp. It was Olive who strode along the path. "How bad?"

Laura gripped Kate's arm and they followed.

"Her leg got caught on some wire. I reckon she's hit her head when she's come off the bike," Graeme called. He strode to the other side of the ute and opened the door. "Thought it best to wrap the leg and bring her here."

"Very sensible." Olive nodded as she joined him and leaned into the ute as Laura and Kate arrived on the driver's side.

Laura gasped again at the sight of her sister's pale face and ripped and blood-soaked jeans. The top of her leg was wrapped in a dirty towel, which also had a patch of something dark that Laura assumed was more of her sister's blood.

Bree frowned. "Hello, Granny. What are you doing here?"

"Just checking up on you all and lucky I did. What's happened?" Her voice was calm.

Bree's frown turned to a wry smile. "Had a bit of an accident."

"I can see that. We're going to get you inside and patch you up." Olive looked across to Laura. "Come round and give Graeme a hand."

Graeme, who'd been known to lug bags of grain under one arm, looked affronted. "I can manage her, Mrs King."

"I know you can carry her but I want Laura to keep pressure on that wound until we can see what we're dealing with." Olive glanced across the top of the ute. "Kate, we'll need the first aid kit and more towels. And clear that mess off the kitchen table."

Laura imagined a severed artery. Didn't people bleed out fast from that kind of injury? She was aware of Kate taking in gulping breaths as she hurried away but Laura's focus was on Bree and how she'd dismissed her request for help that morning. Maybe Bree had cut corners because she was trying to do too much. Laura chewed her lip as she rounded the ute, flooded with guilt and terrified for her sister.

"Put your arms around my neck," Graeme said.

"I could walk." Bree's attempt at stoicism was half-hearted.

"Stop mucking around, Bree." Olive's tone was kind but firm. "Help Graeme as much as you can."

Bree complied meekly. That was the thing about Granny. She gave orders and everyone obeyed, even Bree.

As soon as her sister was clear of the door, Laura gripped the bloodied towel, applying as much pressure as she could.

Bree winced and Laura's stomach churned at the thought of what the leg might look like beneath the bloodied towel. Together she and Graeme manoeuvred Bree inside with Olive leading the way and holding the doors.

"Put her on the table," Olive said.

"Bloody hell, Gran," Bree complained. "We've got a million beds in this house."

"I'm saving your mother a mess to clean up." She gently pushed Bree backward onto the table and an equally pale-faced Kate slid a cushion under her sister's head.

"Make Graeme a cuppa, Kate."

"I'll switch off the ute first."

In their rush to get Bree inside they'd left doors open and the engine running.

"Right you are." Olive dismissed Graeme with a wave. "Laura, find some heavy-duty scissors." She patted Bree's hand. "Hope they're not your favourite jeans but I want to see what the damage is under here."

"The wire went into the front of my leg and ripped sideways." Bree's tone was matter-of-fact now. "Not too deep so no major damage."

Laura came back with the scissors and the first aid kit as Olive gave a slight nod. "Have another towel on standby just in case."

Laura's stomach roiled but she did as she was bid, picking up a fresh towel and gripping Bree's hand as Olive carefully loosened Graeme's makeshift bandage and peered underneath. She pressed the dirty towel back. "You're right. It's messy but you'll live. I think a bandage will do until we can get you to the hospital. You'll need stitches."

"It's not that bad, surely," Bree complained.

Olive tutted and set to work cutting the jeans away and then quickly bound the wounds in a bandage. "You were lucky," she said. "It's not too deep but it's jagged. I still think you'll need stitches. Or at the very least a thorough clean-up and a tetanus injection."

Bree struggled up on her elbows. "Damn. I should be mustering." Her face had colour again and she was sporting a red swelling below her left eye.

"Get her a cold pack for that lump, Laura." Olive inspected her handiwork with the bandage one last time then, satisfied, she sat and took hold of Bree's hand. "I think we could all do with a cup of tea now, Kate, then we'll head in to the hospital."

There was a thud behind them. Kate had plonked back onto a chair so hard it had rocked. She'd lost colour and her eyelids fluttered.

"Get her onto the floor." Olive's usual calm manner when giving orders had gone up a notch, like Dad when he was drafting the sheep.

"What's happened to her?" Bree was propped up on her elbows peering over Olive's shoulders.

"Keep pressure on that bandage," Olive snapped and left Bree to go to help Laura.

Together they tipped Kate gently sideways, Laura taking her sister's weight, and the two of them slipped gracefully to the floor. Well, Kate was graceful; Laura's butt hit the ground with a thud that jarred through her.

"Fu—" She caught a glimpse of Granny's glare. "Fritz," she said meekly and rubbed her behind vigorously.

Olive shoved the fresh towel she'd had on standby for Bree under Kate's head and slapped at her cheek.

Kate's eyes opened. "Ouch." She tried to sit up.

"Stay where you are. Put her feet up on the chair, Laura." Olive was in drill-sergeant mode now. Then, like a miniature replica of the giant from *Jack and the Beanstalk*, she lifted her head and sniffed the air. "What on earth is that smell?"

"Oh no." Laura leaped to her feet. "The cakes are burning."

Seven

In Adelaide, Natalie was desperate to leave the Halbots' apartment and get home. She didn't want to think about Veronica but the more she tried to put the woman out of her mind the more her thoughts returned to her, like a tongue probing a sore tooth.

Milt picked up their jackets and the two of them were moving stealthily across the apartment when Bob let himself into the living room, pulling the bedroom door closed behind him. It had been late when he'd arrived the previous evening and Veronica had flung herself into his arms. Milt and Natalie had retired to the tiny second bedroom to give them some privacy. They'd changed and each climbed into the matching single beds and had tried to sleep. Later, after it had gone quiet out in the lounge, Milt got up and went out. Natalie heard Bob ask if he wanted a beer. Milt had said yes and she'd eventually fallen asleep listening to the sound of the two men talking quietly.

Now Bob's pallor mirrored the grey early-morning light. He glanced over his shoulder then spoke in a low voice. "Vee's gone into a deep sleep at last."

Natalie was grateful, both that Veronica was getting some rest before facing whatever would come today and that they didn't have to make small talk.

Bob didn't look like he'd had much sleep himself. He was one of those men who shaved their heads to avoid the fact that they were almost bald and this morning it made him look much older than when Natalie had last seen him several months earlier.

Milt gripped Bob's hand in both of his. "You call us if there's anything we can do."

Natalie glanced from her husband's concerned face to Bob's sad one. Milt spoke as if Bob and Veronica were their dearest friends when in reality they were distant neighbours who'd avoided each other for years. Even though Natalie had long forgiven her husband she didn't want to play happy neighbours any more now than she had back then. The Halbots would have plenty of other friends they could rely on.

"Thank you both…" There were tears in Bob's eyes. "For staying with Vee." He turned to Natalie and placed a hand on her arm. "I know you and Vee had a big falling-out. But it was all so long ago. Water under the bridge as they say. Silly for it to have gone on for so long. It was decent of you to put it behind you and support her."

Natalie mumbled something placating, unable to hold Bob's tearful look nor glance at her husband, who was standing rigidly beside her. The couples had been friendly once. That was in the time before Natalie's husband and Bob's wife had taken that friendship one step too far. Bob was a good-hearted man but she couldn't imagine even he would be that much of a saint if he knew the truth. She had wondered what Veronica had told her husband all those years ago to keep the families apart. The few times their paths crossed each year Bob was always friendly towards Milt. It was hard to imagine he would act so genuinely if he knew.

Natalie and Milt were both silent as he drove against the tide of traffic travelling towards the city while they headed away. When he suggested a stop in Gawler for a coffee and a bite to eat it took her by surprise. That's when she realised she was hungry again. It had been twelve hours since the slice of pizza she'd eaten last night. She hoped with food in her stomach she would get her mind in order. Normally she spent Thursday afternoons on lesson plans, now she'd have to fit that into the weekend, which would be hard with Laura at home and mustering to be done.

Not that she'd be out in the paddocks much except to run food. She'd learned to shift sheep in the early days of their marriage. Clem and Milt had been grateful for her help then. Money had been tight and she was one less wage to pay. Even after Kate was born she'd left the baby with Olive for short periods and gone out with them but that had stopped once Bree came along. A lot of things had changed after Bree.

Milt stretched his legs, strolling up and down the path in front of the bakery while Natalie ordered takeaway coffees and ham-and-cheese croissants.

"Thanks." He gave her a grateful smile as she handed his over. They sat their coffees on the bonnet and leaned against the car eating in silence. Natalie glanced at her husband as he took another careful bite of the hot pastry. He looked as tired as she felt.

"We should take a holiday," she said.

"We're about to start tailing."

"After tailing, I mean. Straight after," she emphasised. "For a month at least."

Since the girls had grown up they'd hardly taken more than a few days at a time away from the property. Even the new year's break away at the beach had dwindled until this last January when they hadn't gone at all.

"What about school?"

"I've got plenty of leave I've never used."

Milt shook his head slowly. "One day we will, Nat, but now's not a good time." He took another bite of his croissant.

She stared at the footpath. When they were in the Halbots' unit she'd thought all she'd wanted to do was go home. Now she realised all she wanted was to get as far away from home as possible. She'd been given a reprieve and she didn't want to go back to the same life she'd had before. From juggling teaching and its stresses with the property and its demands, to maintaining the huge house and helping Olive with her unit, the committees and meetings – was that all her life would ever be?

Milt scrunched up his now-empty paper bag and picked up his coffee. "Do you mind eating on the way?"

Natalie swallowed her restlessness with a mouthful of croissant and climbed back into the car. She'd let it go for now but not altogether. Getting away for a holiday was the most important thing to her, even if she had to wait a few more weeks.

"I want to call in at Bob and Veronica's property before we go home."

"Why?" She stared hard at her husband as if the answer might be written on his face but he was looking in the side mirror watching for a gap in the traffic to pull out onto the road.

"Bob said Jack was pretty distressed last night by Veronica's news. He thought we might be able to reassure him. Jack's on his own. The girls are still travelling overseas."

"We hardly know him." Jack was the Halbots' oldest child and a year younger than Bree. He'd gone away to boarding school then had done ag studies at uni. He'd only been back on the property a year or so and Natalie's path hadn't crossed his in that time.

Milt flicked her a cautious look. "I've seen him a bit lately."

Unease churned in the pit of her stomach. "Where?" The Halbots lived further north along the Barrier Highway that later veered east and on to the New South Wales border. Their properties were on the same side of the road but to reach each other's houses was a half-hour drive with another neighbour's land between them. Both homesteads were nestled among large gum trees, a long way off the highway. You didn't go there without a purpose.

"Jack's interested in our new drafting yards and our breeding program. He's been to our place a couple of times."

Natalie felt as if someone had punched her. The air left her lungs. She stared at Milt but he was concentrating on the road ahead.

They overtook a truck then, finally, he glanced her way. "Bob's worried Jack won't want to stay on the property so he's keen to let him explore some changes. I couldn't say no, Natalie. How rude would that be?"

She looked ahead, the croissant cooling on her lap and the coffee undrunk. Outside the landscape was familiar and yet alien. Like the pieces of her life she thought she knew so well but that were shifting around her again.

"We can't live that close and not help each other," he said.

"We've never worked closely with the Halbots before."

Milt's big hands gripped the steering wheel tighter. The creases in his knuckles turned red against the brown tan of his skin. "Jack came to me. I didn't have a reasonable explanation for refusing him." He glanced across at her. "The past is the past, Nat. Like Bob said, it's long behind us now."

"Bob doesn't know the real reason for us to keep away though, does he?"

She studied Milt's profile as he concentrated on the road again. He didn't even glance her way. She had an urge to reach across and slap him and that shocked her so much she slid her hands under her thighs in case they moved without her say-so. She had to agree; up until yesterday she'd thought the past was put to bed but now she knew the things you buried had an awful way of surfacing and hitting you in the face again.

She looked ahead like Milt. The white lines flicked beneath them on the black bitumen, drawing them inexorably home. Visiting Jack was the last thing she wanted to do. She'd forgiven her husband for his one mistake all those years ago. And most days she could believe she'd forgiven Veronica, if she didn't have to see her. Once Natalie had made the decision to stay in the marriage she'd thrown her heart and soul into making things right, and she believed Milt had too. They'd had a glitch and they'd survived it. Their love life, if a little less frequent these days, had been better, their lives together with their family richer, she was sure of it, but Jack Halbot was the reason she could never really forget that one blip in their marriage. Born nine months after the affair, could it be that Jack was the one thing Natalie hadn't been able to give her husband – a son?

Not that Milt had ever said anything about wanting a son. Olive hadn't been so discreet about it. She'd knitted little blue matinee jackets for each pregnancy in the hope that Natalie would produce a son and heir. If Milt felt the same, he'd never let on in any way. He'd shown the same delight with the arrival of all three daughters. Natalie knew he loved his girls. Even if he was hard on them at times, it was tough love that showed how much he cared.

She'd prayed that Laura would be a boy, something else she felt guilty about now but back then, like Olive, she'd badly wanted a boy for Milt so he wouldn't ever long for the son he couldn't have. Now here he was, it seemed, working closely with the one person, after Veronica, that Natalie wished was far away on another planet.

"Nat?"

She turned. Milt glanced sideways at her as if he was waiting for an answer.

"Sorry?"

"I said would you prefer I dropped you home first before I go to see Jack?"

Her eyes focused on the passing scenery and she realised they were getting close to the turn-off to their property.

"No, it's all right. That will mean more driving for you and I know you're keen to get out in the paddock." She swallowed her treacherous thoughts and pulled a tight smile. "I haven't seen hide nor hair of Jack since he left for high school. I should say hello at least."

Milt nodded and they followed the highway on past their driveway. Twenty minutes later they were pulling up outside an old stone home, not as big as the Kings' but in much better condition and surrounded by manicured gardens. Natalie took it all in with a mix of amazement and envy. She hadn't been to the Halbots' place since Kate was a toddler and Bree a baby in her arms. Back then Bob and Veronica had only lived on the property for a few years. The house had been in need of repairs and paint, and the grounds had been almost barren. So different now. Natalie drank it all in, thinking of her simple garden, geraniums and gerberas the only colour.

A brown kelpie bounded over to Milt's door as he opened it, and wagged its tail as he patted its head.

"Hello, Buster."

Natalie got out of her side, her heart beating a little faster. Milt even knew the name of their dog. How often had he come here and when? She'd never given a thought to what he did while she was at school. They always talked about their day over dinner and not once had he mentioned coming to the Halbots' and yet here he was greeting their dog.

Milt waited for her and led the way through the back gate, past a neatly clipped rosemary hedge and herb garden to the back verandah. Three pairs of boots were lined up side by side at the back door; two sets large and well worn, the third petite and gleaming with polish.

"Anyone home?" Milt rapped on the wooden frame of the screen door. "Jack?"

"Hello," a voice responded then the screen pushed open. A tall young man smiled at Milt and stepped out in socked feet.

"You remember my wife?"

"Yes." Jack held out his hand. "Hello, Mrs King." His sad eyes were a pearly blue like Milt's.

She swallowed the lump in her throat. "Please call me Natalie."

"You've been with Mum?" Jack's face crumpled.

Without hesitation Milt drew him into a hug. Natalie stiffened. A pain stabbed through her as sharp as any knife. They were a similar height and Jack had fair hair like Milt's had been at his age, and waves like Milt's had sprung into when it grew too long. Even Jack's fingers were long and thin like Milt's.

Jack stood back, struggled and won against tears. Natalie was silent while Milt provided the platitudes. The cancer had been found early, Veronica was strong, much better treatment these days, she'd recover. Jack nodded with each of Milt's offerings like a parched man sipping a drink. He offered a cup of tea and Milt gently refused as they edged their way back towards the gate.

Jack stopped there, his feet still bootless.

"Why don't you come over for dinner tonight?"

Natalie heard Milt say the words and held her breath.

Jack turned to her.

She swallowed the lump that kept returning to her throat, aware Milt was watching her too. "Yes, don't be on your own, come over." Natalie heard herself say the words while she hoped he would refuse.

He didn't, and then they were driving away.

"I hope Bree and Graeme have been managing okay."

Natalie studied Milt as he manoeuvred along the Halbots' track back towards the front gate. Over the years there'd been plenty of strangers at their table. Milt loved inviting people for dinner and she enjoyed it too. They'd entertained family, friends and neighbours, wool buyers, interstate breeders, families visiting the region sponsored by the local church, and once when Milt had been more involved with the farming federation, they'd even had a busload of politicians stop for afternoon tea and a discussion about life on the land. Natalie had taken it all in her stride but the thought of Jack Halbot sitting at her table set all those pieces of the jigsaw of her life whirling again.

"What the hell's going on now?"

Milt's exclamation brought her back to the present. She'd been so lost in her thoughts she hadn't even noticed they'd reached home. Olive's car was parked by the back gate and Graeme's battered ute was pulled in beside it with the dogs barking a welcome from the back.

Natalie followed Milt inside. The wooden door crashed against the wall but she was distracted by the smell of burning and the cacophony of noise coming from her kitchen. They both came to a stop in the doorway. Natalie's mouth fell open at the sight before her. Every surface was covered in some kind of cooking utensil or bowl and half the contents of her pantry. Laura, Olive and Graeme were all standing around the table, Kate, looking pale, was lying on the floor with her legs propped up on a chair and Bree was half lying, half sitting on the table, one leg wrapped in a bandage and strips of bloodied denim scattered on the floor below.

"What in the blue blazes is going on here!" Milt strode forward.

There was a brief moment of quiet, except for the radio, as if someone had pressed a pause button, and then everyone spoke at once.

Natalie was the only one not speaking. She glanced again at Kate then at Bree, not knowing which of her daughters needed her the most. She decided on Bree.

"Quiet, the lot of you," Milt bellowed and Laura had the good sense to turn off the radio.

"What have you done?" Natalie's usual sense of calm in a crisis had deserted her.

Bree gave her a reassuring smile. "I'm all right, Mum. Came off my bike. Granny thinks I'll need some stitches."

Olive gave Natalie the briefest of nods and moved on to her son, who lowered his cheek so she could kiss it.

"And Kate?" Natalie looked to her oldest daughter, who was being helped to her feet by Graeme.

"I'm okay. Felt a bit woozy over Bree's blood."

"She should have a cup of sweet tea." Olive turned to Milt. "Laura's going to drive Bree into town in her car. I'll meet them at the hospital. Bree can tell you all about it when she gets back." She glanced at Natalie. "I'll leave the food for the workers in your hands. I might make it back to town in time to help pack up the trading table. You should have said you were too busy to bake, I would have understood."

Natalie resisted the urge to look heavenward.

Milt nodded at Bree. "I'll help you out to the car."

Kate moved up beside Natalie and slipped an arm around her mother's waist. Her pale face crinkled in a half-hearted smile. "Hi, Mum. Welcome home."

Natalie kissed her daughter's cheek. "Where did you spring from?"

"Surprise visit," she said in a pathetic voice.

"Lucky you're here," Milt said. "We'll need your help with the mustering."

"I don't think she should—" Olive gave a shake of her head.

"I'm feeling okay now, Granny."

Milt turned to Graeme. "Help me get Bree to the car then I'll get changed and we'll head out to the paddock before we lose any more of the day."

Milt and Graeme lifted Bree in a fireman's hold and Olive strode out ahead of them. "I'll get the doors."

Apart from the reference to the trading table she'd hardly acknowledged Natalie. Her nose was out of joint but that was nothing new. Natalie and Olive had had their moments – hardly a surprise with two women living under the same roof for many years. It was the tone of her voice and the stiffness of her stance that Natalie recognised so well. Olive was miffed, no doubt because Natalie hadn't done the required baking.

"Hi, Mum." Laura kissed her cheek. "Bye, Mum."

Natalie looked sideways at her youngest. Her hair was swept up under a ridiculous green hat and escaping from the bottom were strands of bright pink, blue and green. Laura hurried to the door. A slurping, sticking sound accompanied her. Natalie looked down at the mucky footprints across the linoleum.

"Kate, get the old ute out. I'll take my bike." Milt was still giving orders.

Kate made a mock salute to his back then she gave Natalie an apologetic look as she realised she'd been sprung. "I'll see you later, Mum." And then she was gone too.

In the distance Natalie could hear dogs barking, car doors slamming, engines starting. She surveyed the bombsite that was her kitchen and sunk to a chair. All she wanted to do was climb into bed and sleep for a week.

The screen door banged and Milt stuck his head in. "They're on their way."

Natalie turned towards him, unable to summon any words.

"She'll be all right, Nat."

She gave a weak nod. Her initial shock at seeing Bree's bloodied jeans and the bandage around the top of her leg had dissipated. If Olive decreed it was nothing too serious Natalie didn't need to worry. No matter what else might annoy her about her mother-in-law Natalie knew the girls' safety was paramount. Olive was not a fusser but her lack of haste reassured Natalie that Bree's injuries weren't too terrible.

Milt took a small step into the kitchen. "Bloody hell." With everyone else gone it was as if he'd noticed the state of the room for the first time. "Sorry to rush off. Will you be all right with this?"

Natalie nodded again. She didn't trust herself to speak.

"I'll get changed."

"What about lunch?" she managed.

He gave one more look around the kitchen and settled his gaze on her, his lips turned up in a rueful smile. "I'm sure we'll appreciate whatever you can rustle up." And then he was gone.

In the silence that followed, the pieces of Natalie's life shifted and swirled again. She gripped the table in case she was sucked down the plughole with them.

Eight

Bree hobbled from her quarters to the kitchen following the delicious smell of roasting meat. The slow-combustion fire warmed the room and Laura was the only inhabitant.

"Where's Mum?"

"She's gone to have a shower and get changed." Laura turned back from the window. The golden light of late afternoon streamed around her, highlighting the halo of kaleidoscope hair flowing out over her shoulders. "Evidently we're having Jack Halbot here for dinner."

Bree glanced at the table. The good placemats sat in a pile at one end and a pot of freshly picked gerberas took centre place.

"I haven't seen him since primary school," Laura went on. "I don't know why he suddenly got invited."

Bree lowered herself to a chair. "Dad's been helping him with sheep a bit lately."

"It's strange we've never socialised with the Halbots."

"Is it?" Bree hadn't ever thought about it. The Kings' property was large, tucked in a corner of grazing country, bounded by a highway with broad-acre farmers beyond it and a mountain range behind, over which the country was marginal, better suited to cattle. "We have other neighbours to the north we don't see much of but there's always been the Taylors and the Mercers and the Saints." Bree ticked off her fingers as she listed the names of several other families they called 'neighbours' even though they were physically separated by hectares and hectares of land. "And up until recently we've spent any free time with the Fannings." Their nearest neighbours, Brenda and Martin Fanning, had also been their parents' best friends.

"Mum must miss Aunty Brenda. It'd be awful to have your bestie up and leave after thirty-odd years." Laura was missing Spritzi already and they'd only been friends for a short time in comparison.

"She didn't up and leave. She had to sell the property after Uncle Martin died. She couldn't manage on her own and none of their kids were interested."

"Brisbane's such a long way from here though."

"She's got two of her kids there and a sister. It made sense."

"Still, Mum must miss her and with all of us gone it must get lonely, just her and Dad."

Bree gave a snort. "I'm still here and Granny comes out every week."

"But it's not the same as a friend. I think Mum seems a bit quiet."

"You've only been home five minutes."

"Maybe she needs to take a break, go to visit Aunty Brenda."

"Maybe."

"You still look pale," Laura said. "Does it hurt?"

"Like the devil." Bree had fallen into a deep sleep after they'd returned from the hospital. She'd needed several stitches and now the local anaesthetic had worn off and the throbbing pain had woken her. "Would you get me some painkillers from the bathroom?"

"Mum's one step ahead of you." Laura picked up a packet of tablets from the bench and brought them to Bree with a glass of water. "She left these for you."

Bree took two, drank the whole glass of water then grinned at her sister who'd sat down opposite. "You look like a giant lollipop."

"Thanks." Laura dragged her hair back from her face with her fingers. "I washed my hair this arvo. The more I do it the quicker it'll fade. I'll put it up again before Dad gets home."

"You don't think he'll notice?"

Laura grimaced.

★

Natalie sat in her bedroom in front of the dressing table. The shower had refreshed her and her equilibrium had returned. This was the one place in the house she felt was her own, the one room she'd been allowed to make changes to, to make her mark. The walls were the colour of milky coffee and the curtains steely grey. The furniture was oak and, conscious that her husband lived in a house full of women, she'd kept away from florals and frills and always chose a quilt cover and cushions with subtle patterns in greys and whites and splashes of deep red.

Once she'd overcome her despair at the mess in her kitchen she'd tackled the cleaning up. Laura had arrived back when it was nearly all done and had rushed to help. The sight of her daughter tidying away the recipe books had reminded Natalie again about the copy of *The Model Wife* she'd shoved back in the kitchen drawer. She'd asked Laura to mop the floor. Laura hadn't been keen but Natalie had insisted. While her daughter was off getting the mop and bucket Natalie had removed the book and taken it to her bedroom.

She looked at it now with its faded cover, the title barely readable; a harmless old book. She gave a soft snort and turned to the chapter titled 'Managing the Home'. Nat read the first line to herself. *The model wife is proud of the home her husband provides for her and shows her respect by keeping it perfectly clean and without clutter.* It was this chapter that had made her realise how much she'd conformed to the book's rules. The occasion had been Olive and Clem's thirtieth wedding anniversary, the year before Kate was born, and Milt and Connie had thought they should mark their parents' marriage milestone with a celebration. Natalie had convinced them to make it a surprise. She'd done most of the cooking over at their neighbour Martin's place. Those were the days before he'd married Brenda and he'd been pleased to have someone using his kitchen and leaving him leftovers.

The two days before the surprise party Olive and Clem had been in Adelaide. It had been school holidays, so Natalie had thrown herself into cleaning the shared areas of the old house from top to tail. She took down curtains and washed them, had the carpets steam cleaned, washed windows, dusted and polished every surface until everything gleamed. Each night she would fall into bed exhausted and Milt had declared her crazy, said no-one was going to notice a bit of dust on the windows or a smudge on a door handle.

But she was hooked on the sparkling results of her labour. Over the years, between marrying Milt, sharing a house with her in-laws and raising children and teaching, keeping a perfect house had become important to her and in the back of her mind hovered the next line from the chapter – *nothing destroys the happiness of married life more than the lazy, slovenly wife.*

She looked down at the little book gripped in her hands. She'd added her own messages and clippings and photos to prove to herself she wasn't the submissive and servile woman the chapters described. The loose pieces stuck in the back jutted out at all angles. She opened the book quickly to the last page and removed them, slammed the book shut again and put it to one side. On top of the loose pile of pages was Laura's handwritten soup recipe. She turned it over. Next was a battered clipping from a newspaper on how to graft roses. That was from when she'd thought she'd start a rose garden as a surprise for Clem. They'd planted one rose beside the front gate but nothing more had eventuated. So long ago now. She turned it over and put it on top of the soup recipe.

Slowly she worked her way through these scribbled notes and clippings she'd slipped into the back of the book over the years. She paused at a page showing how to fold napkins into swans and water lilies and smiled at the recollection of the rainy afternoon she'd spent with her girls trying to make the designs from paper servi-ettes. Further on there were articles on removing red-wine stains and how to name your pet. That must have been back when they'd got the last dog. Jaffer was eight years old now but it had been such hard work coming up with a name they could all agree on.

Finally she came to the last clipping. It was a full page from a magazine, folded into halves and more recent than the rest. In fact she knew it was four years old and why she'd put it in the book. It was a story on a family of pearl farmers in Broome, an intriguing tale of how they'd started the business from nothing, living in the isolation of the bush north of Broome. She'd cut it out six months before their thirtieth wedding anniversary and looked into fares to Broome. Pearls were the gift for thirty years of marriage and she'd decided a trip to buy them from the place where they were farmed would make the occasion extra special.

She slid the pages back into the book and this time she put it in the drawer of her dressing table. The book might be out of sight but the holiday was not. Milt had said the time wasn't right to get away then but they'd go one day. Life got busy and one day still hadn't come. She'd tried to pin him down as they drove home from Adelaide but he'd deflected her suggestion once again.

Natalie pushed back from the dressing table, tugged her dress down and brushed a piece of hair back from her face. She was not letting him off the hook any longer. Their thirty-fourth wedding anniversary was coming up in July. Bree was more than capable of looking after the property and Natalie was determined to have a proper holiday. It didn't have to be Broome but she and Milt were going away to mark their anniversary and if he wouldn't go she'd darn well go without him.

"Would you be brave enough to do that?" she asked out loud. Her startled face looked back at her from the mirror.

*

Bree sat at the kitchen table with her injured leg propped on a second chair. Laura was opposite her, engrossed in her phone, letting out the odd moan or giggle or tapping out a message. Bree was sure Laura would need rehab if she ever lost her phone.

"You're awake."

They both looked up at the sound of their mum's voice.

Natalie crossed the kitchen and rested a hand on Bree's shoulder. "How're you feeling?"

"A bit sore but I'll live."

"What happened exactly?"

"There was a piece of old wire partly buried on the edge of the track," she said. "It flung up, hooked my leg and off I came."

"Oh, Bree." Natalie's hand gripped her shoulder.

"Don't fuss, Mum." Bree shuffled in her chair, lowered her leg and shrugged off her mum's hand. "I'll live."

"You were lucky," Natalie said softly.

Bree knew she was lucky. The doctor had said a little deeper and further to the side and she would have severed an artery. She wouldn't have made it back to the house let alone the hospital, but that hadn't happened and there was no need to dwell on it.

Natalie turned to the fire.

"I've just added some wood," Laura said and stuffed her phone in her pocket.

"Thanks."

Bree studied her mum as she crossed to the fridge. She didn't look any different. What had Laura noticed? Natalie pushed the fridge door shut with her hip and carried an armful of vegetables to the sink, then took her apron from its hook and slipped it over her head. She was behaving the way she always did.

Laura went to help. "I've put the potatoes in with the meat."

"What about the pumpkin?"

"Not yet. I've cut it up though."

"Thanks." Natalie lined up the carrots.

"I like your dress." Laura hovered at her mother's side.

Bree took in her sister's contrite expression. No doubt trying to atone for the mess she'd created. The kitchen was spotless again, restored to its usual order. She hoped Laura had helped make it that way.

"Do you?" Natalie glanced down as if she didn't know what she was wearing then started to chop.

Bree thought her outfit was rather smart for a casual family dinner with only their distant neighbour as an extra. Still it wasn't often they were all home together and to Bree's knowledge Jack had never eaten with them before. Her mother always liked to make a good impression. Tonight she wore a loose-fitting long-sleeved dress, navy with a white leaf pattern, over tights and flat ankle boots. She'd put on some extra kilos over the last few years but she always looked smart.

"I can finish the vegies, Laura. Perhaps you could open a wine. I'd love a glass."

"Sure. Do you want something, Bree?"

"A beer, thanks."

Natalie glanced around. "Do you think that's wise if you're taking painkillers?"

"I'm sure one beer won't hurt."

Natalie opened her mouth, closed it again and turned back to her chopping.

Laura poured a glass of wine, took the tops off two beers and handed one to Bree.

"Cheers," she said and they all raised their glasses and took a sip. Then the silence was punctuated only by the sounds of Natalie's vegetable prep.

"How was Adelaide?" Bree asked.

There was a pause in the chopping. "Busy." Natalie's shoulders tilted as she continued cutting.

"What did you say you went for again?"

This time there was only a slight pause before the chopping resumed. "Accountant."

Bree frowned. She glanced at Laura who was looking at her phone again, not paying any attention.

"Granny was surprised you went." Bree tried another tack. "She quizzed me about it while we were waiting at the hospital."

The knife thumped on the solid wooden chopping board. "Granny doesn't have to know everything all the time."

Laura glanced up, met Bree's stare and stood. "Are you sure I can't help with the vegetables, Mum?"

"No." Natalie didn't look around. "You could set the table though...for six."

Laura arranged the placemats, set out the cutlery, added a glass to each place and a jug of water to the middle of the table.

The saucepans clattered and banged as Natalie filled them and set them on the stove then turned to her daughters. "I'm going to watch television in the den till the others get back." She picked up her wine and left.

From across the passage they heard the sound of a game show. Laura looked at Bree over the top of her beer, her face twisted into a grimace.

Their mother never watched television during the day unless she was sick. Now Bree was alert. "What's going on?" she hissed.

Laura shrugged. "I don't know. I told you Mum's been quiet all afternoon."

"Did you help her clean up?"

"Of course but she had most of it done by the time we got back. Then I had to run lunch out to the paddock. She hasn't said a word about my hair."

Bree took a sip of her beer and stared at her sister's colourful mop. "That'll be Dad's job."

★

"Hell's teeth, Laura!"

Natalie lurched forward in the recliner at the sound of her husband's bellow. She must have dozed off for a few minutes. She'd been watching a quiz show and now the newsreader was announcing an exclusive headline.

She struggled to her feet and adjusted her apron. The mustering crew were home. Time to finish the dinner preparation.

"What in the blue blazes have you done this time?"

Milt had obviously noticed Laura's hair. Natalie couldn't imagine how he'd missed it before. Even though Laura had kept it stuffed under her cap until this afternoon, pieces of coloured hair were visible around the edges.

"More like psychedelic blazes, I think." Kate was valiantly trying to lighten her father's mood.

"I hope that washes out." Milt again.

"Eventually." Laura's voice was hopeful.

Natalie sighed, picked up her empty wine glass and almost ran into her husband leaving the kitchen. He brushed his dust-coated lips across her cheek. "Have you seen Laura's hair?"

She nodded.

"What on earth will people think?"

Natalie shrugged her shoulders. "Perhaps you should lock her in the shed until it grows out."

He frowned, looked at her closely. "Are you all right?"

"Of course I am." She managed a smile. "It's only hair colour, Milt. It'll wash out."

He huffed and the anger left him. "I'll have a shower. Jack will be here soon. Do you think you should tell the girls about Veronica and tell them not to mention it?"

Natalie opened her mouth but he was already heading for the bathroom. She didn't want to talk to the girls about Veronica at all. It had been his idea to invite Jack, not hers. The last thing she felt like doing was making conversation with a stranger at their table. That's if he was a stranger. She wondered if Bree had also spent time with Jack. She didn't expect Laura or Kate would have as they were rarely home these days.

A stab of guilt made her draw a deep breath. She had her three daughters together under her roof and she'd hardly spoken to them. Seeing Kate had been a surprise. Natalie wondered what had brought her home. They hadn't had a chance to talk yet but she'd been concerned by her eldest daughter's pale complexion, a reflection of her own face she'd seen in the mirror.

And there was definitely something up with Laura – she was as skittish as a newborn lamb. The chaos she'd created in the kitchen had nearly been Natalie's undoing. She'd held herself together and then, once they'd all gone, she'd sat at the table and sobbed. Finally she'd got stuck into the cleaning and, as was often the case in her life, it had been a distraction. Then she'd told Laura about Jack coming for dinner and her daughter had been full of questions. The Halbots had been kept off the family-friend radar for all of Laura's life. Natalie could understand why she wondered about his imminent presence at their dinner table.

She took another deep breath, straightened her shoulders and went back to the kitchen. Kate and Bree were both headed to the door.

"You're awake." Kate grinned. "I stuck my head in earlier. You were snoozing."

"I didn't sleep well last night in a strange bed."

"Kate's going to use my shower." Bree had come up behind her sister.

"Can you wait?" Natalie said. "I need to tell you all something."

The three girls looked at her expectantly. Two sets of deep brown eyes and one set of pearly blue focused on her. Damn Milt. She drew herself up. "Mrs Halbot's just been diagnosed with breast cancer."

"Oh, that's terrible." Bree was the one to speak out; the other two murmured similar comments.

"She and Bob are in Adelaide until they find out more. Jack's fairly upset about it. That's why your dad invited him over...so he's not eating alone tonight."

"Of course." Bree nodded. "His sisters were going overseas. I guess they're still away travelling."

"How bad is it?" Kate asked.

Natalie looked into the worried faces of her daughters. A few days ago she'd thought they'd be hearing this news about her. "I believe it's aggressive but caught early."

"Is that why you were in Adelaide?" Laura asked, her voice sounding so young all of a sudden.

"Why would Mum and Dad go to Adelaide to be with the Halbots?" Bree scoffed. "It's not as if they're good friends."

"We happened to run into them...just after Veronica had received the news. She was...shocked as you can imagine and your dad...well, your dad and I stayed with her until Bob arrived." Natalie felt no need to tell her daughters they'd stayed the night at the Halbots' apartment.

"How did she find out?" Bree had moved closer.

"A routine mammogram."

"In the Breast Bus?"

"I guess so."

"You had a mammogram last week, didn't you?" Bree's eyes were wide with concern.

"Yes."

"That's why you went to Adelaide on short notice. It wasn't for the accountant. They found something, didn't they?"

"Oh, Mum."

"Not cancer." Both Kate and Laura spoke at once.

"I don't have cancer." Natalie felt a weight drop from her shoulders as she said it, relieved to announce it out loud to someone else for the first time. "They found a small lump but it's nothing bad, a cyst."

"Mum," the girls chorused in unison and threw their arms around her.

Natalie fought hard to paste a smile on her face. Until the relief of the call she'd received from the clinic earlier today she'd still held a small fear the biopsy might be positive. "I'm all right."

"Hell's teeth, what's happened now?"

They stepped apart. From the corner of her eye Natalie glimpsed Milt, hands on hips, worry on his face. He'd dealt capably with the girls' histrionics over the years, as long as it was one daughter at a time. More than two at once and he was stripped of his usual good sense and totally flummoxed.

"Mum's been telling us about her scare and Mrs Halbot's bad news," Kate said.

"Yes, well, thankfully your mother's fine."

He shuffled from foot to foot like he did when he felt out of his depth. His hair was slicked back, still damp from the shower, and he'd changed into clean jeans and his favourite checked shirt. He glanced at her but Natalie turned away, moved further into the kitchen, her back to them, and dabbed at her eyes with her apron. He was right. She was safe and she had all that mattered to her in the world, her girls and Milt. She'd lost her way for a moment but she could feel the pieces of her life begin to settle back into place. Perhaps telling her girls she didn't have cancer was what she'd needed. Like opening a valve to release pressure.

"Your mother's told you not to mention any of this while Jack's here."

Natalie composed her face, turned back. "I hadn't yet."

Milt looked at each of the girls. "I think it's best we don't."

"What if he says something?" Laura asked.

Milt frowned. "We respond in whichever way's appropriate."

"It seems an awful thing to say." Kate gripped her hands together. "But I'm glad it's not you going through this, Mum."

"We've got a lot to be thankful for," Milt said. "It's poor Veronica who's drawn the short straw."

The look of sorrow on his face stabbed Natalie as sharply as any knife. She reached a hand for the bench as the off-kilter feeling returned, her brief sense of relief swept away.

There was a knock at the back door.

"I haven't had my shower," Kate moaned.

"Go and have it." Bree gave her sister a gentle push. "The rest of us can look after one visitor till you get back."

"Answer the door, Laura, and take Jack into the den." Milt was back giving orders. "I'll bring in some drinks. We'll get out of your mother's hair."

Natalie turned to the bench and gripped it with both hands.

"Can I help?" Bree asked.

Natalie shook her head. "You go with the others and rest that leg. There's not much left to do here now."

And just like that, she was alone again and the family she loved were welcoming the cuckoo into her home.

★

Kate glanced around the table. The meal had started out a bit quiet but now everyone except her mother was contributing to the discussion about the possibility of Jack changing sheep breeds. Laura had made the two men laugh with her suggestions of brown-and-black ones. She'd indignantly defended her choice saying how much cuter they were than plain old white. It was a safe topic for dinner and they'd thrown themselves into it.

"I suppose you'll be wanting rainbow-coloured sheep next," Bree said, which brought a deep chuckle from Milt. He'd mellowed since his initial reaction to Laura's hair, reassured it would wash out.

It helped that they all had a few drinks under their belts. Kate had gone easy. She was tired enough without throwing alcohol into the mix. Her mother was on her third glass of wine. Not that Kate was counting but Natalie wasn't a big drinker. She sometimes shared a beer with Milt at the end of a hot day or had a glass of red with him in the winter. But she always kept a bottle of white in the fridge in case of visitors.

Still that's what Jack was, a visitor. Not that he was drinking wine and he'd only had two beers but he was talking to her father like they were old mates.

Kate glanced at her mother. Natalie's eyes were glazed as if she wasn't listening to the conversation but was somewhere else. Kate hoped there'd be time over the weekend for a chat, just the two of them, before her mother went back to school and Kate went home.

"Have you thought any more on restoring your tennis court, Bree?" Jack's question dropped on the conversation with all the subtlety of a bomb.

"Are we going to have a tennis court again?" Laura asked.

Kate looked from Bree to her father to her mother, their faces all set like stone.

"I've been talking to Dad about it." Bree turned to her mother, her look defiant. "I know you don't want a tennis court but I think it would be fun to have one again. A while back I called over to see how the Halbots maintained theirs."

Kate was the only one who remembered the time when the tennis court had been the focus of any spare weekends at the Kings' and they were only vague memories, fed by old photos of Granny and Pa holding wooden tennis racquets, standing on the black tar court with neighbours. Her dad had been in some photos and so had the Halbots. By the time she'd turned four the only thing the tennis court was good for was riding her three-wheeler bike and even then she had to dodge the weeds pushing up through the widening cracks. The black tar had been ripped up years ago and now the space was overgrown and the fence that surrounded it was falling down in places.

"It's a lot of work when you don't play tennis," Kate said.

"I played a bit last summer and I really enjoyed it."

"Owen's an excellent pick-up for the team," Jack said.

"Oh, so that's why you took up tennis." Laura made exaggerated winks across the table at Bree.

"Jack and Owen both play number one for their teams." Bree smiled at Jack. "It's a toss-up each time to see who'll win."

"I think I'd better take up tennis then," Laura said. "Sounds like there's lots of talent."

"We have no need for a tennis court here." Natalie sat her knife and fork in the centre of her empty plate. Her words fell like a wet blanket, ending the discussion.

"Will you be able to give me a trim while I'm home, Laura?" Kate thought it best to change the subject.

"Sure."

"Are you a hairdresser?" Jack asked.

"Yep." Laura grinned at him. "If you need a haircut let me know."

"Or a colour," Bree said.

"Careful what you get yourself into, Jack," Milt warned.

Jack dragged his fingers through his hair. "My sisters never have the same hair colour for long and I don't remember what their original colour was any more." He turned to Laura. "But they've never had rainbow stripes. Does it still feel like hair?"

"Of course." Laura tilted her head towards him. "Touch it and see."

He picked up a small lock, rubbed it between his fingers and let it go.

"It's only colour," Laura said. "Just the same as your sisters, only a different colour I assume."

Milt gave a snort. "I can't imagine Jack's sisters dying their hair like a rainbow."

"Perhaps Laura's trying to tell us something." Bree had a mischievous look on her face.

Milt thumped the table. "Hell's teeth. This isn't your way of telling us you're gay, is it?"

"Calm down, Dad." Kate glanced from Jack to her mother who was still staring into the distance as if she wasn't actually present.

"Chill, Dad." Laura shook her head, making the rainbow fluff out more. "If I was going to tell you I was gay I'd just tell you without any props."

Kate winked at Laura then turned back to her dad. "There's no way Laura is gay, Dad."

"Look at all the boyfriends she's had." Bree smirked and wiggled her eyebrows.

"So now you're suggesting I'm a tart." Laura glared at them.

"That's enough of that kind of talk." Natalie pushed back her chair with force, making it teeter a moment before settling back on the floor.

Silence fell around the table once again.

"We're only joking, Mum."

Natalie's face flushed at Bree's snappish response. "Time for dessert." She plucked up her plate.

"It smells good," Milt said.

Kate picked up her own plate then reached for her father's and the others passed theirs. She took the stack to the sink and opened the dishwasher. Her mother was taking an apricot pie from the oven.

"Girl talk," Milt joked. "I'm always outnumbered here."

"Oh, Dad," Laura teased. "You love having a house full of women. It brings out your feminine side."

"Humph!" Milt tried to look affronted. "Your father's lucky to have you, Jack."

Kate glanced at her mother as the pie dish thumped loudly on the wooden chopping board. Her jaw was rigid. "Are you all right, Mum? Shall I serve the pie?"

"I'm fine." Natalie pulled her shoulders back and picked up a knife. "I'll dish up. Pass the plates please."

Natalie cut wedges of pie, levered them up and slapped them into the bowls. Kate had the feeling that everything was far from fine.

*

The bedside lamp illuminated the old book lying open on Natalie's lap. She sat on the edge of the bed and behind her she heard Milt's noisy, deep breaths. Not quite a snore but almost. He'd already been asleep by the time she'd finished in the kitchen and made her way to their bedroom. More words from the managing the home chapter surfaced as she glared at him. *It is the model wife's responsibility to provide her husband a happy home…the single spot of rest which a man has upon this earth for the cultivation of his noblest sensibilities.*

She'd slid down in the bed, her arms rigidly at her sides. Milt got his rest, that was for sure. Wide awake, her own light still on, she'd gone back over the evening and Jack's conversation, his face and the way his gaze had kept returning to Laura. Several times she'd almost tapped Milt's shoulder, to wake him and ask him outright but then she'd drag her hand back. If he said Jack was his son, what then? Could they just go on as normal? She was terrified she couldn't answer that question. Finally Natalie had eased back the covers and sat up. That's when she'd taken the book from her dresser drawer. It was as if it was taunting her. She'd glanced at Milt, still gently snoring, and flipped it open.

Chapter Two stood out in dark print at the top of the page and below that, 'Friends are Welcome.' *The model wife should accept her husband's friends and receive them in her home.* Twenty-seven years ago she'd written NO in bold letters, underlined it several times and then in very small print as if too afraid for it to be easily read she'd written *but not into your husband's bed.*

Stuck on the page beside it was a photo of their tennis court. Veronica and Bob stood at the front beside Milt and Natalie, everyone smiling. She remembered the fun they'd had that day. It had been the last time the Kings had hosted a social tennis match – a month before the glitch.

She gripped her mouth with one hand. Why was she torturing herself with this now? She shook her head at her own silent question but she knew the truth. Somehow she'd forgiven Milt his indiscretion, they'd moved on and made a decent life, but today, when she'd seen Jack Halbot, she knew that the life they'd rebuilt together had been founded on a lie. Jack was so like Milt he had to be his son, and the very thought of it made her feel sick.

She sat, eyes closed, gripping the book in her hands until she was startled by a particularly deep snort from Milt. He made some snuffling noises then flung himself onto his side, his face towards her. She reached out and flicked off the lamp and a new resolve flowed through her. She had three daughters, Milt's daughters, and they were not going to be displaced by a son from the other side of the quilt. Tomorrow she would have it out with Milt and they'd plan a way forward, one which involved keeping their distance from the Halbots...all of them...and a holiday would be the perfect place to start.

Nine

"Morning, Mum." Bree eased herself onto a kitchen chair and tried to find the best position for her aching leg. She'd had trouble going to sleep then slept in and now she felt tired and scratchy.

Natalie looked over her shoulder. There were shadows under her eyes too. "How are you?"

"Sore and sorry."

"Coffee?"

Bree nodded. Natalie put a cup under the coffee spout and turned on the machine. She brought it to the table with the packet of paracetamol. "Take a couple of these."

"Thanks."

"Should I take a look?"

"I already have. There's nothing to see. The plaster is clean, no blood seeping, no redness around the edges."

Natalie swept a lock of hair back from Bree's face and rested her hand on her cheek. "You'll live to fight another day."

Her gentle touch made Bree feel like a little girl again. "It's only a few cuts and bruises." Her tone was sharper than she'd intended and her mum stepped back as if she'd been stung.

"Would you like some toast?" Natalie moved back to the kitchen bench.

"Thanks." Bree took a deep breath and tried to quell the surge of annoyance at being housebound. "I assume Kate's gone with Dad?"

"And Laura. Graeme can't help today. They left an hour ago."

"Perhaps I can go out later." Bree swallowed the tablets and shifted on her seat to find a more comfortable spot.

Natalie glanced at her. "I suspect you were told to rest that leg for a few days." The toast popped and she put it on a plate and set it in front of Bree.

Bree slapped butter on the toast. "The doctor said to keep it dry for twenty-four hours then come back in seven days to have the stitches removed." And he'd also said immobilise it for a couple of days but she didn't tell her mum that.

"Your dad will manage with the crew he's hired. Kate's staying till later in the week and Graeme will be back on Monday."

Natalie went back to the food she'd been preparing and Bree sipped her coffee. She badly wanted to be out there with them. She loved being outside working and especially mustering. She also felt a little guilty that she was going to ask for time off once tailing was finished. She'd said yes to Owen. He was heading north in a week's time and she was going to follow as soon as she could.

Natalie snapped the lid on a container of sandwiches and put them in the fridge then brought her cup and sat beside Bree.

"Since you're housebound for a few days it'll be a good chance to get reacquainted with the computer and the account-keeping."

Bree took another sip of her coffee. This was the perfect time to tell her mother about her plans. Then they could talk to Milt together. Natalie would smooth over any objections he raised.

"Would you mind if we put it off for a bit longer?"

"Why?"

"I'm thinking of trying something different."

"Different in what way? We've got the best software there is, according to the accountant."

"I don't mean with the books, I mean different as in work…off the property…for a while."

Natalie was quiet for a moment then she placed her cup carefully on the table. "When did you decide this?"

"I've been thinking about it for a bit."

"Have you?" Natalie studied her with a concerned frown then rose and took her cup to the sink. She turned and shook her head. "It's just that I was hoping to get your dad away from the place for a few weeks. We haven't had a proper holiday in ages and…well, our wedding anniversary is coming up and I thought we could go soon."

"It's not a special anniversary is it?" Kate was the one who kept up-to-date on those things and she hadn't mentioned it.

"No, but we didn't get away for our thirtieth…or for any anniversary for that matter. I've decided we need a break."

Bree sunk lower in her chair. "You could go when I get back. Take some leave from school." She'd hoped for empathy from her mother, not opposition.

"How long will you be gone?"

"It would only be for a couple of months."

"Months!" Natalie's eyebrows rose. "Where?"

"Marla…with Owen."

"I see." Her mother swung back, put her cup in the dishwasher and shut the door with a thud.

"I'll wait till after tailing, and Laura will be here."

"What do you mean Laura will be here?"

Blast. Bree had thought Laura had talked to her mum. On the way back from the hospital yesterday that had been her plan, to chat while everyone else was out. "She's quit her job." Bree winced at both the worry on her mother's face and the pain in her leg as she straightened up.

"Why?" Natalie shook her head.

"It's complicated."

"It always is with Laura."

It was unlike her mum to be grumpy. Bree felt her own annoyance rise again. Laura had had plenty of time to tell their parents she was staying. "I thought she'd told you. She'd planned to."

Natalie sighed. "Well, I've got accounting to do."

And with that she was gone, leaving Bree feeling angry and guilty all at once. The bloody paperwork was another job on its own. Bree had to admit she'd been avoiding taking it over. Natalie had always done the books and she wasn't going anywhere. Bree couldn't see why she just didn't keep doing them. There was no point in taking it on anyway if she went to Marla for a few months or even more. She'd decided not to say how long it could be when she'd seen her mother's reaction.

Bree hobbled to the sink with her cup. Even though her dad had said the property could be hers one day he was showing no signs of letting go of the reins yet. They had a rough plan in place but nothing was to be finalised until Laura turned thirty. That was six years away. Bree needed this break.

From deeper in the house she heard music. The large dining room rarely got used and a corner of it had been set up as an office. Her mother often played her CDs while she worked up there. Bree pushed away the guilt. It wasn't as if Natalie hadn't done the books for years. A few more months wouldn't matter, surely... unless there was some urgency now. Her mother had remained vague about the trip to Adelaide and continued to be out of sorts. What if there was something she was keeping from them?

*

Natalie stared at the computer screen in front of her but the figures wriggled and jumped as tears rolled down her cheeks. She dabbed at them furiously. There'd been no chance to talk alone with Milt this morning, no opportunity to bring up the topic of Jack again. She'd imagined having it out with Milt and regardless of the outcome regarding Jack's parentage she'd decided they'd rebuild; they'd done it before. She'd been clinging to that thought, and also the chance to get away, but now it seemed raising the idea of a holiday would be pointless. If Bree went off for that long a time there was no way Milt would leave the property. It wasn't that she didn't understand Bree's need to get away, she felt it so strongly herself, but the timing was all wrong.

Natalie took up the clip of accounts from beside the keyboard and started sifting through them. She'd been struggling to stay on top of the account-keeping for months now. Goodness knows how she'd sort it in time for the end of financial year. Somehow her heart hadn't been in it and she'd really hoped Bree would show more interest, but she didn't want to push her and now there was no point. Natalie couldn't shake the worry and the disappointment that overwhelmed her. After ten minutes of fruitless fiddling she pushed back from the desk. Bree had said Laura was back to stay for a while but Laura hadn't mentioned it. Her bedroom door had been shut whenever Natalie had passed. She decided it was time to investigate.

*

Laura leaned against the dual cab, the sun warm on her face, her stomach comfortably full of her mother's sandwiches. They'd all met in a creek bed, dry of water and offering some shelter from the chilly wind. Her mum had been waiting with lunch when they'd all arrived, Milt and Kate and the two blokes all on motorbikes and Laura in the ute. Laura had managed to get through the morning with only a few wrong turns and without her dad losing his cool and they'd finished the paddock. She hoped that meant he might not need her this arvo.

She was only half listening to the conversation; so was her mother, judging by the faraway look on her face. Bree and Kate had been talking about music and Kate was banging on about a show her friend Sarah had gone to in Port Lincoln, but she'd stayed the weekend and Kate hadn't been able to go because she had to work the next day. Kate was acting as if it was a big deal, as if Sarah had planned her weekend to exclude Kate. Laura wouldn't have been surprised if that were true. She'd only met Sarah a couple of times but it had been enough for her to question the friendship. Sarah was gushy and frilly and…pink. Each time Laura had met her she'd been wearing all pink; even her shoes and fingernails were a shade of pink. Laura suspected her underwear would be too. Kate was the polar opposite; never out of jeans, always practical and reliable, a down-to-earth person with a heart of gold. That might be laying it on a bit thick but Laura did admire her oldest sister.

"I guess friendships change," Bree said and looked at her mum as if she'd back her up but Natalie had moved from the fallen log she'd been perched on to pack up the remains of their lunch and obviously had no opinion on the matter.

Laura ventured one instead. "I don't understand why you're even friends with her." She took a bite of the apple she'd whipped from the fruit basket before her mum had taken it away. "It's not as if you've got anything in common."

"We have lots in common."

"Like what?"

"Books, movies—"

"How often do you go to the movies?"

"We do the odd trip to Port Lincoln together, see a movie, go shopping. Well, we used to…" Kate faltered. "I don't know if we will much in the future."

"Why not?" Bree asked.

Kate's pale cheeks went pink. She looked down at her boots. "Bit of a difference of opinion."

"Over what?"

"Nothing much." Kate looked up again. "Anyway we don't have to leave the house to see movies. We do have Netflix. Unlike some other rural dwellers I know." Kate gave her parents a pointed look and Laura, happy to have an ally, joined her in the stare. The Kings' television was old and suggestions they should buy a new model and subscribe to any form of paid entertainment always went unheeded. They'd only installed a wireless network in the last few years. Natalie either didn't hear Kate's dig or ignored it. She had her head in the back of the four-wheel drive packing things away and the two blokes had wandered back to their bikes and were having a smoke.

"We rural dwellers have enough to do without it." Milt took the bait.

"You're always complaining there's nothing to watch," Kate said in the teasy voice she used when she was trying to cajole her dad.

"Then I do something else."

"But sometimes I don't want to do something else," Laura said. "Sometimes it's good to veg in front of a movie."

"Or binge on a series," Kate said.

Milt shook his head and tossed the dregs of his tea to the ground. "Now you're talking another language."

"Maybe you could buy a new TV while I'm home, get Netflix. I could set it up for you." Laura had only just thought of it and she was enthused by the idea. She'd had a Netflix subscription but she'd cancelled when she quit her job. She only had so much money and she had no idea how long it would be before she found something else. Thank goodness she had her parents to rely on till then. "You need a smart TV these days, Dad."

"I don't want any electronic equipment telling me what to do." Milt put his hands to his hips and stretched backward. "Anyway, luckily for my bank balance the shops are shut now."

"There's online shopping these days, you know, Dad. Anytime, anywhere."

"I prefer to support our local shops."

Laura straightened up, warming further to her idea. "We could go into town next week, see what they've got." It was out before she'd thought about it.

"Are you staying longer than the weekend?" he asked.

"Maybe."

"Is it Granny Pork Roast night?" Kate changed the subject.

"I assume so. She usually comes out Saturday night, unless we're not home." Milt looked to his wife for confirmation.

"She hasn't said she's not."

"Yay!" Laura took her sister's hint and enthused over the prospect of another of Natalie's roasts. "I haven't had roast pork since the last time I was home." For as long as Laura could remember they'd had a pork roast on a Sunday night. It had been Pa's favourite meal and by default everyone else's. After he died and Granny moved into town, they'd changed it to Saturday night. Granny would stay over and once a month there was a Sunday morning service at the little local church and they'd all go together.

"We're not having roast pork." Natalie had joined their group again. "We had a roast last night. I've put a curry on in the slow cooker."

There was a heartbeat's pause.

"Whatever we eat will be fine," Milt said. "Granny likes to see you all. Now we'd better get back to work. It'll be dark before we know it. Kate, you go out to the ram paddock and check the water there. I'll do the back paddock and the scrub block. You might as well go home, Laura. After that we're done for today."

At the sound of the bikes the two dogs rose from their rest in the shade of the ute, but no call came from the boss and they sank down to their bellies, heads on paws. Laura turned to her mother but her relief at being exempted from further paddock work was short-lived.

"Are you going to tell me what's going on?" Natalie was rarely so blunt.

"I've come home for a while."

"How long is 'a while'?"

Laura shrugged. This wasn't how she'd thought the conversation with her mother would go. Instead of the easy pouring out of her story she felt reluctant, uneasy under her mother's scrutiny.

"I've seen your bedroom, Laura. All your worldly possessions seem to be occupying every nook and cranny."

"I'm not sure how long exactly." She looked down at the dark-brown soil beneath her boots, still parched from a long, hot summer and not enough autumn rain. "I've quit my job."

Silence lingered between them. A lone crow cawed, the long stretched-out sound underlining the quiet in a sad wail.

Finally Natalie spoke. "I see." Only two words but they carried a load of censure.

Laura looked up but her mother was reaching down to pick up the thermos, the last of their lunch items.

"At least I can help here while Bree's out of action," Laura offered.

Natalie glanced back, a small frown furrowing her brow.

They both knew the truth about that. Laura was no proper replacement for Bree.

"I'll see you at home." Natalie strode away to the four-wheel drive and that was it. No surprise, no gentle questions, no chat about the whys or wherefores of her decision.

The door thudded shut, the motor started and her mother drove away. The dogs rose, half-heartedly this time, and with no response from Laura they settled under the ute again.

Laura had a burning feeling in her chest and the day felt dull even though there were few clouds in the sky. Her mum had said little but Laura had been rebuked as crushingly as if there'd been words. It was the way Granny had sometimes made her feel when she was a child but never her mum. Natalie's way was to calmly outline options and, whichever path they took, Laura and her siblings always knew with sure certainty that there would be consequences for their actions but that the choice was theirs.

Laura stared at the dust trail left in the air by her mum's vehicle. She'd come home to lick her wounds, be fussed over by her mother and to think about the future but nothing had felt right since she'd arrived. It was as if she'd turned up at an alternative family and her place in it didn't exist.

*

Kate had been pleased to find the water trough clean and flowing freely, nothing to clear out or fix, so she was back at the homestead in quick time. She put the motorbike away in the shed and headed for the house. Inside there was silence. She washed up in the bathroom and walked on socked feet to the kitchen. Her mother was standing at the bench, her back to the door, looking out the window.

"I'm back. Dad will probably be a while." He had a lot further to go than Kate and might not be as lucky with the state of the troughs as she'd been. "Where is everyone?"

Natalie didn't move at first as if she hadn't heard, then, slowly, she turned. "Your sisters are in their rooms. Bree's resting and I hope Laura's cleaning up. Did you know she was home to stay?"

Kate didn't recognise the stiff woman who stared at her with a face full of worry. "She told me the night I arrived." She crossed the gleaming kitchen. The delicious smell of curry wafted from the slow cooker. She checked the water level in the kettle and flicked it on. "I'd love a cuppa. Do you want one?"

"Thanks." Natalie sat at the table.

Kate could feel her mother studying her as she took out cups and tea bags, and poured some milk in Natalie's cup. Finally, when she brought the two cups to the table, Natalie stopped looking at her and instead stared into her tea.

"Are you okay, Mum?"

Natalie's fingers wrapped tightly around her cup. "I'm fine." She looked up. A quick smile lifted the corners of her lips. "What about you?"

The question had been asked but Kate could see there was no real request for the truth. "I'm fine too."

"You haven't been home in a while. How's Sean?"

Once again the words were said but Kate could see there was no enquiring look, no desire for any but the simplest of answers. "He's good. Having a boys' weekend at the shack. I had a bit of free time so decided to come for a visit."

"And this fight you've had with Sarah?"

"It wasn't a fight exactly." Kate still hurt from her friend's bombshell. She wanted to talk it over with her mum but now didn't feel right.

"You're good friends. You'll make up." Natalie took a sip of her tea then placed the cup carefully back on the table. "Brenda and I had a few fallings-out over the years."

"Really? You two always acted like bosom buddies."

"We were but even bosom buddies have differences of opinion. Brenda was never one to forgive easily. I usually made the first move even when she was the one who'd started it. You might have to step up, be the bigger person."

Kate gave a noncommittal murmur. She didn't want to phone her best friend and hear more excited gabble about babies. Sarah had exploded with it. There'd been no gentle unfolding to give Kate a chance to take it in. The baby news had rocked her.

"I'd give anything to have Brenda sitting here with me now."

Natalie's words had been little more than a whisper and she was gripping her teacup, staring into it.

"Are you sure everything's all right, Mum?" Kate waited but her mum didn't answer. The knuckles of her fingers were going white. "The tests you had. They were all okay?"

"Yes." Natalie nodded, then she looked at Kate as if she'd only just noticed she was there. She smiled again, but there was no accompanying spark in her eyes. "All results clear."

"That's good."

"How long are you staying?"

Kate faltered. The question had a desperate sound. "A few days. I'll go home later in the week."

"It'll be nice to have a catch-up." The oven timer beeped. Natalie turned, gazed vaguely in that direction. "I've made a baked cheesecake for sweets."

"Granny will love that." Kate smiled.

"Will she?" Natalie rose stiffly from her chair, her look almost vacant as if she was trying to remember something.

"Of course. She's got such a sweet tooth and...cheesecake was always Pa's favourite."

Kate watched her mum walk stiffly across the kitchen. It was as if a stranger had taken over her body. Kate wanted to shake her, ask what had become of her mum, the warm welcoming woman who took everything in her stride, dished out love in spadefuls and took on board anything that came along.

Natalie took the cheesecake from the oven, set it on a wire rack to cool and turned back to Kate. "It's a baked cheesecake served with berry coulis and cream. I haven't made it for years." Then she spun on her heel and left the kitchen.

Kate clutched her cup in the hope the warmth would be some kind of steadying presence while her mother's cup sat cooling on the table.

Ten

Natalie closed the bedroom door, leaned against it and stared at her dressing-table drawer as if it would open of its own accord. It couldn't, of course. The same way the contents of a book couldn't control your life. She left her position against the door, strode to the dressing table and wrenched open the drawer. *The Model Wife* still rested innocently where she'd left it. She snatched it up and flicked the pages open to Chapter Three. 'Parents'. *The model wife respects and cares for her husband's parents and should put their needs before those of her own parents and herself.*

The first time Nat met Milt's parents it was a hot Saturday night in February, after tennis. Milt and his team had won that day, guaranteeing a place in the finals. There'd been plenty of congratulatory drinks and then he'd told her his parents had invited her for dinner. It had only been three weeks since they'd met but Natalie had already fallen in love with him.

"I'll have to go home and change," she wailed. She was wearing a skimpy summer dress that she'd been in all day and she was hot and sweaty, her make-up all melted away.

"No time," Milt said. His eyes were bright from too many beers and he swept her to the car with his big strong arm around her. "We're already late."

"Oh, Milt," she wailed again. She could deal with a class of twenty-eight six-year-olds but she was suddenly terrified of meeting his parents.

"They're used to me coming home like this after tennis."

She wasn't sure if by 'like this' he meant dishevelled and sweaty, or with a few too many drinks under his belt or both.

"Are you sure they invited me?"

"Of course. It was the last thing Mum said as I went out the door this morning. She's cooking a roast."

"Why didn't you warn me?"

"Sorry. I forgot in the rush to get to tennis." He opened the passenger door of his ute for her. "Now that Connie's gone back to uni it's a bit dull at our house. Mum and Dad like to have more than me at the table for roast dinner."

Natalie looked from the open door back to his merry face. "All right, but you can't drive."

"I'll be fine." He leaned in and planted a boozy kiss on her lips. "We'll take the back roads."

She giggled at the brush of his stubble on her cheek but held out her hand for the keys all the same. "I'll drive."

He shrugged his shoulders and handed them over, a cheeky grin on his face. Natalie climbed into the driver's seat and her bravado faltered. Now she knew why he'd given her that look. She'd forgotten the ute was a manual. She'd never driven a gear-shift car before.

Milt grinned at her from the passenger seat. "Foot on the clutch before you start it."

She'd turned away from him, inspected the gear stick and started the engine. They bunny hopped away from the tennis club to a chorus of catcalls and whistles from some of his mates but once on the road she was fine and quite pleased she had a new skill.

By the time they lurched to a stop outside the back gate she didn't feel quite so clammy. She discovered a lipstick in her bag which she applied, brushed her short hair into place with her fingers and ran her hands down her crumpled dress as she stepped out of the driver's seat. Milt rounded the ute. He was chewing some gum and had done an amazing job of sobering up on the thirty-minute journey.

"Ready?" he said and held out his hand.

Natalie hesitated. They'd arrived as the last of the sun's rays illuminated the sky in a soft orange glow and now that she had time to take it in she realised how large the house before her was. She swallowed the lump in her throat and took Milt's hand, grateful for the comfort of his strong, steady grip. She followed him inside, one step behind him, and immediately the temperature dropped several degrees. He shut the heavy wooden door while she took in the lofty ceiling and wide hall. There was light spilling from an open door ahead but beyond that the passage disappeared into shadows. She could see other doors close to them in the solid stone walls but they were all shut.

"Is that you, Milton?" a woman's voice called. "We're in the kitchen."

He winked at Natalie then led her to the open door.

"Mum, Dad, this is Natalie." He stepped aside so she could walk into the room. The woman standing before her was short; she wore a loose patterned dress with an apron tied around her middle and was inspecting Natalie with a sharp gaze.

Natalie held out her hand. "Hello, Mrs King."

Olive gave her hand a quick shake. "I'm sorry about my son keeping you out so late. You must be hungry. Everything's ready. Do sit down."

Natalie followed Milt further in to the huge kitchen. Cupboards ran along two and a half of its walls, punctuated by ovens and a huge fridge with a matching freezer. In the middle was a large solid-wood table and the man who'd been sitting at the end of it rose to his feet. This was where Milt had got his height from. His father smiled a genuine welcome.

"Hello, Natalie," he said.

"Hello, Mr King." She shook the hand he held out. It was rougher than Milt's but his grip was gentle like the smile on his lips.

"Please call me Clem," he said and from then on she had.

Clem offered her a seat, asked how she'd enjoyed her day and made her feel at home. She wasn't quite so comfortable under Olive's appraising eye. Her words of welcome didn't match the sharp, assessing look she kept directing at Natalie, so different to the benevolent gaze she bestowed on her son – a cross between adoration and incredulity, as if she couldn't quite believe she'd produced such a strong, good-looking offspring.

The evening was relaxing enough. Natalie shared a long-neck beer with Clem and Milt. Olive stuck to sherry. The roast had been dry and the vegetables overcooked. Natalie had assumed it was because they were late but came to discover that was how Olive cooked every roast. They'd eaten cheesecake that had a crumbling base and a gluggy filling. When Natalie had been invited again the following week she took a cheesecake she'd made herself. Clem had loved it. Cheesecakes had become her trademark dessert and even though they'd dropped in and out of fashion over the years, she often made an old favourite or searched out a new recipe to try.

Now she ran her finger down the glossy page she had cut from a magazine and glued onto the blank page before Chapter Three in the book. It was a recipe for New York–style baked cheesecake with berry coulis. She hadn't made it for years and yet tonight she'd whipped it up without even looking at the recipe.

"Nat?"

She jumped up from the bed.

Milt's footsteps thudded up the passage. Even though he would be bootless and there was a carpet runner over the wooden floorboards, he still couldn't manage to walk quietly. Never had been able to.

She shoved the book under her pillow as he pushed open the door.

"Here you are." He paused. "Everything all right?"

"Fine." How many times had she said that today? "Fine." She couldn't help herself. Resentment seethed inside her. "Everything's fine."

Milt opened his mouth, the puzzlement on his face almost comical. Then he changed tack mid-thought. She could read him well. Or at least she'd thought she could. She took a deep breath.

"Milt, I want to—"

"You need to talk to the girls." He cut her off. "Have you seen the state of the bathroom? There's not a surface spare, bottles without lids, a line-up of hair machines in the power board, they'll blow a circuit if they all start up together, and there're rainbow strands of hair all over the floor and the basin." He growled but there was no real depth to it.

"You usually wash your hands in the laundry."

"The trough was full of clothes."

Natalie thought about the en suite she'd once tried to have added to their bedroom. It had been back when the two older girls had reached teenage years and the bathroom had become a battleground. Milt had raged like a bull at their clutter. After one particularly busy weekend when they'd had girlfriends staying over and he'd raved on to her for ten minutes, Natalie had hatched a plan to build an extra bathroom under the verandah outside their bedroom. Milt had said it was a waste of money and Olive had backed him as she always did. Clem had sat on the fence as he always did. Olive had said they'd always managed with one bathroom. Of course she and Clem were living in the quarters by then and money had already been spent to bring that bathroom up to scratch.

Natalie had even gone in to the bank and organised a personal loan, much to the amusement of the manager at the time who was also a family friend. She was prepared to pay it back out of her teaching wage. Clem had convinced her in his quiet way she'd be wasting her money. Best to save it for a rainy day when it might really be needed for something important. It had certainly been helpful to have her own money when it came to tough years on the farm and there'd been other expenses: Kate's ongoing treatment after she'd fallen from a tree; Bree's extra study trips; Laura's braces. Natalie's off-farm income had helped with many things over the years.

She studied Milt as he rummaged for clean clothes. Her strong, unfaltering Milt, although she doubted that again now. Not his strength but the unfaltering part. She'd swallowed her pride and her hurt all those years ago, forgiven him, moved on with their lives but now she questioned her trust. Did she really have the confidence in him that she showed to the rest of the world?

"The tanks are getting low." He pushed a drawer shut, opened another. "The girls have to remember we're not on mains water here." By that he would mean she had to remind them. "Laura especially, she—"

"I'll suggest Laura share Bree's bathroom. That'll remove some of the clutter."

"Do we know how long she's staying?"

Natalie shook her head. "Milt, we need to talk."

"What about?"

"Jack."

"Not again, Natalie. I told you he's only interested in expanding his farming knowledge. There's nothing more to it." He took a clean shirt from the wardrobe. "I'd better get through the shower. Mum will be here soon."

He left and anger bubbled in Natalie's chest. She could think of nothing but Jack, and Milt was oblivious.

She took a deep calming breath, let herself out into the passage then paused at Laura's door. It was shut. She'd been brusque with her youngest. Her words had discouraged conversation when she could see from Laura's look after lunch she'd wanted to unburden, but Natalie hadn't given her the option, hadn't had the strength to deal with Laura's dramas.

She'd seen the same pressing look in Bree's eyes when she'd talked about going away with Owen and in Kate's when she talked about her falling-out with Sarah. She should have asked if it was that or something more that created the air of lethargy she noticed around Kate. Natalie wanted to listen, to offer motherly soothings and words of wisdom, but it was as if that ability had been suctioned from her.

The damned book declared it was *her duty to devote her time to taking care of her family and putting them before her own needs.* She'd done that all the girls' lives so why couldn't she summon the energy for it now? It was as if Natalie was an outsider watching her family from a distance and all the while she was drawing away, the facade of her life brittle, curling at the edges like an old photograph that had been left in the sun.

The voices from the kitchen were bright, loud, the girls all talking at once and then Olive's chuckle. Natalie drew a deep breath, steeled herself for the evening ahead and stepped into the kitchen.

There was a pause in the conversation as she entered. Bree's brow furrowed. Kate's smile was encouraging, but Laura's look was tentative.

"Have you been sleeping?" Olive inspected her. "You're still looking pale."

"Are you all right, Mum?" Kate asked, her dark eyes searching.

"I'm fine." She crossed to stand beside Bree and reached for her apron. "You should be resting that leg."

"I hope you girls haven't been wearing your mother out," Olive said.

"How would we wear her out?" It was Laura who asked, sitting between Kate and Olive at the end of the table. "We're all grown up now, Granny."

"Of course you are, darling." Olive's voice held only the slightest hint of sarcasm. "But mothers never stop worrying about their children. And with her teaching and the city visitors next week she's got plenty on her plate."

"What city visitors?" Kate asked.

"Is that next week?" Bree said at the same time.

"They can't stay here, Olive," Natalie said.

"Of course not. I wouldn't allow that without asking you first but we did discuss the picnic in the creek." Olive drew back her shoulders. Her sharp gaze pinned Natalie. "We have to do our bit for those less fortunate than ourselves."

"We're mustering then tailing, Granny." Bree shook her head. "Next week's not a good time for Dad or me to help out."

"It's just a picnic in the creek. Your mother and I can manage."

"I can help," Laura said and gave Olive a playful nudge. "Is it sausages and damper like last time?"

"Yes, and if you're going to be there perhaps you could give rides on one of the bikes or the four-wheeler. They're all younger women and I'm sure some of them would enjoy that."

"I can do it if I'm still here," Kate said.

"If you're still here we'll need help with the tailing," Bree said.

"What day is it likely to be?" Kate ignored her sister.

"Not till Thursday or Friday. I wouldn't book for early in the week when your mother is teaching." Olive sounded affronted as if she was doing Natalie a favour by committing her precious days at home to works of charity. "The day is still to be confirmed."

Natalie set the container of cauliflower rice she'd prepped earlier on top of the steamer with a thud and gripped the sides tightly. Behind her Laura was full of excitement.

"I haven't helped out with a farm visit for years. It'll be fun."

"And not too much work if we all pitch in," Olive said.

"Can someone set the table?" Natalie's request was sharp. She glanced over her shoulder to see all eyes looking in her direction. She took a calming breath. "Your dad's having a shower; he won't be long then I can serve dinner."

Bree moved to the cutlery drawer.

"I'll do it." Kate stood. "You should be sitting down." They swapped places.

"Anyway, I'm glad you're here now, Natalie," Olive said. "I'd rather like a wine if you're having one."

And just like that Olive changed the subject, dismissing any discussion.

"You should have said before, Granny. I could have got you one." Laura jumped up then frowned. "Although I think the bottle was emptied last night."

"There should be another in the bottom of the fridge." Natalie pointed to the crisper as Laura opened the door.

Laura rummaged then lifted a bottle triumphantly. "Yes. Do you want one, Mum?"

"Thanks." Natalie nodded. Suddenly a glass of wine looked like a lifebuoy thrown to a drowning woman. Behind her the conversation picked up and went on, Olive pressing the girls for details about their lives. Natalie wiped down the sink. Normally she'd be part of the conversation but tonight she felt as if she was drifting somewhere beyond it. She checked the progress of the curry then took her seat at the table.

Olive smelled the air. "Is that curry?"

"It is." Laura passed her one of the two glasses of wine she'd poured. "We had roast with Jack Halbot last night so Mum didn't want to cook one tonight."

Olive paused, her hand midway to the glass Laura offered. She looked at Natalie, a glint of irritation in her eyes. "Why was Jack Halbot here and why would he get my roast?"

"Don't worry, Granny," Kate said. "It was only mutton, not pork."

"I love roast mutton. Saturday night is always roast night. It's tradition." Olive sniffed and took a sip of her wine. "Never been one for curry. It was always used to disguise rabbit in my younger days."

"It's chicken," Natalie said.

"There's cheesecake for afters," Laura said brightly.

"And where am I to sleep tonight?" Olive glanced between Laura and Kate. "I usually take the guest bedroom but I assume one of you will be in there."

Natalie blew out a quiet breath. She hadn't thought about sleeping arrangements.

"I'll move in with Laura for the night," Kate said.

"Or you can sleep in my spare room, Granny," Bree offered.

"Thank you, Bree. No need for a whirlwind in a teacup. Your spare room would be best. Then I won't be putting anyone out."

Natalie gritted her teeth. Normally she ignored Olive's sulking, which had become worse since Clem died, but she wasn't in the mood for it tonight.

"Hello, Mum." Milt strode in and bent to kiss his mother's cheek.

"Milton, darling, don't you smell nice." Olive smiled at him with that adoring look reserved for her firstborn, her petulant look dispersed.

He took his seat at the top of the table.

"How's the mustering going?" she asked and Milt filled her in on the day's progress while Natalie rose to organise the meal.

Kate stepped up beside her. "I can help."

"There's no need."

"Plates or bowls?" Kate stood her ground, opened the crockery cupboard and looked back, eyebrows raised.

"Bowls." Natalie checked the cauli rice and handed it over for Kate to serve while she carried the slow cooker full of curry to the sink. Outside, around the property, her girls had worked beside their father since they were young. She had to remind herself that they were also capable of transferring those skills to household duties. She'd always expected them to make their beds, help keep the place tidy, but cooking and cleaning had been her domain. She did it without even thinking. She paused, one hand on the lid of the pot, and recalled the little book tucked away in her drawer. Or had she simply been conditioned?

The phone rang and Laura answered then waved the cordless receiver in the air. "For you, Mum."

Natalie swapped a serving spoon for the handset and walked away from the activity to a quiet corner of the kitchen. "Hello."

"Natalie? Hello, it's Paul."

She glanced back at the girls dishing the curry, hoping they wouldn't put too much in Olive's bowl. There would be no end of complaint if the serving was too big. "What can I do for you?"

"I'm just checking everything's okay."

"Watch you don't slop it." Kate's tone was rough.

"You worry about what you're doing," Laura countered.

Natalie moved out into the passage. "Yes, everything's fine."

"That's good." There was a pause before he went on. "I thought I'd give you a ring because the other day you said there was a family problem and then someone mentioned in the staffroom they'd seen your daughter and mother-in-law at the hospital."

Natalie took a deep breath. Nothing was ever private in a small town. "Bree had a bit of an accident on the bike. She's okay." Her voice sounded brusque. She softened her tone. "We're all okay, Paul. Thanks for your concern."

Once more there was a pause, a deep intake of breath. "It's just that you seemed a bit upset when you left on Wednesday. Not your usual self." Paul's words had come out in a rush but he stopped again abruptly, took another deep breath. "I can arrange some time off for you if you…if you still need some. I'd be happy to organise it."

Natalie's initial irritation was replaced by remorse. It was good of him to check on her after she'd been so abrupt with him. "That's kind of you."

"Dinner's on the table, Mum."

She turned at Kate's whisper from the door behind her and nodded in acknowledgment. "I have to go, Paul. Thanks, I should be fine but..." She'd planned to go back to work on Monday. After all, there was nothing wrong with her but perhaps a few days off would help her find her equilibrium again. "Can I let you know tomorrow?"

"Sure." He sounded relieved.

"Thanks." Natalie returned to the kitchen where Olive was about to say grace and replaced the handset in its cradle.

Olive murmured grace as soon as Natalie sat. "No point in our food going cold," she added as an addendum to the amen. Then she poked at the meal in front of her with her fork. "I don't know why we can't have proper rice."

Natalie stiffened and from the corner of her eye she saw Milt pause with his fork halfway to his mouth. He wouldn't even know it was cauli instead of rice if Olive hadn't mentioned it.

"Cauliflower's better for you, Granny," Laura said.

No-one else spoke. Milt put a forkful of food into his mouth, a slightly puzzled look on his face. Natalie tucked into hers and the rest followed.

The girls were full of chat. They'd finished the curry and Kate was helping Natalie serve the cheesecake when Olive asked why Jack had come for dinner.

"Dad asked him," Laura said.

Natalie turned in time to see a glance pass between Milt and Olive. It was only the briefest of glimpses but Natalie was sure her mother-in-law's look had been questioning and Milt's chastened. Surely Olive didn't know. All these years Milt's indiscretion had been a secret kept between him, Natalie and, to her eternal mortification, her father-in-law, Clem. Did Olive know about her son's cheating too? And if she knew about that, did she know the truth about Jack? Nausea squirmed in Natalie's stomach.

"Dad didn't want Jack to be on his own," Bree said. "He'd just got the news his mum has cancer."

"Oh, well…" Olive looked down at the serve of cheesecake Natalie had placed firmly on the table in front of her. "That's sad news." Her tone implied Veronica had died. There was silence around the table as Natalie and Kate delivered the rest of the bowls.

Damn Veronica, Natalie thought, she's casting her shadow over my family again. Natalie had worked so hard to eradicate her, thought she'd succeeded.

"Hey," Laura said brightly. "I've brought the *Mamma Mia!* sequel DVD. Why don't we watch that tonight after dinner?"

Bree groaned.

"I'd love to see it," Olive said.

"I'd rather have a tattoo," Bree moaned.

"Don't be silly, Bree." Olive gave her granddaughter a disapproving look. "It's lovely when we're all together and a cheerful movie would be just the thing." She shifted her gaze to Laura. "I assume it is cheerful?"

"Of course it is." Laura beamed. "It's so long since we had a family movie night."

"I'll pass," Milt said.

"Oh come on, Dad." Kate gave him a gentle poke. "You know how much you love a good love story."

Milt snorted and Olive gave a soft clap of her hands.

"Why don't you girls take your dessert into the den and get started? I need to talk to your dad. I won't be long."

"Are you dismissing us, Granny?" Kate asked affectionately.

"Of course not, but you won't be interested. Get the movie started and I'll be there before the introductions have finished."

"If I have to do this I'm getting into my pyjamas." Bree limped to the door.

"Great idea." Laura bounded to her feet, her halo of rainbow-coloured hair bouncing with her. "Nothing like a movie night in our PJs. Do we have chips and chocolate?"

"In the storeroom." Natalie waved a hand towards the other door off the kitchen, which led to the room where all excess supplies were kept. It was nearly as big as the bathroom with thick walls and no windows, a miniature supermarket Natalie always kept stocked. It was too far to go to town if you ran out of something.

"What about you, Mum?" Kate asked. "Will you watch it with us?"

"Your mother should stay too." Olive smiled but there was a steely look in her eye.

"I'll come in later." The curry did somersaults around Natalie's stomach. What was this about? Surely not Milt and Veronica. Natalie studied her mother-in-law's face but she gave nothing away.

Laura came out of the storeroom triumphantly waving a block of chocolate and a packet of chips. "Caramello chocolate and salt-and-vinegar chips."

"Weren't there any barbecue?" Bree asked as they left.

"Should I stay and help with the dishes?" Kate was the last to reach the door. Her eyes were dark in her pale face.

"No need," Natalie said. "There's not much left to do."

"I'll help your mother then I'll be in."

And that was it. Just as if they were still children, Olive had herded the girls from the kitchen.

Milt finished his cheesecake and pushed his empty bowl to one side. Natalie poked a spoon into hers but didn't eat, no longer hungry for her favourite dessert.

"What's this about, Mum?" Milt asked.

Olive took the last mouthful of her cheesecake and set her spoon neatly in the middle of the bowl. "You know I'm not a fan of curry but I enjoyed that and dessert was delicious, thank you, Natalie."

No matter what went on between them over the years Natalie could not fault her mother-in-law's sense of correct protocol. She had impeccable manners.

"It was, thanks, Nat." Milt gave her a tender look.

Natalie's heart crumpled. He wasn't one for big displays of emotion, especially in company, but it was the little gestures that she appreciated.

"What did you want to talk about, Olive?" she asked, her voice gruffer than she'd intended.

"Constance called in today."

"Again?" This time Natalie's tone was a mix of brusque and surprise.

"It's good of her to come." Olive looked down her short, pointy nose.

"Sure is." Milt shifted in his chair. "What's that…three visits since you moved in?"

"There's no need for sarcasm, Milton. She's been more often than that. Anyway, it's easier for me to drive to her place and visit. I can help with cooking."

Olive was looking at her son but the words were for Natalie who'd fallen in love with the big farmhouse kitchen, not long after she'd fallen in love with Milt. There had been no room for two women in the kitchen in spite of its size and once the children had come along Olive had much preferred to look after them than cook. It was an arrangement that had worked for both women. Natalie's girls were close by and lovingly looked after, while she had free rein to cook. It was an enjoyable outlet for her and while no-one had ever voiced it, she secretly felt she was a much better cook than her mother-in-law. Olive had always pitched in with food prep at the busy times and was on hand when it came to cleaning up. Natalie was happy to take one of Olive's jibes once she realised the topic of Milt and Veronica's past wasn't on the agenda as she'd feared.

"Anyway," Milt tapped the table in front of him. "What was the purpose of her visit?"

"You make your sister sound like an outsider." Olive's face formed the pout she'd perfected when she wanted to chastise her son without using words. "She just called in to see me."

"Connie doesn't *just* call in. There's always a reason for her visits."

Olive humphed and shifted in her chair. "We did talk about wills and funerals."

"That's cheerful."

ABBA music blared from the den opposite as if to mock him.

"Granny, it's starting," Laura called as Bree hobbled past the kitchen door.

"Tell Laura to keep going without me, Bree," Olive said. "I'll be there soon. And would you shut the kitchen door, please. No point in letting out the warm air."

Bree did as she was bid and the music became muffled.

"Whose funeral?" Milt said.

"Pardon?" Olive looked back at her son.

Milt took a breath. Natalie could see he was struggling to be patient. He wasn't close to his sister. He always said Connie had been spoiled but Natalie recognised Olive and Clem's indulgent parenting had also extended to Milt. They'd both been spoiled, if perhaps in different ways.

"Whose will and funeral were you and Connie discussing?"

Natalie could tell by the look on his face they both knew the answer to that question. Connie had been resentful ever since the reading of her father's will. The farm went to Milt, who had worked it all his life, that had not been a surprise, but Connie, who had received a parcel of well-performing shares, had muttered about unequal divisions. Milt was to continue to support his mother. Olive had a decent nest egg put away of her own that had remained untouched when the unit in town was purchased, which the farm had also funded, as it did her car and household bills. When Olive went, Connie would also inherit her mother's money but Connie hadn't felt that was fair.

"It's best to talk about these things so you're not lumbered with problems when I'm gone. Look at the worry we had over your father's funeral."

Clem had left no instructions regarding his burial wishes and it had been a three-way tussle between Olive and her two children over the details. It had been a difficult time and Natalie had kept out of it, simply making cups of tea and providing food when needed. Connie had insisted Clem should be cremated and his ashes scattered on the property. Milt had said he should be buried in the town cemetery. And Olive, submerged in grief and lost for ideas or words of her own, had eventually gone with a compromise. Connie hadn't been happy but conceded for her mother's sake. There'd been a well-attended celebration of Clem's life, overflowing their little local church, after which a cremation had taken place and the ashes more recently interred at a private family gathering in a plot purchased in the town cemetery.

"You made it clear you are to be cremated and your ashes put with Dad's." Milt was struggling to remain composed. He hadn't dealt well with the haggling after his father's death, which had been enough without the worry of what to do with his remains.

"I did."

"Have you changed your mind?"

"No." Once more Olive shifted in her chair. "Not about that."

"Would you like a cup of tea, Olive?" Natalie could see this was causing discomfort for her mother-in-law. Whatever this was.

"Thank you." Olive flashed a brief smile and Natalie stood, relieved to be excused from the tension at the table.

"Mum, just spit it out, whatever it is that Connie has been meddling in." Milt would not be distracted now.

"When I go…"

Natalie glanced back. Olive was stumbling over her words now. Perhaps it was this talk of dying.

"Connie thinks she should have the unit."

"What in the blazes for? She wouldn't use it."

"I assume she'd sell it."

"The unit that's being paid for by the farm?" Milt shook his head.

Natalie carried the teapot Laura had given her for Christmas with the rest of the tea-making items on a tray and came back to the table. Colour had risen in Olive's cheeks. Natalie put milk in a cup and poured, passing the tea on to Olive who took it with an aggrieved smile.

"Your sister thinks her inheritance is much less than the farm is worth."

"Oh she does, does she?" Milt placed his hands on the table. He wasn't a violent man but the firmness of it made the cups rattle on their saucers. "Dad paid her out when she left to go to university. She always said she never wanted to work on the farm."

"I suppose in those days your father and I always encouraged you to take on the property. It's different these days for girls."

Natalie thought about that. The future of the property was a topic she and Milt had discussed between themselves and with their girls after Clem had died, but there was no firm plan in place yet. They'd given Bree, the only one interested in running the property, a few years to decide what she wanted and they had discussed ways of making it fair for the other two, but it wasn't settled by any means. She wondered what would have happened if one of their children had been a boy. An image of Jack sitting at their dinner table chilled her heart. Milt had been so at ease with him, so welcoming. And why was Olive so curious about Jack's attendance at their table?

"Dad was generous to Connie on many occasions over the years." Milt's face was drawn, but in his eyes a fire smouldered. "Their family holiday to America and Disneyland, for instance."

Natalie gasped. Connie and her family had made that trip with their three boys when they'd all been primary-school age. She remembered thinking they must have been doing all right to afford it. "We paid for that?"

"Some of it," Olive said.

"Most of it." Milt's gaze was locked on his mother. She twisted her teacup on its saucer.

Natalie recalled that trip. It had been before she'd taken over the farm bookkeeping and around the time she'd tried to convince Milt and Clem she wanted an en suite. There'd also been talk of a short holiday to Queensland. Neither of those things had happened but Connie's family had gone to America.

"Your father was always conscious that Connie would get less," Olive said.

Milt shook his head. "They went at a time when we'd just struggled through several years of low rainfall, Mum. It was me—" he stabbed at his chest "—working for virtually no wage that pulled us through and gave Connie's family a holiday. My family didn't have one."

And Natalie's teaching wage had put food on the table, but she said nothing, instead swallowing the bitter seeds of jealousy that she'd never had cause to taste before. Olive straightened the cup on its saucer. A log shifted in the fire with a thud and a crackle of sparks. Where do we go from here? Natalie wondered.

The phone rang and she leaped up to answer it.

"Hi, Nat, how are you?"

Natalie pressed the phone to her ear, relieved to hear the cheerful tone of her sister's voice. She moved out into the corridor where the sounds of the movie playing from the den made better background noise than the tense rumbling voice of her husband talking to his mother.

"Fine, Bron." She'd said it again. *Fine* seemed to be the only word in her vocabulary when it came to describing how she felt. "How are things there?"

Her sister, her husband and their four children lived in Victor Harbor. Natalie and Bronwyn's parents had bought their retirement home a few blocks away. They'd all been together last Christmas for a day but there'd only been brief phone calls since.

"Not so good."

Natalie's heart skipped a beat. "What's happened?"

"Mum's had a fall. Nothing broken, thankfully, but she's a bit battered and bruised."

Natalie pressed her back against the wall. She wasn't close to her parents. As a young woman she'd always pushed their boundaries, tested the strength of their love and sometimes found it came up wanting. They'd been disappointed when she'd chosen teacher training over nursing, sad when she'd broken off with her previous long-term boyfriend for her whirlwind romance with Milt, and surprised when that had been followed by marriage; upsets that they'd never fully recovered from. Not long after the wedding they'd moved interstate for her dad's work and even though they were now back in South Australia they only caught up a few times a year.

"Did she trip?"

"She's not sure but she thinks so. She was in the street and the pavers are a bit up and down. The doctor wants to keep her in hospital overnight, perhaps two nights, and run some tests. Dad's not a hundred per cent either. Still recovering from pneumonia."

Natalie put a hand to her head. "When did he have that?"

"A week or so ago. Didn't we tell you?"

"No." Natalie tried to recall the last time she'd rung her parents or they'd rung her. She vaguely remembered her mother saying her dad wasn't feeling the best. How long ago had that been?

"He spent a couple of days in hospital. He's doing okay now, just not fully back to his old self."

"Things have been busy here. I should have been in touch." Natalie's excuse sounded lame even to herself.

"Anyway, Nat, I know you're working but I wondered if you could possibly come down and help for a few days."

"When?" Natalie's mind went into overdrive trying to think how she could manage a trip to Victor Harbor.

"Monday."

"As in this week?"

"Yes. I'm sorry, I know you've got lots on your plate. It's just that I've promised the twins' teacher I'll go on camp with them and we leave on Monday for three days. Mum will need collecting from hospital. I'm not sure Dad should be driving and they'll need help with meals and getting around. Dad's got a check-up on Tuesday. I can take over as soon as I get back."

"Hell's teeth, Mum." Milt's voice rumbled loudly from the kitchen behind Natalie, above the sounds of her daughters, well, two of them at least, singing along to ABBA music in the den.

"Move over, Laura." Bree's complaint was louder than the music.

Natalie put a hand over her free ear and moved further along the passage. Bronwyn's now ten-year-old twins had been a surprise addition to the family when their older brother and sister were six and eight. Bronwyn had a busy time helping her husband run a small business, looking after four children, all still at school, as well as helping their ageing parents when needed.

"Of course I'll come," Natalie said, her mind still turning over the implications of her promise. At least she knew Paul would organise cover for her class. "I'll drive down tomorrow."

Putting a few hundred kilometres between her and home might be just what she needed to put herself back together again.

Eleven

Bree leaned on the back fence, her arms folded across her chest against the cold morning air, her injured leg propped out in front of her. A chilly easterly wind blew. It made an eerie sound in the gum trees by the dog kennels and turned her ears and nose numb. Her sisters and her dad were nearby but no-one spoke. They'd all come out to wave off her mum as she left for her trip to Victor Harbor and, as the sound of her car faded, her family faded with it. They all milled around the back gate as if they were rudderless.

Milt took a position in front of them and clasped his large hands together as if he was about to say his prayers.

"You girls will have to step up while your mother's away." He eyeballed each of his daughters.

"That's a given," Bree said.

He ignored her and went on to explain the work that needed to be done. Bree bristled. It wasn't as if she was a rookie who couldn't manage a day's work on the place. Kate and Laura were having trouble keeping straight faces as her dad reiterated some of the tasks but she didn't see the funny side.

"So tomorrow Kate will be out in the paddock with Graeme and I...and I think Jack's going to come for a while as well."

"He's been around a bit lately," Bree said.

"He's determined to make changes to the Halbots' stock line and..." Milt fixed a piercing look firmly on her. "He's keen to learn."

The hairs on the back of her neck prickled. Was he intimating she wasn't?

Milt's focus shifted to his youngest daughter, and having spelled out the jobs that would be Bree's and Kate's he moved on to matters of the stomach. "Do you think you can manage the food side of things, Laura?"

"Yes." Laura's eyes widened and she sucked in her lips. Her heavy make-up and colourful hair reminded Bree of the Bratz dolls they'd had as kids. "I'm sure Granny will help."

"She's gone home."

"Already?" Kate said. "She must have been up early."

"She wanted to get back to town in time for church."

"I'll give her a call later," Laura said.

"You're not to bother your grandmother." Milt's tone was gruff.

Laura pulled a face. "Okay. Keep your shirt on. Usually Granny likes to help, that's all."

"Not this time. She's got a busy week ahead."

Bree raised her eyebrows. That was news to her. Her grandmother was a bit of a committee-goer but she didn't usually let that interfere with helping when there was work to be done on the farm and last night she hadn't said anything about a full week. She was always one to provide a long list of what she was doing so everyone knew how busy she was.

"Granny loves to come out and help." Kate echoed Bree's thoughts.

"She's not as young as she used to be and it's a long drive in and out from town." He looked to Bree. "There's still cleaning up in the shearing shed to do."

"I know." Bree gritted her teeth.

Milt glanced at the other two. "So we're all clear on our jobs?"

"Aye, aye, Captain." Laura giggled.

He gave a snort and headed off to the dog kennel.

"It's freezing out here." Kate stamped from foot to foot then headed inside with Laura right behind her.

Bree stayed where she was, annoyance flowing through her body like a charge. Her dad spoke as if she were a minion at his beck and call. He wouldn't speak to Graeme like that or bloody Jack Halbot. It irked her that he didn't see her as a partner in the business.

She pushed off from the fence and a sharp pain tugged at her thigh.

"Damn it," she hissed.

She was glad she'd made the decision to go away with Owen. Let her dad run the place without her and see how he got on.

★

Natalie looked out the window of her parents' unit where wind and rain lashed the tall Norfolk Island pine trees across the road. The day had turned wild. She glanced back at her dad who was dozing in his recliner. It was one of two set up in front of the television, which had been on when Natalie arrived, a never-ending game of lawn bowls playing. Her father had turned it down but not off as they'd chatted over their tea and the fruit cake Natalie had brought with her. It was her father's favourite but he'd only eaten half the piece she'd given him. Said his appetite hadn't recovered since the pneumonia.

Natalie's guilt had deepened at the sight of him when he'd first opened the door to her. He looked much thinner than he had at Christmas and he'd felt frail beneath her embrace. Their conversation had dwindled and after he'd nodded off Natalie had stayed in her chair, thinking she could shut her own eyes after the long drive, but she was restless and found herself taking in the neat and modest furnishings of her parents' small lounge room; gazing at family photos on cupboard tops and walls, recalling the life events that the pictures represented. There were far more of Bron's family than of hers. Natalie could have sent others, of course. Another thing to feel guilty about. She picked up a more recent photo of her parents, taken at Kate's wedding with the bride and groom. Ray and Althea Turner beamed at the camera, their arms linked with Kate and Sean. They'd been so proud and happy that day.

She replaced the photo frame, silently picked up the cups and plates and took them to the kitchen. It was a modest room but big enough for a square table and four chairs in the middle. She wiped down the bench and returned the milk to the fridge. There were several cards and invitations on the door, held in place by magnets from her parents' travels to various parts of Australia. The invitations were for a high tea at the bowling club, an eightieth birthday from a name she didn't recognise and then a sixtieth. She frowned at that and lifted it off the fridge. It was to Ray and Althea and was for a dinner in two weeks' time in Adelaide, to celebrate Tony's birthday. There was no surname but the invitation was from Marcia and girls and Natalie was pretty sure her old boyfriend had married a Marcia and that his birthday was in June. Why would her parents be getting an invitation to his birthday?

A car pulled up in the driveway. Natalie stuck the invitation back on the fridge and turned as her sister came in the door, her hair damp from the rain.

"Damn, that smells good." Bronwyn drew Natalie into a squeezy hug. She was Natalie's younger sister, and shorter, so her head rested briefly against Natalie's neck.

"It's only slow-cooked lamb. I made plenty so you can take some home." Natalie had taken the big chunks of lamb from the freezer the night before and then this morning had set the slow cooker going with the lamb, onions, garlic, frozen tomatoes from her summer vegetable garden, the remains of some red wine from the previous night's dinner and assorted herbs.

Bronwyn pulled back. "I am capable of feeding my family."

Natalie was surprised by her change of tone. "I know. But you've got a lot on your plate. I do so little to help with Mum and Dad, I thought at least food would be useful. It's a big pot so enough for us all to share or I can freeze it if you've got something organised."

Bronwyn looked contrite. She sighed. "To be honest I haven't even thought about tonight's meal. Karl's at the shop. Paying wages on a Sunday at this time of year nearly kills us so we mostly work it ourselves. I've been cleaning up the house and packing ready for this camp. Lina's home with the twins and Marcus is who knows where. I'd say surfing but even he wouldn't go out on a day like today." She dropped the plastic bag that swung from her fingers to the table and flicked on the kettle. "It must have been a wild drive down."

"It was. Wind and dust until I got close to Adelaide then wind and driving rain from there onwards."

"I don't suppose you've been to see Mum yet? Where's Dad?"

"He's snoozing in his chair and we haven't been out yet." Natalie closed the door between the kitchen and the lounge. "I told Dad we'd go before dinner but I'm not sure he should be out in this weather."

"Good luck stopping him."

"How is Mum?"

"I called in on my way here but she was sleeping so I didn't disturb her. Brought some washing back." She waggled a finger in the direction of the plastic bag. "This fall has knocked her a bit. Doc wants to run some tests so she could be there a few more days. Dad can manage but I'm worried he's not back to his old self since the pneumonia."

"I didn't realise. I could have come earlier."

"You've got the farm and teaching."

"You've got a business and four kids."

They eyed each other across the kitchen table. There was six years' difference in age and two very different upbringings between them. Natalie had been raised with strict rules about what she could and couldn't do, exact timelines for coming and going and warnings of what might befall a girl if she didn't listen to her parents, all of which went out the window when Bronwyn came along, but they were sisters and they'd been close once. Crazy how life stretched relationships and changed them.

"I live nearer." Bronwyn smiled, the brief tension between them dispersing once more. "Don't beat yourself up. I'd honestly do anything to avoid going on another school camp but I'm committed. We've organised extra staff hours to cover me at the shop. And the twins would be disappointed. I've hardly been on an excursion let alone a camp since they started school. I used to do so much more for Marcus and Lina." She waved a tea bag in the air. "Tea?"

"Thanks." It would be Natalie's fourth hot drink for the day but if it meant they could sit and chat for a few minutes before her sister dashed off she'd drink it. She took out the milk then recalled the invitation stuck to the fridge door. She waggled a finger at it. "Mum and Dad got an invite to Tony's sixtieth."

Bronwyn gave her an odd look. "They keep in touch."

"With my first boyfriend?"

Bronwyn wrinkled her nose. "I caught Mum sending him a birthday card only last year."

"You're kidding!" Natalie sunk into a chair. "That's odd, isn't it?"

"I suppose in one way. But...well, they liked Tony and even after you were no longer going out he used to come over sometimes."

"Did he?"

"Well, until Mum and Dad moved to New South Wales. After that I don't know but they obviously kept in touch."

Natalie was shocked to think her parents had maintained a relationship with her ex-boyfriend. Still did, by the sound of it. How could she not have known?

The kettle boiled and Bronwyn carried their cups to the table. "Listen, thanks again for coming at such short notice. I didn't want to let the kids' teacher down. She deserves a medal, that woman. She's nearly as good at her job as you are."

Natalie smiled. She'd always loved teaching, since her very first prac teaching experience. A young boy had been sitting beside her reading in the stop-start fashion of someone who can decode but not really understand what he's reading. But as he'd read his tone had changed, his fluency had improved, and with it came understanding. He'd leaned forward over the page then turned bright eyes to her. "I can read," he'd said, in a voice so full of awe it was as if she'd given him open access to a room full of chocolate. "I can really read," he'd said again.

"Yes, you can," she'd replied and he'd dropped his gaze to the page and continued on, the funny repetition of Dr Suess's *Green Eggs and Ham* coming alive on the page as his confidence grew. She'd heard the difference in his voice, the moment when a chore had turned to something exciting, the secret code of letters and spaces and punctuation suddenly making sense, and just like that a door had opened to a whole big world for him. She'd been hooked on helping children to open doors ever since but lately, just this year probably, she hadn't felt that same enthusiasm that always enveloped her at the start of each new school year.

Bronwyn blew on her tea. "I feel bad taking you away from your class."

"I've got plenty of leave up my sleeve and it's only for a few days. We've got a new principal; he's going to take some of my lessons this week." Natalie allowed herself a small smile. "He wasn't even born when I started teaching."

"Like the doctor who's looking after Mum. I swear he looks younger than Marcus." Bronwyn groaned. "I feel so old."

Natalie chuckled. "Trust me, fifty-two is not old."

Her sister dragged her unruly curls back from her face, something she'd inherited from their father while Natalie had straight hair like their mother. "It feels old when you're the mother of teenagers and two ten-year-olds."

"Well, my girls are definitely grown up. They don't need me like your kids do and Milt's mum is managing fairly well on her own." Natalie thought of Olive's rather sad, stilted farewell after a quiet breakfast with only the two of them and Milt at the table. Their conversation had been about Natalie's trip, the weather and the upcoming ram sale. Milt and his mother had been painfully polite. You could have cut the air with a knife. The girls had all slept in and only appeared as Natalie was ready to leave for her drive to Victor.

"How are my gorgeous nieces?" Bronwyn asked.

"They're good." Natalie rattled off the response, in the same manner she described herself as fine, but were they really all good?

A week ago Natalie would have said her girls were settled, healthy, happy, leading busy lives doing what they wanted, which was all that she'd ever hoped for them but now…She recalled Kate's pale face, dark eyes and bloodless lips that had turned up in a forced smile this morning as Natalie had climbed into her car. Bree had been quiet too; Natalie wondered when she was planning to tell her father about her imminent departure. And Laura, well, dear Laura had been chirpy, the one bright spark among them, but she'd thrown in her job and come home without, it seemed, any plan for the future.

"I don't suppose Milt was happy for me to drag you away for a few days."

"I'm staying the week, at least. I'll be here when Mum comes home and stay on. Take the pressure off you. Besides, all three girls are home at the moment so Milt has plenty of help."

She wouldn't admit her husband hadn't been pleased to hear of her plans to go to Victor for a week. That would only add to Bronwyn's load and also made Milt seem churlish. He wasn't usually like that. He was often the one who suggested she visit her parents or invite them to stay at the farm. But last night had been different. After Bronwyn's phone call Natalie had returned to a tense standoff in the kitchen. Obviously more words had been said in her absence.

Olive had been fussing over the dishwasher and Natalie had urged her to leave the last of the tidying up to her and to go and join the girls in the den.

Milt had still been sitting at the table, a brooding presence, when she'd told him about her mum and her plans to go to Victor the next day. He'd baulked when she'd said she'd be gone for the week.

"We're tailing," he'd said, with such a shocked look she may as well have told him she was planning to dance naked down the main street of town.

"The girls are all here. Bree will be fine in a day or so, Kate's more than able to help and Laura can do food. There's plenty in the freezer and I'm sure Olive would help if you asked her nicely." She'd smiled at him but he'd harrumphed, said good night and taken himself off to bed. She'd joined the others for the end of the movie and by the time she'd climbed into bed he'd been asleep.

This morning, with no local church service to attend, he'd gone off to the sheds first thing. They'd only had a brief time alone in the bedroom after breakfast when he'd come to find her as she'd packed her case. The damn *Model Wife* book had been on the floor where it must have fallen in the night from under her pillow. She'd shoved it in her case so he wouldn't see it.

There were other things they should have discussed. She'd wanted to ask him then about what was going on with Connie and his mum. And there was Jack. If he was Milt's son she'd thought she could deal with it, make a plan for the future so that everyone was taken care of, but sometime during her restless night, reality had hit her like a slap on the face. Natalie knew she was no longer strong enough to deal with a future where Milt confessed Jack as his son.

And there was Veronica. She must know the truth. Had she and Milt maintained a private connection over the years? Doubt and distrust had stripped her confidence in having a conversation with her husband. Better to go on as they were. She couldn't envisage a future with everything out in the open and so she'd said nothing when he'd wrapped his arms around her and pulled her close.

"I'll miss you," he'd said.

She loved Milt's big bear-like hugs. She'd nestled her face into his jumper, savouring his warm male scent mingled with the smell of oil from whatever he'd been working on in the shed. It was his words that had surprised her. She rarely went away alone, but he never admitted to missing her. She'd reciprocated, of course, felt remorse at the lack of feeling in her response. He'd picked up her case and they'd had no more time alone.

Natalie was startled from her reverie at the sound of the door opening behind her. She stood quickly, knocking the back of her chair. Ray Turner had one hand on the door handle. With shoulders slightly stooped, he blinked slowly, taking in the kitchen.

"Hello, Dad," Bronwyn said. "Fancy a cuppa?"

"No thanks, love." He glanced at Natalie. "You are here. I thought perhaps I'd imagined you."

"Nat's come to stay with you while Mum's in hospital," Bronwyn said.

"I don't need looking after."

"I thought I might be able to do a few jobs for you." Natalie tried to put breezy into her voice. "Cooking, shopping, washing. Bron's off on camp with the twins tomorrow, remember."

"Of course I remember. I've had a cold but I haven't lost my marbles."

"Not many, anyway." Bronwyn grinned and then slowly, as if he'd just got the joke, so did their dad. "You'll enjoy Nat's cooking better than mine while Mum's out of action." She winked at Natalie.

"We should go and see your mother." Ray leaned on the back of a chair and took a few deep breaths. "I haven't been in today. Waited for you, Natalie. She'll think I'm lost."

"I called in," Bronwyn said. "She was sleeping. Give Nat and I a chance to finish our cuppas then we'll get going. I have to go home and pack."

At the hospital Natalie's mother was propped up in bed looking as fresh as a daisy. Apart from a bruise above one eye, a few down her arm and a bandage on her elbow she didn't look any the worse for wear. She was surprised to see Natalie.

"Bronwyn asked her to come." Ray bent to kiss his wife's cheek. "To look after me."

"She's going away on camp," Althea said. "She's such a good girl worrying about us but we would have managed. Aren't you teaching?"

"I took leave," Natalie said. "I wanted to come anyway as soon as I heard you'd both been unwell."

"I tripped, that's all," Althea said. "Hurt my pride more than anything else, and your father is on the mend."

"I told them I could manage." Ray picked up his wife's hand, gave it a pat.

Althea smiled at her husband. "Still, it was good of Natalie to come. Nice for you to have company."

"I certainly liked the smell of dinner cooking." Ray patted his stomach and indicated the only chair in the room.

"You have it," Natalie said.

"I wondered how long you'd last on Bronwyn's cooking." Althea lowered her voice. "She has many talents, your sister, but cooking's not one of them. Don't you dare tell her I said so. Now do sit down. It's a long drive. You look worn out. Are you well?" She pointed to a space at the end of the bed. "Tell me all about the girls. What are they up to? No babies for Kate yet?"

Natalie perched on the flat space beyond her mother's feet and felt her shoulders relax just a little as she filled her parents in on life at home. It was a while since they'd had a proper catch-up, just the three of them.

Later that night, alone in the spare room after dinner, Natalie rummaged in her case for her nightie and found the old book she'd tossed in. Once more she was drawn to it. She flipped it open to the chapter on looking after your husband's parents. At the bottom of the page she'd written *AND YOUR OWN* in big letters. She'd written those words and stuck a photo of her parents on the blank page opposite just before Christmas one year when the girls had been small and she'd had words with Olive.

It was the time her parents were travelling back from inter-state and were having Christmas at Victor with Bronwyn. They'd wanted Natalie, Milt and the girls to join them. It wasn't a big ask, they'd had few Turner Christmases together since Natalie had married, but Olive had planned a particularly big King Christ-mas that year, with Clem's brothers and their families, and she'd almost demanded Milt and Natalie's presence at home. Natalie had been angry. Her own family get-togethers were so rare she'd been determined to get to that one.

Milt hadn't been much help: it had been a late harvest, he and Clem were both working around the clock and he was bone tired. In the end he'd had to stay home to finish reaping and she and the girls had driven to Victor alone. It had been a terrible trip. Laura was still a baby and had cried all the way, Kate had been carsick everywhere on the last leg of the journey, and Bree had spiked a temperature Christmas morning and come out in a rash and Natalie had spent part of the day in the hospital waiting to see a doctor.

Bronwyn and Karl didn't have children then and their house was small. After a couple of days with fractious children and little sleep, Natalie had packed up her girls and driven home. The fam-ily that had waved her off had tried not to show their relief but she'd seen it, even on her parents' faces. Her mum had been the one to encourage her to go home, saying the girls would soon settle in their own beds and give Natalie a chance to sleep too.

This afternoon she'd seen that same look on her mother's face as they'd said their goodbyes. "It was lovely to see you," Althea had said, "but don't feel you have to stay for long. We know how busy you are and we can manage, can't we, Ray?"

Her parents lived their lives perfectly well without her. She felt just as much an outsider here as she had in her own home.

Twelve

A whirlwind of leaves and dust whipped across the main street as Laura drove into town. She passed the pub on the corner, scene of many a get-together on weekends, basketball presentations, birthday dinners, and social events over the years. There were two other pubs but this one was her favourite. Bert Hinder had owned it for as long as she could remember. It didn't look much from the outside but there was always a friendly welcome, a cold beer and hearty pub food available inside.

She slowed at the intersection as a dusty four-wheel drive crossed in front of her towing a camper trailer. It pulled in at the shady grassed area beside the new toilet block. Being on one of the main routes between Adelaide and the popular tourist destination of the Flinders Ranges meant the town often had extra visitors.

Laura continued on along the main drag, divided by a wide strip dotted with peppercorn trees, then pulled abruptly into an empty parking space in front of a small, freshly painted shop. She peered at the neat white building through her windscreen. It was a shoe shop. That hadn't been there last time she was home. She got out and glanced at the smart styles displayed in the window.

Eight o'clock on a Monday morning was too early for anything
to be open, except the school and the coffee shop – and she was
here for both. She dragged her gaze from the shoes and moved on,
stopping in front of the hairdressing salon. She glanced around.
There was not another soul in the street. She put a hand to the
window of the hairdressers and peered in.

She took in the fresh white walls and the floating wood floor.
The interior had been made over since she'd been in last. Gone
were the large black-and-white linoleum and the hot-pink swivel
chairs. Now it had a rustic but modern look with square black
armchairs on large silver bases, mirrors surrounded by wide silver
frames and track lighting fitted above each station. She liked it,
and found herself wondering if they needed staff. She didn't know
the owner but one of her old school friends still worked here.

A car burbled along the street behind her. A shiver wriggled
down her spine. She spun around. It had sounded like Kyle's fancy
Subaru but the car was a different colour. Silly to be jumping at
shadows but he'd given her a fright outside the gym. She was
thankful again she'd never told him much about home and they
hadn't been together long enough for her to bring him for a visit.

She shoved her hands into her jeans pockets and moved on past
the stone facade of the bank. At least they still had a bank, unlike
a lot of other small country towns. A few leaves swirled at her feet
as she made her way along the footpath towards the cafe, which
was definitely open judging by the number of cars parked out the
front and the colourful banner that fluttered in the brisk morning
breeze above the tables and chairs set on the edge of the footpath.
Laura's first job of the day after clearing up the breakfast dishes
had been to run her mother's teaching notes in to the school. Her
mum had also left a list of top-up vegies to buy at the supermarket. But first a real coffee.

She reached for the door handle just as the door flew open. She smiled. The guy with the surprised look smiled back.

"Laura, hello," he said.

"Hi, Owen. In for a caffeine hit?"

"Sure am."

Another bloke came up behind Owen, wanting to get out. They both stepped to one side. Owen peered over her shoulder. "On your own?"

"Yep." She grinned. "Bree's on shed duties. Mum's away. There's still mustering to be done and the boss-man has us all on a roster. Are you coming out for a meal this week?" Laura wasn't sure how often her sister met up with her boyfriend. "I'm in charge of food so you may wish to back out if you are."

"Sounds like your dad might appreciate another male at the table."

"Wouldn't we all?" Laura gave him a cheeky grin and Owen laughed. She could see why Bree liked him – besides his good looks Laura got the impression he was also fun. One of the downsides to returning home would be the shortage of guys.

"I've got a busy week ahead. I'll let Bree know which night I can come out."

"Great." Laura watched him saunter away, then turned and walked smack-bang into another man coming out of the coffee shop. His cup squashed against his chest and a brown stain spread across his white shirt and deepened the blue of his tie before the takeaway cup fell to the ground at their feet, splattering his shiny black lace-up shoes.

"I'm so sorry," she wailed, flailing pathetically at the fabric as he tried to tug it away from his skin. "Are you scalded?"

"No." He had the shirt between his fingers now, flapping it in and out. "Milk coffee. Not too hot."

He was a head and shoulders taller than her so when he lifted his face to look at her he was still looking down. She knew she was gaping but she couldn't help herself. His thick dark hair was gelled back from his forehead in a luxurious up-swirl as if he'd just stepped out of a salon, and his eyes stared back at her through a set of large blue aviator glasses. He flapped the shirt again then bent to retrieve the all-but-empty cup just as she bent down too, and her cap fell off.

"I'm so sorry," she said again as she shoved the cap firmly back on her head. "I should buy you a new shirt." She grimaced. "If there was anywhere in town I could get one from, we don't run to…" She could tell the shirt was expensive. The only men's clothing available in town was country workwear. "…fancy menswear here," she finished lamely.

"I'll go home and change."

"Let me at least buy you a replacement coffee." Laura wasn't keen to let him go just yet. Not without finding out his name. "My name's Laura…"

"I'm running late. Please don't worry." He looked flustered now, as if he'd been the one to tip coffee down the front of her.

"Another day then?"

"Sure. I have to go." He spun away.

"Do you at least have a name?"

"Sorry…it's Paul, Paul Brown."

"Nice to meet you, Paul, and I'm sorry about the coffee." Laura waggled a finger at his stained shirt.

An alarm sounded from his pocket. He tugged out his phone and stabbed at the screen. "Sorry," he said again. "I have to go." He spun on his heel and hurried away.

Laura watched as he climbed into a new-looking RAV4. She wondered where he worked. To her knowledge he wasn't a local and dressed like that...perhaps the bank, an accountant or something to do with the hospital. Maybe he was only in town for the day. She felt a pang of disappointment. She'd been quick enough to notice there was no wedding band on the hand that had clutched the cup. New local talent was hard to find. Her lucky sister had snared one of the few recent arrivals.

The RAV4 sped off down the street and Laura's face lit up in a slow grin as she recalled his brief words. He'd said he was going home to get changed. With any luck that meant he lived in town. She needed to find out more about Mr Paul Brown.

*

Kate tucked her phone back into her jeans pocket. She'd tried to ring Sean last night with no luck and this morning his phone had gone straight to voicemail again. There was phone reception at the shack but it wasn't reliable and as soon as she got out to the paddock she'd lose coverage too.

She'd spoken to him the night she'd arrived to let him know she'd made it safely, full of chat about Laura's rainbow-coloured hair and interrupting Bree's dinner with her new fella. Sean had been interested in Owen, pleased to know there might be at least one more bloke at family gatherings. He'd called her Friday before he'd left for the shack with last-minute queries about where the spare torch was and his new fishing rod. She'd smiled at that. She doubted they'd get any fishing done.

She made her way across the yard to the ute. Dragged herself really. She was the last to leave the house. Laura had gone to town early, Graeme and her dad had already left for the paddock and Bree was working on something in another shed somewhere. Bree loved to be outside. She would happily fix a dodgy pump, change a tyre, muster stock, help a ewe deliver a lamb; whatever it took to work the property.

The three of them had been brought up in the same house and yet they were all so different. Kate liked to think she was practical and she didn't mind getting her hands dirty but she preferred inside work. She was happiest in the office of Sean's family business but also enjoyed being on the road with him, helping with stock-work from time to time. And then there was Laura, who didn't like sheep and showed her creative talents with hair and make-up. Sometimes that extended to cooking too, but she would still get outside and help if she had to.

Several sharp bangs echoed from the storage shed. Bree was no doubt taking out her frustration at being banned from the paddock, whereas Kate struggled to find some enthusiasm for the day's work ahead. Mustering wasn't a job she enjoyed and her energy levels were still low in spite of plenty of sleep. She was beginning to think maybe there was something wrong with her. She'd have talked to her mum about it but she'd be gone all week.

Once again her hand slipped over the bulge of her phone. Hearing Sean's voice would be a tonic. She wanted to know how his blokes' weekend had gone. No doubt he'd be full of Damo stories to make her laugh. Damo really was an accident waiting to happen.

She stopped mid-stride. Maybe something had gone wrong and that's why she couldn't reach Sean. She allowed a brief niggle of concern to rise before she pushed it away and set off again. He was a truck driver, on the road a lot, and she'd learned not to worry. When he was away overnight he rang her from wherever he was regardless but a weekend at the shack with his mates was a different thing. He'd have had plenty to drink and be distracted by his mates. Sean was usually a sensible bloke, she never doubted his reliability, and the rational explanation for his lack of communication was that he was sleeping off a big weekend or perhaps was somewhere out of range. He'd know she'd be waiting to hear from him.

*

Bree tossed her phone on the bed, sad to let go of the brief connection she'd had with Owen. He was putting in long hours at the garage, getting caught up on as much work as he could, and packing up his house. He'd suggested they catch up Thursday night. She'd thought he meant in town. She had to go in to the doctor Thursday afternoon to have the stitches removed, but Owen had mentioned Laura's offer of a meal.

"You could stay the night again," she'd said and he hadn't hesitated to agree.

Bree belatedly thought about the logistics of that then berated herself. She was twenty-eight and had her own quarters. If she wanted to share her bed with her boyfriend she damn well would.

She did a slow stretch, conscious of the slight tug of the wound on her injured leg. It had been a bit tender when she'd finished her day getting everything sorted in the sheds but since she'd showered and laid down on her bed to talk to Owen it had settled again. She was sure she'd be right to get back out into the paddock for mustering tomorrow.

Before she reached the kitchen she heard banging. Laura looked up as she entered, a meat mallet poised mid-air.

"What the hell are you doing?" Bree asked.

Laura grinned. "Making pork schnitzels."

Bree wandered closer. The length of the bench was covered, as was usual when Laura cooked; egg shells dribbled gooey trails of white across the bench, which was scattered with small jugs, bowls and cups, and flour overflowed from a plate onto the work surface. Laura's meals had been enjoyable so far but she made a hell of a mess preparing them. Bread slices fell forward from an open bag beside the food processor. Bree picked the bag up, found the tag under the butter tub, twisted the top and slipped the tag back in place.

"Don't think I've had a pork schnitzel before." She watched as Laura took a piece of the meat she'd been hammering, dredged it in flour then slipped it into a bowl of beaten egg. "Mum usually buys chicken or beef ready made from the butcher. Looks like a process."

"Not that bad." Laura dropped the viscous meat onto a plate and smothered it with a breadcrumb mix. "Spritzi's mum makes the pork ones from scratch, just like her Oma made them, and they're delicious. The butcher in town had pork loin steaks on special so I thought I'd give them a go."

"Do you need help?" Bree preferred to keep out of the way of food prep but as the only other person present she felt obliged to offer, like she did with her mum, but Natalie rarely accepted help.

"I'm fine with the food. I've made a potato salad to go with it and a green salad. Maybe you could set the table." She blew a wisp of wayward red and yellow hair from her face, rubbed her shoulder against the tip of her nose and grinned. "You can help when it comes to cleaning up."

Bree shook her head and went to the fridge in search of a beer. "Where are Dad and Kate?"

"Kate's up in her room, I think. She had a shower a while ago, and Dad hasn't come in yet. He's doing something with Jack." Laura raised her neatly textured eyebrows. "Who is staying for dinner again, by the way."

Bree ignored the question in her sister's look. She had no more idea why her dad was so chummy with Jack than Laura did. She couldn't put it all down to his parents still being in Adelaide. Jack had been over to their place on several occasions prior to his mother's diagnosis. Not for meals or cups of coffee but paddock work and sheep inspections. Bree waved a beer at her sister. "You want one?"

"No thanks. I'm going to make a Floradora in a minute."

"Do you wear it, eat it or drink it?"

"Drink it. Gin, lime, raspberry and ginger ale. It's divine. I'll make you one."

Bree screwed up her nose and popped the top off her beer. "I think I'll stick to what I know."

Laura had finished her food prep and prepared her fancy drink when Kate arrived in the kitchen. Bree stared at her. "Make-up! I hope that's not because Jack's coming for dinner again."

"I didn't know Jack was coming for dinner." Kate's response was snappish. "What's that?"

Laura had placed a tall glass on the table.

Kate leaned in to inspect the pretty pink drink, which sported a segment of lime on the rim. "Since when do we run to lime out here?"

"It's a Floradora. Mum's got gin in the storeroom and I bought the other ingredients this morning when I was in town. Do you want one?"

"No thanks." Kate headed for the fridge. "I'll stick to beer."

"Have either of you heard of a guy called Paul Brown?" Laura asked.

Kate withdrew a beer, then swapped it for a lemonade and joined them at the table. "Nope."

Bree put her head to one side. "The name rings a bell."

"Tall, dark-brown hair, glasses." Laura wriggled those carefully brushed eyebrows of hers up and down again. "He lives in town."

"Oh yeah. If it's the guy I think it is he's Mum's new boss. I've seen him but never actually met him." Paul was rather forgettable in Bree's opinion. A bit of an odd one out in the community. Didn't play sport, though she'd seen him occasionally at the pub on a Friday night with some of the school staff. "Don't think she fancies him much."

"Ooo." Laura's button nose wrinkled. "Thank goodness. He's way too young for her."

"Not to mention she's already married to our dad," Kate said.

"I thought he was…" Laura twirled her fingers in the air. "Attractive in an intellectual kind of way."

Bree gave a snort. "Each to their own."

Laura turned away. "Hey, speaking of hunks, Kate, did you see that picture of Sean on Facebook?" She started scrolling on her phone.

Kate placed her lemonade on the table untouched. "He barely looks at Facebook, let alone posts photos." A slight frown creased her brow.

"I think he was tagged in it." Laura hunched over her phone, which was gripped in both hands now. "Yes, there it is. He's got the cutest little baby in his arms and the woman peering over his shoulder isn't a bad looker."

Bree and Kate leaned forward to look at the phone. It was indeed a photo of Sean sitting in a deck chair grinning widely for the camera. He was holding an adorable baby dressed in a pink growsuit, and the woman wasn't just looking over his shoulder. Her chin was resting on it.

"I have no idea who that is." Kate sat and pulled her own phone from her pocket.

"Her name's Erin Fleming. She's from Port Lincoln."

Bree shook her head just as Laura looked up.

"What?" Laura said. "If she's got my brother-in-law on her page I can stalk her."

"That's why I don't do Facebook." Bree slid into a chair and propped her leg on the vacant seat beside her.

"You do."

Bree shook her head. "I deleted my account last year."

Kate and Laura both looked up from their phones.

"You see. You didn't even notice. I have a real life, not a virtual one."

Laura rolled her eyes and looked back at her phone. "There're more photos, Kate. Looks like Sean had a party weekend. Is that..." Laura tipped her head to one side and peered closer. "Is that Sean's friend Damo sitting in an esky with a fish-shaped hat on his head? It's hard to tell."

"That's him." Kate's head was lowered over her own screen again. "They were at the shack over the weekend."

"That would have been entertaining." Bree drained her beer. "Your Sean is a saint to put up with a friend like Damo."

From beyond the kitchen the back door banged. They heard the low rumble of Jack's voice followed by a hearty laugh from Milt.

"Sounds like Dad's in a good mood." Laura tucked her phone into her pocket and stood up. "I'll start cooking the schnitzels."

Bree hoped his mood had improved. She hadn't seen him since the middle of the day when she'd been the one to drive their lunch out to the paddock. He'd been testy then because they'd been having trouble with a breakaway mob who'd spread out into some prickly scrub. The way he'd spoken it was as if it was Bree's fault the sheep had done a runner and she hadn't even been there.

Milt's chuckle rumbled cheerfully again. Obviously Jack Halbot didn't annoy him like she did. She looked over at Kate who was staring at her phone as if it was about to reveal the meaning of life. "You okay?" she asked.

Kate looked up, her dark-brown eyes pools of uncertainty. "Yeah." She stood up as the two men arrived in the kitchen. "I'll get the drinks."

★

Dinner was over, and Jack had gone home, Bree had retreated to her quarters and their father disappeared to bed when Kate's phone rang. She dragged herself up from her chair in the den where she and Laura had been watching some reality TV show about dating. She glanced at the phone she'd been clutching in her hand since the last time she'd tried to ring Sean straight after dinner. She blew out a soft breath before she answered, relieved as much to see the picture of his smiling face as to be released from that appalling show.

"Hey, Katie-Q," he said as she put the phone to her ear.

"Hello yourself." She made her way to her bedroom and shut the door. "I've been trying to call you."

"And I've tried to call you."

"I was probably out in the paddock."

"We've been playing phone tag." He chuckled, lightening the mood. "I've been in and out of signal range myself. I didn't leave the shack till this morning then Dad had work lined up for me."

He was speaking quickly and she could hear cupboards banging in the background.

"Have you eaten?" she asked, realising it was after nine.

"Just throwing something together now."

"How was the weekend?"

"Great…exhausting really. I feel like an old man compared to Damo and Shortie. I'd forgotten how much they can toss back and then line up and do it all again the next day."

"Poor you." She sat on the edge of the bed and waited to find out more, not wanting to ask.

"Do we have any tomatoes?" Sean said.

"Try the crisper."

"How're your mum and dad?"

"They're good. Mum's had to go to Victor to help look after the grandparents but they're doing okay. Dad's his usual frantic self during mustering so I've decided to stay on, at least till Mum gets back."

"Great idea. I'll let my mum know."

"Already done it. She's got the office under control till I get back."

"If you're staying I'll call in your way. I've got to take sheep up north and I'll have an empty truck on the way back. I'll need to stop somewhere and I'd rather share a bed with my wife than the bunk in the truck."

Kate's spirits lifted at that. "When are you coming through?"

"I should be there by Thursday evening…in time for dinner."

There was a clattering sound and Sean swore.

"What's that?" she asked.

There was a grunt then, "The bloody crisper just fell out of the fridge."

"Did it break?"

"No, but there was something rotten in the bottom." He groaned. "It's gone everywhere."

Kate wrinkled her nose. "I thought I'd had a thorough clean-out in the fridge before I left."

"This resembles something that might once have been a cucumber."

"Ugh!"

"Yep. It's putrid. I'd better go. I'll have to clean this up or everything else will be tainted with it. I'll ring you tomorrow night."

"Okay. Love you."

She flopped back on the bed, replaying their conversation in her head. He'd sounded tired. No doubt still recovering from his male-bonding weekend. She picked up her phone, selected Facebook and scrolled till she found the pictures again. Sean's job meant he was away from home a lot and she'd never once doubted his faithfulness but as she stared at the photo of him with another woman and a baby in his arms a huge lump of jealousy lodged in her chest. It wasn't so much the woman as the way he held the baby, and the big bright smile on his face.

Thirteen

Natalie pulled her jacket tight against the stiff breeze rolling along the street from the Great Australian Bight with the chill of Antarctica on its breath and wished she'd brought her thick coat. Regardless of the weather, after three days with her father – wait, no, it was Thursday, so that made four days – she needed to get out. They'd picked up her mother on Tuesday and with three of them confined to the unit Natalie wanted some escape from their enquiring and sometimes censuring conversations.

She ducked into the sanctuary of a little coffee shop and let the warmth wash over her.

"Same as usual?" the bright young thing behind the counter asked.

"Gosh. Have I been in that often?"

The young woman smiled warmly. "I like to remember regular customers. Flat white, no sugar."

"Thanks." Natalie chose a piece of lemon slice to go with it, paid and found herself a table in the corner, her back to the wall. Her dad had brought her here the morning after she arrived. She'd come twice more with him and then yesterday on her own when she'd needed to escape the confines of her parents' unit, and here she was doing it again.

Usually when they were together there were more family members present and Natalie had the buffer of others, and it had been a tricky few days with just the three of them, their few topics of conversation exhausted. Her parents were outwardly welcoming but she felt on tenterhooks the whole time, being careful about what she said, and she could see them doing the same. She reassured herself her parents did love her, and she them, but there was a distance between them that may as well have been as wide as the ocean outside for their – or her – lack of ability to cross it.

Last night Bron had called in briefly after dinner. Full of chat about the highs and lows of school camp and the antics of her twins, she'd brought a breath of fresh air to the unit and an animation to her parents that had been lacking when it was just Natalie with them. Bronwyn was their favourite. She always had been, it was so obvious even Bron had picked up on it, but she was never smug about it. Natalie didn't feel real jealousy – perhaps a bit when she was younger but not now, and not of her sister. If she felt anything it was disappointment that her parents didn't see Natalie or their granddaughters as much as they could. She was simply resigned to their stilted relationship and even more thankful that she was close to her own girls.

Her coffee arrived, a tiny biscuit nestling in the accompanying teaspoon and a generous serve of slice on a plate. "Thank you," she said as the waitress whipped away to serve another customer. It wasn't quite ten o'clock so the early-morning coffee rush was over and the mid-morning partakers not yet arrived.

Natalie found herself itching to get back to the property again, knowing her girls were all there together. Giving herself space had been a good thing. The concerns that had been stirred about

Milt's past with Veronica had eased. Laura had kept her filled in on events at home, and evidently Jack had been for a meal again, but here, with only her parents in need of her – and they asked for little – Natalie had been able to put the events of the last week into perspective, of sorts.

It had been a shock to go through the tests for breast cancer and then another shock to find Veronica in Milt's arms, but she'd replayed it a million times and had decided it was as Milt had said. He couldn't ignore Veronica in her time of need. Natalie had convinced herself her fear that Milt and Veronica had kept in touch behind her back was ridiculous and had made the decision to believe Jack couldn't be Milt's son. It was the only way to keep her family and her sanity intact. She sometimes thought about her life as being in two parts, pre and post glitch. Maybe now she could add a new branch and call it before and after the anomaly. It was as if a curtain had been drawn to reveal a new scene, one in which she wasn't sure she knew herself.

"BA and AA." She pressed her fingers to her lips and glanced around but no-one had noticed her talking to herself.

She took a sip of her coffee and pushed her absurd thoughts away. Instead she pictured home and her husband and wondered what he was thinking of her time away. Their conversations had been brief while she'd been in Victor. Since they'd first been together they'd spent so little time apart that phone calls, other than requests to collect something or messages regarding their whereabouts, were rare, and so Natalie found it difficult to gauge Milt's mood from his stiff tone and getting information was like pulling hen's teeth. He'd muttered something about his mother and Connie but said he was dealing with it.

It worried Natalie to think Connie could want to take more from the property than she'd already received but it was best sorted between mother and son. As long as Natalie's girls didn't lose out, and if that looked likely she'd put up a fight. She'd mentioned taking a holiday again to Milt but that had been met with more grumbles.

She glanced down at her bag where a pile of travel brochures poked from the top. She'd felt so annoyed at his last rebuttal she'd suggested she might go by herself. That had silenced him, then one of the girls had called out and their talk had ended. Another unsatisfactory conversation with her husband.

Besides Laura's updates, there'd been one text from Bree and a call and a text from Kate. They were all managing without her so she was to stay as long as she needed, according to Bree, but they missed her and hoped she would be home soon, from Kate.

Natalie took a sip of her coffee and reached into her bag, drawing out the bundle of brochures and piling them on the table in front of her. On her walk yesterday she'd called into a travel agency and collected a wide selection of holiday options. Regardless of Bree going away – Natalie wondered if she'd told her dad about that yet – and Milt's rumblings that there was too much to do, there was definitely going to be some kind of holiday this year. Not to the usual beach, not to Victor, but to somewhere far away, interstate or even overseas. Her friend Brenda always said you had to put two state borders and a body of water between you and home to have a proper holiday.

Natalie pictured Brenda's vibrant smile. Dear Bren, they'd been through a lot together, helped each other through the good and the bad. Brenda had never known about Milt and Veronica though. That had happened before she married Martin and moved to the property next door. Natalie was glad her friend didn't know. Brenda thought Milt was a saint second only to her own dear Martin. There'd been times over the years when Natalie had felt angry with Milt over something and Brenda with Martin and they'd vented their annoyance together. Sometimes Natalie had been sorely tempted to confide in Brenda, let her friend know about Milt and Veronica, but she'd always held back. Once that cat was out of the bag there was no putting it back and the past was the past.

Natalie picked up the top brochure. It was well thumbed; they all were. She'd pored over them last night after her parents had gone to bed, excited by each new possibility, looking for something that would be so irresistible that Milt would want to go without putting up an argument. Hong Kong had always fascinated her, and Singapore. She'd toyed ever so briefly with the idea of a teaching position in an international school there once but she would've had to commit for two years and that had been out of the question.

The lush green of an island rising out of a turquoise sea attracted her attention. Thailand was a possibility, or Vietnam. Anywhere in Asia was enticing and it wasn't that far to go for their first trip overseas. She'd made sure they had passports a few years back but at this rate they'd be out of date before they'd had a chance to even get a stamp.

She put the European tours to one side, too far for now, and picked up another on the Northern Territory. They could escape the harsh cold of winter for the warmth of the tropics. It was the brochure with the camels mirrored in the glassy beach, a golden sun low in the sky, that she kept going back to. Broome and the Kimberley region intrigued her and she thought with more hope than surety it might interest Milt too.

"Dad said I might find you here."

Natalie looked up at her sister in surprise then glanced around. She'd been so absorbed in her brochures she hadn't even noticed the tables around her had filled with the mid-morning coffee crowd.

"What are you doing out?"

"It's not that busy at the shop and my darling husband suggested I catch up with you while you're still here."

"Am I going somewhere?"

"I rang Mum to say I was calling in to catch up with you. She thought you'd be off home later today."

"Did she?"

"Milt's under the pump with lamb tailing, she said."

Natalie sighed, recalling the conversation over breakfast. "I said Milt was mustering then tailing. Mum thought he'd be needing my help but I said I would have been at work the last three days anyway and only helping at home today. Mum said she didn't want them to be an extra burden for me and I said they weren't. She said you were here if they needed…" Her shoulders slumped. Her mother had bustled her out of the kitchen when she'd offered to cook the previous evening. She'd done her best to be the dutiful daughter but Natalie was no longer required.

Bronwyn shrugged her shoulders. "They're fiercely independent. Don't take it personally. I don't usually get to do too much."

"I bet you'd be allowed to cook for them."

"Ha. You've tasted my food, right? I didn't get the cooking gene from Mum like you did. She won't let me in her kitchen and insists on bringing food when she comes our way. It's just they've both had a bit of a setback. They're not as young as they used to be but they'll be fine." Bronwyn picked up her empty cup. "Fancy another coffee?"

"Thanks."

"Do you still take milk?"

Natalie nodded. "Evidently I'm a regular. The young lady behind the counter knows how I like my coffee."

She had to admit while her parents seemed to have aged markedly since Christmas they weren't quite in their dotage. She'd become used to her dad's gaunt appearance and realised he wasn't as frail as he'd first appeared. If they hadn't been visiting her mum or having a coffee in this shop and he wasn't watching sport on TV, he spent a lot of time tinkering in the garden shed he'd set up as a workshop. Funny really, because she'd never thought of her dad as the practical type but he'd taken to restoring kids' toys for a local charity. And in spite of her mum's trip or fall, the doctor had given her the all-clear and she was talking about playing golf again in some competition tomorrow. Natalie's help was no longer needed.

She picked up her brochures, gave one last look to the image of camels walking on a beach against the backdrop of a golden sunset and slipped them back into her bag as Bronwyn slid onto the seat opposite.

"Planning a holiday?"

"I'd like to. Getting Milt away from the property is the hard part."

"Where would you go?"

"I don't know, anywhere really. Overseas might be a push for Milt so somewhere warm like Broome perhaps."

"I dream of holidaying, anywhere at all, as long as I have to do absolutely nothing but lounge around and be pampered by attentive waiters." Bronwyn gave a soft snort. "School camp wasn't quite up to scratch. The kids had a ball though. I wish there were camps that took them for school holidays. You know, like you hear American kids do. My boys would take to it like ducks to water and it would be a holiday for me without them for a few days. I love them to bits but they're full on."

Natalie studied her sister. Her hair could do with a cut, there was a hint of grey at her temples she'd not noticed before and her make-up didn't mask the dark shadows under her eyes. She looked like a woman who needed a break. "Why don't we take a holiday together?" It was impulsive but they could both do with getting away.

"What?"

"It's been a long time since we spent some proper time together where we weren't juggling kids…" She twisted her lips in a wry smile. "And now parents. We wouldn't have to go far, but at least interstate." Natalie glanced out at the bleak day. "Somewhere warmer than here." Enthusiasm for her idea grew, lifting her lagging spirits.

Bronwyn held her gaze. "You're serious."

"Yes, I am. Wouldn't it be great to get away?"

The waitress arrived with their coffees. "You're not waiting for anything else?"

"No, thanks," they both said together.

The waitress whisked away the number that had stood in the middle of the little table between them. Natalie smiled at Bronwyn, wondering why she hadn't thought of it before. If Milt wouldn't leave the bloody property, she could, and she'd take a holiday with her sister.

"Where would you like to go?" She'd taken Bronwyn's silence for interest in the idea.

Bronwyn lifted her cup, took a sip of her coffee then leaned in, lowered her voice. "We can't afford a few days off let alone going away on a holiday. Marcus wants to go to uni next year and I don't know how we're going to manage that."

"You haven't put money aside?"

"Keeping the business afloat takes all our time, money and energy." Bronwyn's normally cheerful outlook was nowhere to be seen.

"I can relate to that." Natalie thought of the years they'd done it tough. At least in between there'd been good years, a little cash put away.

Bronwyn gave a soft snort. Took another sip of her coffee.

"What's that mean?" Natalie frowned at her.

"I know your overheads are much bigger than ours and there are huge fluctuations in income on the land but have you ever truly had to worry where your next mortgage payment was going to come from? Do you even have a mortgage?"

"There're constant ongoing costs in running a property. It's like having a mortgage, a huge one."

Bronwyn clutched her cup and stared into it. "Have you ever lain awake at night, staring into the dark, a lump as big as a beach ball in your throat, wondering how you were going to pay the school fees…put another meal on the table?"

"Sometimes my teaching wage was all we had."

"Well…at least you had that."

Natalie stayed silent a moment. She understood the look of despair on her sister's face. There were other things besides lack of money that could keep you awake at night. "It hasn't always been easy."

"I'm not saying I envy you but from where I'm sitting it looks like you're doing okay."

Discomfort built in Natalie's stomach. Was she doing okay? Looks could be deceptive and there were some things one sister couldn't tell another. She wondered briefly if Karl had ever cheated on Bronwyn and immediately pushed the idea aside when she pictured her easy-going brother-in-law. Still, what had she just thought about looks being deceptive?

"I did envy your Christmas holidays down here though," Bronwyn said. "You'd take several days around Christmas and I know you pitched in with cooking but it was a holiday for you."

"You came our way some years."

"Only when Christmas coincided with an extra day's holiday and then it would be a quick overnight trip. We rarely get time away from the business."

"Nor do we."

"What about the two weeks at the beach each January?"

"We didn't get there this year."

"And when your girls were younger you took them to the Gold Coast."

Natalie thought back to that. They'd had a couple of excellent years on the property and Clem had pushed them to take a break. It was two years after Connie's family trip to America and Natalie hadn't been slow in saying yes. Even Milt hadn't taken much convincing. It wasn't much but she conceded in comparison to her sister she had notched up more holiday time.

"This isn't about our families. It's about us. What do you think?"

Bronwyn's dark eyes met hers across the table. "No offence, Nat, but if I could afford a holiday I'd be going with Karl." She took a big slurp of her coffee. "Speaking of whom, I must get back. I said I'd only be gone for half an hour. What are your plans?"

"I don't know." Natalie was still feeling a little stung at Bronwyn's rejection of her idea of a holiday together. But, to be fair, a week ago her response would probably have been the same. If she was taking a holiday somewhere she wanted it to be with

Milt but what if he wouldn't go? And, she was shaken by her next thought…what if she didn't want him to?

"You don't have to stay on, you know. Mum and Dad will be fine. I just panicked when they were both acting a bit clueless."

Natalie shrugged. "I don't think they want me here anyway. Mum seems to have no adverse effects from her fall apart from a couple of bruises. Must have strong bones. And Dad's picked up since she's come out of hospital."

"I'm sure it's because you were there." Bronwyn grinned. "And your good cooking."

Natalie smiled at that. "I'm not allowed in the kitchen now that Mum's home."

"You can come and cook dinner for me!"

"Really?"

"Well, not tonight. Everyone's got basketball so it will be pizza on the run."

Natalie thought about spending another night in her parents' compact, tidy unit: the stilted conversation, Dad with half an eye on the sports channel, Mum with her knitting. They had a routine and her extended presence upset that. "There's not much for me to do. I think Mum and Dad would be happier if I went home." She'd asked her mum about the invitation to Tony's birthday and that had caused a stir. Her mother had become defensive, saying they could be friends with anyone they liked and they liked Tony. When Natalie had next gone to the fridge she noticed the invitation had disappeared. There was so much about her parents she didn't know, so much about her life they would never be privy to. They were acquaintances rather than parents and daughter.

Bronwyn stood up, came around the table and hugged her tight. "I've enjoyed seeing you and, in their own way, they have too."

Natalie smiled and nodded, thankful for the sentiment but not sure of its validity.

"Do you want a ride back to the unit?"

"No, thanks. It's only a few blocks and I need the walk if I'm going to be in the car half the day."

"You're definitely going then?"

"Unless the wheels have fallen off big-time when I get back to the unit, yes." Now that she'd made the decision to go home the uncertainties crowded in on her again. She squeezed Bronwyn's hand and stepped back, forcing a smile to her face. "I'll call in and say goodbye to you and Karl at the shop on my way out of town."

Fourteen

Easy conversation drifted around the table and for a change male voices outnumbered those of female in the Kings' kitchen. Bree slid into the vacant chair between her dad at the head of the table and Owen, who was in conversation with Jack seated on his other side. Kate sat opposite her and beside her was Sean. That had been a surprise. Not so much his arrival, Kate had said he was coming, but it was the way she had thrown herself at him and clung to him that was weird. Kate wasn't usually the outwardly fussy type.

"Anyone for a red with dinner?" Milt raised the wine bottle he'd just opened. Only Owen accepted the offer. The others were sticking to beer or, in Laura and Jack's case, the Floradora cocktail she was keen on and had talked him into trying.

"What happened about Granny's picnic?" Bree asked. "Wasn't that meant to be tomorrow?"

"Yes, damn, I forgot all about it," Laura said.

"She knows we're busy," Milt said. "And with Nat away she found someone else to host it."

"We should have invited her out tonight," Kate said. "She must find it lonely on her own after all the years of being in this house."

"She wanted to move out." Milt's tone was gruff. "I spoke to her this morning. She had a meeting this afternoon and she was planning an early night."

"Perhaps I should go in and see her tomorrow," Laura said. "Mum usually calls in regularly and she's not here."

"It's a pity she's not." Milt glanced around and lifted his glass. "Cheers," he said. Everyone joined in, taking a sip of their chosen drink. Milt nodded. "Nat loves lots of people at her dinner table."

"Although not someone taking over her kitchen." Bree eyed the mess Laura had left.

"Laura's done a great job."

"She needs to work on keeping to one spoon and one bowl," Kate said.

"A top chef can't do everything, little red hen." Laura waggled her head at her sister. Her rainbow-coloured hair was swept up in a bun tonight, and she wore a peasant-style shirt that showed off her pale, elegant neck and shoulders. She could be a model for outrageous hair but Bree didn't say anything. Her dad seemed to have got used to the colour and she didn't want to remind him by drawing attention to it.

Laura waved a spoon in the air and juice flicked.

"Careful," Kate said.

"I'll mop it up," Laura said.

That was something Bree very much doubted.

"It's ready now," Laura said. "Who's helping me dish?"

Kate stood. "I will."

Bree was happy to leave them to it. The stitches in her leg had been removed and the doctor had declared it was healing well but tonight, after a lot more activity today than she'd done for a while, it was feeling stiff and a bit tender.

"That lamb ragu smells pretty good," Owen said.

Bree gave him a nudge. "I love anything I don't have to cook."

"Are you hinting that I'll be on cooking duties?" Owen looked like he was going to say more.

Bree cut him off. "Has anyone heard from Mum today?"

"I sent her a text a while ago." Laura lifted the lid from the pot responsible for the delicious aroma. "She didn't answer."

"I'll ring her after dinner," Milt said. "Your nanna's home from hospital and Aunty Bronwyn's back so your mum will probably come home tomorrow. And you said your parents will be too, Jack?"

"Yep. Mum wanted to come home for a couple of days before she...before her treatment."

"Yes, well, that's good." Milt shifted in his chair. "Good idea. Give her some space to get herself together."

Bree decided to change the subject. "So you had a big weekend at the beach, Sean."

Her brother-in-law grinned back at her across the table. "Just a quiet one with the boys." He sat back as Kate slipped a plate of steaming hot ragu in front of him.

"We saw pictures," Laura said as she brought more plates to the table. "It looked like there were a few others there besides the boys."

A puzzled look crossed Sean's face.

"Laura's referring to the baby and the blonde. There were photos on Facebook," Bree said.

"Oh, right. That would have been the people in the shack next door. They joined us for a barbecue one night."

Bree saw the looks that passed between Sean and Kate as she took her place at the table. His was sheepish, hers worried.

"Be prepared, Owen." Milt took a sip of wine. "There's nothing private in this family."

"It was on Facebook for everyone to see." Laura sat on Bree's other side.

"Bloody Facebook," Milt growled. "As if there aren't enough problems in the world."

"You need to get off the ark, Dad," Laura said. "Everyone's on Facebook." She looked at Bree. "Except Bree of course."

"And me."

They all turned to Jack.

"It's too toxic," he said.

Milt gave Bree then Jack an appreciative look. "Thank goodness some people have some common sense."

Bree was happy to take his praise for a change, even if she did have to share it with Jack.

★

It was dark and Natalie was feeling weary by the time the tyres of her car rumbled over the familiar stock grid and she pointed the nose of the vehicle to the garage. The headlights highlighted several vehicles lined up at her back gate and further away she'd glimpsed a stock truck with the distinctive blue and red logo of her son-in-law's family transport company.

At least Olive's car wasn't among them. Milt had said he'd sort the situation with Connie but Natalie didn't like the sound of it. Connie was percolating something and it filled Natalie with unease. Not that she would expect to see her mother-in-law on a weeknight these days but she wondered who else she'd find inside.

She took care to keep hold of the door so it didn't swing and bang as she went in. Male voices carried along the passage; a rumbling chuckle, perhaps Sean, Laura's higher-pitched voice complaining.

"The local grapevine works fine here." Milt's voice rose above the others. "Your neighbours look like they're putting a plan together to help out while your mum's...away. If there's anything more that we can do to help let us know, Jack."

"People are being great."

Natalie paused. Her heart gave an extra thud. Jack! At the sound of his voice her determination to continue on as if he didn't exist was swept away. It was easy to ignore him when he wasn't sitting at her kitchen table. Once again she wondered how often he'd come their way on visits she'd been unaware of.

"Dad wants to stay with her...while she's having the treatment."

"How long will it take?" Laura's question was gentle, full of empathy.

"She's having the operation first and then treatment...I don't know."

A chair scraped. "Your mum will fight this, Jack, and she'll get through it."

Natalie peered around the kitchen door, which was slightly ajar. Through the gap she saw Laura put a hand on Jack's shoulder. Her rainbow-coloured hair hid the lighter colour that would be the same fair shade as Jack's, the same as Milt's used to be.

"She's a strong woman, your mother." Milt was looking at Jack with such, what would she call it? Compassion or...love?

Natalie pushed open the door.

"Hell's teeth, Nat, where did you spring from?" Sitting opposite the door, Milt was the first to see her. They'd all been focused on Jack.

Then there was a clamour of voices as they all welcomed her, Sean the only one to get up. He came to her and kissed her cheek. "Good to see you, Natalie."

She forced herself to smile and murmured a response but she was finding it hard to breathe. They were all staring at her – her husband, her daughters, Owen. Jack.

Laura came to give her a hug. "You look worn out, Mum. Have Nan and Gramps been running you ragged?"

"Have you eaten?" Kate asked. "Laura's made a passable lamb ragu."

Natalie glanced around the table at their empty plates then to the mess on the benches. She was home and yet it brought her no sense of relief.

"I snacked on the way," she managed. "I'm not hungry but…I am tired. I'm sorry…I…"

Laura peered at her. "You don't look well. Are you okay?"

Milt got to his feet.

She waved at him to sit down. "I'm fine." She was saying it again. "Just tired. It has been a bit hectic." Another lie. It had been like a holiday at her parents' place compared to home.

"I ran into Claire while I was in town," Bree said. "She covered one of your days off. She said to tell you the kids are fine and she had your program folder and gave it to me to bring back."

Natalie glanced at the desk in the corner and the green folder perched there. She didn't want to think about school or anything else really. Her head hurt from thinking.

"Thanks. I'll leave you all to it and head straight to bed." She backed away.

"I'll bring you a cup of tea." Kate looked concerned.

Natalie gave what she hoped was a reassuring smile. Kate and Laura were quick to empathise, and Bree had said a quick hello when she'd arrived but sat back now, so like her father, who was doing the same. Poor Owen must think her a lunatic and Jack, well, Jack was watching her steadily, those pearly blue eyes searching. She couldn't bear to meet his look.

"Thanks…sorry to disappear. I'll be fine…after a decent sleep." She turned away from their gazes, made her way to the bedroom. Normally this room was her haven but not tonight. There was no peace here as she stripped off, no comfort as she slid under the covers.

She'd felt an outsider in her parents' home and now that she was in her own, she still couldn't find that elusive peace. The sight of Jack in her kitchen, Laura bending over him, her hand on his shoulder, had made the pieces of her puzzled life jumble again and now she doubted her decision to not ask Milt the question she'd tried to avoid.

*

"Are you sure your mum's okay?" Sean shut the bedroom door and began to strip.

Kate watched him. Normally she'd be hungry for his strong, lean body after a week without him but tonight the lethargy clung to her, dampening any stirrings of desire. "Yes. I guess." She slipped down in the bed, trying to focus on his question. "Although I thought she seemed a bit…" A bit what? Kate spent each day struggling to keep her own head up and she didn't have a lot of energy left for her mother's mood.

Sean switched off the light and slipped into bed, drawing her to him. She relaxed in his comforting embrace, so glad he was there. "She had to go to Adelaide for tests the same time as Jack's mum. Everything was fine, she said. Maybe it's been a bit of a shock… Mrs Halbot's news."

"I didn't think they got on."

"It's not that they don't get on. They just…I don't know. I think there may have been some kind of falling-out when I was little. We've not really mixed much with the Halbots until…" Kate thought about that. Bree had muttered something about Jack turning into Dad's golden-haired boy while they'd been out mustering. Bree was often touchy and Kate hadn't thought much about it. "Until recently." She slid a hand up Sean's chest and rested it on his shoulder. This wasn't what she'd wanted to talk to her husband about. "You haven't said much about your weekend."

"Nothing much to tell. No luck fishing, although I enjoyed trying. I drank too much trying to keep up with Damo and Shortie. Woke up Monday morning with a sore head and crook guts and decided I'd never do it again." He patted her back. "That should make you happy."

"I don't mind you having a boys' weekend, once in a while."

Sean groaned. "No, I mean it, please be the wife that says I can't ever do it again."

Kate laughed, gripped him tighter. "So who were the neighbours?"

"A couple and their baby, Adelaide friends of Tom's from the next-door shack. They were staying for a week. We had a barbecue with them on the Saturday night."

"The baby looked cute."

"She was." Sean rolled away, flicked on the beside light.

Kate blinked at the sudden brightness.

"When were you going to mention Sarah and Nick's baby?" He studied her.

"I…" She shrugged, looked away from his gaze. "I haven't seen you since then."

"There was no argument with Sarah, was there? It was hearing about the baby that upset you the day you met her for lunch."

Kate looked into Sean's deep brown eyes studying her closely and crumpled with remorse. "We'd made a pact," she whispered. "We'd be the childless couples. You know how hard it is when everyone else in the district has kids. Sarah and I were each other's buffer."

He continued to gaze at her then shook his head. "You're a goose." He reached out, pulled her to him. "You can't make that kind of agreement with someone else." He kissed her.

She rested her head on his shoulder. *Not even your own husband.* The words echoed inside her head. She'd believed Sean when he'd said they didn't need a child if nature didn't intend for them to have one; they had each other. His brothers had produced nieces and nephews who adored him. Maybe her sisters would have babies one day. She was happy to be that doting childless aunt but was he truly happy to remain childless?

Only a few weeks earlier one of his nieces had been baptised. It had been a big family celebration with aunts and uncles and cousins. He'd been holding the baby cocooned in the crook of his arm, and one of his cousin's wives had declared him a natural and wanted to know when he was going to be a dad. "There're plenty of kids in this family," he'd said in a jokey voice. "We're not having our own." Kate had been near enough to hear and she'd seen his look. He meant 'she' not 'we'. It had hit her like a bolt out of the blue. Her refusal to try IVF was the reason they didn't have children.

She turned to him now. "You and I made that kind of agreement."

He sighed. "That's not what I meant. You and I are husband and wife."

"But it's not so different."

"It is. I haven't changed my mind about children…unless you have?"

She shook her head. He'd said *unless*. A heavy weight settled around her heart.

Once more he moved away from her, this time to turn the light off. "I'll need to get an early start in the morning." He kissed her lips and slid down in the bed, reaching to pull her close as she did the same. "Good night."

Kate lay perfectly still, wanting to say more but not sure how to begin. Perhaps this wasn't the right time. Once they were both back at their place, maybe. It would be difficult but perhaps they needed to revisit their decision, or had it really been her decision and Sean being the supportive guy that he was had simply agreed? His hand felt heavy across her belly and his breathing deepened. She moved his arm to the side, and he snuffled and rolled away.

The sadness inside her swelled and added to the deepening lethargy she felt. She decided she should make an appointment to see the doctor tomorrow. Her childhood GP still practised in town. She felt more comfortable unburdening her woes to the woman who'd seen her through her teenage years, rather than to the GP where she lived. She took a deep breath and let it out gently. Just making the decision to visit the doctor eased the weight.

*

Bree and Owen were finishing the last of the kitchen clean-up when Milt returned from the bathroom. He paused, watching Owen who was wiping down the bench while Bree put dishes away. He hovered looking lost. In her lifetime Bree had rarely seen her dad pick up a tea towel. He'd clear the table, put plates in the sink or the dishwasher, but that was about the extent of it.

"Thanks for cleaning up." Milt shifted from foot to foot. "Laura's food's not bad but she does create a bit of havoc."

"No probs," Owen said, his face wide with his easy smile.

"I'm glad you're not driving back to town tonight. Probably shouldn't have opened the second bottle of red."

"I enjoyed it."

"And Bree's got you somewhere to sleep." Once more Milt's feet shuffled.

Bree shut the cupboard with a thud. Was her dad being diplomatic or did he really believe Owen wasn't spending the night in her bed?

"Yep," Owen said. "All under control."

"Well...great." Milt nodded. "Will we see you again before you head north?"

"Probably not."

Milt moved closer, reached out a hand. "Good luck then. I'm sure Bree will keep us posted on how it goes."

Owen shook his hand. "Yeah." He glanced sideways and gave Bree a look, eyebrows raised.

"I'm off to bed." Milt turned away.

Bree looked at Owen and nodded her head towards the door, adding a slight wave of her hand.

"Hang on, Dad," she said. "I want to have a quick word."

"I'll say good night then." Owen took her hint and left them to it.

Milt turned back. "What's up?"

Bree could see his eyes were red and weary, partly from a hard day's work and partly from the red wine, which had also added a ruddiness to his cheeks.

"I'm going to go to Marla while Owen's there."

He scratched his head. "It's a long way to go for a visit but we can work it so you get some extra time, maybe take a week. See what happens after tailing." He went to turn away.

"No, Dad, I mean I'm going up there to stay while Owen's there. It could be several months."

Milt turned back, the look on his face suggesting he didn't understand what she was saying. "But you've got work here."

"I spoke to Graeme. He's happy to fill in for me."

Milt's head went up, understanding dawned. "At a cost."

"You can pay him what you pay me."

"And what will you live on?"

"Owen reckons I could get work at the roadhouse. Or maybe on a nearby station."

Milt shook his head. "Owen's leaving next week."

"I'll wait till tailing's finished. Give you time to work something out with Graeme."

Milt's shoulders drooped. In the silence the fridge began to hum. "If it's what you want," he said brusquely and turned away. "I'll see you in the morning."

Bree stood alone in the kitchen. Pleased to have finally told her father, excited to admit she was going on this adventure with Owen, and yet there was a part of her that felt as if she'd lost something and she wasn't sure what it was.

*

The cup of tea Kate had brought Natalie sat cooling on the bedside table. She watched Milt now, his tall frame stripped naked. He carried a few extra kilos around his middle but he was still fit for a man approaching his sixtieth birthday. She'd always loved his body, even when they'd gone through the rough patch after the affair. Her head and her heart had found it easy to feel the pain of his infidelity but her own weak flesh had found it difficult to reject his body. Eventually it had been the sex that had brought them back together and then they'd worked hard to make the rest right.

Now he was rummaging in his underwear drawer, muttering about not being able to find anything and then lifting a pair of superman boxers into the air in triumph. They'd been a Christmas gift from one of the girls, probably Laura. He'd given up wearing anything to bed once the girls had left home but had the funny habit of putting on a pair of boxers when they returned. Not that Natalie would complain. She was in pyjamas and sex was the last thing on her mind tonight, the same as most nights these days. Menopause had changed her body and her libido. It had coincided with Milt slowing too but she did wonder how long it had been since they'd last made love. There was always intimacy and cuddles, but not sex for perhaps a couple of months.

She pushed those thoughts away. She'd made up her mind to ask her husband the question that had come back to haunt her ever since they'd visited Jack on their way back from the city. Pretending all could go on as usual wouldn't work. Now the pressure of it built inside her with a ferociousness she had to expel.

Boxers on, Milt climbed into bed beside her and kissed her cheek. "Did you know Bree's planning to go off to Marla with Owen?"

His question took her by surprise. She'd worked herself up to ask her own question. "She mentioned something about it before I went to Victor."

"Hell's teeth, Nat. This property is her work. I can't leave it on a whim and neither can she. Didn't you tell her that?"

"Didn't you?"

He looked at her, mouth open as if to respond and then he closed it.

She felt sorry for him. He still thought of his daughters as little girls and had no idea how to have a grown-up conversation with them. Natalie was to blame in some respect. She'd always stepped into the breach. It was so easy for her to talk with her girls. A few leading questions and they usually spilled all.

"There's a bigger problem," Milt said. "Connie's agitating for some kind of payout."

"What? You told her there won't be, I assume."

"I haven't spoken to Connie. This has all come from Mum."

"Connie's had handouts and she'll get an inheritance. She's not getting an extra share. It belongs to us now, to our girls."

"I know all that, Nat." He held up his hands. "Settle down."

Natalie bristled. "What are you going to do about it?"

"There's nothing I can do about it until I find out exactly what she wants." He reached for his glasses. He only used them when he read his book, too stubborn to take a pair with him for everyday use.

"Are you going to read?" she asked. Reading was rare for her other than professional development journals and papers. She couldn't remember the last time she'd read a book for pleasure, probably last summer, but it was Milt's nightly habit, his way of switching off. They were always fat tomes: biographies, Australian history or war memoirs. Usually he came to bed first and by the time she'd finished her jobs he'd be ready to put out the light.

"I was."

She swallowed the urge to slap him. She'd been doing that a lot lately, swallowing her urges. There had to be another outlet for her anger.

"I wanted to talk."

"About?"

Natalie took a breath, her heart thumping. There was no easy way to ask the question she wasn't sure she wanted to hear the answer to.

"Jack."

Milt plumped the pillow behind his head and settled back against it. "What about Jack?"

"You seem to have taken quite an interest in him."

Milt let out a tired sigh. "We've talked about this, Nat. He's a neighbour and, in spite of the past, a neighbour that needs some help through a difficult time at the moment."

"I don't mean now. Before Veronica's diagnosis, he'd obviously been here on occasion and you there."

Milt folded his arms, tugging the sheets tight as he did. "I told you he's interested in our breeding program. He wants to learn and we're right next door. He came to our last sale."

"Did he?" Natalie thought she would have remembered that.

"Yes. He asked a few questions and we got talking. He's been keeping in touch ever since."

Natalie swallowed. She was about to raise a topic they'd agreed never to raise again.

"We agreed…after…well, we decided never to socialise with the Halbots."

"And we haven't. Jack's visits have been business."

Natalie had started now. She couldn't stop until she had her answer. "And the dinners, the cups of coffee?"

"Hell, Nat, you're splitting hairs. He came last week because I didn't think it was good for him to be alone. You know that."

"And tonight?"

"He was here today while we were yarding sheep. It was Laura who invited him to stay."

Natalie's stomach twisted tighter until it felt like a solid lump had formed inside her and then it lunged upwards, forcing the words from her mouth, opening an old wound that had never properly healed. "Is Jack your son?"

Milt's face went slack except for the small frown that furrowed his brow. He gave the slightest shake of his head. "After what we went through, Nat, why would you even ask that?"

"Because I have to know."

"He's not my son."

"How can you be sure?"

"Because…" He looked down, his legs shifted under the sheet. "I told you why…we didn't—"

"You had an affair with his mother." She kept her voice low, never wanting her girls to hear those words.

"There was no affair exactly." His response was a harsh whisper. "You know that. We settled all this a long time ago."

Natalie snorted with pent-up rage mixed with terror. She was having none of his cover-ups now. "Perhaps you told me what I needed to hear."

"What the hell does that mean?"

"Jack was born nine months after you and—"

"Jack was premature." Milt's chin jutted forward. "And I'd bloody well know if he was mine."

"How?"

"You know how." His face contorted in a mix of disbelief and anger. "Hell's teeth, Nat, it's in the past. Why are we even discussing it?"

Natalie shook her head. Dread was spreading cold fingers down through her body and out to her limbs, prickling the back of her neck. She'd rebuilt her marriage and had thought the glitch was behind them but Milt couldn't see how much Jack looked like him. The pearly blue eyes, combined with Laura's fair hair and Milt's waves. It was as plain as the nose on his face but Milt was never quick to see what was right in front of him.

"You were the one who betrayed our marriage." She couldn't stop herself. Her words were sharp, barbed, aimed to hurt.

Milt threw back the covers and rose from the bed, the ridiculous boxers hanging low on his hips, below his paunch. He glared down at her. "Yes, I know," he growled. "And I've been paying for it ever since."

Natalie recoiled. "What do you mean? Once we sorted things out I've never mentioned it until now."

"And we weren't going to tell anyone but you told Dad."

"I did not." Natalie was firmly back on the high moral ground again.

"How did he find out then, when not even Mum knew?"

Natalie sat up. She remembered the day so well. Clem had come to her, hat in hand literally. He was such a gentleman. Always took his hat off if there were women present. "You were off in the paddock and your mum in town. I was home with Kate and Bree. He came and sought me out, said he knew. He was so understanding, so kind. It was a relief for me to have someone to confide in."

"Did it have to be my father?"

"He'd overheard us arguing a few days before. He didn't take sides."

Milt humphed. "Not what he said to me."

"Well, he said nothing against you to me. Your dad kept things close to his chest but he offered me a choice. He asked me to forgive you and stay but he said if I couldn't do that and I had to leave the marriage he'd make sure the girls and I were well looked after."

"Dad said that to you?" Milt sagged to the bed. "I got a right royal telling-off. I'd never felt so bad in my life, first for the hurt I caused you, then for my father's disappointment and then the anger...well, I assumed you'd been the one to tell him."

"You were angry with me?" Natalie struggled to contain her own simmering rage.

Milt shrugged, put his head in his hands. "Hell, Nat, it was so long ago. Why are we doing this to each other again?"

Colours swirled before her eyes, and she couldn't breathe. She threw back the covers and strode to the window, throwing up the sash and letting the cold night air waft in around her, welcoming the chill of it prickling over her skin. Her marriage had a question mark over it again but this time she doubted her wisdom in staying. What had it been for? She turned back to Milt. He was still slumped on the edge of the bed, his back to her.

"Perhaps it was a mistake to try to bury it," she said. "You know what they say, lies come back to haunt you."

He turned to her. "There have been no lies. You know all there was to know."

"Jack?"

"He's not mine, Nat." Milt sighed, crawled back into bed and pulled up the covers. "I'm tired. We're just going round in circles. Let's get some sleep. We've got another early start tomorrow."

Natalie studied him as he turned away to switch off his light. Since his affair and the patching up of their marriage they'd rarely rowed openly or raised their voices at each other. Milt was quick to anger but just as quick to cool. He'd growl about something then calm down and they'd talk, but tonight he wouldn't and she couldn't. Nor could she stand to lie beside him, not feeling like she did. She had to get away or she'd go mad. She took her dressing-gown from the hook on the back of the door.

"Where are you going?" he asked.

"I can't sleep. I'll only keep you awake. I'll go to the spare room in the quarters."

"Owen's in there."

Nat looked back at the dark outline of his frame in the bed. "Milt, you can be so blind." She spoke in a low voice. The rest of the house was in darkness. "He won't be in the spare bedroom, I can assure you."

The dark shape sat up. "You think he's with Bree?"

She shook her head, pulled the door to behind her and set off down the passage. That Owen and Bree were an item, as they say, and Milt hadn't noticed was one more piece of proof that he couldn't see the bleeding obvious.

Fifteen

Laura buzzed around the kitchen making extra noise to compensate for the lack of it coming from her two grim-faced sisters sitting at the table clutching their cups, tea for Kate, coffee for Bree. She switched the radio to Triple J. Her father was already up and headed out around the same time as Sean and Owen by the sound of it. Her two sad-sack sisters had made breakfast for the men but not for themselves. She put a plate of toast on the table between them with a thud fuelled by a small burst of jealousy that there was no man in her life for her to even miss slightly, let alone moon over like these two were.

"Cheer up, you two. It's not as if you're never seeing them again."

Bree was the first to reach for the toast. "I'm not upset because Owen's left. It's Dad. I told him last night I'm leaving."

"Leaving!" Laura plonked into the seat beside her. "I thought you were going for a few months."

"I am." Bree took a despondent slurp of her coffee.

"Leaving sounds permanent."

"Well it's not…unless Dad wants it that way," she muttered. "Anyway I'm not going for a while yet. Not till tailing's done at least."

They were silent a moment then Kate spoke. "I can understand how he feels." It was that knowing big-sister voice of hers.

Laura glanced at Kate, catching a glimpse of Bree's scowl as she did.

"Of course *you* would," Bree snapped. "It's all right for *you*. You're not here often and you don't work for Dad."

"But I do work in a family business. Lucky for me I can job share with my in-laws and I've earned some time off. You're Dad's only worker."

"There's Graeme."

"And me," Laura chipped in. She hated tension between her sisters.

They both turned to look at her, Bree's face full of disdain and Kate's slightly surprised.

"I can help." Laura snatched a piece of toast and began to spread it with chunks of butter. The solid lumps tore at the cooling toast, pulling it apart as she wielded the knife. "I'm not going anywhere for a while."

"How long do you plan to stay?" Kate's tone was gentle.

"I don't have a plan."

"What about your job?" Bree asked.

Laura's confidence waned under Bree's piercing gaze. "I quit."

"So this is not just a holiday?"

"No."

Bree pushed back her chair and stood. "Well, there we are." There was a smug smile on her face. "You can take my place. Easy done." She took her cup, strode to the coffee machine and set it going again.

"No need to be so huffy," Kate said. "Talk to Dad about it more."

"I've tried."

Laura met Kate's look across the table. Her sister gave her an encouraging smile.

"I'm going to stay on for a few more days too," Kate said.

"How come?"

"I've hardly seen Mum so I'll stay till the weekend, maybe into next week. I've taken some more leave." She looked pointedly at Bree as she sat back in her chair.

"Well, aren't you lucky to accrue leave," Bree snapped. "I can't seem to find the piece of paper that records how much I'm owed."

Kate opened her mouth then closed it again. Music blared from the radio, filling the silence, and then Kate spoke. "Shouldn't we be out with Dad now?"

Bree glanced at the kitchen clock. "Give him a few more minutes."

*

Natalie blinked at the numbers on her mobile phone until they came into focus. She sat up quickly as she realised it was after seven. Milt would probably be up and gone. It was the first day of tailing and he'd want to make sure everything was ready. She hoped one of the girls had cooked him some break— She stopped, berated herself. Why should she care? Then the other part of her felt guilty because she did.

She groaned and swung her feet to the ground, shivering at the cold boards beneath her feet. Bree's spare room in the quarters was a junk room really. The place she'd dumped anything she didn't need. The scattered boxes and bags had been pushed against one wall in an obvious attempt to tidy up. Bree must have done a quick rearrange when she'd made the bed for Olive. At least the bed had still been made up.

The night had been chilly and Natalie had been awake for half of it, at war with herself, going over her life and what had brought her to this moment. She'd moved on from worrying over Jack being Milt's son and the implications of that, to questioning her marriage all over again, and that had made her ponder her life and what she'd done with it. Even the thought of going back to her teaching didn't inspire any excitement like it once had. She was fifty-eight; surely there was more she should have achieved by now. The anomaly in her breast had started the questioning and then had become jumbled with the uncertainties that Jack's presence had evoked.

It occurred to her in the night that she'd been abducted by aliens and returned to someone else's body. That was a better explanation than facing the truth: her life was not what she thought. With a burst of clarity the words *paradigm shift* repeated in her mind. She'd first heard of a paradigm shift at a conference she'd attended many years ago. The presenter had explained that a paradigm is the way each person sees the world and a paradigm shift enables you to view the world from a totally different perspective.

Natalie hadn't really understood but now it was clear. The busy yet settled and happy existence she thought she had been living was not the reality. She'd thought herself a caring and competent teacher but the new principal had eroded her confidence in her abilities. Her husband's long-buried affair had produced a son, she was convinced of that now, no matter how Milt denied it. The kitchen was no longer her domain and the property they'd worked hard to build up was under threat from Milt's sister, who'd done nothing to deserve it. Then there were her girls. Natalie had faltered at the thought of her three precious daughters. They were her world but they had their own lives to live and even though they were all under her roof at the moment, they wouldn't continue to be. They no longer needed a mother. A chill went through her at the thought of nothing to look forward to.

She groaned again and gripped her head in her hands. The constant turmoil in her head and the tightness in her chest were driving her crazy. In the early hours she'd decided she needed to get away, give herself some space to think, and immediately she imagined the face of her dearest friend, Brenda. It had hit her like the proverbial ton of bricks how much she missed her friend. They would have talked everything through, not the stuff about Jack but everything else. Since Brenda had left she hadn't had a proper heart-to-heart talk with another woman like she'd always been able to do with her dear friend. They emailed and chatted on the phone but life got busy. It had been two weeks, maybe three, since she'd heard from Brenda last. Natalie didn't know why she hadn't thought of it earlier.

At three o'clock this morning she'd made the decision to visit Brenda in Brisbane. She didn't care that it was tailing. Laura was managing the food. Natalie had plenty of leave up her sleeve from school. Paul would just have to arrange more cover for her.

With that all decided she'd finally slept, but now as daylight crept into the room her determination to get away faltered. Only one week and tailing would be finished, and then it would be only three more till school holidays; she could take a break then. She slipped her arms into her dressing-gown and felt the weight of common sense and duty settle with it on her shoulders.

Out in the corridor she stopped to listen. No sounds from within the quarters. Owen would have left early and Bree was no doubt out with her father by now. She opened the door that separated the quarters from the house and was greeted by music coming from the kitchen radio. It wasn't on the ABC so Milt had definitely gone. She made her way towards the kitchen in desperate need of a cup of tea, but just before she reached the door she stopped. The girls were talking.

"I suppose you'll be inviting him for dinner again." Bree's voice had a teasing tone.

"He's good eye candy." Kate chuckled.

"Lay off, you two." Laura's annoyance was accompanied by the crash of cutlery in the sink.

"Dad thinks he's it and a bit," Bree said. "And he lives close. It'd be a match made in heaven."

A chair dragged sharply. "Hey, watch it," Bree called. "Mum won't be happy if she finds you throwing wet dishcloths around."

Natalie pressed a hand to the wall. They had to be talking about Jack. Laura couldn't have feelings for him. He could be... her empty stomach churned and she pressed her fingers to her lips.

"It's weird, don't you think?" Laura said. "We've been neighbours of the Halbots all our lives and never had much to do with them till now."

"Dad's sure taken a shine to Jack. He's like the golden-haired boy." Bree's voice was full of irritation.

"Perhaps he likes having another bloke around the place," Kate said. "And we did see the Halbots back when Dad played tennis. It was before your time, Laura."

"So why did it stop?" Laura asked.

There was a short pause as if they were all thinking about that.

"I don't know," Kate said.

"Has anything more happened about reviving the tennis court?" Laura asked.

"Dad's thinking about it," Bree said.

"I don't think Mum's keen on the idea," Kate said.

"What's Mum got against tennis anyway?" Laura said. "She's always encouraged our sport but tennis is this big voodoo we're never allowed to mention. Dad's got a cupboard full of trophies."

"You're right," Bree said. "I've never thought about it much but it's been Mum who's not wanted us to resurrect the tennis court."

"Do you think she's okay?" Kate asked.

Natalie leaned her body against the wall, worried her legs would fold beneath her.

"Now that I think about it she's been quiet ever since she came back from having the tests in Adelaide," Bree said.

"I said that the other day," Laura huffed.

Natalie stayed where she was, unable to make herself move away.

"I guess it would be a shock to get the all-clear and then to discover your neighbour wasn't so lucky," Kate said.

"Maybe Mum's got that weird thing," Laura said.

"What weird thing?" her sisters asked in unison.

"You know when people wish they had what someone else did to get the attention."

Natalie put a hand to her head. Her daughters thought she was going crazy. Maybe she was. Nothing had seemed right in her life since the discovery of the anomaly. It was like she'd thought back in the coffee shop in Victor; there was some kind of dividing line across the path of her life and now she was living AA – After Anomaly.

"Don't be ridiculous. Mum's just Mum," Bree scoffed then a chair scraped. "Bugger, look at the time. She'll be here soon to organise food and Dad will be chomping. We'd better get out there, Kate."

More chairs scraped across the kitchen floor and Natalie only had time to straighten herself up before Bree pulled open the door.

"Mum?" Bree glanced behind her and back again. "Hi…bye. Gotta go." She brushed a kiss over Natalie's cheek and dashed past.

"Morning, Mum." Kate stopped to look at her more closely than her sister had. "Did you get a good sleep?"

Natalie twisted her lips up in a smile. "Yes thanks, love."

"See you later." Another kiss grazed her cheek.

Only Laura was left, framed in the doorway, her rainbow hair fluffed out in a wild halo and a puzzled expression on her face. "I didn't know you were up. Dad said we should let you sleep."

Natalie wondered if he'd said she was in Bree's spare room.

"Would you like some breakfast?"

"Yes."

"I'll put the kettle on, then you can tell me what you want me to do for food today. I can give you a hand if you like."

Natalie watched her youngest cross the kitchen. They all assumed she'd go on as usual but could she…would she? She was desperate for a cuppa and a piece of toast but she needed time to compose herself. "I'll have my shower first. Don't worry about me, I'll get myself something once I'm dressed."

By the time she'd showered and returned to her own bedroom Natalie was determined again to go to Brisbane to see Brenda, and she was going to go now before she changed her mind again.

She made the bed, paused at Milt's side, his reading glasses perched on his current book, something about the explorer Hubert Wilkins who'd been born just up the road. Milt often shared little snippets of information he discovered from his reading. Natalie traced her fingers over the cover and felt a sudden yearning for the luxury of time to read a book. It would be the first thing she'd buy when she got to the airport. Excitement fuelled her now as she tipped out the clothes she hadn't unpacked from her Victor Harbor trip and repacked with clothes better suited to the warmer climate in Brisbane.

"Mum?"

She froze at Laura's call as if she was about to be discovered doing something illicit.

"I'm taking coffee up to Dad, back in a while."

"Okay."

Natalie rushed, determined to be gone from the house before Laura returned. She'd ring Paul and Brenda from the car once she was down the highway.

She typed a text for Milt.

Have decided I need a break to clear my thoughts. Going to have a week or so with Brenda in Brisbane. Haven't told the girls. Will leave it to you.

Her finger hovered over the arrow to send. She doubted he'd look at his phone until morning tea but just in case she decided to wait until she was on the road before she sent it. She re-read her text and felt like a coward but there was also a small dash of pleasure in that last statement. It was always her job to fill in the girls. He could do it for a change.

At the bedroom door she paused, a bundle of dirty clothes tucked under her arm and her suitcase handle in the other hand. Nothing out of place. She hurried down the corridor, risking a glance in the other bedrooms, both with unmade beds, and came to a stop at the kitchen. She should go in, clean up. It was a big job for Laura on her own, but if she stayed Laura would come back and find her and then she'd have to explain.

And there it was again, *The Model Wife*, controlling her. She couldn't do anything unless the house was clean. Or could she? Natalie took a deep breath, turned away from the plates and cups still spread across the table, and the pans and more plates and mugs piled around the sink, dumped her dirty clothes in the laundry as she passed and let herself out the back door. She paused to give Bubbles a pat, glanced over her patch of gerberas. There were few flowers on them now; they didn't like the cold. Before she could succumb to more backward glances she loaded her case and drove away feeling as if she was escaping, or more truthfully running away from home.

★

Laura did the morning tea shift on her own. She'd been surprised her mother hadn't made another appearance but perhaps she'd gone back to bed. She'd looked tired and Laura had decided to leave her alone but when she got back from the shed with the empty baskets there had been no sign that her mother had even been in the kitchen.

Laura set herself to cleaning up and, knowing how particular her mum was, she even mopped the floor. She plucked the fading gerberas from the vase on the table and replaced them with some sprigs of lavender. When she finally stopped the house felt empty around her, as if no-one else was home. She jiggled her shoulders to disperse the ominous prickle that nagged her and went in search of her mother.

She trod softly along the passage, pulling her own bedroom door closed to hide the mess as she passed. There'd been no time to deal with any of her things since she'd arrived home. Outside her parents' bedroom she hesitated. The door was slightly ajar. She pushed it slowly inwards, peered around then stepped straight in. Everything was neat and tidy, the bed made, not a thing out of place. The window sash was open just enough to let in some air and the lace curtain wobbled in the soft breeze.

"Mum?" It was stupid to say it, as if her mother was suddenly going to materialise when it was obvious she wasn't in the room.

Laura retraced her steps. She called louder and checked each room. Kate's bed was unmade like hers and the rest of the house was empty with no sign of her mother. She yanked the band from the ponytail she'd made while she was cleaning, dragged her fingers through her hair and tied it up again then stood in the middle of the passage, hands on hips, frowning at the back door. Her mum must have gone to the sheds. It was pretty mean of her to leave all the food prep to Laura.

*

Kate came back to the house just before lunch break. She was going to grab a quick bite then head into town. The receptionist at the surgery had been able to fit her in with Dr Strauss later that afternoon. She'd made up an excuse for her dad about needing a script, but as she removed her boots at the back door she braced herself for her mum's response. It wasn't easy to get things past her. In some ways Kate didn't want to. It would be a relief to talk through her concerns with her mum; maybe she'd even go with her to town.

If she was back at her own place Kate might have talked to Sarah about her health concerns but not now, since their...what would she call it? Friends had disagreements, patched them up and went on but this was different. It wasn't an argument but Sarah having a baby would change their relationship forever. The baby would always be a point of difference between them. She would normally share her feelings with Sean but she was too frightened, worried they were on different pages too. Her mum was the only one she felt she could talk to about all this. Kate sighed and moved her weary body into the house.

Laura was alone in the kitchen. She was loading the esky and a box with containers.

"Where's Mum?" Kate asked.

Laura looked up. Her face had lost the usual Laura sparkle. "I don't know. She's not in the house. I thought she might have gone up to the shed. I haven't seen her since breakfast."

"We haven't seen her. Did you check the house?"

"Yes." Laura locked the lid on the esky. "Can you help me? I've got to get this lot up to the shed."

Kate looked at the load of items to be transported. "I'll bring my car to the back door."

"Thanks." Laura's face crumpled into a grateful smile. "I thought Mum would be here to help."

Kate took her keys from the rack beside the door. "Won't be long."

★

Bree strode towards the house. Tailing was going well and her dad was keeping his cool. He was usually edgy on the first day of any big job, always watching for potential problems, but today he was almost a different man, as if his mind wasn't fully on the task. She'd had to remind him a couple of times to move the sheep on.

With only a short time till lunch, she'd slipped away for a quick bathroom break and she planned to call Owen.

Ahead of her Kate hurried through the back gate towards the car shed. Bree let herself inside, went to the bathroom and arrived in the kitchen to find Laura lugging a box towards the back door.

Bree looked around the chaos that was their kitchen. "Where's Mum?"

"Bloody hell," Laura spat. "I don't know. I'm not the mum police."

"Steady up."

Laura shoved the box at her. "Make yourself useful and take this to the car. Kate's driving to the back gate."

"Mum's car's not in the garage." Kate had come in behind her.

"Perhaps she's gone into town," Laura said.

"Not without telling anyone, surely." Kate's brow creased in a frown. "Are you certain she didn't say anything to you before she left, Laura?"

"I didn't even know she had left."

"Your mum's gone on a holiday." Milt stood just inside the kitchen door, his phone clutched in his hand. A grubby damp mark circled his brow where his hat had been. "She's gone to Aunty Brenda's for a break."

The three of them stared at him as if he'd started speaking in another language.

"It's not school holidays yet, is it?" Kate broke the silence.

"Does that mean I have to do all the cooking?" Laura gaped at him.

"But we're tailing," Bree said.

"Yes we are, and we've a hungry team to feed. Let's get going." He clapped his hands and they galvanised into action, carrying lunch to the car.

Bree was the last to leave the kitchen. Knowing her mother wasn't there, hadn't really been there for a while now, left her with a hollow feeling as if her mum had simply evaporated, gone for good. She shrugged away her unease and strode out the door, pulling it shut with a thud behind her.

★

A hundred kilometres south Natalie was sitting in a bakery making up for last night's missed dinner and the breakfast she hadn't eaten that morning. There was a glitch in her escape plan, well, there'd been two but she'd dealt with the first one. When she'd spoken to Paul he'd said it was short notice for her to take three days' leave. She'd surprised herself and him by firmly declaring she had plenty of leave and she was taking three days of it and he'd have to organise it, whatever it took. That done, she'd tried Brenda again. She'd got her voicemail the first time. The second time she'd tried, a breathless Brenda had answered. She was on her way to the airport. Her daughter and son-in-law did business in Thailand and they were taking Brenda along as babysitter for their one-year-old.

"As if that would be a hardship," Brenda had chortled. Her only grandchild was the centre of her world these days. "We'll be gone a couple of weeks and there'll be time to have a look around, see some sights. We're going to finish up in a resort in Phuket before we come home."

Natalie swallowed the gloom of her own disappointment and instead focused on the joy she heard in her friend's voice. Losing her husband, selling the property and moving halfway across Australia had been such a tough time for Brenda. She deserved some happiness.

Trouble was, it had foiled Natalie's escape plan. She hadn't said anything to Brenda, of course. After she'd rung off she'd been close to the little town where she was now having lunch. She'd pulled in and sat a moment in her car. Her eyes had filled with tears for the loss of the opportunity to be with her friend. The visit had been whisked from her grasp and had taken the excitement of her escape with it. Heavy legs had carried her inside the bakery where the smell of pastries stirred her hunger.

Now as she nibbled carefully at the piping hot pasty she considered her options. She could simply turn around and go home again but a feeling of disappointment accompanied that idea. Or, she could keep driving and simply pick another destination. The thought of that both thrilled and terrified her. She'd never gone off on her own before, couldn't imagine what that would be like.

The brochures were still on the back seat of her car but she took out her phone instead and googled holiday destinations. She added 'escape' and 'winter' and the first thing that appeared on her screen was *Best Winter Sun Holiday Destinations in Australia* and at the top of the list was Broome, Western Australia. Perhaps Google had read her thoughts, like it tracked her online history. She'd wanted to go to Broome since the article on pearls had piqued her interest along with the idea of a thirtieth wedding anniversary holiday. That hadn't happened but she had only thought of it as deferred, and had imagined Broome would be a place she and Milt would explore together, but now…The doubt washed over her again.

Outside a shower of rain blew in along the street. Not enough to be of any use. She stared out at the bleak day. Several people rushed past, huddled against the cold. In the warmth of the bakery, Natalie was trying to make a decision when her phone rang. The sudden sound startled her. She stabbed yes to accept without looking to see who it was.

"Natalie?"

She stiffened.

"Natalie, are you there?" Nancy Phelps's voice boomed in her ear.

"Yes." Damn! Why had she answered without checking the caller ID first?

Nancy kept talking, her voice loud in Natalie's ear. "You missed the netball meeting last week but I've still put you in charge of the catering. Young Bonnie said she'd do it but she's so unreliable. I said she could help you. You've got more common sense than the rest of the committee put together."

Natalie's insides churned and then two words popped into her head – After Anomaly. She'd never said no to Nancy in her life but this was Natalie's AA life and planning to escape on a holiday on her own made her bold. "Thanks for thinking of me but I can't do it this time." She took a breath. "In fact I don't think I'll be on the committee at all any more."

"But—"

"My girls haven't played netball for years. I think it's time to let someone else who's more involved take a turn." She bent to pick up her handbag. Her fingers trembled. Her initial strength in standing up to Nancy was fading fast. "Must go. I'm on my way to Adelaide."

"But—"

"Nice to chat, Nancy." Natalie pressed end, gathered her things and strode quickly from the shop. She'd said no to Nancy Phelps and it felt as if she'd won the lotto.

Sixteen

Thirty-eight thousand feet in the air, Natalie pressed herself against the back of her seat as the man in front flung his seat back, trapping her in the small pocket of space left between it and the men on either side of her. She glanced from one to the other. They'd both said hello then plugged earphones into devices and, apart from accepting refreshments, they'd hardly moved since.

She shifted in her seat, moved her legs up and down, scrunched her toes, and finally took the inflight magazine from the seat pocket and began to flick, disappointed there'd been no time at the airport to browse the bookshop. She still had nothing to read. She'd plucked a copy of the newspaper from the stand in Perth as she'd boarded the second leg of her flight to Broome but it was difficult to open in the small space and she'd given up.

The glossy magazine held little interest either. She flicked past ads for jewellery worth more than her year's wage, cars that would be useless on rough dirt roads, watches that appeared to do everything but tell the time clearly and holidays to places overseas she knew she was unlikely to take. Opulence had never been her thing. She saw nothing her heart desired, except perhaps the holiday but it didn't have to be fancy to fulfil that dream. Head-lines urged her to 'Be ready for tomorrow', 'Tap in and tune out'. There was even one urging her to buy a 'sexy ceiling fan'.

She had to smile at that. There had been no ceiling fans in the farmhouse when she'd moved in. The summer they swapped with her in-laws from the quarters to the main house she'd organised ceiling fans to be installed in the kitchen, the main bedroom and the bedroom next door they used as a nursery. She'd paid for it from her own savings. Olive had declared it a terrible waste of money but by next summer she'd had fans installed in every room including the quarters. No further comment was made, and when Laura was a baby Olive had also arranged air conditioning for the bedrooms and the kitchen. Natalie thought of those fans now and contemplated the picture in front of her. She wondered about the advertising person who'd used the word *sexy* to describe a ceiling fan.

She continued to flick then paused at the section called 'Travel Insider'. At the bottom was a picture of a beautiful beach with no-one on it and the heading 'Exploring Dampier Peninsula'. She'd never heard of Dampier Peninsula but the article boasted unspoilt landscapes and the promise of a spiritual awakening. She put her head back and closed her eyes. She wasn't sure about a spiritual awakening but her heart and soul were in need of some kind of restoration and she hoped a holiday in Broome would do that for her.

She opened her eyes again at a change in engine noise. The pilot said something about seeing whales in the bay. Past her neighbour's head, the tiny window was filled with the aquama-rine of the Indian Ocean stretching to the horizon as the plane did a slow loop and lined up with the airport runway.

"There." The young man stabbed at the window.

She leaned closer. She caught a glimpse of a tiny dark shape and a splash of foam but wouldn't swear on her life it was a whale.

They zoomed lower over white sand dotted with beachgoers, next came glimpses of bush and vibrant red earth, and then the wheels shuddered onto the tarmac. She gripped her hands tightly in her lap. She'd done it. She'd left her family, her work and community, and the cold of a South Australian winter behind and flown halfway across Australia to Broome. She seesawed from excitement to disbelief to panic.

The heat hit her as soon as she stepped from the aircraft. She was totally unprepared and overdressed in jeans and a lightweight jumper she'd dragged on in the pre-dawn chill of Adelaide. She squinted into the mid-afternoon glare reflecting from the tarmac and hoped her sunglasses were in the bottom of her bag somewhere.

Inside the terminal there was no relief from the heat as she joined the press of people waiting to collect their luggage from the single carousel. Another flight had landed just after hers, adding to the crowd. She watched through a gap for her bag. The few times they'd flown, short trips for business or a wedding, she'd left the luggage to Milt. She was always the one to hold the tickets. It was odd being on her own with no-one else to think about and yet nerve-racking she had no-one to confer with; would her bag be there, was she in the right place, had she booked the correct dates for the hotel?

Her blue case with its vivid red name tag burst from the flaps, halting her wayward thoughts. She squeezed her way forward to grab it then, bags in hand, she found the complimentary transport to her hotel.

Once settled aboard a minibus with several others, the cheerful driver entertained them, pointing out the sights and telling them all to relax, they were now on Broome time. She did her best but the last twenty-four hours had exhausted her and even though the bus was air-conditioned, she was generating an internal heat that overwhelmed her. Perspiration dampened her back and her chest felt tight. She drained the last of her water bottle and glanced at her fellow passengers, all couples. She was the only one travelling alone. The drive from the airport was through an alien landscape of red dirt and unfamiliar bush, adding to her apprehension. The further they got from the airport the more she thought how stupid she'd been to have come all this way on her own. A spur-of-the-moment whim fuelled by her husband's infidelity twenty-seven years ago come back to haunt them, and instead of facing it head-on like she'd done most crises in her life she'd run away.

The previous evening, after she'd settled into her room at the airport, she'd sent Milt another text. *Arrived safely at airport, flying out first thing tomorrow.* She'd owed him that at least, and she'd sent the girls a good night message, generic for all three with an extra request for one of them to take her green folder back to school for her first thing Monday. She hoped Claire might be able to take her class again, or one of the more experienced relief teachers as Natalie hadn't touched the folder to update or elaborate on her program. The girls had each replied immediately, quick messages of goodnight, very brief except for Laura, who added she'd make sure the folder was delivered.

Much later, when she was in bed and almost asleep, Milt had replied. *First day tailing went well. Have good flight.* His texts were always brief and left out the little in-between words. She'd only realised that morning she hadn't told him about her change of plans, that she was flying to Broome instead of Brisbane. And now here she was and feeling so foolish that, if she wasn't so tired, she would jump on the next plane heading south and go home again.

The bus followed a long curving road then swung into a driveway lined with tropical plants. She caught a glimpse of the brilliant blue ocean she had so recently flown over and then they came to a stop at the grand entrance of the hotel. The luggage was unloaded as Natalie walked over the wooden footbridge. Beneath her, water trickled softly and as she stepped up to the huge wood-and-glass doors they swung open and the relief of cool air rushed out to meet her.

Inside the lighting was subtle. Vibrant artwork adorned the walls, the wooden floor was polished to a dark rich hue and the plush leather lounge chairs looked deep and inviting. Beyond a second set of glass doors on the other side of the room she could see lush green plants and the backs of pool chairs beside a large water feature. Natalie took another breath and approached the smiling young woman behind the check-in counter with a sense of relief.

"Welcome," the woman said. "Checking in?"

"Yes." The weight slid from Natalie's shoulders. Perhaps it was possible to escape reality. It would be silly to turn around and go home now when she felt as if she'd just stepped into paradise.

*

The cavernous farm bedroom was like an igloo. Kate had forgotten how hard it was to keep the old house warm. She should be under the covers but then she knew she wouldn't want to get up again and she still had to face dinner. Instead she lay on top of the bed, a blanket over her legs, hands clasped across her stomach, staring at the ceiling.

They'd knocked off early on the second day of tailing and she'd made straight for the house and the shower. It had been a bitterly cold day and that, along with the doctor's diagnosis from the previous afternoon, ensured she'd stayed chilled to the bone. She'd dug out a pair of trackpants from the drawers of her old bedroom chest, pulled on a long-sleeved t-shirt, a windcheater and a pair of thick socks, and then added the blanket before she began to feel warm.

Last night and today she'd run on autopilot, with her head full of swirling thoughts and her body, her betraying body, numb. None of the others seemed to notice. Her mother would have but she wasn't here. Gone off on a sudden holiday with Aunty Brenda. Dad had muttered something about her needing a break.

A tear rolled down Kate's cheek and she batted it away. She badly wanted her mother here, to tell her what the doctor had said, to feel the reassurance of her mother's arms around her.

Dr Strauss had gone over her with a fine-tooth comb and had thought there was little wrong with her but had ordered blood tests and taken a urine sample. That had produced the shock. The doctor was sure the blood test results would confirm what the urine test had revealed: Kate was pregnant. Dear, kind Dr Strauss had been delighted for her and Kate had been in too much shock to ask any questions.

Now her head was brimming with them. Why, after years of infertility, would her body suddenly decide it was fertile? She and Sean had accepted a childless life and even though she doubted his commitment to that plan she was in no doubt how she felt. Her life was satisfying; she had no longing for a child. Kate did not want to be pregnant, did not want to be a mother. She had not one inkling of maternal feeling towards this clump of cells grow-ing inside her. Sean wouldn't understand. He'd think her reaction totally mad. She knew what his response would be to the news.

"Kate, dinner's ready," Bree called from the passage.

Kate let out a deep sigh. She'd been feeling a bit off her food for a while. Now she knew there was a reason for it she only felt worse. Laura had muttered something about making pizza tonight. It seemed she was getting fed-up with doing the food too and had said they could get their own tomorrow.

Without their mum they'd lost their cohesion. Dad's lecture on giving her some space, and they would manage, and pull together as a team in their mother's absence, had a hollow ring to it, as if he was saying the words but didn't believe them. Yet again she wondered what was behind her mum's sudden departure.

The kitchen was full of the smell of crusty dough, melted cheese and cooked tomato. The others were all seated at the table when she arrived and studied her as she took her place.

"Are you all right?" Bree asked. "You look like shit."

"How kind of you to say," Kate snapped back and pulled her hands up inside her sleeves. She was grateful for the fire warming the kitchen but she still felt chilled after leaving the warmth of the bed. She reached for the jug of water and poured herself a glass, noticing everyone was on water tonight.

"Are you coming down with a cold?" Laura asked.

"No. It's been a freezing day, that's all. I couldn't warm up." Kate looked around, realising someone else was missing. "It's Saturday. Where's Granny?"

"I rang her," Laura said. "She wanted to stay home in the warm."

"Do you think she's okay?" Bree's question was directed at her dad.

"As far as I know," he said. "I rang her Thursday and Laura spoke to her today."

"She sounded fine," Laura said. "She's going to Aunty Connie's for lunch tomorrow."

Milt gave a soft snort and shifted in his chair. "This food will be going cold."

"Help yourselves." Laura waved a hand over the pizzas arranged down the table. "There's one with chicken, one ham and pineapple, and the other two have a selection of meat and veg." She took a slice from one of the plates. "What do you want, Dad?"

Milt lifted his gaze from the empty plate in front of him. "Any," he said.

Kate knew her dad wasn't a fan of pizza but he accepted a slice from the plate Laura offered him and began to eat.

"Have you heard from Mum today?"

He put his head to one side as if her question required deep thought. "Not yet."

"She and Aunty Brenda will be talking non-stop," Bree said.

"Can you imagine it?" Laura grinned. "They haven't seen each other since Aunty Brenda sold the property."

"They ring each other often," Bree said.

"But it's not the same as sitting down for a good chat." Kate took a nibble of her slice of pizza.

Bree gave her an odd look.

"I agree," Laura said. "There's nothing like a face-to-face chat. I know I'd much prefer to sit and talk with my friends over a coffee than on the phone."

Kate nodded and stared numbly at her plate. Right now she wished her mum was here so they could do just that, rather than be thousands of miles away with Brenda.

They lapsed into silence. Kate surprised herself by eating a whole slice of pizza, took a second piece and then wished she hadn't as she remembered the reason for her feeling unwell in the first place.

"What are we going to do tonight?" Laura asked. "There's nothing on TV."

"Must be a footy game on." It was Milt's first contribution to the conversation.

Laura groaned. "If we had Netflix there'd be plenty of options."

"We don't need other options," Milt grumbled.

"Have you got TV in the quarters, Bree?" Laura looked expectantly at her sister.

"No. I use the one in the house. Mum and I have a few favourite shows we watch together and I don't mind the footy."

"But there's an outlet for a TV there, isn't there? Granny and Pa had a TV when they lived there."

"Yes."

Kate could tell by the look on Laura's face she had an idea brewing.

"Could I take over the quarters while you're away?"

"No." Bree gave an adamant shake of her head.

"Why not? You'll be gone a while. I could have my own space."

"You've got your own space."

"But I—"

Milt's chair pushed back abruptly. "You can have the TV to yourself. I'm turning in." He carried his plate to the sink.

"Me too." Bree stood. "I'm going in to spend the day with Owen tomorrow." She glanced at her dad who was on his way out. "I won't be home tomorrow night."

Milt paused, half turned.

"I'll be back first thing Monday morning in time for tailing," she added quickly.

He gave a nod and looked to Laura. "Good pizza, love, thanks." And then he was gone.

"Night." Bree glanced from Laura to Kate and then she too left.

"I'll help with the dishes," Kate said, the pizza in her stomach swirling as she moved.

"You look really tired," Laura said. "Why don't you get an early night too? It won't take me long here."

Kate glanced around; as usual there were dishes and containers and cutlery spread in all directions. "I'll help," she said.

*

Once the kitchen was tidy Kate went to bed and Laura slumped to a chair. Cooking was like hair dressing: you were on your feet all day and your hands were often in water. She was grateful for Kate's help but she was over the role of cook and kitchen-hand. The fridge hummed a lonely tune in the big empty room. She hoped her mum wasn't going to spend too long at Aunty Brenda's.

Laura glanced restlessly around the tidy kitchen. She was weary but not tired and wished she hadn't been so hasty in cancelling her Netflix subscription. She was desperate enough to have watched it on her phone. Her gaze halted at the desk in the corner. There was a pile of her mum's school stuff stacked there and she remembered the folder. She got up, strode to the desk and picked up the only green folder among her mother's things. She flicked it open and the first thing she saw was a bright yellow post-it note. Laura smiled, lifted the note from the folder and tapped it with her finger as an idea formed.

"Why not?" she asked the empty room and dug out her phone, punching in the numbers for the mobile her mother had scribbled. A little flutter of nerves made her question her decision but a deep male voice answered and before she could change her mind she responded.

"Is that Paul Brown?" she asked.

"Speaking."

"I'm Laura…I bumped into you last week…the clumsy coffee incident."

"Oh…yes…the rainbow hair."

Laura's hand went to her head. His tone was censoring.

"So you're calling because?"

"Oh…because Mum asked me to bring her folder to you—"

"Mum?"

"My mum's Natalie King. She teaches at the school."

"Oh yes. That would be great, thanks." He sounded like he was going to end the call.

"I was wondering what you're doing tomorrow," she blurted. "I owe you a coffee."

"There's no need to worry about the coffee but the folder will be helpful for the relief teacher."

"I thought I could deliver the folder and buy you a coffee."

"Oh…right."

"But if you're busy I—"

"What time?"

"Two o'clock at the cafe?"

"Fine. I'll see you tomorrow…Laura, did you say?"

"Yes."

"Right."

Laura stared at her phone. He was gone. She let out a squeal then paused to listen, but no-one came running to see what that was about. She gave one last look around the tidy kitchen and made her way to the den with a spring in her step. Tomorrow she had something, or should she say someone, to look forward to and tonight, since she was getting the TV to herself, she'd watch a good old favourite, something romantic. She rummaged through the DVD collection and pulled out *27 Dresses*.

"Perfect." She settled on the couch, snuggled into a soft alpaca blanket and pressed play.

★

In her Broome hotel room, Natalie lay in the middle of the king bed and watched the fan turning slow circles above her. She smirked. The fan had three wooden blades, each curved in the shape of a teardrop. She wondered if the advertising guru would call this fan sexy. Her stomach gurgled, and she placed her hands on it. She'd done nothing but eat all day and then tonight had ordered linguine, with a creamy sauce full of prawns, clams, mackerel and squid.

It had been delicious but rich, and now it was burbling inside her along with the two glasses of wine she'd consumed.

Dining out alone had been a new experience. She'd eaten on her own many times, of course, but never out at a restaurant. She'd felt self-conscious at first but the staff were welcoming, the sound of the ocean just across the road soothing, and the breeze caressing her bare arms liberating. The restaurant had been full and the staff so busy she'd had to fight the urge to offer her help. How silly would she look then, a guest clearing tables? Besides, this was her After Anomaly life. She'd avoided watching them and turned her attention to the view across the lawns towards the towering palm trees. She'd made herself relax and had enjoyed her meal then she'd taken a stroll around the gardens before returning to her room.

She glanced around it now, taking it in from the comfort of the bed. It was spacious – even though there was such a huge bed dominating the room it also boasted a desk, a fridge and a large television, another small table and scattered chairs, yet there was still room for her to dance if she wanted to. She smiled and nestled her head into the soft pillow.

When she'd first arrived in her room she'd been in a hurry to strip off, unpack and slip into shorts and a t-shirt. Then she'd thrown open the louvred shutters on the glass door and paused in amazement. She had her very own deck and beyond it was a huge pool where people swam or basked in the sun on the assorted lounge chairs. That was when she'd realised there'd been no bathers in her case.

I'll just have to shout myself a new pair, she'd thought, vaguely recalling a shop in the foyer near reception. The bed had looked so sumptuous she'd lain down to test it and it had been much later when she'd opened her eyes to the view of a sky that had turned to gold. The bedside clock said she'd slept for two hours. She'd taken her time rousing herself, showering and dressing for dinner. Already she'd felt at home.

Home! She sat up with a guilty start, wondering where she'd left her phone. She hadn't taken it to dinner and she hadn't thought of home or her family since she'd arrived. Her mobile was on the desk where she'd left it plugged in to charge, the blue light of a message flashing. She padded across the wooden floor. Being barefoot and wearing only her loose dress felt luxurious after the confines of winter layers at home.

She picked up her phone. There was a text from Milt. She closed her eyes. Did she want to read it? The crack in their marriage that she thought had healed had been ripped open. There could be no denying Jack's presence. It was as if Milt had cheated on her all over again. At home the weight of it had been intolerable but here, thousands of miles away, she felt like a different woman.

Her eyes flew open. Determined to hang on to the sense of freedom being here had unleashed she put the phone firmly back on the desk, whisked off her clothes and slipped into the silky summer nightie she'd brought with her. She raided the bar fridge, took a chocolate and a can of lemonade and settled back in the middle of the bed, propped up by all four pillows, then switched on the TV. With the addition of pay-TV channels there was a long list of movies for her to choose from and no time frame in which to watch them. She popped the top off the lemonade and felt giddy with the sense of freedom that fizzed over her.

Seventeen

Natalie was later than she'd intended to breakfast. She'd sat up watching *My Cousin Rachel*. Dark and brooding, it was something she'd never have watched at home but she'd enjoyed it nonetheless. It was definitely not Milt's kind of movie and she couldn't imagine her girls watching it either. She'd flicked through a magazine for quite a while afterwards before she'd felt sleepy, her wakefulness a combination of the heavy presence left from the movie and her afternoon sleep, and then this morning she'd slept in, despite the time difference. Nine o'clock here meant it was ten-thirty already at home. The indulgence of doing things when she wanted instead of when someone else did was taking a bit of getting used to.

She wore sunglasses against the bright light of the Kimberley morning and paused to take in the busy dining room open on all sides the beautiful day. Her gaze extended outside, beyond the garden and the lawns to the white of the sand and the vivid blue of the ocean. Her best intentions to walk first thing hadn't come to fruition but she had all day to visit the beach.

"Would you like to join us?"

She looked down. Two women were studying her expectantly, one with twinkling blue eyes and a smile, the other with piercing grey eyes and a jutting jaw.

"Only we noticed you ate alone last night," Blue Eyes said.

"Oh." Natalie glanced around. Every table seemed to be occupied.

"You're welcome to join us." Grey Eyes spoke this time. "But if you'd prefer to eat alone—"

"Thank you." Natalie took the spare seat and placed her plate of bacon and eggs on the table.

"I'm Dot," the blue-eyed woman said. She had a neat, short bob haircut, blonde from a bottle. Natalie guessed she was in her late sixties. "And this is Faye." Dot waggled her fingers at her friend.

"Natalie." She smiled at both women and took off her sunglasses. They weren't needed in the shade of the dining room.

"Are you travelling alone or waiting for someone?" Dot asked.

"Alone," Natalie said confidently, as if it was something she did every day.

"You're so brave. Faye and I always travel together. We're both from Perth. What about you?"

"South Australia."

"Oh, whereabouts? We're going there next, aren't we, Faye?"

"Let Natalie eat her breakfast, Dot. You know how quickly it cools."

Faye's tone was brusque and the glance of her grey eyes equally sharp, but Dot didn't take offence. She simply smiled sweetly. "Of course." She leaned in. "The food's nice but we don't like the coffee."

"Dreadful filtered stuff," Faye said, not worried about lowering her voice. "But I refuse to pay extra for a proper coffee. We're paying an arm and a leg for this place already."

"Oh, but it's worth it," Dot said. "How's your room, Natalie? Ours is simply divine."

Faye pursed her lips and blew a breath through the gaps. Her closely cropped grey hair matched the grey of her eyes. Natalie felt a bit wary of her but Dot was delightful and continued to talk, with only the odd interjection from Faye, while Natalie ate her breakfast. They were retired teachers, Dot a widow, Faye a divorcee, both liked to travel. They'd been overseas on several trips together but had decided it was time to see more of their own country. This holiday had been to celebrate Dot's seventieth and it was their first visit to Broome.

"Silly really when we're Western Australians. It's wonderful to escape the cold back in Perth. I guess South Australia is freezing too. The pool is divine here," Dot said. "Have you been in yet?"

Natalie shook her head. "I only arrived late yesterday." She sipped the last of her coffee. It wasn't the best she'd ever had but it was drinkable.

"The water's a bit cool for my liking," Faye said.

"You said you found it refreshing," Dot countered.

"Hmm." Faye poured herself more water.

"We both love to swim." Dot turned back to Natalie. "We haven't tried the beach yet. We thought this afternoon. Would you like to come with us?"

"Easy up, Dot," Faye said. "Natalie's probably got her own plans."

"Not really," Natalie said quickly as she saw the anticipation fade from Dot's face. "But I have to buy some bathers first. I forgot mine."

Dot's face lit up again. "We're going into town to the shops this morning. You could come with us. I don't know about you but a friend's opinion is always welcome when I'm buying bathers.

I know we've only just met but we'd be happy to help, wouldn't we, Faye?"

Faye's look was impartial but she gave a nod. "We're taking the bus in."

"We've been here three days already and we're getting to know our way around," Dot said.

"I will join you, if you don't mind."

"Oh good." Dot gave a playful clap of her hands. "We love spending time with new people, don't we, Faye?"

Once again Faye's nod was noncommittal but Natalie thought she'd like to tag along, at least till she found her way, although the thought of the steely-eyed Faye helping her to buy a pair of bathers put a falter in her step.

Back in her room Natalie stuffed her purse and sunglasses into her tote bag and reached for her phone. She hadn't looked at it in her rush to get to breakfast and the little blue light still flashed. She swiped the screen to find last night's unread message from Milt and nothing from her girls. Milt's message was brief. *Safe travels. Say hello to Brenda. Behave yourselves.* And a smiley face.

She tossed the phone in her bag without replying, not sure what bothered her the most. The fact that she hadn't yet told him she was not in Brisbane or his glib message to behave. If he'd behaved twenty-seven years ago they wouldn't be in this mess now.

Natalie applied her brightest lipstick and strode off to meet Dot and Faye. There was no way she was going to bloody behave. She walked through the lush gardens filled with towering palms, pandans perched on stilted roots and colourful hibiscus. An ornamental bridge took her over a small stream leading to a trickling water feature and she slowed to take it in. It was all so different to home, so soothing. She let her anger go and laughed. Her companions were both close to seventy, Dot celebrating her special zero birthday and Faye only a couple of years her junior. Not likely there'd be too much misbehaving but Natalie was determined to let her short hair down.

By the time they'd done a wander up and down the main street her enthusiasm had waned a little. The heat and the brightness of the sunlight and cloudless sky were still a surprise. Her brain was still set to winter even though her eyes took in the glare and her body the warmth. At breakfast a steady breeze from the ocean had kept the temperature down but now she was dragging her feet. There were several women's clothing shops and she was grateful for their air conditioning but they were also busy with other shoppers.

Feeling sweaty and having to squeeze between racks and other customers hadn't put her in a conducive mood for trying on clothes but Dot was a trooper, working out what suited her and running things to and from the change room. Faye kept to herself, much to Natalie's relief, and only offered an opinion if Dot dragged her to look. In the end Natalie came away from one shop with a pair of bathers and a floaty dress to wear over the top, and from another a broad-brimmed hat. At the last shop she bought an olive-green-and-bronze patterned shift dress and a sarong. The sarong had been Dot's suggestion.

"So useful," she'd said. "You can wear it to cover up bathers or as a wrap to keep out the sun."

Even though Natalie was used to beach holidays she'd never bothered with sarongs and over-bather outfits. She'd always worn shorts and t-shirts. The two other women bought a top each and when Natalie enquired about a newsagency to buy a book they took her instead to a delightful bookshop where Dot and Faye were astonished to find she didn't read much. They plied her with suggestions and as she was in Broome she chose two that had local settings, one historical, set during World War Two, and the other more contemporary, about a woman living in Broome and a proposed mining development. Dot and Faye chose another book each, complaining they had too many already but then deciding there was always room for more. They shared their books so it was like two for the price of one, Dot had laughed.

They ate lunch off a small lane that served as Chinatown, enjoying the shade created by leafy trees and a wide verandah, then wandered past souvenir shops to catch the bus back to the hotel where Dot urged them to head to the beach.

"You've got to try out those new bathers, Natalie," she said.

Faye made a wry face. "The pool's right outside our rooms."

"But we haven't been in the ocean yet," Dot persisted. "The tide's in now so it's the best time."

"All right," Faye huffed.

Natalie couldn't resist Dot's enthusiasm and the thought of wearing her new bathers. She'd better get some use from them considering the price. Back in her room for a quick change she looked at herself in the bathroom mirror. The bathers were patterned with green foliage and splattered with bright tropical birds. The neckline was far more revealing than what she was used to but *behave* had been whirling in her head when she'd tried them on. She was fifty-eight and while her gaze swept quickly over the bulge around her middle, she liked the way her bust filled them out. Behave indeed, she'd thought as she bought them. Now she decided she liked the shape the bathers gave her and the freedom of wearing so little.

Across the road from the hotel they looked down on the brilliant white beach that stretched away in both directions.

"We have to swim between the flags," Dot informed her and pointed ahead to where the surf lifesavers were set up. It would be them and a thousand other people, it seemed. Faye led them down the steps and over the sand, her tall frame completely covered by a long-sleeved white shirt and beige linen pants. Natalie had tied the sarong around her waist and slipped on a t-shirt and Dot's shorter physique was covered by a long-sleeved sundress patterned with vibrant pink-and-purple flowers. They must make an odd-looking trio for anyone watching on.

Natalie trailed behind Dot and Faye as they dropped their towels and both strode confidently towards the ocean, which surged up the beach in powerful waves. She'd only ever swum in pools and the calm waters of the bay where they took their annual summer holiday. The water was cold at first but once submerged Natalie relaxed. The three of them floated along, doing occasional lazy strokes, bobbing up over the waves, enjoying the ocean. Even out here Dot didn't stop talking, telling Natalie how much she and Faye enjoyed swimming. They were both regular swimmers at home – Faye had a heated pool and Dot sometimes swam there or at her local swim centre.

"We don't swim in the ocean so much any more though, do we, Faye?"

"No. Too damn cold for me these days."

"What about you, Natalie?"

"I live a long way from the nearest beach and there's a town pool but I never use it. It's probably been well over a year since I swam last."

Natalie floated on her back. Even on their beach holidays she rarely swam these days but she was enjoying this. Around them several people bodysurfed and Faye caught a wave and joined them. She made it look so easy that by the time she'd made her way back to them, Natalie had decided to give it a go.

"My ears don't like it any more and I'm trying to keep my hair dry." Dot patted her neat bob as a wave began to unfurl behind them.

Natalie lunged forward as the foaming water surged above her, suddenly looking much wilder than she'd expected. She'd hardly taken a breath when the roaring curve of the wave crashed over her and carried her forward in its turbulence then spat her out as it flattened towards the beach. She rose to her feet in shock. The power of it had surprised her but also woken a yearning to do it again. She caught her breath, shook the water from her ears and waded out.

Only half an hour later the three of them were staggering from the ocean, laughing, well, Natalie and Dot were. Faye was giving a kind of strangled chortle that could have been a laugh, though Natalie couldn't hear properly for the swishing in her ears. They were all waterlogged. Dot had done her best to keep her hair dry but had been surprised by a wave and had ended up drenched. She'd been mid-sentence when the wave had struck and the look on her face when she'd finally surfaced had been hilarious.

Natalie turned back to watch the ocean as she towelled herself dry. The power of the waves had surprised her, frightened her sometimes, but left her invigorated and refreshed. She felt a surge of inner energy she hadn't felt in a long time.

"Back to the hotel pool now?" Dot asked. The other two had already covered up and were collecting their bags. Dot gave her an enquiring look. "We like to spend a few hours reading by the pool in the afternoon. Will you join us?"

Hours reading by a pool. Natalie had trouble comprehending such idle indulgence. Faye looked up and grimaced, which Natalie now knew was the closest she came to an encouraging smile.

"I'd love to," she said.

"Oh good," Dot said as they set off. "Then at four we order drinks. I had the most divine cocktail yesterday. I think I'll try it again today."

"You also had a headache last night," Faye said.

"I think that was the second glass of wine at dinner. I should have stopped at one."

Natalie trailed along beside them, enjoying both their company and the new sense of abandon the swim had unleashed. She wasn't a wife, mother to three daughters, a teacher, a housekeeper or cook, she was simply a woman on holiday.

★

At home in South Australia, Laura had driven into town. The main street was quiet. All the shops were closed on a Sunday afternoon except for the cafe and another takeaway business further down the street. She smiled as she pulled her dusty Hyundai in to the curb beside the gleaming RAV4 already parked outside the cafe. She looked at her reflection in the rear-view mirror and tucked a tendril of hair back in under her cap. Paul Brown had struck her as the conservative type and she'd thought it best not to flaunt her hair.

She let herself into the shop. Paul was the only other customer. He was sitting at a table studying his phone. Even on his day off he was dressed neatly in woollen jumper and chinos. She only had a few seconds to take him in before he looked up and saw her. He tucked away his phone and stood.

"Hi," she said, then cleared her throat at the squeaky sound she'd made.

"Hello." He nodded and adjusted his glasses on the bridge of his nose. Laura couldn't believe the simple gesture could be so sexy. "You brought the folder?"

"Folder?" She blinked. "Oh, Mum's folder, yes. It's in the car."

He took a step as if he was going to head that way now.

"Coffee," she said. "I promised you coffee."

"Yes." He glanced at his watch. "I've got half an hour."

"Right, well, I'd better order. What will you have?" Then she remembered the coffee she'd tipped all over him. "Flat white, right?"

"Yes." And for the first time his lips curved up in a smile.

Once they were seated, with the table and two coffees firmly between them, their conversation was, at first, a little stilted. Then they got onto music and lost track of time. They both liked the same things, an eclectic mix of musicians and retro music, and realised they'd been at shows at the same venues.

"What was the last show you went to in Adelaide?" she asked.

Paul scratched his ear. She'd noticed he'd done that a few times when he was thinking. She thought it was cute.

"It was at the Thebbie back in March…" He stopped, fiddled with his empty coffee cup.

Her mouth dropped open. "No way. March. Don't tell me you were at the ABBA show?"

He nodded sheepishly.

"So was I. I love ABBA music."

He smiled widely then. "So do I, but not many of my friends do. I went on my own."

"A couple of my girlfriends are fans too." She laughed. "We could have been sitting right beside you."

"You could have."

They held each other's gaze across the table.

He glanced at his watch. "Jeepers, it's late, I have to get going. Sorry." He stood.

She was still hanging onto *jeepers*. Who said that any more?

"Thanks for the coffee," he said.

She stood too and followed him to the door. He held it open for her and she shivered as she stepped outside into a blast of icy wind. It had been warm in the coffee shop.

"Well...thanks," he said again and took a step towards his car.

"I'm home for a while," she blurted. "We could catch up again, share some music."

He stopped. "Sure." He pulled out his phone.

"I've got your number."

He nodded. "Of course. You rang me." A quick smile and he hurried away.

Laura jumped into her car. Her door slammed shut with the wind. Wow, she thought and leaned her head back against the rest. She closed her eyes then flicked them open at a tap on her window.

Paul was there, leaning down, arms folded against the cold.

She lowered it.

"The folder," he said.

"Oh yes." She reached behind and grabbed the carry bag she'd slipped it into.

He smiled. "Thanks." Then he hurried back to his car and drove away.

Laura nestled into her seat and sat a few more minutes, savouring the enjoyable hour she'd just spent, not looking forward to returning to the property, her gloomy dad and her despondent oldest sister. Lucky Bree had escaped for a day and a night. Laura recalled Paul's smile and wondered how long she could leave it before calling him again.

Eighteen

Natalie closed the book on the final page, disappointed to be leaving the characters yet relieved to be released from the evocative story she'd been reading. She lifted her gaze to the pool where Dot and Faye were swimming up and back, as they liked to do every afternoon before drinks. Natalie usually joined them but she'd been so close to finishing the book and unable to put it down. She found it hard to take in, that among all the other things she and the other two women had done over the last five days, she'd also managed to read two books. She was hungry for more and glad that Faye and Dot had offered some of theirs.

The pool spread out before her and to one side there was a raised deck where people came and went all day, relaxing on the couches, enjoying company or simply snoozing the day away. The rest of the pool area was lined with padded sun-lounges like the one she lay on. There were small tables for drinks, and umbrellas and sails for those who, like her, sought some shade. Around her the steady but muted tones of cheerful music played, and she caught murmured conversations, the chink of ice and the distant whir of the cocktail maker. No-one splashed or called out in this pool, which was for adults only. The only raised voice was that of a bird trying to outdo the background music.

She rose, stretched languorously and felt the full heat of the Kimberley sun as she stepped from the shade and slipped off her kaftan, a new addition to her sun wardrobe after another visit to the shops. She'd swum every day, sometimes two or three times, between beach and pool visits. Now she stepped carefully into the pool, allowing her overheated body time to adjust to the cold. The pool wasn't heated but was warmer than the ocean and a far gentler alternative.

She submerged herself to her shoulders as Dot and Faye came to a stop beside her.

"I'm going to miss this place." Dot's expression was glum. "We go home tomorrow."

"Oh." Natalie was brought back to reality with a painful thud. In this bubble world of her holiday, spending her time with Dot and Faye, seeing the sights, indulging herself, relaxing with not a thing to do but to wonder where and when to eat her next meal, she hadn't given a thought to time passing but now she realised this would be her sixth night. She'd booked eight to get a special rate.

"How much longer are you here for, Natalie?" Faye asked.

"Three more nights."

"I don't want to go home. Perhaps we could extend our stay." Dot's face brightened.

Faye gave a snort. "We've already spent our annual holiday budget on one week here, and the flights! It would cost us almost as much again to change them."

"I know, and we do have bridge tomorrow afternoon." Dot smiled at Natalie. "I know everyone says it but it's true, once you retire you become so busy you wonder how you fitted in work.

I help out at an op shop and there are a few of us away at the moment so they'll be looking out for my return, and Faye volunteers at a school for children with special needs."

"And one of my sons will be home from overseas in a week. He's planning on living with me till he finds his own place." Faye snorted again. "Forty and still sponging off his mother."

"Still, it will be nice for you to have company for a while." Dot floated in the water between Natalie and Faye, and caught Natalie's eye with a knowing look. "He's been gone for two years; you'll be glad to see him again."

"Humph!" Faye sniffed. "I'm doing another lap then I'm getting out. This water is too cold for me." She pushed away and began to stroke across the pool.

Dot watched her go and gave her own version of a snort. "She'd have you believe she doesn't care two hoots about her sons but she's only covering up how much she misses them. She was like a lioness protecting her cubs through a messy divorce from her alcoholic husband then raised them singlehandedly. Her boys both ended up working overseas and she misses them terribly. Although it has been handy for us to have a bit of free accommodation in London and Singapore over the years."

"Do you have children?"

"No. It wasn't to be for Ted and me. What about you?"

"Three daughters."

"Are you going home once you leave here?"

Natalie's stomach churned at the thought. She'd sent a dutiful text to her family each night. She'd kept it general, not sure how to say in a few words that she'd ended up in Broome instead of Brisbane. Milt responded briefly each time but they'd not spoken on the phone since she'd left home, and there'd only been a couple of short texts from the girls hoping she was having fun. She wasn't ready to go home yet. So far she'd only seen the sights of Broome. There was so much more to the region.

"Perhaps I'll find somewhere cheaper in another part of town for a few more nights. Or maybe take a tour to Derby and the Mitchell Falls. I haven't booked my flight home yet."

Faye arrived back then and they all left the water.

"What about that Horizontal Falls trip?" Faye said as they towelled themselves dry.

They'd perused many tourist brochures together over the last few days, looking for places they could explore together. "It did look fabulous."

"A bucket list item, they say." Faye turned her hard stare on Dot.

"You could have gone on your own," Dot responded with an equally steely look. Natalie had learned over the last five days Dot wasn't the pushover she'd first seemed. "You know I won't fly in anything small. The plane here from Perth was bad enough and we have to get in another sardine can to go back yet."

"Was it a little plane?" Natalie hadn't looked at plane sizes when she'd booked. She'd simply picked the cheapest and quickest option to get her to Broome.

"If you call a Boeing 717 with over one hundred seats little, then yes."

"Oh."

"Why don't you go up the Dampier Peninsula?" Dot said. "Visit that beautiful pearl farm we read about. They had accommodation, didn't they?"

"Buy yourself some pearls," Faye said. She wore no jewellery during the day but each night at dinner Natalie had noticed she wore a short string of pearls.

"A gift from my father to my mother," she'd said when Natalie had commented on how lovely they were, prompting a long discussion about pearls.

"It's not something I think I'd buy for myself," Natalie said now.

"Don't wait for your husband to do it," Faye declared. "If you see something you like buy it. A celebratory gift to yourself."

"What's she celebrating?" Dot asked. "Is it your birthday?"

"No." Natalie lowered her gaze under the scrutiny of both women. Yesterday, over afternoon drinks while Dot had gone back to the room for something, Faye had asked her outright why she'd travelled alone. For some reason, probably something to do with her second cocktail, Natalie had confided that Milt wouldn't leave the property so she'd come without him. She may have also mentioned how cross she was with him but not gone into any detail. Faye had obviously read between the lines.

"Independence," Faye said.

Dot's mouth fell open and her eyes widened. "You're not getting divorced."

"No." That word shocked her. Her marriage wasn't over. This was another glitch surely, just a hiccup. She and Milt would work it out and yet – a dawning realisation hit her – did she care enough to want to?

"Good grief, don't jump to wild conclusions, Dot. Natalie's learning to take some time for herself, that's all."

"Oh, of course. Silly of me, only Faye has an independence celebration every year on the anniversary of her divorce."

"And another on the anniversary of our joint retirement from the Education Department," Faye said.

"There's always something to celebrate," Dot said.

"How long since you retired?" Natalie asked, glad to change the subject.

"Ten years."

"Eight for me but we share the date," Faye said.

"Are you thinking about retiring?" Dot asked.

And once again two sets of eyes were focused on her. Dot's gently enquiring, Faye's probing, as if she could read things in Natalie's mind she hadn't admitted to herself.

"I…" Natalie shrugged her shoulders. "I haven't thought about it yet." It was a lie; she had but was terrified by the concept. What would she do with herself if she didn't have school?

"Oh well. You must be happy doing what you're doing." Dot smiled. "You'll know when the time has come, won't she, Faye?"

Faye nodded and continued to look at Natalie with a steady gaze. "You'll know."

"Oh blast!"

They both looked at Dot who'd sat then shot back off her seat as if she'd been bitten. She reached down and plucked her sunglasses from the lounge. One arm dangled.

"And another pair bites the dust," Faye said.

"Why do I have so much trouble with sunglasses?"

Natalie smiled. The last five days had been punctuated with searches for Dot's glasses.

"I'm popping back to the room for my spare pair," Dot said. "Don't start drinks without me."

Natalie and Faye settled themselves on their sun-lounges. Faye stared off after her friend and gave a shake of her head. "She won't be able to find them." Natalie expected Faye to say something acerbic as she often did but was surprised when her next words were gentle instead. "I don't know what I would have done without her friendship over the years."

Natalie immediately felt the deep sting of Brenda's move away; close neighbours and best friends, they'd shared the highs and lows of life, like Dot and Faye.

"How long have you known each other?" she asked.

Faye pondered a moment. "Thirty-five years. She's reliable in a crisis, is Dot."

"I imagine you are too."

"Hmmm." Once again Faye seemed to ponder. "Fifteen years ago both my sons got jobs overseas and in a flash they were gone. They'd been my reason for getting out of bed each day for so long, I fell in a big hole. I was fifty-three and all I'd done with my life was teach and raise two boys."

Faye's words were like a can-opener peeling back the lid on her own life. "What did you do?"

"I took up swimming." Faye raised her sunglasses, looked steadily at Natalie and grinned. "Some people buy fast cars. I have a heated lap pool in my backyard now."

Natalie tried to think of something she was so passionate about that she would invest that kind of money in it and came up blank.

"I also went to a life coach," Faye said. "I only lasted one session but I came away with a nugget I've stuck by. Don't let anyone *should* you. Even people close to you with the best of intentions will want you to do things their way. Accepting that I had a right to do things my way helped me deal with the guilt of my marriage failure, of raising two sons without their father."

Natalie studied Faye. Never in a million years would she have thought her the kind of person who felt guilt about divorcing an alcoholic husband. She appeared so composed and in control of her life but perhaps she hadn't always been like that.

"I had to turn the room upside down to find my spare glasses," Dot's bright voice called as she approached.

"Surprise," Faye muttered and sat her own glasses firmly back on the bridge of her nose.

"Oh, here comes that nice waiter again." Dot waved and gave a girlish titter as the young man who'd been bringing them drinks each afternoon approached. He was young enough to be Dot's grandson but she flirted outrageously with him and he was sweet enough to play along.

They ordered their drinks and settled back onto their sun-lounges. Natalie found herself thinking over Faye's midlife crisis. Is that what was happening to her? She was a wife, a mother, a daughter, a teacher, all things she'd felt she'd been mildly successful at to this point – well, maybe not the daughter part – and yet she found herself wondering if that was it. Surely there was more to life.

"Are we going to yoga again this afternoon?" Dot's question broke through her thoughts.

Faye lifted the brim of the hat she'd placed over her face. "Are you kidding?"

"No." Dot sat up. "I enjoyed it, didn't you, Natalie?"

"Yes, but—"

"See, Faye."

"I'm not going." Faye settled back under her hat. "Don't let me stop you two though."

Dot had convinced them to go to the free sunset session of yoga the previous afternoon. Natalie had not done yoga before, another thing she'd never found time for. The room was tucked away in a quiet corner of the resort and she'd soon relaxed and enjoyed herself, but their session had ended rather abruptly and she wasn't sure she could face the instructor again.

"I don't think I'm in the mood now." Natalie tried to let Dot down gently.

There was a snort from beneath Faye's hat.

"Oh, I'd rather go with you girls than on my own." Dot pouted. "Bother you, Faye."

The hat flew up again. "You don't seriously want to go back after what happened?"

"It was nothing abnormal."

Natalie chewed her lip to stop from laughing. The class had gone well until Faye and Dot had been so fully relaxed that Dot had dozed off and Faye had let one rip, at which point they'd gathered their belongings while the rest of the class, all much younger women, avoided eye contact. They'd bolted from the room, collapsing in hysterical laughter as soon as they made it outside.

"No, me farting and you snoring is par for the course but not usually in a full class of lithe young things." The hat went down again.

"It was rather funny." Dot began to laugh.

Natalie joined in and from under the hat came the strangled chook sound that had startled Natalie the first time she heard it but she now understood was Faye's happy laugh.

"Your drinks, ladies." They composed themselves as the young man handed out their cocktails. "Are you heading downtown to watch the Staircase to the Moon tonight?" he asked.

"It'll be our only chance," Dot said, giving Faye a hard stare.

"Wouldn't miss it," Faye replied.

"I'd like to see what it's all about," Natalie said.

"It's pretty spectacular," their waiter said. "And also popular, so don't forget to book a space on the bus." He flashed them a big smile. "Enjoy, ladies."

Dot raised her blue concoction in the air. "Here's to good friends." Natalie and Faye chorused after her.

Natalie sipped the mojito she'd become rather fond of. While she savoured it she pondered what to do once Dot and Faye had left. Nothing appealed. So much of the last four days had been fun because of their company. She was going to miss them.

★

Laura sat in another cafe in a different town, down the highway away from home towards Adelaide, and watched out the window for Paul to arrive. The tailing had been all finished by lunchtime, thank goodness, so when she'd got Paul's text asking if she'd like to meet for a late coffee here, she'd jumped at the chance. Outside the day was bleak. Sleety rain had fallen on and off and the temperature had barely risen higher than the overnight low. Thankfully the coffee shop was warm, although if Paul didn't hurry up the flat white she'd ordered him would be cold.

Just as she thought it she saw his car pull up out the front. He'd been here during the afternoon for a principals' meeting. It was a longer drive but she didn't mind where they met.

He pushed open the door, looked around and smiled as she waved to catch his attention, even though at this hour on such a miserable day she was the only one occupying a table. She took in his smart appearance. Today he was wearing dark pants, a checked jacket and a woollen scarf that revealed a tie beneath as he tugged it away from his neck and sat down.

"Sorry I'm late," he said. "These departmental meetings always drag on."

"I got your coffee."

"It was meant to be my shout."

"Next time," she said and he smiled.

"Thanks for coming down here to meet me."

"I don't mind. It's nice for a change." Laura glanced around at the industrial-look decor. The cafe had changed hands and had a makeover since the last time she'd been here.

"It's just that there are some parts of my life I like to keep private. I find that hard living where I do. I feel very…" He scratched his ear. "Visible."

Laura grinned. "That's the country for you. Everybody knows your business even if you don't." She liked the idea that he considered their meeting private.

"Speaking of which, is your mum's friend okay?"

"Her friend?"

"The one she's gone to visit?"

"Oh, Aunty Brenda."

"She's your aunty?"

"Mum's close friend, and I'm sure she's fine, why?"

"Your mum sounded a bit…stressed when she rang to tell me she was going and I haven't heard from her. It all seemed a bit sudden and I thought perhaps something was wrong."

"No. Nothing wrong. Mum hasn't seen Brenda since she moved away last year. They're very close."

"Luckily her co-teacher Claire has filled in for a few days. It's not easy to get relief teachers at the moment, especially on short notice."

"She made it tricky for you too." Laura was still annoyed her mum had left her with all the food prep. Even though there was a lot of extra food prepared in the freezer she still had to defrost it, deliver it and clean up.

"We're managing." Once more Paul scratched his ear. "I hope it wasn't me that's driven her off."

"You?"

"We had a bit of a discussion about curriculum the other week. I think I may have put her offside."

He looked so concerned she reached out and placed a hand over his resting on the table. She smiled. "Don't let it bother you. Mum's not easily upset. She just needed a break…" Laura twisted her lips. "From everything I guess."

"Well, when you talk to her please send my best. She's been mentoring a couple of new staff and one in particular is missing her support."

The conversation changed then but on the drive home Laura had time to ponder her mother's swift departure again. They'd all been so busy there'd been no time to think too deeply about it but now that tailing was over she'd quiz her dad a bit more. He was the only one who would know what was really going on. There was certainly nothing in her mother's brief texts to indicate there was anything more happening than two old friends catching up.

Nineteen

Natalie did slow strokes to the deep end of the pool then gripped the edge and hung there a moment. Last night she'd been restless and hadn't slept well. She'd eaten dinner alone again now that Faye and Dot had gone, but she'd found it too quiet and returned early to her room. She'd watched another movie then started the book Faye had left with her but the lack of company gave her plenty of time to think about other things, like home and her inevitable return. Part of her wanted to go home to her girls if not to Milt but she knew if she did she'd be back in the weird mixed-up mood that she'd left in. She was determined to continue her holiday but where next?

She pushed off from the edge of the pool and began to swim back the other way, passing a man who was doing the same languid lengths of the pool as her, but in the opposite direction. This morning she'd caught the bus to the Courthouse markets where she'd wandered aimlessly through the colourful stalls. She'd enjoyed a mango smoothie, picked out a couple more books from a second-hand stall, bought some soap the colours of a Cable Beach sunset and, at a busy jewellery stall, she'd selected a bracelet for each of the girls sporting a single pearl. The photos of the Staircase to the Moon she'd taken on her phone were a blurry mess so she'd bought a wine bottle cooler with a picture of it as a memento of the spectacular phenomenon she'd enjoyed with Dot and Faye. After that, she'd called at the tourist centre and made enquiries about where to go next then returned to the hotel armed with plenty of suggestions. The Dampier Peninsula was her first choice but she wouldn't be able to get a seat on a tour there for a few more days and she needed new accommodation from tomorrow night.

She reached the other end of the pool where the cafe deck overhung it and heard the sound of the cocktail shaker. She wondered what Faye and Dot would be doing. Back into their busy lives already, from what she'd gathered. She wasn't rushing back for that. She'd hardly given school a thought, although she'd sent Paul a text to let him know she would need the extra week away, and her mind had also lingered on a couple of children who she knew would be missing her. Joel in particular didn't cope well with change and she hoped whoever was replacing her would be able to continue their work on fire and flood with care. Her program was detailed but perhaps Paul would've got her replacement to do something else altogether. And she wondered how Eloise was coping. Natalie was sure she had the makings of a valuable teacher, she just needed confidence and time.

"Hello again."

Natalie stood abruptly in the shoulder-deep water to avoid bumping into the man in front of her. "Sorry, I was miles away." She went to move around him.

"This is an excellent place, isn't it?" he said.

She looked more closely at him. Dark-brown eyes watched her steadily from below a balding pate; a moustache etched his upper lip. He could be her age, maybe older.

"Yes, lovely." She felt uncomfortable under his gaze. She glanced around. There were plenty of people about but she felt very alone.

"Your husband's not a swimmer?" he said.

Natalie frowned.

"Only I noticed you doing laps yesterday afternoon on your own."

"Oh."

"I *lurve* the freedom of water, don't you?" He raised one eyebrow. "I'm Bazz, by the way. Maybe I could buy you a drink?"

Natalie made a choking noise as she gasped and swallowed at the same time. Was this guy trying to pick her up? Dear God, she didn't even know what that looked like any more.

"I'm late actually, Bazz." She spun away, teetered momentarily in the whirlpool motion of water she'd created then strode to the steps. Not daring to look back, she wrapped herself in a towel, gathered up her things and strode to her room, latching the door firmly behind her.

Once inside she sat for a moment, gobsmacked – firstly because he'd appeared to be chatting her up and second because she'd bolted like a startled rabbit. Why hadn't she simply told him no thanks to the drink and kept swimming? She looked at her surprised face in the bathroom mirror and laughed. "Bloody Bazz," she muttered then shuddered as a chill rippled over her. The air conditioning was cold on her damp skin.

She ran a warm shower and stepped in. When she closed her eyes she saw Milt's face. From the moment she'd first met him he'd been the only man she'd ever wanted. Now when she thought of him she was filled with…She pursed her lips. How did she feel about her husband? Angry? If she really narrowed it down, suspicious too. The trust she'd thought was there…perhaps it had been false? It had been blown away in the face of Jack Halbot's intrusion in their lives.

Out of the shower and dressed again, Natalie reluctantly decided to pack her bags. Regardless of her destination she needed to leave the hotel the next morning. Her case was empty except for a few items she hadn't needed, and she was surprised to find, tucked in one of the zipper pockets, *The Model Wife*. She'd had such a blissful few days she'd not given it a thought.

She tossed it aside on the bed and as if to mock her it flipped open at Chapter Four. The heading leaped out at her – 'Managing the Home'. She sat on the bed, picked it up and read. *The model wife is proud of the home her husband provides for her and to show her respect she should keep it perfectly clean and without clutter.* The word *should* jumped out at her, and she heard Faye's voice saying *don't let anyone should you*. But she had, hadn't she. Stuck on the blank page opposite was an old black-and-white photo of the farmhouse. She'd pasted it there not long after Olive had given her the book. She ran her finger over the vast roofline. The kitchen had been updated when the girls were in their teens but it hadn't been a complete remodel, just replacing outdated items like the oven and the dishwasher. They were almost past their use-by date again. The dishwasher had played up a few times lately and the last time the plumber fixed it he said they'd need to think about replacing it.

How she'd love to give the kitchen a complete makeover. It had been her guilty wish when Olive had announced she wanted to move into town. At last, Natalie had thought, she could make some changes, but it hadn't happened and lately she didn't have the energy it would take to renovate. There was enough work just keeping it clean. She did love that house and yet she'd become its employee.

She read the next line in the chapter. *Nothing destroys the happiness of married life more than the lazy, slovenly wife.* She gave a snort. From the safe distance of another state she could see how she'd adopted that mantra. It was a huge house and she'd kept it as clean and neat as possible, never going out or going to bed until everything was done. Milt had teased her sometimes, saying a few grains of dust or a smear on a window didn't matter but he'd never understood how much work it took to keep the old house clean. If you let it get away you'd never keep on top of it. Now she thought perhaps he'd been right.

She glanced around her well-appointed hotel room. How easily she'd become used to the indulgence of having someone to clean and tidy up after her. Perhaps if she gave up her teaching she could spend some time doing up the house. The thought was both enchanting and repelling. If she gave up work she knew she truly would become a slave, not only to the house but to the needs of the property.

She skipped down a few lines and stopped at another sentence. *It is the model wife's responsibility to provide her husband a happy home… the single spot of rest which a man has upon this earth for the cultivation of his noblest sensibilities.* Hell, she'd done that and what had it all been for? Where was her happy home now? She slapped the stupid book shut. Why was she torturing herself with it again?

There was a tap on her door. She jumped, shoved the little book between the others she'd bought at the second-hand stall and opened the door.

Bazz stood on her balcony, highlighted by the glow of the fading sun behind him. His smile was wide. "Hello, lovely lady. Have you finished what you hurried off to do?"

"Yes…well…no…" A shiver prickled down her back. "How did you know I was here?"

"You came here after you left the pool." He stepped closer and glanced over her shoulder. "All alone? I thought perhaps you'd like to join me for a pre-dinner drink."

"I…" She stood taller and put the edge of the door between them. "I'm getting ready for dinner, meeting friends."

"Perhaps after dinner then? A nightcap?"

Natalie found it hard to drag her gaze from the moustache that looked like it had been pasted on above his lip. It was what her girls would deem 'porn star'. Another shiver rippled down her spine.

"No, thank you." She began to push the door.

"Tomorrow perhaps?" he asked.

"I'm leaving," she said and shut the door firmly, her heart making a loud thud in her chest.

She pressed her fingers to her lips and listened as his footsteps retreated across the wooden deck of the verandah. The persistence of the man was incredible, she'd give him that much, but never in a million years would she have a drink or anything else with him. She turned to her case and began to pack with renewed fervour. She'd had a wonderful interlude here at Cable Beach but with Faye and Dot gone and strange men making advances, the shine had gone from her stay.

*

Laura heard her dad come into the kitchen behind her. When she turned he was staring at the table, a puzzled expression on his face.

"What's up?" she asked.

"Who's the extra for?"

He waved a hand over the table she'd just set with five placemats.

"Granny."

He frowned.

"It's Saturday night and I'm cooking pork roast."

"I didn't think she was coming?"

"Who?" Bree asked as she joined them.

"Granny." Laura and Milt spoke at once. His tone was a little sharp.

"Why wouldn't she be coming?" Bree said as she took a beer from the fridge and passed it to her dad before getting one for herself. "It's Granny Pork Roast night, isn't it?"

Kate walked through the door yawning.

"You okay?" Laura asked. Her sister always looked pale these days.

Kate gave a half-smile in return. "Just a bit weary."

"That's rich considering you've slept for half the day," Bree said.

"I've been doing other things."

"Like what?"

"She prepared the vegetables," Laura said.

"That'd be right, you two always stick together."

"What's got up your nose?"

"That's enough," Milt rumbled but his words were lost in Bree's tirade.

"You've been late most mornings, you work at half pace sometimes and—"

"She hasn't been feeling well." Laura defended her big sister.

"What's wrong with you?" Milt asked.

"Nothing."

"Girls, girls, girls!" Olive strode into the room, silencing the noise with a clap of her hands. "What's going on?"

They all stopped.

"Hello, Granny." Laura broke the brief silence.

Olive eyed them all suspiciously then kissed each girl's cheek. She hesitated in front of her son.

"Hello, Milton."

"Mum." He bent to brush a kiss across the cheek she offered then turned and sat in his chair.

"Can I get you a wine, Granny?" Kate asked. "I think we've got some."

"That'd be very nice, thank you."

Olive hooked her handbag over the back of a chair. "I could smell that roast from the door."

"Can you look at it?" Laura pleaded. "It doesn't seem to be crisping up."

Olive went to the oven and peered in. "It might need a hotter oven. I never mastered the art of good crackling. Your mother's the expert." She turned back to the others. "Where is she?"

They all paused.

"She's gone to visit Aunty Brenda," Laura said.

"In Brisbane?" Olive looked to her son for confirmation.

He nodded.

"I would have come out earlier and helped if I'd realised she was leaving today."

"She's been gone all week." Kate set a glass of wine in Olive's place.

"But..." Once more Olive looked to her son. "What about school?" Her shoulders went back. "How on earth have you managed with tailing?"

"I've got three other grown women here to help."

"We made quite a team." Kate glared at Bree.

"But the food—"

"I did it." Laura grinned.

"Very well, I might add." Milt raised his beer in a mock salute. "You all did very well."

Bree opened her mouth as if she was going to say something then took a mouthful of beer instead and sat at the table.

"Well!" Olive said. "Fancy that. Your mother's left you and gone all the way to Brisbane."

"We can look after ourselves, Granny," Laura said. She hadn't had a chance to prod Kate into asking their dad about the Brisbane trip and obviously Granny knew nothing.

"Let me help you now, at least." Olive turned back to Laura.

"No need. Everything's under control. Once the meat's cooked Dad can carve and Kate can help me serve. I'm just making an apple sauce." She waved her hand towards a pot that was steaming hard on the stove.

"Don't let it catch," Olive said.

"Oh no." Laura whisked the pot from the stove and somehow the force of it flung the lid to one side, touching her hand. She jerked the pot forward and boiling liquid slopped down her front. She wasn't wearing an apron and the hot apple soaked straight through her jumper.

"Get that top off quick," Olive commanded.

Laura ripped it over her head and behind her there was a collective gasp.

"Hell's teeth! Laura, is that a tattoo?"

She cringed at her dad's bellow and turned slowly, hugging her bunched jumper to her chest. Olive whipped a tablecloth from a drawer and draped it around her shoulders.

Milt pushed back from his chair. "What in the blazes would you do that to yourself for?"

Her two sisters remained silent, Kate wide-eyed and Bree with a smug look on her face.

"Let's deal with this first." Olive waved a hand towards Laura's midriff. "Did you burn yourself?"

Laura shook her head. "It barely soaked through." She looked down at a red patch stinging on her wrist. "Only steam on my arm, I think."

"That's just as bad. Come here to the sink and run it under cold water."

"A bloody tattoo," her father muttered behind her. "The world's gone mad."

Beside her Kate cleaned up the splattered apple sauce and Olive saved what was left in the saucepan.

"Worse things happen up creeks without paddles," she said.

Kate made a funny noise in her throat and gave Laura a grin behind Olive's back. "A tattoo!" she mouthed.

"So what made you get a tattoo, little sis?" Bree had retrieved a thick work shirt from the laundry and put it on the bench beside Laura.

Laura turned off the tap and patted her hand dry. She glanced at Bree who was leaning on the bench beside her. "Seemed like a good idea at the time."

"Christ!"

"Milton, I'll not put up with you blaspheming," Granny said. "Make yourself useful and carve this meat."

He glowered at his mother a moment, opened his mouth, closed it, then took a deep breath and did as she asked.

Bree and Laura shuffled away from the activity and Laura picked up the shirt, letting the tablecloth fall away.

"What is it anyway?" Bree peered at her shoulder.

"A moth." Laura grimaced. It had been Kyle's idea. He had flames tattooed up one arm and he'd joked about her being a moth to a flame. She'd thought it funny at the time but the next day, sore and sorry, she'd hated it. Hadn't even told Spritzi about it.

"I think it looks like a butterfly," Kate said as she passed with an armload of plates.

"It's a moth." Laura slipped the sleeve of the shirt gingerly over her wrist.

"No." Bree shook her head as Laura shrugged the shirt over her shoulders. "Definitely looks like a butterfly." She flipped the lid off a beer and passed it to Laura with a grin. "Drink?"

Laura didn't say much over dinner. She was aware of the odd glare from her stony-faced dad but he said nothing more about the tattoo. She got compliments for her roast but she'd been disappointed. There was no crispy crackling like her mum made and the apple sauce was runny.

Olive was full of questions about tailing and more admonishments for not letting her know Natalie was away. "How long will she be away for?" she asked.

"I don't know," Milt said.

Laura risked a glance at her dad. He sounded fed-up.

"Have you spoken to her?" she asked.

"Not lately."

He'd said that the last time she'd asked him. He startled her by lunging forward and peering across the table to the far wall.

"Hell, what's the date? It's nearly the end of the financial year and the BAS will need to be done soon."

Laura glanced in the direction of the calendar, too far away to read.

"I can do it," Bree mumbled.

"It's not even the end of the month yet," Kate said. "But I can help so it's up-to-date when Mum comes home."

Bree's look was sceptical.

"Account-keeping is my job, you know. I can do BAS."

"I think it's a bit selfish of Natalie really." Olive started to stack plates and Laura felt the collective breath held by the rest of her family. Olive went on, oblivious. "It's not like her."

"No, it's not." Milt stood and almost snatched the stack of dirty plates from his mother's hands. "She usually puts everyone else first before doing something for herself."

Laura glanced at her sisters, who were looking at their dad as if he'd just revealed a dark family secret.

"Yes, well." Olive stood and rested her hands stiffly on the back of her chair. "That's a mother's lot in life. Now we should get these dishes done. Isn't there a home football match on the television tonight?"

Kate and Bree both leaped to their feet but Milt surprised them all as he dumped his load of dishes on the bench. "It's only a few pots, I'll do them."

Olive opened and closed her mouth then gave a sharp nod of her head. "Thank you, Milton. I'll put the kettle on."

Bree and Kate helped clear the rest of the table and pack the dishwasher. With everyone busy Laura snuck her phone from her pocket and opened up Facebook. Her mother didn't use it but Aunty Brenda did. She was often posting photos of her grand-daughter or family get-togethers. Maybe she'd posted something about Natalie's visit. Laura had been so focused on everything else in her life she hadn't thought to check. Five minutes later she'd given up all pretence of hiding what she was doing and was staring at the pictures on the screen in front of her.

"No phones at the table," Bree teased as she did a final wipedown.

Laura looked up, ignoring her. "Dad, have you spoken to Mum at all since she left?"

Everyone stopped what they were doing and looked at him. His shoulders drooped. "We've been texting."

"But her text said she was going to Brisbane?"

"Yes, why?"

"I've just checked out Aunty Brenda's Facebook page and she's travelling with her family – in Thailand."

Four puzzled expressions looked back at her then they all started to speak at once. Finally it was her dad whose voice rose to the top.

"Quiet!" He moved up beside her and held out his hand. "Show me."

Laura lifted the phone and showed him pictures of Brenda at the beach, by a pool, riding an elephant. "Her post from last Sunday was from Brisbane airport."

"Mum wouldn't have flown up there as a surprise, would she?" Kate asked. "And not contacted Aunty Brenda first?"

"Surely not," Olive said.

"Maybe she offered to house-sit?" Bree said.

Olive's hands went to her hips and she glared at her son. "Are you truly telling me your wife has been gone a week and you have no idea where she is?"

A deep blush coloured Milt's ruddy cheeks. He dug his own phone from his shirt pocket and strode from the room. Laura's sisters stared from her to each other.

"Well," Olive said. "That's a fine affair of the state. I think I need a strong cup of tea."

Twenty

Natalie glanced around the dimly lit restaurant as she settled in the chair the waiter had pulled out for her. There were several places to eat at the hotel and for her last night she'd chosen a smaller restaurant with Italian-themed dining but before she'd asked for a table she'd done a reconnaissance. There'd been no sign of Bazz. He'd rattled her by turning up at her door but here, in the company of other people in the restaurant, she could almost laugh about it. Fancy someone asking her out. It was just a little bit flattering. She pictured Bazz's moustache wobbling over his lip, recalled the oily tone of his voice, and knew he was definitely not her type.

She picked up the menu then took in her surroundings again. The restaurant wasn't as popular this evening as she'd noticed in passing on previous nights but it was possibly her last chance for some fine dining for a while. Across from her sat a pair of young lovers with eyes only for each other and to her right sat a man, perhaps several years younger than her. He was alone and reading a newspaper. Further away there were a couple of tables of four and that was it.

She ordered then spent time flicking through a couple of the tour brochures she'd brought with her. She'd found a few options for cheaper accommodation closer to town overlooking Roebuck Bay and planned to spend the next day transferring and settling in and booking tours to fill in the week. And after that…well, who knew?

The barramundi salsa verde was delicious with the fennel, rocket and orange salad and she was pondering the recipe when the waiter brought her a fresh glass of wine and removed her plate. She declined the offer of the sweets menu and had just raised the wine to her lips when she noticed the flare of a flame from the corner of her eye. She turned, gasped as she realised the newspaper the man had been reading had brushed a candle and was starting to burn. He noticed just as she did and began to pat at it with his hand. On instinct Natalie tossed her glass of wine over it, soaking the paper, the cloth and part of his shirt.

She put her fingers to her lips. "Oh, I'm sorry."

A set of amused dark-brown eyes studied her. "It was my fault. Shouldn't read the newspaper at the table."

She smiled. "Not one with a candle on it anyway."

The waiter returned and helped clean up.

"Please bring the lady another glass of wine," the man said.

"Oh no." Natalie shook her head.

"I insist."

The waiter hovered.

"All right, thank you," she said.

The man got up from his table and reached out a hand. "I'm Gabe."

"Natalie." She shook his hand.

"You're on holidays?" He sat back down.

"Isn't everyone here?" She chuckled then felt silly. She'd noticed over dinner the staff had been chatty with him in a different manner to that they used with other guests. "Are you connected with the place?"

"No. Tour guide. I stay here from time to time when I'm picking up or dropping off a group. They know me here."

The waiter brought her wine and refilled the water glass Gabe had emptied before the fire.

"You planning some trips?" He glanced at the brochures she'd spread along the edge of the table.

"Yes." She stacked them up. "I haven't made up my mind exactly where yet. It will depend on what's available but I'm leaving here tomorrow so my first job is to book somewhere else to stay. It's lovely here but I need to find something a bit cheaper, especially if I'm going to be out for most of the day on tours."

"Bookings are at a premium this time of year."

"So I've discovered. I wanted to take a Dampier Peninsula tour. I'm keen to visit the pearl farm at Cygnet Bay too, but everything's booked out for the next week and I'm not sure how much longer I'll be staying."

He nodded, then dropped his gaze back to the table where he twisted the water glass in his hand. She had time to take in the close crop of his dark hair and the neatly trimmed dark shadow of stubble across his jaw.

He glanced up, caught her studying him. "There's more to the peninsula than pearls."

She reached for her wine, took a sip. "Do you take tours there?"

"Sometimes, but it's also home for me." He paused as if he was pondering his next words. "I'm heading home tomorrow."

"Home." Natalie thought about the detailed map she'd studied of the peninsula. It was a large expanse. "Which part do you come from?"

"It's a small community up the top of the peninsula." He paused again. "If you want to see the real peninsula I could give you a ride."

"To Cygnet Bay?"

"No, my country. My people are Bard."

Natalie shifted in her seat. Was Gabe another Bazz? She hadn't got that feeling about him.

"It's a special place. Much better than here. Although the accommodation's not as luxurious."

"Are there pearls?"

He shook his head. "No need for pearls. Not far to Cygnet Bay though if you really want them."

"Oh...no...I..." Natalie shook her head. "I was just curious what people did there."

"Chill, mainly. That's why I don't stay for too long." His face split in a wide grin. "There's just the beach and kilometres of nothing. Too boring for me."

Natalie thought about the pictures she'd seen of the peninsula. Lots of white sand, turquoise water and red dirt.

"Anyway, the offer's there." He stood, took a worn card from his wallet and put it on top of her brochures. "That's my number. Call me if you want to come. I'm checking out of here at nine in the morning, going to the supermarket. If you're coming with me you'll need to get some supplies too. There're shops but they're basic and expensive."

He thrust out his hand. She shook it.

"Nice to meet you, Natalie. Thanks for putting out the fire." Once more he grinned. "Good night."

She sat a while after he'd gone, staring at his card. What an odd evening. Natalie hadn't expected she'd be putting out a fire from her dinner table. She smiled at the thought of Gabe's kind offer. Tempting as it was, there was no way she was setting off with a complete stranger to go bush on her own.

She signed her account, gathered her things and strolled slowly back along the path that meandered through the well-maintained gardens to her room. It was another glorious evening. She'd thrown a wrap around her bare shoulders but it wasn't really necessary. The nights had been so mild. Something rustled in the bush beside her. She stopped, looked around. It was a dark part of the path and there were no other guests about. She had a sudden image of Bazz. Would he still be around? She quickened her steps, fumbled her card at the door and finally pushed it open.

No sooner was she inside than she heard her mobile ringing. It had gone flat with all the internet searching she'd been doing before dinner and she'd left it to charge. She picked it up just as it stopped and Milt's name faded from the screen.

"Damn." She tried to work out what time it was at home. One-and-a-half-hours difference so eight-thirty in Broome meant ten at home in South Australia. It was late for Milt to be ringing. She looked at her call history and her heart skipped a beat. He'd rung her ten times over the last few hours but he hadn't left a message. She stabbed at his number and put the phone to her ear.

He answered on the first ring. His phone must have been still in his hand. "Natalie. Where are you?"

She took a deep breath. The gruffness in his voice both annoyed and alarmed her.

"What's wrong?" she said.

"What do you mean what's wrong?"

"Why have you been ringing and not leaving a message?"

"Why haven't you been answering?"

"I was out for dinner. I didn't take my phone."

"Hell's teeth, Nat. I've been that worried. Where are you?"

She felt the pangs of guilt stirring again. "I'm in…Broome."

"Where?"

"Broome, Western Australia."

"How the hell did you get there?"

Natalie suppressed the urge to laugh. "On a plane."

"But why? You were going to Brenda's. Then tonight I find out Brenda's in Thailand with her family."

Natalie sunk to the bed and kicked off her shoes. So that was what the sudden panic was about when all week a simple text message once a day had been enough.

"Why would you lie?" Milt's tone was icy.

Natalie's mirth evaporated and she stood up again, the polished wood of the floor cool beneath her feet.

"I didn't lie."

"You omitted to tell me the truth then. Is that better?"

Natalie began to pace. Pot, kettle, black, Milt, she thought. Anger burned fiercely in her chest. "When I sent you that text I was planning to go to Brenda's. It wasn't till later I found out she wouldn't be home."

"You should have told me where you were."

Should echoed in her head.

"What if something had happened to you?" Milt's voice was getting louder.

"I am quite capable of looking after myself."

There was silence, then a sigh. "I know you are." His tone had softened. "I miss you."

She gripped the phone tightly. What could she say? Occasionally she thought of home, missed her girls but…not Milt. When she thought of her husband all she felt was a simmering anger.

"Tailing went well." He filled the silence. "The girls did an excellent job. Bree knows what she's doing, of course, but I don't know how much longer she plans to stick around. Kate was a big help although she did disappear from time to time. Do you think she could've had a fight with Sean? She's been moping around a lot and says she's going to stay on for a bit longer."

Natalie wanted to know what he meant by moping exactly, but he went on.

"Laura's kept up with the food. She's not a bad cook but, hell, the mess she makes and…" His tone sharpened. "Did you know she's got a bloody tattoo?"

"No." It didn't surprise her though. Laura was always the one to push the boundaries. She hoped it wasn't somewhere too prominent; couldn't be, surely, or she would have noticed it.

"When's your flight home?"

She opened her mouth. Closed it again.

"The BAS is due soon."

"I'm not ready to come home yet."

"What do you mean by 'not ready'?"

She sighed. "I've only been gone a week, Milt. I need more time."

"You're not still going on about Jack, are you? I'll never invite him for dinner again if that's what you want."

She sunk back to the bed, her body suddenly too heavy for her legs. She'd given him an ultimatum once before and now she thought how futile it had been. "It's not about inviting him for dinner." And it wasn't just about Jack. She couldn't explain to her husband how she felt when she didn't know herself. It was as if she'd been swirled around in her mixmaster and flung out the other side into a world she didn't recognise. This After Anomaly life that she didn't quite fit. Resentment festered inside her. She'd always done her duty: to her parents, her husband, her girls, her in-laws, her work, her community. Everyone had a piece of Natalie and somehow she'd lost herself in the process. She'd never done anything outside anyone else's expectations of her.

"Obviously we should talk this through," Milt said. "Tailing was not the right time."

There was that *should* again. Natalie pictured Faye's steely stare then looked at the brochures she'd tossed on the bed beside her. Gabe's card had slipped off. She picked it up, gripped it tightly. Escape beckoned. Was she brave enough to do it?

"Natalie, did you hear me? Come home so we can talk."

"I'm leaving Broome tomorrow…but I'm not coming home," she said. "I'm going somewhere more remote, a place up on the Dampier Peninsula. Not sure how reliable the phone signal will be but I'll get a message to you when I can. Give my love to the girls. Goodnight, Milt." She pressed *end* and then turned off her phone for good measure. Her heart thumped in her chest. She knew nothing about Gabe or the place he called home but she was damn well going to go with him.

Twenty-One

Kate pulled her dressing-gown tighter around her and let herself out of the bedroom. Last night's call from Sean had given her a reprieve. He had a Queensland job on and would be gone for two weeks. No sooner had he hung up than Kate rang her mother-in-law and organised to extend her leave. She'd bought herself some time but what she was going to do with it she had no idea. She couldn't imagine feeling any different about this baby than she did now, and to add to her misery she felt so sick. Staying in her bedroom helped; there was no fire there. She found she felt better if she kept the room around her cool and herself rugged up. The heat of the kitchen and the den only made her nausea worse but she couldn't stay in her room forever.

Hushed voices reached her from the kitchen. The door was pulled to but, as often happened, it hadn't latched. Her dad was talking and then Granny said something about her mum. Kate pressed herself to the wall and listened. She was in desperate need of a cup of tea but curiosity got the better of her.

"Did Natalie tell you?" Milt asked.

Kate held her breath. Maybe Granny knew something about her mother's hasty departure after all.

"Of course not," Olive said. "Your father did. Do you think he would keep that kind of secret from me?"

Milt groaned and Kate leaned closer, puzzled. If this was something Pa had known about it must have happened a while ago.

"No point in putting your head in your hands, Milton," Olive snapped. "The past is past. Have you done something else to upset your wife?"

"No." A chair creaked. "And it's none of your business what happens between Natalie and me."

"If it affects the property it is."

"Oh for f—"

"Milton!"

Bree stepped into the passage from the quarters. Kate put a finger to her lips and waved her over. She took up a position on the other side of the door.

"You don't have to worry about the property any more," Milt said.

"Connie's worried."

"Hell's teeth, don't tell me she knows."

"Knows what?" Bree mouthed and Kate shrugged.

"Of course not. Her concerns are about me."

Milt snorted.

"And an income for her," Olive said.

"Tell her to go out and earn one then."

"There's no need to be snappy. The world has changed since you took on the property. Ideas about sibling reparation have changed."

"Connie was well compensated and Dad's will made it clear."

The bathroom door opened. Laura stepped out. "What's—?"

Bree and Kate both put urgent fingers to their lips, silencing her. She came to stand beside Bree, her hair enclosed in a swirl of towel and her eyes wide. She leaned in.

"She feels this place is still partly hers," Olive went on.

"She can think what she likes but it's not. This property is an asset, Mum, not a bottomless pit of money. You know that. Connie knows that. She's married to a farmer—"

"With much more marginal land and three sons."

"And I've got three daughters. I have to think about their future."

Kate looked from Laura to Bree. Both stared back at her open-mouthed. It sounded as if Connie was after a piece of the property. That had never been mentioned when they'd had a family meeting about the future a year ago.

"You're right," Milt continued. "Times have changed and maybe we would have set things up differently today than we did forty years ago but it's not as if Connie's had no recompense. We can't go back and change things now. Bree has a few more years to make a decision. If she wants to continue running the place, her sisters will have to be compensated, but unless we sell it's never going to be equal value. As well as that there's you to be looked after and Nat and I when we eventually retire."

"Perhaps we need to revisit your plan."

"No-one can walk away with a big bucket of cash unless we sell and divide the lot between us." Kate could hear the frustration in her dad's voice. "Hell's teeth, Mum, is that what Connie wants? A part of this property?"

"Not exactly a part, but something more."

Once again the three sisters gaped at each other. Kate had always liked her aunt Connie. She'd always been so friendly and had bought lovely gifts when they were kids.

"After everything Dad's given her already," Milt growled. "And what she'll get once you're gone."

"I don't plan on going any time soon," Olive huffed.

"I'm not wasting any more energy on this futile discussion. I've got work to do."

"It's Sunday morning."

"Yes it is." A chair scraped.

The three girls dashed into the bathroom and closed the door as they heard the kitchen door squeak open. There were muffled thuds as their dad made his way outside. Bubbles miaowed and the back door banged shut.

Bree lowered herself to the edge of the bath. "I can't believe Aunty Connie would be such a bitch." She looked from Laura to Kate. "You two aren't going to be like that if I do take over the place, are you?"

"It's not the same for us," Kate said. "Dad's made it clear from the start we could all work here if we wanted to."

Bree snorted.

"You're lucky Laura and I don't want to work the property," Kate said, the churning in her stomach replaced by anger. Bree could be so self-righteous "You can have it to yourself."

"Yes, but Dad's made provision for you and me," Laura said. "Your uni and my courses were all paid for."

"Bree went to uni too," Kate said, knowing it sounded petty.

"You got help to buy your first house," Laura said. "And I will when the time comes. We've got a small parcel of shares each in our names and..." She twisted her lips and wrinkled her nose. "One day, a long way off, we'll get whatever Mum has when she goes."

"Bloody inheritances," Bree spat. "It'd be better to have nothing to fight about."

"We're not fighting, are we?" Laura looked from Bree to Kate.

"She's right," Kate said. "Dad and Mum have made everything clear, involved us all in the future planning."

"Maybe Aunty Connie didn't get much," Laura said. "And she's not worked off their farm since she had the boys."

Bree folded her arms. "Like Dad said, she could get a job."

"There was something else," Kate said as she remembered the first part of the conversation she'd eavesdropped on. "Granny said something happened between Mum and Dad."

"What?" Laura and Bree asked as one.

"I don't know but Granny and Pa knew about it."

"That narrows it down." Bree's hands went to her hips. "Did they say anything more specific?"

Kate shook her head, trying to remember. "Granny said something about Dad upsetting Mum again."

"Hell, he's probably done that a million times over the years," Bree said.

"This sounded serious."

The door opened behind them. Olive looked at each of them, surprise on her face. "What are you all doing in here?"

"Cleaning my teeth." Laura snatched up her toothbrush.

"Waiting for the shower." Kate winced. They all looked towards the empty cubicle.

"I was just chatting." Bree, the only one dressed, stood up.

Olive eyed them suspiciously. "Well, I'll use the bathroom in the quarters then."

"Okay." Bree smiled.

Olive gave them one more searching look and left.

"Waiting for the shower?" Bree glared at Kate.

"It was the best I could do," Kate hissed. "We'd better get out of here." She opened the door and peered out. The passage was empty. She waved to her sisters and by the time Olive re-entered the kitchen all three of them were tucking in to breakfast.

★

In Broome, Natalie sat on the verandah of a cafe with an empty coffee cup and half a slice of orange cake. The cake had looked so tempting but she'd barely had two mouthfuls; nervous tension mixed with anticipation was creating havoc with her stomach. Over her head, hanging baskets full of lush green plants swung gently, stirred by the fans and the breeze gusting along the street. She would have been hot without the movement of air.

Once more she glanced at her watch and looked across the street but there was no sign of Gabe. She'd phoned him first thing this morning and he'd arrived before nine in a large four-wheel drive to pick her up. They'd driven into town where he'd taken her to a supermarket, made suggestions about what she might need and loaded her purchases and his into the back of the vehicle. Then his phone had rung and he'd moved away but she could tell from his manner he wasn't happy about something. He'd ended the call, apologised, said there was something else he had to do before they left and suggested she might like to have a coffee while she waited.

Now she realised an hour had gone by. The tables around her on the narrow verandah had filled and emptied and refilled. Everything she owned in Broome was in the back of Gabe's vehicle, except for the tote bag at her feet. Once again she reconsidered the sense of heading off with him. He was still a stranger really. This morning she'd been worried she wouldn't even remember what he looked like but his smile had been warm as he'd crossed the driveway to greet her and she'd felt reassured, but here on her own again her confidence was waning.

On a whim she'd agreed to travel with a man she barely knew to a remote community that she'd only seen as a dot on a map. She wasn't sure how she would fit in or what would be expected of her. Gabe had said there was accommodation but did they truly welcome strangers?

She looked around at the people sitting at other tables. She knew no-one here in Broome, let alone further afield. The last time she'd sat here it had been for lunch with Dot and Faye. She wondered what they'd make of her decision to head north with a stranger. She smiled. Faye would have said go for it.

"Natalie."

She looked up. Gabe was waving at her from the pavement. Now was her chance. She could say she'd changed her mind, find another place to stay, book some tours. She grabbed her tote and made her way to the footpath.

"The car's over here." He waved to the parking spaces in the middle of the street and began to walk in that direction.

She hesitated.

He stopped and glanced back, his resolute look softened. "Sorry I've been so long," he said. "Are you okay?"

She nodded. Started to follow.

"You must have thought I'd gone without you." The smile spread across his face again. "My aunty Rosie found out I was coming home and she had a list of jobs for me that kept getting longer."

"You're sure there's accommodation for me?"

"Yeah. Aunty Rosie said it's busy up there but there're some empty rooms. You'll be right."

"Great," she said and, remembering his pleasant interactions with the staff who had clearly known him well, she swallowed her anxiety.

They followed the highway out of town, passing four-wheel drives towing every kind of caravan from monster-sized to compact pop-tops. Thick bush crowded to the edge of the road, so different to the scattered scrub at home. Home! Natalie dug in her bag for her phone. She hadn't sent a text and she'd told Milt she would.

"I forgot to ask if there was phone signal at your community," she said.

"Yeah, no problems, but along the way it'll drop in and out."

"I'll send my family a message now then. To let them know I'm on my way." Just in case things went awry someone else would know where she was.

A signpost indicated Cape Leveque and Gabe turned north, the bitumen stretching out long and straight ahead of them. Natalie typed a message, deleted it, retyped and re-read it then pressed *send* and watched the signal fade from her phone and change to emergency only. For the first time in her life she wondered how that actually worked.

The vehicle bounced and this time, when she looked up, the road had changed to red dirt. It billowed around them, a stark contrast to the green vegetation and the brilliant blue of the almost cloudless sky. The car had been coated in red dust inside and out when she'd got in. Now she knew why.

The vehicle dipped and then continued to bound up and down, giving the feeling they were in a boat zooming over waves. She glanced across at Gabe, who was focused on the road. Too late to turn back now, she thought, and gripped the armrest tightly.

"Do you go home often?" she asked.

He took his time answering and she thought perhaps he hadn't heard her. Finally he glanced her way.

"No. Most of my family's in Perth." His look was reflective then he grinned again. "I told you. Too quiet for me up here. Maybe when I'm an old man I'll come back to stay."

Natalie considered that. She guessed he was around fifty. A long way from being an old man.

"Are you on holidays from work or just getting away from your family?"

"Both," she said before she had time to think.

"What's your work?"

"I'm a teacher."

"Little kids or big?"

"Year three."

"I loved school when I was that age."

She glanced at him. "But not when you were older?"

"No. Didn't want to be there."

"Well, you seem to have done okay."

"Thanks to Aunty Rosie."

She waited for him to go on but he didn't elaborate and they lapsed into silence. Roadworks slowed their progress intermittently.

"The bitumen will go all the way from Broome to the Cape soon," Gabe said while they waited at a stop sign to let traffic pass in the opposite direction.

"That would be an improvement, wouldn't it? Easier access?" Natalie thought of the dirt roads at home she had to drive over and how happy she would be if someone bitumenised them but it was unlikely to happen.

"Better access is good for the people who live there – they can come and go more easily, especially in the wet – and good for the tourists." He kept his gaze focused ahead as they bounced over cor-rugations. "At the moment this road is really only four-wheel drive access and not many caravans try it, only the true off-roaders."

Natalie thought about the vehicles they'd seen. He was right, not many towed anything and if they did it had been camper trailers, with only the odd caravan crawling along.

"It's called progress," Gabe said. "I work in the tourism industry but I'm not sure if people are ready for how big it will get once the new road is complete. At the moment they manage the small number of tourists who come but once the road is finished it will mean almost all-year access and a lot more people wanting to visit. It could mean more jobs for our community but I'm not sure we've got the infrastructure to cope with a big increase. And there are those who don't like the visitors we have now."

Natalie thought about what he'd said as she stared out at the passing landscape. All she could see were trees and red dirt, different to home and yet not. She wasn't sure what the attraction was for tourists but she kept that to herself.

The road changed from red dirt back to bitumen but there was still little to be seen other than the bush and trees that hugged the edges. At last, just as Natalie was beginning to think they surely couldn't go much further or they'd end up driving off the end of the peninsula, Gabe slowed and turned off the highway. Then once again the bitumen ran out and they sliced through a soft dirt track. Up ahead a roofline appeared through a gap in the trees, and then another and then a clearing with houses and sheds, workman-style huts and a couple of camper trailers set up on grass. Every structure was coated in red dust. They came to a stop in front of a building that had *Office* marked on the door.

"Gabe." A young woman rushed forward and drew him into a hug as soon as he got out. "Great to see you."

"Hey, Tika," he said.

Natalie stepped out, stretched, looked around. There was red dirt as far as she could see and no sign of the beach Gabe had promised.

"Natalie, this is my cousin, Tika. She works here in the office."

Tika shook her hand. "Not usually at this time on a Sunday." She gave Gabe a playful pat. "I've been waiting for you and Natalie. Come in and fix up for your room, Natalie, then Gabe can take you down there. All the cabins are booked but you can have the lodge to yourself. It's got an outside bathroom and a camp kitchen."

"Thanks, that'll be fine," Natalie said with more enthusiasm than she felt. Tika seemed friendly enough but was keeping her distance. Was she one of the locals who didn't want strangers visiting her community?

Natalie paid for her accommodation and picked up a couple of brochures while Tika printed the receipt and organised keys. Outside again Tika locked the door behind her.

"You take Natalie down and get her settled then get yourself over to Aunty Rosie's quick smart," she said. "She's got a big barbecue planned for tonight."

Gabe groaned.

"You know everyone wants to see you." She waved and walked away without another look at Natalie.

"Hop in," Gabe said and they set off again, following the red dirt track between buildings and finally pulling up beside a metal-clad dwelling with a verandah stretched across the front.

Natalie stepped out onto more red dirt. The bricks of the paved verandah were ingrained with it; even the walls had a kind of rusty red glow. She unlocked the door and stepped inside. It was hot with a musty closed-up smell, basic but neat. She was relieved to see no sign of the red dust inside, at least. Gabe helped her carry her things to the door then hovered on the verandah.

"Will you be right?" he asked.

"Fine." That word again.

"Aunty Rosie's expecting me."

"Of course."

"I can show you around tomorrow."

"Thanks, but don't worry about me. You go be with your family."

He went to leave then turned back. "I'm going for a kayak in the morning down at the creek. It's pretty good down there. Would you like to come?"

"I've never kayaked before."

He smiled. "It's easy. Out with the tide then in with the tide. We won't have to paddle." He started to walk away. "I'll call past around seven. See if you want to come."

He jumped back into the vehicle and drove off, leaving a cloud of dust in his wake.

Natalie put on the air conditioner, relieved to find that in spite of its looks it was soon blowing lovely cool air through the room. She unpacked, found the bathroom, winced at the sign saying keep the toilet lid down to keep out the frogs, took her food to the well-equipped camp kitchen then sat on her verandah taking in her surroundings. It was peaceful here. Birds called, and there was the odd noise of a distant vehicle but other than that so quiet. She wondered where the beach was, found the map Tika had given her with the keys and realised the road that went past her door led there.

A swim would freshen her up. She'd become used to her daily sojourns in the water. Wearing her new bathers under her cover-up and lathered in sunscreen she stuffed her phone and the striped Turkish towel she'd bought at a little shop outside the supermarket back in Broome into her bag and set off along the track. She was slowed down by the soft red dirt, tried to find firmer ground and eventually made it to the edge of the sandhills where her struggling steps continued on over stark white sand.

By the time she got to the top of the first hill she was puffing hard. The sea was a thin blue line in the distance. She caught her breath and set off again and at the top of the next ridge of sand she stopped again, puffing harder. The distant blue line looked no closer. She struggled on for a few more metres then stopped. Behind her came the sound of a vehicle labouring up the sandhill. Perhaps she could catch a ride. She caught a glimpse of a four-wheel drive roof then it veered off, heading away from her on one of the many trails that had split from the main track. She recalled the words printed on the map: visitors were to stick to the main beach track. Access to other roads was prohibited.

She stumbled on for a few more steps, then her feet sank in a deep patch of sand and she fell to her knees groaning in frustration. Even if she managed to make it to the beach she'd have to come back and already she felt exhausted. What had brought her to this point? She'd been so determined to do something different, turn her back on Milt, and…what? Prove she didn't need him? So much for Faye's declaration of independence. Tears rolled down Natalie's cheeks. A breeze cooled her skin and rippled the sand. It was already hard to see her footprints in the sand behind her and she'd forgotten to put a bottle of water in her bag. She struggled to her feet and began to labour back across the stark white landscape, batting at the tears that continued to flow.

Inside the cool cabin she flung her bag down in disgust, took a swig of water from her bottle and slumped into a chair. Her stomach gurgled and she realised she hadn't eaten lunch so she set about cooking herself an early dinner, chicken shasliks and salad. It had smelled inviting as she cooked it but she ate it with little enjoyment. Around her the late-afternoon sky turned to gold and a flock of screeching white cockatoos whirled overhead and found themselves a roost in the spreading arms of a towering tree.

Vehicles moved in the distance, doors banged, laughter carried across the still evening and then the sound of music. Natalie was often on the property by herself but she never felt so alone as she did here even though there were people not far away.

She cleaned up her dishes, had a shower then went back to her room and shut herself in. It was too cool now. The air conditioner had done its job. She turned it off, set the fan going over the bed and slid under the sheet. In the relative quiet she heard the music again and raised voices. It was a happy sound, heightening her sense of loneliness. Is this how life would be if she left Milt? And where would she go? Not into town. Perhaps the city, but she had no connection there any more. She could move to Victor Harbor, be closer to her sister and her parents. An image of her mother's self-satisfied look popped into her head.

Her parents had never wanted her to marry Milt in the first place. She'd still been going out with her childhood sweetheart, Tony, when she got her first teaching job in the country and met Milt. She recalled the first time she'd seen him like it was yesterday. It had been at a tennis club fundraiser cabaret: tables made up of people from each club in the district and beyond, everyone brought plates of food, plenty to drink and there was a toe-tapping band. He'd asked her to dance and they'd stayed together all evening. He'd been charming, funny and she'd enjoyed the sensation of his arms around her as they danced. Everything about him had seemed solid, from his strength to his commitment to courting her. Love had developed quickly over the next few weeks, so different to the love she'd thought she'd felt for Tony, which was a schoolgirl crush in comparison.

Her parents had loved Tony. She hadn't realised they still did until her recent trip to Victor. He'd been the son they'd never had and they'd been devastated when she'd come home for a visit and broken it off with him. She'd felt terrible, of course. Tony hadn't taken it well either but she'd known she and Milt were meant for each other and less than a year later they were married. She rolled on her side, curled into a ball. Life together had been wonderful until the babies. Not that she blamed her girls. She loved them more than life itself, but when they were born it had been different. She'd been depressed, she knew that now, and a part of her had blamed herself when Milt had strayed.

She put one hand to her head and gripped it tightly. Coming here had not helped. There were other tourists here but she still wasn't sure she was welcome. Gabe hadn't said how long he was staying. She wondered how quickly she could get a ride back to Broome. She could book those tours she'd liked the look of, be with other people and keep herself so busy for a few more days she would be too tired to think about home.

Twenty-Two

Natalie awoke in a dark room. She squinted at her surroundings until her brain cleared and then remembered where she was. She found her phone and looked at the time. It was six-thirty already and Gabe had said he'd call by at seven. She flicked on the light and dressed while she waited for the kettle to boil. Once more, nervous energy coursed through her. At some point before sleep had claimed her she'd determined to go on the kayak trip but now she worried how she'd manage. She had little experience on the water other than swimming and going for the occasional boat ride with friends when they stayed at the beach over summer. Sitting low in the water in a kayak was a totally different thing.

By the time she heard a vehicle coming down the track she'd drunk her coffee and eaten a banana, smothered herself in sunscreen and put shorts and t-shirt on over bathers. Gabe was in a different vehicle. This one had a roof rack and two kayaks strapped to the top. A young man sat beside him; there was a sullen slump to his shoulders and he didn't look Natalie's way but in contrast a woman smiled and waved at her from the back passenger seat.

"Ready to go?" Gabe called. "Charlie and Aunty Rosie are coming with us."

Natalie climbed into the back seat and the smiling woman extended her hand. "It's nice to meet you, Natalie. I'm Rosie."

She squeezed Natalie's hand. Her touch was gentle and warm like her smile and Natalie relaxed.

"And this bundle of laughs is Charlie." Rosie gave the lad in front of her a gentle poke. He half turned to Natalie, nodded, but didn't make eye contact.

"Did you sleep all right in that room?" Rosie asked. "Sometimes it can get a bit hot."

"The bed was very comfortable and the fan was enough to keep me cool." When Natalie had finally fallen asleep it had been deep and restful.

"I hope you don't mind us tagging along," Rosie said as they bumped forward along the track. "I haven't been out in the kayak for ages and Charlie wants to give it a go."

Charlie said nothing to confirm or deny this statement.

"I've never been."

"You'll love it."

Leaving the red dirt behind, they ploughed up the first of the sandhills Natalie had struggled to walk up the previous afternoon. At the top she got another tantalising glimpse of the water in the distance.

"I started walking to the beach yesterday," she said.

"It's a bit of a hike," Gabe said.

"One kilometre it says on the brochure."

"Hmm." He scratched at the stubble on his chin, not so neatly clipped today. "That might be right."

Rosie chuckled. It was a warm friendly sound. "But it's through sandhills. Hard enough in a vehicle. We can go that way when we come back, can't we, Gabe? Show Natalie the beach."

"Sure."

Natalie settled back with a feeling of anticipation rather than the unease that had plagued her the night before. The idea of having another woman along instead of being out alone with Gabe was reassuring. When she realised she was to share a double kayak with Rosie she was even happier. It would have felt quite intimate sharing the small space with Gabe and she was glad he and Charlie took the other.

Once they got the kayaks in the water there was very little paddling to do. As Gabe had said, they arrived on an outgoing tide, which carried them to an exposed reef. Rosie walked her across it pointing out all kinds of rock pool and reef life while Gabe and Charlie snorkelled. Gabe had a spear gun that he was showing Charlie how to use. They speared a fish each. Obviously it was something Gabe had done before but the whoops of delight from Charlie when he brought his wriggling fish to the surface brought smiles to all their faces.

"I've got lunch, Aunty Rosie." Charlie held the fish aloft, his face beaming with pride.

"He grew up in Perth." Rosie's eyes shone as they watched the lad's excited romp through the water to put his fish in the bag Gabe had brought. "He's never done anything like this before."

They all gathered around the bag, looking in. It now contained two large bluefish. Gabe gave Charlie's hair a playful ruffle but nothing could wipe the wide smile from the lad's face.

"Gabe can show you how to cook them," Rosie said.

Gabe looked down at the water lapping at their feet, which was now coated in a dirty scum. "Tide's turning."

They climbed into the kayaks and were swept along back towards the creek entrance, passing over an octopus, huge stingrays with tails as long as the kayak and reef sharks that darted after fish of every description. They even spied a distant sea turtle. Charlie's cries of delight echoed Natalie's pleasure. The sea life was abundant and amazing to view from where they sat, only centimetres above the water in the kayak. She was sorry when the tide eventually nudged them to the edge of the creek. Like the tide that had turned, she felt as if something inside her had changed direction. She'd forgotten her worries and lost herself in the sheer delight of observing the abundance beneath her. A sense of calm had enveloped her, something – she realised as she settled in to the back of the four-wheel drive again – she hadn't felt in a long time.

Then on the way back they stopped at the beach and she couldn't decide which experience was better. It was as Gabe had described, white sand stretching away in a long slow curve in either direction. The pristine beach was lapped by the Indian Ocean, which sparkled under the glare of the sun, and they had it all to themselves.

Rosie wandered the edge of the water while the two blokes and Natalie swam. Gabe and Charlie jumped and splashed, chasing each other like puppies playing. The waves were gentler than they'd been at Cable Beach and Natalie stretched out on her back and let herself float. Gabe had been right, this was beautiful country.

Later he dropped her back at her room and told her to come over to the camp kitchen when she was ready. By the time she'd showered and changed she was hungry and arrived just as he and Charlie had their heads down inspecting the fish in the coals.

"See that pink flesh there," he was saying to Charlie. "It needs a couple more minutes."

Rosie arrived with a potato salad and Natalie brought out her leftover ingredients to make a tossed salad. Her stomach groaned at the delicious smell of baked fish and beside her Rosie laughed. "You sound hungry, girl."

Gabe brought the fish to the table and sat it on the large plate Rosie had set out. Natalie was offered the fish first and waited impatiently while the others served themselves then they all tucked in.

"Mmm!" she groaned happily through a mouthful. "That is divine."

Gabe grinned. "Not bad."

They added salad, finished what they had and picked more flesh off the carcass. Natalie wanted to lick her plate she'd enjoyed the food so much, even more than the fancy restaurant barramundi.

"How long are you planning on staying?" Rosie asked. "We can take you fishing up the creek if you like."

Natalie sat back. Last night all she'd wanted was to head back to Broome but now...She hardly knew Gabe and Rosie. They made her feel so welcome and yet... "I don't know." She looked at Gabe. "I didn't even ask how I'd get back."

"I'm staying till Saturday," he said.

"We can get you a ride before that if you need." Rosie set her cutlery on her empty plate, her deep brown eyes locked on Natalie. "But why don't you stay? It's a good place. Even our beach is better than Broome."

Natalie pictured the beach where she'd just swum with its pristine white sand, like Cable Beach but bigger and no rocks, the beautiful turquoise water, and not another soul in sight. Sometime during their morning expedition a sense of release had settled over her and the swim had been liberating. The sheer relief of this new buoyant feeling was intoxicating. Perhaps here she could find some peace from everything that troubled her. Natalie dragged her gaze from Rosie's searching look and glanced at Gabe.

"I...it's certainly beautiful here."

"You stay as long as you like," he said. "And you don't have to go back to Broome when I do. Rosie's right. It won't be hard to find you a ride back when you're ready."

Charlie sniffed, sat back in his chair and folded his arms, his look sullen again.

"What about you, Charlie?" Rosie said. "You going back with your cousin tomorrow or sticking it out a bit longer?"

Silence fell around the table. Natalie shifted in her chair, unsure what to make of the surly Charlie. He'd seemed to enjoy the morning like she had but now his earlier moodiness had returned. She felt she understood teenage girls so well after three of her own but boys were different.

He pushed up to his feet, arms crossed. "I'll stay."

"Good." Rosie gave a satisfied nod. "I've got a few jobs need doing." Charlie frowned and opened his mouth but Rosie cut him off. "And Uncle Ron will need someone to help with the kayak tours."

"Okay." His eyes showed a suggestion of interest before he turned away.

"Hey," Gabe said. "Take your plate to the sink before you go."

Charlie came back, his face serious but at least not quite as hostile, and took his plate into the kitchen. He went out the other door without speaking.

Natalie caught the wink Rosie gave Gabe. There was something going on here that she wasn't privy to. The rumble of a helicopter sent her gaze skyward, surprised by its throbbing intrusion into this peaceful existence.

"You'll hear a lot of them," Gabe said. "There's an airstrip nearby and the rigs out at sea use it as a refuelling point."

The machine vibrated closer then faded into the distance. A reminder she wasn't as isolated as she'd imagined.

Rosie collected their plates and Natalie rose to help clean up. The two women started on the dishes while Gabe got rid of the fish carcass.

"You a reader, Natalie?" Rosie asked.

"Since I've come on this holiday I've read three books and started a fourth which is more than I would have read…" Natalie paused. Shook her head. "In two years."

"I love reading. I've got a little library back at my place if you run out." Rosie laughed. "Plenty of time for it here."

Gabe came back inside. "I'm going to visit Uncle Ron."

"I'd better get going too." Rosie wiped her hands on the tea towel. "You sure you're happy in the lodge? It's pretty basic."

"It's all I need," Natalie said and waved them off.

Back inside her room she paused to look around. It was so different to her Broome accommodation, not grand or luxurious but comfortable and clean. She'd meant what she said. The morning out paddling had swept away any concerns she had about staying here. While the indulgence of the resort had been enjoyable, in a strange way this basic room was all she needed. She stretched out on the comfy bed and closed her eyes.

Later in the afternoon, after a refreshing sleep and just as she had settled to read, Gabe called in again.

"There's a cabin empty," he said. "Tika and Rosie reckon you'll be more comfortable there. It's got its own kitchen and bathroom."

Although the thought was appealing Natalie didn't want to bother moving. She was already settled in her room even though she hadn't really unpacked.

"There's a group of blokes coming tonight," Gabe said. "Fishermen. They're nice enough but they can get a bit rowdy and they like to take over the camp kitchen. You might prefer your own space. And you won't have to go out for the bathroom."

Natalie had a sudden recall of Bazz. Perhaps having her own cabin where she could keep to herself if she wanted was a better idea. "If it's no bother."

Gabe shook his head.

"Thanks."

"I'll help you shift."

He waited on the verandah while she threw her things back in her bag then he loaded his vehicle with her belongings and drove to one of the colourful cabins she'd noticed from the camp kitchen. He pulled up in front of one painted a vibrant shade of purple.

"You'll like it here. Bit more comfortable than your other room."

Natalie stepped inside and felt instantly at home in the neat little cabin. Gabe brought in her case while she carried her assorted bags.

"I'll clear the remains of my food from the camp kitchen," she said.

Once again Gabe offered to help. By the time they were done Natalie was hot and sweaty.

"I can't offer you much to drink," she said as she put the last of her perishables in the fridge. She waved a bottle of mineral water. "It's cold at least."

"Suits me." Gabe took two glasses from the cupboard.

She poured and they took their drinks outside where they settled into the outdoor chairs and sipped the cool fizzing water in silence. Across from the verandah was a small garden plot containing assorted shrubs and beyond that was patchy lawn, coconut palms and much larger broad-leafed trees. The sun had slipped below the giant sandhills creating a golden glow across the sky.

"Thanks for bringing me here," Natalie said. "I can understand why you'd want to come back. It's beautiful."

He turned, his look searching. Natalie felt he could see right inside her.

"I like to visit. This is home but there's not much to do here."

"That sounds good to me." Natalie broke away from his gaze and watched a small bird flitting in and out of a leafy shrub.

"Are you running away from something?"

His question took her by surprise. She glanced back. He was still studying her, his look solemn. They'd only just met. She felt comfortable with him, as if they'd known each other for years instead of days, and yet she wasn't about to confide in an acquaintance, least of all a male one.

"No, I just needed a holiday. Some downtime."

"You'll get that here." He watched her a moment longer then stood suddenly and drained his glass. "I'll leave you to it."

"Thanks for your help." Natalie waved him off. There was something about Gabe that she found — how could she describe it — attractive? That she even thought it surprised her. Not that there hadn't been other men she'd found attractive over the years but none of them had compared to Milt or made her even think of straying. She shook herself. Her husband had crossed that line but the idea had never entered her head before. She rolled her shoulders, stretched languidly in the warm air and pushed thoughts of men from her mind.

Back inside her cabin she unpacked, everything this time, made herself a coffee and curled up on the couch with her book.

Once again she was overwhelmed by the indulgence of sitting and reading on a...she had to struggle to remember what day it was. Monday! She'd been kayaking, swimming, eaten the most delicious fish cooked for her straight from the ocean and now she had nothing to do but relax and enjoy the pleasure of reading a book.

She glanced at her phone. There was plenty of signal here. She should send a message, say she was staying longer, but her last text, when she'd been leaving Broome, had said she wasn't sure how often she'd be able to make contact. They were managing without her. Natalie opened her book. She'd send another message once she knew what her next move would be.

Twenty-Three

Bree slid out of her boots and sat them beside her dad's. He'd knocked off early. She wondered if he had a meeting to go to. She hadn't noticed anything against Wednesday when she'd checked the calendar that morning. Bubbles was curled in his usual spot on the chair by the back door. She scratched him under the chin and let herself inside where she was greeted by the sound of an ABC newsreader blaring from the den.

"Bree," a voice hissed.

She turned. Laura was beckoning her from the kitchen.

Bree frowned. "What's up?" No sooner had Bree stepped into the kitchen than Laura closed the door carefully behind her.

"When are you leaving?" Laura said.

Bree bristled. "I don't know." Her dad had asked her only this morning when she intended to head off and now Laura was nagging her. If the truth be told she was reluctant to leave now. After the conversation they'd overheard between Granny and Dad, she was worried about her mum and also the future of the property. She couldn't bring herself to make plans to leave when things were so messy at home. "Has anyone heard from Mum today?"

"I haven't and Kate and Dad haven't mentioned it."

"Where is Kate?"

"In her room."

Bree shook her head. Kate might as well go back to her place for all the help she was being.

"And Dad's watching TV. He came in about an hour ago, had a shower and went to the den. He never watches TV at this time of the day." Laura gripped Bree's arm. "What are we going to do?" she hissed.

"About what?"

"For goodness sake, Brianna."

Bree raised her eyebrows. "Calm down."

"Dad's miserable." Laura began to pace. "Kate's miserable. You're leaving any minute and Mum's gone off to some remote place where we can't contact her."

"Have you tried?"

"I sent a text this morning but she didn't reply. Do you think she's all right?"

"Why wouldn't she be?"

"After what Granny said about Dad doing something to upset her." Laura got to the end of the table and wrung her hands. "What if he has?"

"They'll work it out."

Laura stalked back down the kitchen and stopped right in front of her, eyes wide. The sickly sweetness of her perfume wafted on the air around her. "What if Mum's actually left him and this holiday thing is all a cover-up."

Bree paused at the thought then brushed it aside. "Don't be ridiculous. Mum and Dad have a rock-solid marriage. She wouldn't leave. I'm more concerned about the stuff with Connie. That's probably playing on Dad's mind too."

They both froze as the door opened behind them. Kate stuck her head in, looked from one sister to the other. "What are you two up to?"

Bree frowned. She hadn't seen Kate at breakfast this morning or at lunch. Her face was pale and her skin blotchy, as if she'd been crying.

"We're keeping the heat in," Bree said.

Kate came all the way in and shut the door. She was huddled inside a thick sloppy jumper and even though the kitchen was warm, she looked almost blue with cold.

"We're talking about Dad," Laura said.

"I've just looked in on him. He's asleep in his chair. Do you think he's okay?"

Bree groaned. "He's probably tired. It's been a big couple of weeks."

"We think he and Mum have had a fight," Laura said.

"What?" Kate said.

"We do not," Bree snapped.

"Granny thinks they did. Why else would Mum go off without telling us?"

"She told Dad where she was going, not us," Bree said. "If she'd been mad at him it would have been the other way round, wouldn't it?"

"Perhaps she's mad with us too."

"Why?" Kate slumped into a chair then got up again, switched the kettle on and put a tea bag in a cup. "Anyone else want one?"

Both Bree and Laura shook their heads.

"I guess she might not be happy about you leaving, Bree." Kate spoke in that know-all older sister voice that annoyed the hell out of Bree. "She's been trying to get Dad to take a holiday," Kate went on. "But I can't imagine she'd be that upset. And your hair was a bit of a shock, Laura, but it's Dad who flies off the handle about those kinds of things, not Mum. And unless someone's told her I presume she doesn't know about the tattoo."

Bree bristled again at the suggestion her joining Owen at Marla was such a selfish act. Her parents had had plenty of chances to take a break and she wouldn't have made a fuss if they'd gone off, in fact she'd welcome the opportunity to run things her way. She went to the fridge and got a beer then glared at Kate. "Perhaps she's worried about you, moping around all day looking like something the cat dragged in and not helping much."

Kate clutched her cup. "If she was worried about any of us she'd be here, not thousands of k's away." Tears brimmed in her eyes.

Bree got a daggered look from Laura. She felt a stab of guilt. She hadn't meant to sound so mean. "Look, I'm sure Mum's doing just what Dad said. She's gone on a holiday. Maybe they're both miffed 'cause he wouldn't go too."

"But she was going to Aunty Brenda's," Laura said.

"It was a bit of a surprise to find out she was in Broome." Kate rested her behind against the kitchen bench and took a sip of her tea.

"Dad told us about that," Bree said. "Mum's decision was last minute and she didn't know Brenda was going to be away."

"But it's all a bit weird, isn't it?" Laura said. "You'd think she'd have let us know the minute her plans changed. It's almost as if she wouldn't have told us she was in Broome if we hadn't caught her out."

They were all silent then until Bree plonked her beer on the table and sat. "I think this is all ridiculous. You're worrying over nothing."

"We could just ask Dad what's going on." Kate came and sat down again. The tears were gone and her face was returning to a healthier pink.

"Like how?" Bree said.

They all froze as the handle rattled and the door opened. "Hello, started drinks without me?" Milt's eyes were bleary but his voice was cheery.

"A beer?" Bree leaped to her feet.

"Thanks, love."

"Jeepers, look at the time. I'd better get tea started." Laura jumped up too. Bree glanced at her. Her little sister said the strangest things sometimes but *jeepers* was new.

"Everyone happy with chops for tea?" Laura asked.

"I'll do the vegetables," Kate said.

Bree passed her dad a beer then set the table and for a while the kitchen was abuzz with activity. No-one brought up their missing mother and soon the smell of meat cooking wafted around them.

Kate made a sudden dash for the door. "I'll be back in a minute."

Bree looked up as the door banged sharply but her dad and Laura didn't seem to notice. She took a deep breath. "Have you heard from Mum today?"

Milt looked surprised by the question. "No." He patted his pocket. "But I haven't checked my phone tonight. Must have left it in the bedroom." He too let himself out into the passage.

Laura gave Bree a questioning look.

"What?" Bree said.

"I thought we were going to ask him about Mum," Laura hissed.

"I was working up to it."

"Jeepers, keep your hair on."

Bree took a swallow of her beer. "Anyway, it was Kate's idea. She can do it."

Bree folded her arms and looked away from Laura's baleful expression. Even though the colours were fading it was still hard to take her seriously with that rainbow of hair cascading around her head.

*

Kate reached her room and took a deep calming breath of cooler air. The warmth of the kitchen combined with the smell of meat cooking had upset her rebellious stomach. It seemed to be just the smell of red meat that troubled her and it had come over her so suddenly. She took a couple more deep breaths then all of a sudden her stomach spasmed and she retched.

"Kate?"

She'd barely pulled the door to behind her in her haste to reach her room. Now her dad pushed it open and looked in.

"Are you all right?" he asked.

Tears filled her eyes again. Why couldn't her mum be here? She clenched her jaw trying to keep the contents of her stomach from rising.

"What is it, love?" Milt strode into the room and put an arm around her. "Aren't you well?"

His comforting action was her undoing. She leaned into his chest and sobbed. She'd been crying on and off for days but she'd fought the tears. Now she let them fall. She cried for this little human inside her and the terror of not wanting it. She cried for Sean because she knew how much he would and she cried for her mum because she needed someone to help her understand these feelings that she didn't understand herself.

Milt didn't say anything, just held her close against his solid chest and let her cry. Eventually her sobs began to fade. He lowered her to the bed and reached for a box of tissues.

"Here," he said.

She took several, wiped her face and blew her nose. She felt the pressure on the bed beside her as he sat too.

"Is this something to do with Sean? Have you two had a falling-out?"

"No." She shook her head then nodded. "Kind of." Fresh tears rolled down her cheeks.

"Right...well." He shifted on the bed and put an arm around her again. "I guess you wish your mum was here."

Kate could hear the discomfort in his voice.

"Would you like me to go and get one of your sisters?"

She shook her head and pressed it into the nook of his shoulder. He was warm and solid. "No."

"Okay...well. I'm afraid I'm not much chop when it comes to relationship advice but I can listen if that would help."

She looked up at him. "Are you and Mum okay?"

A shadow passed over his face then he smiled and pulled her in close again. "We are. Now, what's this all about?"

"I'm..." Kate let out a deep sigh. Gulped in some more air. Willed her stomach to settle. "I'm pregnant."

"Hell." Her dad squeezed her arm then held her away from him. "Hell," he said with awe in his voice. "My little girl's having a baby."

The relief of telling someone was instant. She gave him a watery grin and blew her nose. "I haven't been your little girl for a long time, Dad."

"I know, love." He grinned then pulled her close again. "So what's the problem? Has it caught Sean by surprise? He'll come round, you know. The toughest blokes always fall the hardest."

"It's not Sean. At least I...I think he'll be pleased." She took another deep breath, wiped her nose. "It's me. I feel so tired and so sick and I don't want to have a baby."

He patted her arm. "You poor thing. You know I remember your mum being like that."

She tipped her head back and looked up at him. "Not wanting a baby?"

"No, not that exactly, but she was really crook with both you and Brianna. And all she wanted to do was sleep. She felt much better once she got past the early stages but she never enjoyed being pregnant."

"But she wanted the babies, didn't she? Us?"

Milt frowned. "Of course. It was just that she felt so miserable it was hard to be excited." He pressed his hand to her cheek and guided her head to his shoulder again. "You'll be a good mother. You'll see. Once you feel better and the jolly hormones settle down...your mum was always going on about rampant hormones."

Kate knew he was trying to help but he only made her feel worse. "I won't." She pressed her fingers to her lips but they didn't hold back the words. "I don't want to be a mother." A fresh surge of misery washed over her. She couldn't believe she had more tears to shed but her eyes filled again. Once more she sobbed into her dad's shoulder and he remained silent, gently rocking her back and forth as if she truly was his little girl again.

Twenty-Four

Natalie finished the final page of her book, closed it and placed it on the table beside her. It had been an enjoyable read, one that Rosie had loaned her, about a mismatched Irish family. She'd laughed and cried over it and now that it was finished she missed the characters. Or perhaps, if she was truthful, the story of a domineering grandmother and sibling rivalry underpinned by solid family love made her miss her own family. She stared out across the space beyond her cabin, focused on nothing in particular. Life here had become easy. She was both energetic and slothful in equal measures. Her skin was lightly tanned and her body felt strong and fit.

Here under the verandah she was protected from the late-afternoon sun by the tall trees that edged the sandhills but there was still some heat in the day. Her body soaked up the warmth like those of the little lizards sunning themselves on the rocks edging the garden. She took a sip from her water bottle, pressed the cool of it to her cheek, thought vaguely about going for another swim then looked up expectantly at the sound of a vehicle.

She smiled and waved as a familiar four-wheel drive pulled in with a kayak poking out the back. They'd made no formal arrangement but she'd grown used to Gabe turning up to take her somewhere. And if she was being honest she enjoyed his company and their casual conversations that made no demands of her. To him she was simply a visitor to his country and he was passionate about that. She'd learned so much about the area and its history from him.

The passenger window went down and he leaned across, his smile so familiar now. "Want to come for a paddle?"

"I'd love to." She scooped up her hat and climbed in, her bathers already on under her shorts and t-shirt.

"How was your day?" he asked as he drove off towards the sandhills.

"Great thanks. I've been lazy and enjoyed it."

He chuckled. It was a contented sound she'd grown fond of.

"Are we going to the creek again?"

"No, the beach. It's a perfect evening for a paddle down there."

"Oh, you're right," Natalie said as they rolled to a stop high above the waterline. The ocean was pearly blue and calm, and the sun hung like a golden ball low in the sky. "What a beautiful evening."

"We'd better get the kayak in quick. The sun will be gone soon."

She tore her gaze from the view and helped him lift the kayak and carry it down the beach. The freshness of the water against her legs took her breath away but her body soon acclimatised.

"I'll hold it while you get in."

She did as he bid then clutched the sides as the kayak rocked wildly under his weight as he climbed in behind her. He paddled them away from the shore. Natalie glanced back and realised there was only one paddle.

"You're doing all the work," she said.

"It's not hard." His strong arms dipped from side to side.

Natalie turned away. They were paddling parallel to the shore now, their four-wheel drive like a discarded toy on the vast expanse of sand, and beyond it the pale blue sky was brushed with hints of pink as the sun sank lower.

"This is so beautiful."

She trailed her fingers in the water. Gabe was easy to be with and she found herself so much more relaxed in his company now than she had been the first time they'd kayaked. Perhaps it was silly but she felt as though life AA had given her permission to test the boundaries. When she was with Gabe she felt different, younger and freer, and she was enjoying those feelings. He knew little about her personal life, nor she about his except that he was divorced, a result of being away from home too much on tours, he'd said, but not whether there was anyone else in his life.

A fin cut the water a few metres away. She pulled back her hand.

"Dolphins," Gabe said and she relaxed again.

He stopped paddling and let the kayak drift. Two more appeared and swam under them, broke the surface and disappeared again. The sun dropped lower and slipped behind clouds, turning everything golden. They continued to drift.

"How can you bear to leave this place?" she asked.

He didn't answer. She twisted round to find him studying her. "It's not easy."

They floated further, lulled by the gentle rock of the kayak, with the vast expanse of the Indian Ocean beneath them as if they were the only two people in the world. She thought of her family and turned her gaze back to the expanse of bay ahead of her.

Behind her Gabe dipped the paddles once more and with the help of the current swept them towards the shore. They worked together to get the kayak back in the vehicle then drove across the sandhills to the community in silence. It was a companionable quiet but with a slight edge to it as if they were both waiting for the other to speak. Natalie's elbow rested on the door and she turned her face to the wind, enjoying the sense of freedom she felt as it blew through her hair and billowed her loose shirt around her shoulders.

Back at her cabin she shut the door and leaned in through the open window.

"Thank you for taking me. Can I offer you a lemonade, cool water?"

Gabe studied her as if considering her offer. The pause between them was broken by his mobile ringing. The screen glowed and the phone vibrated, adding urgency.

"Thanks, but I'd better get going."

He reversed away, putting the phone to his ear as he went.

Natalie wandered inside, sad that he hadn't accepted her offer. Gabe was easy to be with and she enjoyed his company but perhaps a little too much. She was playing with fire but she couldn't let go of the invigorating feeling being with him brought.

The next day she was disappointed when lunchtime came and went and he still hadn't turned up. Not that they'd had a set time but after their paddle the night before she found herself watching for him. The day was hot and, desperate for a swim, she hitched a ride to the beach with an older couple who were on a daytrip. They didn't even get out of their vehicle, were only there for a look, they'd said, before they moved on to the next place.

Natalie stayed on the beach, had a swim and read her book. Four-wheel drives came and went but none of them were Gabe and eventually, as the sun lowered in the sky, no more came. She watched the water for a while – there was a strong breeze and it was rough compared to the previous evening. Finally she turned her back on it and walked over the sandhills to camp. It took her a while and it was hard going. By the time she reached her cabin her calves were aching but she was proud of herself. It had been good exercise but she was quite sure it was way further than the one kilometre suggested in the camp brochure.

Hunger drove her inside. She inspected the contents of the fridge, wondering what she'd make herself for dinner. There were some sausages in the freezer, and a motley collection of vegetables, cheese and eggs. She took some cheese and a packet of crackers from the cupboard. They'd do for starters and she could scramble some eggs later if she felt like it. She'd either have to get more supplies soon or go back to Broome. The idea of travelling back with Gabe was agreeable but then this holiday would be over. She looked around her little cabin and through the window to the garden of assorted flowering shrubs, the palm trees that towered high overhead, and she knew she wasn't ready to leave.

She poured herself a glass of mineral water, wishing today for the first time since she'd arrived that it was wine, and took her plate of nibbles outside. The sun had slipped further, leaving an orange glow on the horizon merging to a deep purple sky as night descended. The helicopters that often thundered across the sky to and from the nearby airstrip had stopped and there was only the distant sound of other campers.

She nestled into her chair sipping her drink and glanced at the battered little paperback she'd been reading. She picked it up and studied the cover. The main character was resonating with her. A married woman with a family who'd been almost destroyed by a tragedy. To survive she was going to have to make some changes in her life that hadn't sat well with some of her family. Could Natalie be like that?

"Can you read in the dark?"

Natalie jumped, splashing her drink down her shirt. "Gabe!"

"Sorry." He stepped closer. "Didn't mean to give you a fright. I thought you would have heard me. I kicked my toe on a rock back there."

"I was miles away." She put her book and glass on the table.

"Sorry I've been gone all day."

"You don't have to be worrying about me."

"I went with Uncle Ron to check out a few ideas for tourist trips and we had car trouble. We've only just got back but I bring food and wine." He lifted a plastic bag into the air with one hand and a bottle in the other. "I can't vouch for the wine. It's been in Uncle Ron's fridge for a while, but the steaks are excellent. I bought them myself." He stopped, his arms dropped to his sides. "I'm raving on and you've probably made other plans."

"Oh yes." Natalie chuckled and waved a hand at the plate on the table. "I have so many options."

He glanced at her lump of cheese and scattered crackers. "Steak then?"

"Yes please. I might even have enough ingredients for a passable salad."

He held out the wine, which she accepted gratefully, and while she tossed an assortment of vegetables with some lettuce, he started the barbecue and opened the bottle.

Natalie took a sip, winced at the sharp taste. "It's a while since I had wine."

"You don't have to be polite." Gabe took a second taste and ran his tongue over his lips. "It grows on you."

They sat outside with just the light from the kitchen window to see by.

The steak melted in Natalie's mouth. "Oh, that's divine. I haven't had steak in a long time."

"I'm glad you're enjoying it." He grinned and watched her take another bite before he started on his.

While they ate he told her about his trip with his uncle. "Charlie came with us. He was the reason we got stuck out there. Left a door open and flattened the battery. It took us a while to get help."

"Bad luck."

"It was a useful lesson for Charlie. Consequences for actions."

"But you and Ron had to suffer the consequences too."

"Yep, and Uncle Ron sure let Charlie know." Gabe laughed. "Charlie's ears will still be ringing."

Natalie sat back from her empty plate and took another sip of the wine. It was a sauv blanc semillon with last year's date so it couldn't have been in Ron's fridge for too long. "You're right, it does grow on you."

Gabe finished his meal and they sat in silence for a while, both of them staring out into the night.

"I have to go back to Broome tomorrow."

Natalie wasn't prepared for the wave of sadness his words provoked. "I thought you had one more day here."

"Plans have changed. It's short notice I know, but if you want to go with me you'll need to be ready early."

She turned back to the scene before her: the night sky, a sprinkling of stars and a palm tree making a darker silhouette.

"You're not ready to leave yet, are you?"

She shook her head. Gabe got out of his chair and bent over her, took both her hands in his. It was a shock. They'd touched before of course, shaken hands, and he'd helped her across rocks on several occasions or brushed her arm in passing, but this felt intimate. She didn't pull away. He grinned. "I knew you'd like it here." She looked up at him. His eyes sparkled with the light from the window. It was a look of friendship but still she felt a warm thrill spread through her chest.

He squeezed her hands a little tighter, leaned a little closer. "This isn't reality, you know that. You have another life back home, family...a husband."

She knew he would read the surprise on her face. She'd not mentioned Milt once to Gabe, she was sure.

"Sometimes it's the things people don't say that speak the loudest."

She felt embarrassed then. "I'm not hiding anything. My husband...Milt...I'm not sure..."

He let go of her hands, and even though the night was warm she felt cold, the spell cast by his proximity broken.

"This is the place to find yourself. Stay on; Aunty Rosie will look after you. When you're ready to go back to Broome she can organise it. I'm glad I met you, Natalie. Let me know when you come back to WA next."

He left her then, striding away into the dark. She heard a soft thud, heard him swear. She smiled. He'd found the rock again.

Twenty-Five

Kate huddled over her first cup of tea for the morning, her hands circling the mug for warmth. Around her the kitchen was silent except for the occasional tick of the fridge and beyond that, outside, the distant sound of a tractor moving back forth.

At the moment her stomach was settled. It was her nerves that were on edge. Before he'd gone outside her dad had convinced her she needed to tell her sisters she was pregnant. They'd all been worried about her and keeping it a secret wasn't helping. He'd wanted to ring her mum too but she'd said no, she preferred to tell people face to face. He'd agreed to let her do things her way before he'd gone outside to do whatever he was doing on the tractor.

Kate gripped her mug tighter. At least she had a week up her sleeve before she had to tell Sean. It wasn't the kind of conversation she wanted to have over the phone. His interstate job had bought her time.

"Good morning." Laura breezed into the kitchen then shut the door, twice, the second time with a thump to make sure it stayed shut. "It's freezing in here. Have you let the fire go out?"

Kate glanced towards the slow-combustion fire in the corner of the kitchen. The room had been warm when she'd come in to find her dad eating his breakfast.

Laura poked at it, then put some more wood on and strode across to the kettle. Her outfit brought a temporary smile to Kate's face. She'd obviously been going through drawers of old clothes. She sported worn ugg boots with a hole in one toe revealing a stripy pink sock, a pair of purple trackpants and her old school jumper, topped off by her hair, which, although beginning to fade, was a crown of colour around her face.

"Hell, look what the cat's dragged in."

Kate's smile faded. Bree had let herself in. Of course she was dressed in her standard denim and thick blue jumper; her hair shone and was pulled back in a neat ponytail. She stopped to look from Kate to Laura. "Should have worn my sunglasses."

Kate sighed, put her head in her hands. She'd peered in the bedroom mirror when she'd slipped on her dressing-gown. She knew how terrible she looked.

"It's bloody freezing in here." Bree strode to the fire. "Have you let the fire go out?"

"I've just added wood," Laura said.

"Where's Dad?" Bree asked.

"Haven't seen him," Laura said.

"He's doing something on the tractor." Kate lifted her head.

"What?" Bree went to the window.

"I don't know." Kate looked at her sisters who both had their backs to her. "I need to tell you something."

They turned. Bree's look was expectant, Laura's full of concern.

"You're sick, aren't you?" Laura slid into a chair next to her, and slipped her warm hands over Kate's. "I knew something was wrong."

Bree remained standing, arms across her chest. "Let her talk, Laura."

Kate took a breath. "There's nothing wrong with me. It's just that I'm…I'm—"

"Pregnant!" Laura squealed.

"Yes." Kate breathed out. Another hurdle crossed.

Laura threw her arms around her and pulled her close, then sat back and looked up at Bree. "We're going to be aunties."

"So that's why you haven't been looking so good?" Bree said.

"I feel like crap."

"This is so exciting." Laura bounced up and down on her chair. She was squeezing Kate's hands so tightly she had to extricate them before they lost circulation. "Have you told Dad?" Laura stopped bouncing, her eyes wide. "What about Mum? Does she know?"

"You two and Dad are the only ones I've told."

Bree sat on the chair on her other side. Her dark eyes locked on Kate. "What about Sean?"

Kate shook her head. "He's driving interstate. I want to tell him…in person, when he gets back." She turned to Laura, avoiding Bree's questioning look. "That's why you mustn't say anything. I don't want him hearing about this from anywhere else."

"Like Facebook," Bree said.

Kate grabbed Laura's hand. "Oh, hell no. Laura, you mustn't breathe a word…to anyone."

"Of course I won't until you tell me I can." Laura huffed. "I can keep a secret, you know. But why haven't you told Sean? I thought he'd be the first person you'd tell, even if it was by phone. He loves kids. He'll be over the moon."

"Laura, stop," Bree said.

"What?"

Kate had her head down, scrabbling in her pocket for a tissue. She was trying to hide her tears but Bree had seen them roll down her cheeks.

"What's the matter?" Laura's tone was hushed this time.

"I don't want it." The words fell from Kate's mouth in a ragged whisper. She squeezed her eyes shut. Neither of her sisters spoke. The fire whooshed as a log ignited. Something banged outside as the wind picked up and beyond that there was the drone of the tractor.

"Why would you not want a baby? Is there something wrong with it?"

"Shut up, Laura." Bree's arm went around Kate's shoulder and she could no longer keep her sobs silent.

"I'm sorry, Kate." Laura's voice was heartbroken.

"It's all right." Kate dabbed at her cheeks and blew her nose. "It's not your fault. I've been a bundle of mush since I found out. I'm healthy and pregnant. The doctor sees no reason for concern over the…its health. I have to have a scan in a week or so."

"It must have been a shock," Bree said.

"Why?" Laura looked from one to the other.

"Sean and I both have problems…health issues that…nothing serious but…" Kate sniffed. "We didn't think we'd ever be able to conceive naturally."

Bree squeezed her shoulders then let her go. "I'll make you a fresh tea."

Kate gave her a grateful smile. She'd forgotten the heart-to-heart they'd had one Christmas several years ago. Everyone else had gone to bed but Bree and Kate had stayed up drinking. It wasn't long after Kate and Sean had agreed no IVF and no babies for them. Kate had told Bree about it and Bree had supported her decision. All on practical grounds, of course. She was of the theory that assisted pregnancies weakened the gene pool, survival of the fittest, she'd said.

Kate looked at Laura who was still watching her, eyes wide with worry. "I know it seems weird to some people but I've never wanted to be a mother."

Laura twirled one lock of purple hair in her fingers. "What about some toast?" Her look was so hopeful Kate nodded.

While they were busy behind her she took some deep breaths, wiped her face again, pulled herself together. Now that she didn't have to try to hide how she felt, some of the tension that had gripped her since her visit to Dr Strauss abated. Her shoulders relaxed. Bree came back with another cup of tea and coffees for her and Laura. Laura brought assorted condiments and a plate piled high with toast. Kate had a sudden desire for toast smothered in butter and some of her mother's apricot jam.

"What's Dad doing out there anyway?" Laura asked.

"I don't know," Kate said through a mouthful of toast. "He didn't say."

"Tractor's stopped." Bree leaned back, listening, and the other two did the same. The back door banged.

"Hell's teeth."

They all grinned at each other as their dad burst through the kitchen door. He stopped mid-stride. "What's going on here?"

"Breakfast," Laura said. "Want some?"

"It's nearly morning tea time." He looked pointedly at his watch.

"It's Saturday morning," Bree said. "What's the rush?"

He paused then held up his muddy hands. "I'll wash then come and join you for a quick cuppa but you'll all have to get your skates on. There's bookwork needs doing this weekend and then we've got a tennis court to build."

He clattered back through the kitchen door, banging it shut behind him, leaving his daughters to gape at each other in surprise.

*

Natalie leaned on the kitchen bench and peered out the window at the bright day. It was the first windy day since she'd arrived and she knew the red dirt would be creeping its way inside. It did most days anyway but today it had help.

Yesterday she'd been restless after Gabe had left. Knowing he wouldn't be calling in took the shine off the day but not her decision to stay. She'd tossed aside the book she'd been reading. The main character had decided she must leave her husband and Natalie wasn't sure if she was making the right decision. The story had unsettled her.

Today she wanted to get out and do something. She glanced around the tidy cabin. She'd cleaned out the fridge and scribbled a list of items she needed. The bed was made and the floor swept. She knew Rosie would do it again. It was her job to clean the cabins and although Natalie had said she was happy to do her own, she always knew when she returned after her morning walk or a swim that Rosie had been there. The coffee and tea were topped up, a chair straightened, the fresh smell of pine in the bathroom.

A vehicle rolled to a stop outside.

She opened the back door as Rosie climbed out of her four-wheel drive.

"Hi, Natalie. Sorry I haven't seen much of you the last few days," Rosie said. "I've been busy. My cousin's been away and I've been doing her jobs as well as mine. She's back now." Rosie stopped below the step, looking up at Natalie. "I wondered if you'd like to come to my place for a cuppa?"

Natalie was grateful for the distraction. "I'd love to, thanks." She pulled the door shut behind her and followed Rosie to her vehicle.

Rosie lived with her mother in a new house on the other edge of the community. Natalie had only seen it from the distance on one of her walks. The map of the community had been clear about where visitors could and couldn't go and she respected the privacy of the locals who lived here. Her time with Gabe had always been spent out away from the community or at her cabin. She didn't even know if he had his own place or stayed with someone else when he was here.

They pulled up under a carport that was lined with bright-leafed plants and Natalie followed Rosie past a garden overflowing with lush tropical vegetation and taller frangipani, and then under an arbour of bougainvillea leading to the front door.

"Come in."

Inside she felt the instant relief of cool, clear air. There was a sleek air conditioner purring from high on the wall, so different to the old machine in her cabin, which was efficient but made a heck of a racket.

"This is lovely," Natalie said, taking in the simple lines of the modern home.

"Much better than my old house. Especially on days like this. The windows keep most of the dirt out. I hate windy days here. Damn pindan gets into everything."

"Pindan?"

Rosie cast her arm towards the window. "Red dirt."

Natalie nodded. "I envy you windows that close snugly. I live in an old farmhouse and nothing fits properly any more. It's impossible to keep the dust out."

Rosie brought mugs of tea to the table with milk and sugar. Natalie sat, then noticed the dresser at the end of the table was crowded with photos, mostly of men and boys. Among them she recognised Gabe. He was quite a lot younger but the camera had caught that bright smile of his and a glint of mischief in his eyes. She turned away, surprised by how much she missed him.

"They're all my family." Rosie placed a plate of biscuits on the table and came to sit beside her.

"All of them?" Natalie glanced back. There had to be about thirty different photos, if you included those scattered over other surfaces in the room.

Rosie laughed. "I call them my family. I've got four kids of my own. Three boys and…" She looked to the photos. "A daughter."

Natalie followed her gaze and saw an old photo of a much younger Rosie beside a man and four young children, one a baby in her arms.

"The others are my lost boys." There was pride in Rosie's voice.

"Lost boys?"

"Gabe was one of them." Rosie pointed a finger towards his photo, in prime place, middle front of the dresser. "He's my brother's boy. He went haywire in his young days. My brother and his wife couldn't cope. They were living in Broome then but my brother was working away a lot. Gabe got in with a bad crowd. Did some stupid stuff. Drank too much. You know. Could have gone to jail."

Natalie tried to imagine the Gabe she'd met doing stupid stuff, as Rosie put it.

"I went and got him. Brought him back here. Found him some work." Rosie's eyes sparkled. "There's always something needs painting here. He did all those cabins." She blew on her tea, took a sip. Looked back at the photos. "I got one of my cousins to take him bush, remind him who he was and where he comes from.

He's doing well for himself these days but he likes to come back and visit. Touch base with home. He was my first success." She looked lovingly at the photos then a sadness settled on her face. "Some of them couldn't adjust, didn't stay, went back to their bad ways. I thought maybe...well. Charlie's another lost boy. He wasn't doing so well, wanted to go back, but that kayaking trip we took together was a turning point for him."

Natalie could relate to that. The kayaking trip had been for her too. She'd been set to leave that first day. The release she'd felt out on the water, her delight in all the sea creatures and the sheer bliss of simply enjoying herself had been her reason to stay.

"Charlie went out again this morning with a group and my cousin Ron. Ron takes kayak tours, and mud crabbing and fishing trips. He said Charlie did a good job." The smile returned to Rosie's face.

"I saw mud crabbing on the list of things to do."

"Would you like to go?"

Natalie screwed up her nose. "I'm not sure about that. Gabe showed me some pictures of the crabs. They're huge."

"Monsters." Rosie tipped her head back and laughed. Natalie took a sip of her tea and the restlessness she'd felt all morning dropped away. Being with Rosie was like being in the company of someone she'd known for years instead of a few days. It reminded her of Brenda and the huge hole her move had left in Natalie's life. Brenda had been one of a kind.

"Have you got kids?"

Rosie's question shifted her thoughts to the family she'd run away from.

"Yes, three girls."

Rosie's gaze strayed back to the photos.

"You have a daughter, you said."

"Angela. Now she's my angel." Rosie wasn't looking at Natalie but somewhere into the distance. "She died in a car accident along with her dad."

"Oh, Rosie." Natalie felt bad for raising such sad memories. "I'm so sorry."

"It was a long time ago. We lived in Perth then. My sons were all under ten. I brought them back here. They've grown up now. Doing well for themselves. They're always wanting me to go and live with them but two are in Melbourne and one in Perth. I visit them. I've got grandies now but I won't leave here for long. My mum's here." Once more she glanced at the photos. "Coming home healed me when I thought I wouldn't be able to go on living. There's something about this place...I don't want to leave."

"I can understand why," Natalie said. "It's beautiful country."

"I'm glad you stayed." Rosie fixed her penetrating gaze on Natalie. "You seem to be a lot happier."

"How can I not be happy when I'm holidaying in paradise?" Natalie glanced away from Rosie's stare to the frangipani tree she could see through the window.

"You're carrying something inside you that's causing you to hurt."

"Am I?" Natalie tried to make light of it but didn't shift her gaze from the tree, still sensing the intensity of Rosie's look.

"Gabe noticed it too."

"Did he?"

"You remind me of my lost boys when they first arrive. Some of the things they've seen and done shouldn't happen to kids. Their eyes are like the shutters we use to keep out the wind in cyclone season and then, as this place works its magic, you can see that light begin to shine out from inside them again."

"They're lucky to have you." Natalie risked a look at Rosie, who shrugged.

"All I can do is provide a roof over their head and decent food to eat; it's being here that makes the difference." She leaned closer. "I've seen that change in you since you first arrived with a face all shut up. Is it being here, or Gabe who's made the difference?"

Natalie shifted on her chair. The backs of her legs had stuck to the vinyl upholstery in spite of the cool of the air conditioner. Her first reaction was to say 'the place' but then she pictured Gabe's smile and a wave of guilt swept over her.

"Listen to me." Rosie's laugh broke the tension. "If my mum was here she'd be telling me to mind my own business. I've always been a stickybeak. Poking my nose into things I shouldn't."

Natalie stood up. "Thanks for the tea, Rosie. It's been lovely to chat."

"Any time." Rosie followed her to the door. "Gabe said you want to stay longer."

Natalie paused, the door still shut against the windy day outside. "I'm not in a rush to go. I'd better let them know at the office though."

"You'll be right. I already told Tika to pencil you in for another week." Rosie smiled and opened the door. A blast of hot air greeted them and Natalie hurried outside, not wanting to allow the dirt into Rosie's lovely clean house but Rosie stepped out after her and shut the door.

"Would you like to go fishing?" she said. "I wouldn't mind some fresh fish again and Charlie's nagging me to take him."

"I'd love to." Natalie was pleased to have something to look forward to.

"I reckon this wind will drop out by early afternoon. We'll pick you up after lunch."

Twenty-Six

Bree stood under the back verandah watching the rain pelt down. Not the drifting drizzle that had been taunting them on and off since early May. This was the big, heavy, pounding drops of a soaking rain they badly needed. The tennis court where they'd been working all morning to get rid of the weeds and make it level was a quagmire. The others had all come inside for lunch when the rain started but Bree had gone to the shed to tinker with a bike she'd pulled apart. Now she was greasy and wet.

Tomorrow they'd start seeding the small part of their property they cropped but there'd be no more outside work today which meant she'd have to tackle the BAS. Reluctantly she let herself inside where she was greeted by a burst of hammering, a grunt and then swearing. She swallowed her grin as her dad flapped one hand back and forth in the air and clutched a hammer in the other.

"What are you doing?" The kitchen door had been removed and was now lying along the passage wall.

"Fixing this bloody door so it will shut properly."

She was surprised at that. Normally with a break in the season he'd be out making sure everything was ready to start seeding.

Even though they'd been ready for a month, he'd usually be double-checking.

Kate came out of the bathroom, a towel around her head. "You're here," she said. "I'll just get dressed and dry my hair and we can start on the BAS."

"I can do it." Bree looked begrudgingly at her dad but he ducked away, making a big show of inspecting the doorframe.

"I'm happy to help."

At least Kate was smiling again. Bree knew how difficult this pregnancy was for her. She could relate to her lack of enthusiasm for a baby. Being a mother wasn't how Bree saw her future either. Parenthood wasn't something she'd discussed with Owen. She had no idea what his feelings were on the subject of children. They weren't at the stage of making any kind of commitment but now she wondered when the right time was to broach such an important topic.

Kate and Sean had gone into it in detail when their likelihood of becoming parents naturally had been almost zero. They'd been firm in their decision to ignore IVF and have a childless future. Discovering she was pregnant must have been a huge shock for Kate. Working together on the farm paperwork would be a useful distraction, like working together on the tennis court had been this morning.

"Okay, thanks," Bree said. "I'll change out of these wet things first."

The den door opened and Laura came out. As soon as she saw her dad her hands went to her hips. "Haven't you put that door back yet? I need to start dinner and you're making a racket and letting all the warm air out." She went into the kitchen. "It's Granny roast night you know."

Milt muttered something under his breath.

"I'd forgotten Granny would be here tonight." Kate had come back down the passage. She had that guarded look again. "I don't want to tell her about the baby. You know how much she adores them. I'm not ready for that."

"Whatever you say, love." Milt patted her shoulder. "We'll leave it to you."

"Your lunch is still here, Bree." Laura came back to the door carrying a plate with a sandwich covered in plastic wrap. They all turned to look at her.

"What?" she said.

"Remember to keep your mouth shut about the baby when Granny comes," Bree said.

"I told you I can keep a secret." Laura shoved the plate at Bree and strode back into the kitchen.

"Thanks." Bree's stomach gave a welcome growl. She was hungry.

*

Laura had the roast on and the vegetables ready to go. She was planning dessert but so far nothing appealed and it was hard to concentrate with her dad muttering and mumbling between intermittent hammering. He'd stopped for the moment and was inspecting the inside of the doorframe. She flicked idly through the pile of cookbooks she'd spread out on the table in front of her. She was tired of being responsible for meals: organising the meat, the fresh fruit and vegetables, cooking every night, cleaning up the inevitable mess that seemed to come from her every attempt. This wasn't why she'd given up hairdressing and come home. Although she was still no closer to resolving what the future looked like, she knew it wasn't being a full-time cook for the family.

"How's it going, love?"

She hadn't heard her dad come up beside her.

"I'm trying to find something for dessert but I'm fed-up. I don't know how Mum does it. She makes it look so easy."

Milt sat down beside her. "Years of experience. And she does enjoy cooking."

"So do I. But not day after day, night after night, trying to come up with something interesting." Laura put her head in her hands and groaned. "What am I going to do?"

"Are we still talking about dinner or something else?"

Laura groaned again. "My life is a mess."

"Not from where I'm sitting."

She looked up, tugged at her hair. "You've seen my hair, my tattoo."

"Yes, I have. You're braver than me on both counts."

"Stupider, you mean."

"I don't think that's a word." He grinned. "That's all superficial stuff anyway. You said the hair would wash out and you were right, it's fading already. I guess you're stuck with the tat, although I believe there're ways to have them removed if that's what you want. But they're not the sum of who you are, love. You're bright, creative and talented in so many ways."

He was studying her with such love in his look it brought a lump to her throat. "I've thrown in a perfectly good job and now I've got nothing."

"Don't ever say that." He put a hand on her shoulder, gripped it firmly. "You've worked hard to learn a trade and you're good at it. It's not as if you've lost those skills just because you've left where you work. There are plenty of other salons. I never liked that bloke you worked for. You can do better."

"You don't really know him." She'd never realised her dad had given her job a lot of thought, let alone taken any notice of Gareth.

"We called in to visit you a few times and I got his measure. The way he spoke to his staff wasn't right, as if you all belonged to him. He was a bully, Laura."

"You never said."

"I knew you'd work it out eventually." His phone rang. He took it from his pocket. "Hello, Phil." He nodded. "Right, okay, thanks. I'll come and check it out." He ended the call and put his phone back in his pocket. "Sheep on the highway. Phil from across the road thinks they could be ours. I'd better go and check. Will you be okay?"

"I'll find something to cook."

"I meant about the bigger picture. You can take as long as you want to decide what you want to do. You might even get something local to tide you over but don't give up on your chosen career yet. You've got a world of talent and not every salon has a Gareth. Maybe there'd be a way to start your own business. We gave Kate money towards her house and we'd be happy for your share to be put towards a business if you came up with a plan. I'm sure your mum would agree."

Tears brimmed in Laura's eyes.

"Don't worry if it's not something you'd want to do though." Milt gave her a concerned look.

"I'd just never thought about my own business."

He shrugged. "Why not? You'd need to present me a decent plan if I was going to invest money in it but I'm sure you're capable. Kate's good at that sort of thing. You should talk it over with her."

He patted his stomach as he stood up. "And don't worry about dessert. We don't need it. Your mum only cooks it sometimes."

Laura dragged her thoughts from her own worries to her mum. "Is she all right, Dad?"

He'd begun to move away but he stopped, turned back. "Last I heard, yes. She misses us but she was in need of some time away."

"I miss her too." Laura sucked in her lip, fighting back tears again.

"I know, love." He came back, brushed a kiss across her forehead. "We all miss her but sometimes you need to give the ones you love some space."

Laura's heart lurched. Her dad had the same sort of look after Pa had died, sad and lost. "She's coming back soon though, isn't she?"

"I hope so but I'm not sure what her timeline is yet. And don't worry about the food. I appreciate what you've done and so do your sisters." He lifted his hand in a wave. "I shouldn't be too long."

She listened as he let himself out the back door then she started flicking through cookbooks again. A wave of cool air drifted across the kitchen. The door was still off its hinges. She wasn't sure what she was going to make for dessert or how she was going to keep the kitchen warm for dinner but at least her dad had given her something to hope for. Even though her mum wasn't here he was on her side and that was a comforting feeling.

*

Bree shifted her plate to sit on top of the empty mugs so she could check out the pile of papers underneath. She'd munched on the sandwiches while she and Kate had worked their way through accounts and invoices, diaries and notes, sorting through three months of paperwork. Outside the rain continued to fall. They'd had to turn on the overhead lights and the desk lamp to be able to read. The dining room was freezing and they'd huddled in front of a small heater blowing warmth around their feet.

Kate sat back from a paperclipped pile of invoices, blew on her hands and rubbed them together. "If this got done every week it wouldn't be so bad." She picked up the next pile of papers, bank statements they'd just printed.

"I know." Bree sighed. "Mum usually does it more often but with everything that's been going on lately…"

"It's freezing in here and the light's terrible. I don't know how Mum stands it."

"There's the desk in the kitchen. We talked about moving the computer there when we got wireless. I don't know why we didn't. Something to do with cables."

Kate didn't look as if she was listening. She kept sifting through the pages in front of her, the pile of bank statements. She paused to look closer then moved on.

"There shouldn't be any surprises though," Bree said. "Everything matches up, doesn't it?"

Kate stopped, looked at a page, went back to another.

"What are you looking at?" Bree asked.

"Well, I'm wondering why Granny is getting two monthly payments."

"Where?" Bree reached for the statements and Kate handed them over, tapping the top of the page with her finger.

Bree glanced at the entries. On the first day of the month there was a transfer to their grandmother's new account. "That's Granny's living allowance. That account was set up after Pa died." She looked further along the dates. A few days later a larger amount was transferred to an account in Pa's name. She lifted the pages until she came to the start of the previous month and saw the same entries.

"So unless the bank has a direct line to heaven I'm assuming that's a joint account that Granny can access." Kate tapped the page with her finger again.

Bree looked at her sister. "You think she's double dipping?"

Kate shrugged. "I don't know. I'm only guessing, but the amount going to the old account is slightly larger so it was probably Granny and Pa's joint allowance. Maybe when the new account was set up they overlooked stopping payments to the old one."

"Hell." Bree sifted through the papers. "That's probably been going on for..." She glanced up at the calendar. "Nearly a year. That's a lot of money."

"Maybe it's just sitting there."

"You think Granny's forgotten it."

"Or she doesn't know the account's still open."

"Mum pays most of her accounts."

"I see that. Talk about double dipping. The farm pays for everything and she gets an allowance."

"She buys her own food and clothes. She'd have the hairdresser, gifts." Bree stopped at that. Her grandmother had always been generous with her gift-giving but since Pa had died she only gave cards for birthdays and they'd all got chocolates last Christmas. Bree had assumed she'd decided to cut back and keep it simple.

"Wish I had her budget." Kate was staring at the bank statements again.

"Statements are all online these days and I doubt she looks at them. She may have assumed one account was closed when the other was opened." Bree tugged open the drawer beneath the computer, forcing them both back in their chairs.

"What are you doing?"

"Mum would have set up the account for Granny." Bree reached in and felt around at the back of the drawer. "She keeps a little book with usernames and passwords."

"Surely not for bank accounts?" Kate looked horrified.

"Not hers, but I wonder if she might have written down Granny's in case she had to access it."

Bree tugged out the little book. It was slim and well worn. Her mother had jotted down the usernames and passwords for every online shop, business and rewards program she'd ever subscribed to. Bree began to flip through the pages of notes in her mother's neat print with the occasional hardly legible entry in between. Her dad used the little book as well but she could see nothing that looked like it referred to Granny. She flicked to the back and there it was, her grandmother's new account details. She kept looking and found other entries: Mum's share portfolio, Dad's share portfolio, and then finally jammed between the password for Nespresso and one for Myer was the details of Granny and Pa's joint account. She turned to Kate.

"It's here." She minimised the spreadsheet on the computer screen and brought up the internet browser.

"You're not going to log into Granny's account?"

"Why not? She won't know and at least we'll be able to see if the money's still there or not."

Bree opened the shortcut to their online banking page and typed in the number and password for Granny and Pa's joint account.

The screen opened up and they both leaned forward.

"It's empty," Kate said.

Bree opened the transaction history. It only showed the last month, the money going in and then the money going out. Beside her Kate gasped. The transfer out went to an account in the name of C L Daly.

"Aunty Connie." Kate's voice was a whisper.

Bree extended the dates for the transaction history to include the last year and there it all was in black and white. Each month a payment had gone in and had accumulated untouched until three months ago when the whole amount had been transferred to C L Daly. Since then, a few days after the money was paid in it was transferred to Connie's account.

"How could Mum and Dad have missed this?" Kate asked.

"Maybe they haven't missed it. Maybe they know about it." Bree tried to remember what they'd overheard her dad and Granny talking about last Sunday morning when they'd all listened outside the kitchen door. "Granny was talking to Dad about Connie wanting more from the property."

"Well, these bank transfers look like she's getting it."

They looked at each other. "We could stop the payments," Bree said.

"Not without talking to Dad first. There might be some explanation we don't know about."

They both stood up. Their afternoon at the computer had been punctuated by banging and sawing and the occasional burst of swearing but it had gone quiet out in the passage now. The kitchen door was still lying prone against the wall as they walked past. The tantalising smell of roast pork wafted out to greet them. Bree glanced at Kate but she didn't seem bothered by it. Laura was alone in the kitchen, bending over the open door of the combustion fire.

"Where's Dad?" Bree asked.

Laura's face and jumper were streaked with blotches of white flour. "He got a call from the neighbours across the highway. There were some sheep out so he's gone to investigate." She frowned. "I thought he'd be back by now. It's nearly dinnertime. Granny should be here soon too."

As if Laura had conjured her up, Olive's call reached them from the back door.

She stopped in the empty frame of the kitchen door. "What's going on here?"

"Dad's trying to fix the door so it stays closed," Laura said.

Olive harrumphed. "His father didn't have any luck either. That door has always had a mind of its own." She strode into the kitchen. "Is he going to put it back tonight? Hard to keep the heat in here with no door."

"He's gone to check on some sheep."

Once more Olive harrumphed. Bree studied her closely, trying to imagine her sweet, sensible granny doing something as underhanded as siphoning off money to Connie.

"How much rain have we had here? It's been steady all afternoon in town."

"Close to an inch last time I checked," Bree said. "If it keeps up it might be another day or so before we can start seeding."

"Very good," Olive said decisively as if Bree was responsible for the rain that had fallen. "What are you cooking, Laura?" Olive moved over to inspect Laura's mess spread along the benchtops.

"I was going to make lemon dumplings but we don't have any lemons so I've changed it to golden syrup dumplings."

"Oh, I used to make them a lot. Easy way to feed a family." Olive looked proudly at Laura. "I haven't had them for years."

"Well, you haven't tried them yet. They might not be any good."

Olive tickled Laura under the chin. "If I can make them anyone can."

Bree heard the back door open, waited for the bang but it didn't come and then her dad appeared in the doorway. "Hello."

"Thank goodness you're back," Laura said. "The roast's nearly ready to carve."

"I'll wash up and be in." He went out then came back and stood in the empty doorframe. "Sorry about the door. I'll fix it tomorrow."

Olive gave another soft harrumph before she busied herself setting the table.

Milt's phone rang. He glanced at it, stabbed at the screen and put it to his ear. "Hello, Natalie." Behind him four women all stopped what they were doing and listened.

*

When Milt answered within seconds of Natalie pressing *call* she shifted anxiously in her seat, feeling even more guilty for her long silence. She'd hardly given her family a thought for days. Earlier the wind had dropped to a gentle breeze as Rosie had predicted. They'd had a successful fishing expedition and now Natalie sat in the shade of the cabin verandah, fresh from a shower and wearing the dress she'd bought in Broome. It was a change from a week of nothing but bathers, shorts and t-shirts. *The Model Wife* sat on the table beside her. She'd found it again when she'd searched her all-but-empty case for a pair of earrings.

She'd picked it up, sat it on her lap, trying to resist the urge to open it but couldn't help herself. It was her past, part of her Before Anomaly life but also an heirloom, even if a desecrated one, and she'd made it into a record of so many happy times. Eventually she succumbed and slowly turned the pages, reading the chapter headings, the words that had been scribbled in laughter and in anger over the years. She'd paused at the photo of the house – not just a house, her home, her family's home – then stopped at the career page where she'd stuck her individual school staff photo. It was dated 1999, the same year Laura started school. Natalie had smiled at her hair – it had been longer then and she remembered she'd had it styled the day before the photo so it was all fluffed out around her face. How young she looked.

She'd flicked to the last chapter, the one about family. 'Family before all else' was the title. *The model wife bears children and cares for them diligently.* Well, she'd certainly done that. *The model wife spends her time taking care of her family and putting them before her own needs.* Olive wouldn't agree that Natalie had followed that golden rule, and if Natalie was being honest, neither did she. And now it was too late. They were grown up, they didn't need her any longer, not really.

That's when she'd reached for her phone, eager to look at their faces. She'd scrolled through photos, stopping at any she found of her girls, and once they'd run out she'd re-read the text she'd last sent home. It seemed like only a few days ago but she realised a week had gone by, and she'd selected Milt's number.

"How are things there?" she asked now, feeling like she was asking an acquaintance rather than her husband.

"Good. Everything's good," he said. "We've had an inch of rain today."

She could hear the smile in his voice. He'd been watching the sky for a decent rain for months.

"That's good."

"We'll be out in the paddock seeding as soon as there's a break. It's already a bit too wet so might be another day or so."

"How're the girls?"

There was a slight hesitation. "They're good. All still here with me. And Mum. Laura's cooked a pork roast."

"Of course, it's Saturday night. How is Olive?"

Once more there was a pause and then. "She's fine."

And there was that word she'd learned was code for anything but *fine*. Now she found herself wondering what he really meant.

"What about you?" he said. "You must have a suntan by now."

"I'm f..." She stopped herself, refusing to hide behind that word any more. "I'm well but I haven't resolved anything yet."

There was silence. She looked at her screen, the call was still connected. She put the phone back to her ear. "Are you still there?"

"Yes. Listen, Natalie, whatever it is you need to work out, don't you think it would help if we talked?"

"It's too hard over the phone."

"No, here at home."

Natalie gripped the phone tighter. "Eventually."

"How long is that going to be?" Milt asked.

"I don't know."

"The girls...well, they wish you were home."

"Has something happened?"

"No, but we miss you...I miss you. I'm worried."

"I'm perfectly fine, Milt." She chewed her lip, so cross she'd said that word again despite her best intentions not to. "I'll call you again in a week."

"A week!"

"I'm going to a friend's place for dinner. I have to go. Give my love to the girls and Olive."

She ended the call. The flock of white cockatoos whirled overhead, screeching at her lie. Well, it wasn't all a lie. She was going to Rosie's to eat the fish they'd caught today but not for an hour or so yet. There was no rush. There was never any rush here.

She looked across the grass and shrubs to the trees that edged the sandhills. The sun was low in the sky, turning everything golden with its rays. She loved this part of the afternoon here. Everyone had knocked off for the day, the throbbing of distant helicopters had ceased and there was little to be heard but the odd voice from another camper, a distant vehicle and the chirrup of birds. Everything was settling, waiting for night to fall.

A bird swooped in and perched on the branch of a nearby shrub. It had done that each afternoon since she'd arrived. Gabe had told her it was a bowerbird scouting for objects to decorate its bower. Natalie never had anything that caught the sharp-eyed bird's interest. It craned its long neck forward, inspecting her with its beady look.

"Sorry, nothing for you," she said and as if it understood the bird swept away on silent wings. She envied it its resolute purpose in life. Her new start had no direction at all.

Twenty-Seven

Dinner at Rosie's was a happy affair. The fish had been devoured with much bragging from Charlie and then as they'd settled back, replete from their meal, he'd started telling jokes. It was hard to equate the happy young man, whose face was split in a grin with a mischievous spark in his eyes, to the sullen boy she'd first met on the kayaking expedition almost a week ago. He'd been quiet when they set out on their fishing trip today but as soon as he caught his first fish he'd become animated and the smile had hardly left his face since. Now he was making them laugh.

Natalie had enjoyed their trip to the creek as well. She'd managed to catch one fish but Rosie had declared it not good for eating so they'd had to throw it back. Tonight's dinner had been courtesy of Rosie and Charlie's skills, not hers. Natalie's contribution had been to open her last packet of lettuce leaves and create a tossed salad to go with their pan-fried fish and oven-baked chips.

Out of jokes, Charlie got up from the table and collected their plates. "I'm going to my room now," he said.

"Thanks for catching me some dinner, Charlie," Natalie said.

"No problem." He grinned. "Anytime you need fish you just ask me."

"Ha!" Rosie laughed. "Suddenly you're an expert."

Natalie was surprised to see Charlie bend and give Rosie a swift kiss on the cheek.

"Night, Aunty Rosie," he said. "Natalie."

By the look on Rosie's face as she watched him go, the kiss had taken her by surprise too.

"I didn't think I was going to have any luck with that one," she murmured once they heard the clunk of his bedroom door closing. "But there's something there after all."

"He's a bright young lad."

"Very. He just needs to believe it himself." Rosie stood up. "Cup of tea?"

"I'd love one."

"It's a nice night. Let's go outside. You go ahead, I'll bring out the tea."

Natalie let herself out onto the verandah that ran all the way around Rosie's house. It was dotted with plants in pots and comfy outside chairs. She sank into one, settled into the soft cushions and closed her eyes, breathing in the sweet scent of frangipani wafting on the cooling breeze. She'd become used to the easy rhythm of life here but her conversation with Milt earlier had unsettled her again. She'd said she wanted another week but what if another week wasn't enough?

Rosie arrived with the tray of tea things, interrupting her thoughts.

Natalie looked at the plate of biscuits between the mugs of tea. "Mint slice!" She'd seen the high cost of items like chocolate biscuits at the roadhouse when she'd called in there with Gabe. They'd had ice cream that day.

"Gabe bought me up a few packets. He knows what a sweet tooth I am." Rosie grinned. "I keep them in the back of the crisper. Not many of my lodgers think to look among the vegetables for treats."

Natalie took one, bit into the cold rich chocolate coating and savoured the tang of the mint. She hadn't had chocolate since Broome. Here she'd been living a simple existence on fruit and salads, some steamed vegetables along with the meat she'd been eking out.

"Can I get a ride out to the roadhouse?" she asked. "I need more supplies."

"I'm going to One Arm Point on Monday," Rosie said. "You could come with me. There's a supermarket there and they've got a bigger selection."

That settled, they drank their tea and munched their biscuits in silence, both staring out into the black night. From somewhere behind them came the repetitive thud of rap music.

Rosie sighed. "They all like their music, my lost boys. I like music too but rap is one thing I can't take to. The words are clever but the noise that goes with it..." She put a hand to her head and groaned. "I'm getting too old for this."

"How old are you, if you don't mind me asking?"

"Sixty-eight."

"I thought you were more my age. I'm ten years younger."

"The numbers don't mean much." The music rose a notch. "Unless there's rap music, then I feel a hundred."

Natalie chuckled. "There was always a battle over the radio stations when all my girls were at home." Like they were currently. She wondered who would be winning that fight now. "The constant changing of the channels used to drive Milt mad."

"Milt your husband?"

"Yes."

"You miss them?"

Rosie's face was in shadow but Natalie could feel the intensity of her look.

"My girls, yes."

"But not your man?"

"We argued before I left. It was something...something big. I'm not sure how we're going to overcome it."

"Stuck between a rock and a hard place?"

"Yes."

"My Gabe's a good man."

"I know."

"He wasn't after his break-up with his wife though. Set him back a while." Rosie leaned forward. "You going to leave your husband, Natalie?"

Natalie's breath caught in her throat. "No." She looked away. "I don't..."

Rosie sat back in her chair. "It's a big decision. I had another fella once the kids had grown up, but we didn't stay together. Too different in the end."

Charlie's music continued to thud behind them. Natalie stared up at the night sky where a million stars glittered back.

"Do you ever wonder what we're doing here and why?" she said.

"That's a pretty big question."

"Before I came on this holiday I had a bit of a scare. They found a lump in my breast. Thankfully it turned out to be nothing to worry about, an anomaly, they called it. A woman who lives near me wasn't so lucky." Natalie couldn't bring herself to mention Veronica's name or how she'd found her in Milt's arms. "It was a shock. You hear people say when they have a near-death experience their life passes before their eyes. Mine wasn't that serious but it made me question my life. Shouldn't I have done something more than be a wife and mother and teacher? I decided my AA life would be different."

Rosie looked at her blankly.

"AA stands for After Anomaly. I don't want things to go back to the way they were BA."

There was a pause then they both spoke at once. "Before the anomaly."

Natalie nodded.

"What would you want to do?" Rosie asked.

Natalie sighed. "That's just it. I don't know. I think I'm ready to give up teaching but if I did that what would I do? There's always plenty to do on the property but we're heading to retirement. Our daughter will take it on."

"On her own?"

"Not to start with. I guess Milt will stay on and help but I don't want us to be like his parents. They never really let go of the place and my father-in-law, Clem, literally dropped dead in his boots. Surely there's more to life than working till you die."

"What would you do if you weren't working?"

"Travel." The word was out without her even thinking. "I've wanted to travel for years, I don't care where. Milt and I have hardly been anywhere. We took the girls for a beach holiday each summer and we've been interstate for a couple of trips, mostly for business or for family events. Whenever I've raised the topic of taking a proper holiday Milt's always said one day we will. Then I found myself saying it when other people told us about their travels and then I realised..." She turned back to Rosie who was still watching her. "One day meant never."

"Holidays are good but you still have to go home."

Rosie's words dropped like rocks. Natalie shifted in her chair. She wasn't ready to do that.

"What else would you do?"

Natalie looked at all the pots around her on the verandah and recognised a yearning she'd long neglected. "Create a proper garden. We have a basic one, a few shrubs and a bit of lawn, a couple of flowers. I plant a few veggies in the summer and I have a patch of gerberas that I manage to keep alive and one rose that was my father-in-law's. Milt calls them my weeds."

"He's not a gardener?"

"No. His parents weren't either so I guess he never had the chance."

"I love my garden."

They both sipped their tea, gazing at the oasis that surrounded Rosie's home.

"Is there something else," Rosie asked. "Something that you want more of in your life?"

"A slower existence that doesn't involve juggling my work between everyone else's, maybe do up the house or even buy somewhere near the sea and get Milt to retire. I want the chance to hold grandchildren but…before that I want more time with my girls. That sounds crazy 'cause they're all home at the moment and here I am on the other side of the country." Natalie pictured their faces and felt the stab of the guilt that had plagued her since she'd returned to teaching. *The Model Wife* had been partly responsible for that, with its stern command to give up work beyond the home for the sake of her family. Olive had added her disapproval, asking Natalie how she would manage, and Natalie had worked especially hard so that her mother-in-law could never suggest she wasn't coping. "I've always worked. Either teaching or jobs that were needed for the property. I was lucky my mother-in-law lived with us so she often looked after the girls when I had late meetings."

That was true, she would have needed after-hours care if it hadn't been for Olive, who'd also done a few extras such as bringing in washing or doing some pre-preparation of meals, but she always made sure Natalie was aware of how much she did, adding to the weight of Natalie's guilt.

"I wanted to work but I couldn't stop the self-reproach I felt at leaving them, palming them off to their grandmother to look after while their mother did other things."

"I know that feeling."

"It's with me now, even though they're grown up. And now I feel as if I've let them down all over again."

"Why?"

"When I left, Kate, my eldest, was bothered about something. She doesn't open up easily but I could see she wanted to and I didn't let her. Bree, who's in the middle and wants to take over the farm, feels restricted by Milt's way of doing things. They're so alike but they rub each other up the wrong way and now she's saying she wants to leave. And then my youngest, Laura, I don't know what's up with her. She's thrown in the hairdressing job she's had for six years to come home and...well, I'm not sure what."

"I'm the same with my sons. They're all settled now but they've had their moments. I think it's a mother's lot to worry about our kids, feel we should have been there more, done things differently. I've reconciled with the fact that we can't go back. We just have to learn to carry the guilt as best we can." Rosie cradled her mug in her hands, staring into it. When she spoke again her voice was distant. "When my husband and daughter died in that crash I blamed myself for the death of my little girl."

"You weren't there, were you?"

"No, but I'm the reason they were on the road. I'd been offered some temporary work at one of the resorts in Broome. It was day-time work for a couple of months. The boys were all at school but my husband was working too and we had no-one to look after our little angel. He was driving her up here to stay with my mum when they had the accident."

"Oh, Rosie." Natalie reached out and laid a hand on her friend's arm. "I'm so sorry."

Rosie kept staring into her mug. "I was a mess for a long time. Eventually my mum came and got me and the boys, and brought us up here. Driving past the place where my man and my angel died nearly killed me as well. Once I got here I didn't want to leave. I couldn't face travelling along that road again. This place became both my escape and my prison."

"So you've never gone south?" Natalie couldn't imagine this self-contained woman never leaving the peninsula.

"Oh yes." Rosie chuckled. "Once my boys went to Perth for high school I missed them too much. I had to overcome my fear of that road. I moved to Perth, lived there for a few years, that's where I met my other fella, but I still wasn't in a good place. Once the boys finished school I came back here. I was like you. Search-ing for some kind of purpose but I didn't know what.

"I got a job up the road at Cape Leveque. I enjoyed that and then my sister-in-law rang me desperate for help with Gabe. He came up here and somehow between me and my mum and his uncles and cousins we helped him find the strengths inside him. Living in this place helps. It's beautiful here but it's also isolated and quiet. Plenty of time and space to work out who you are. I've made peace with my demons and I'm happy. Working with my lost boys has helped me as well as them."

They lapsed into silence with only the thud of the music punctuating the night.

Rosie raised her eyebrows. "I don't always have success."

"He seems to be coming around."

"Maybe. He's got a long way to go. It just depends whether he can stick it. I can keep them busy, improve their life skills, but it's the isolation that wears them down. If they learn how to deal with that it makes them stronger."

"There's certainly a difference in Charlie since I first met him. You're amazing to take them on. It can't be easy."

"I think the same way about teachers. What a terrific job you do. I only take on one boy at a time. You have a whole class full."

Natalie stared off into the night. "I've always loved teaching. Helping children to find their potential…"

"But?"

Natalie looked back at Rosie, took a breath. "It's so much admin now. I spend less time with the children and when I'm with them I'm teaching them to standards I don't believe in. I've lost faith in the system." She stopped, took another deep breath. She'd never said that out loud before. "Once I would have fought to change it but now…I think I'm too jaded. There's no fun in it any more. I met some retired teachers while I was in Broome. They said I'd know when the time was right to retire. Perhaps my time has come."

"You don't sound sure."

"I'm not. That's what's so hard. I've built up a rapport with my class and there're a couple of young teachers who I've enjoyed supporting this year but there's a new principal and I can tell he thinks I'm old-fashioned."

"But you obviously care about the kids. Could you use your talents somewhere else?"

Natalie shrugged. "Like you do with your lost boys? I don't know if I can deal with teenagers."

Rosie laughed, a rich warm sound that echoed in the night air. "But you'll find something that makes use of your gifts and perhaps it will be the thing that helps you find the purpose you feel you've lost."

Natalie thought about that. Teaching had been something she'd felt enabled her to make a difference. Travelling and gardening would keep her busy, but if she stopped teaching what could she do that made her life meaningful and of benefit to others? And what was she to do about her marriage? Once more she looked up at the starry night and found no answer forthcoming.

Twenty-Eight

Kate pulled on an extra jumper. Sometime in the night the rain had stopped but the air in her bedroom was cold and damp. There'd been no chance the previous evening to tell her dad about the bank transfers. Laura's dinner had been a huge success and even though Kate hadn't eaten a lot, she'd enjoyed a small serve of pork, and the golden syrup dumplings had been melt-in-your-mouth delicious. This morning her stomach was rebelling again. She'd loved to have waited for the cup of tea and toast Laura had been bringing her the last few mornings but Kate had forced herself to get up early in the hope of catching her dad in the kitchen alone.

In the passage she was met by even colder air. At the other end of the long hall the back door was half open and Bree was standing just inside the screen door looking out.

"What's going on?" Kate asked, coming up behind her sister.

"Dad's out in the garden." Bree turned to look at her, her voice low. "He's weeding. I've never seen him do that before."

Kate peered over Bree's shoulder. "That's Mum's gerbera patch, isn't it?"

"Yep."

They watched as their dad added another weed to the bucket beside him and rested back on his heels. He studied his handiwork a moment then lurched to his feet.

Bree pushed Kate back and gently closed the door. They both strode into the kitchen where the door was still off its hinges and busied themselves getting breakfast. Out in the passage the back door opened.

"We should tell him about the accounts," Kate whispered. "Before Granny gets up."

Bree nodded. There were sounds of water running from the laundry and then their dad joined them.

"Good morning." His tone was cheerful.

"Hi, Dad." Kate faltered at his bright smile. She didn't want to spoil his good mood.

"Coffee?" Bree asked as she removed her own cup from the machine.

"Thanks." Milt sat in his usual spot at the head of the table.

Kate brought a plate of toast and her cup of tea and sat beside him. "We need to tell you something." She kept her voice low. Granny was in the spare room in the quarters but with the kitchen door off they might not get any warning of her arrival.

Milt looked from one to the other as Bree put a cup of coffee in front of him then slid into the chair on his other side.

"Fire away," he said.

Kate glanced at Bree who gave her a brief nod.

"It's about Granny."

He frowned. "What's she been up to this time?"

"We're not sure that she's actually been up to anything," Bree said. "It might be Aunty Connie."

"Hell's teeth."

"Don't get cross, Dad." Kate shot him a pleading look. "Just listen."

Between them they started to fill him in on the financial discrepancies they'd found the day before. They paused when they heard a sound in the passage but it turned out to be Laura. Kate beckoned her in and she listened to the end of the story.

"Hell." Milt flung out his arms and sat back in his chair as they finished. "That original payment was for your pa and granny together. Your mum must have forgotten about it in the process of setting up a new account for Granny. I just assumed she'd stopped it." He looked from Bree to Kate again. "And now you reckon the money's going to Connie's account?"

Kate pursed her lips in a sad smile and nodded.

Milt surged forward and thumped the table with his fist, making the liquid in their untouched cups wobble. "Well, that stops now. My sister's not getting another free cent from our hard work." He scratched his head. "Can one of you stop the payments?"

"Easily," Kate said.

"Good."

"Dad, what's going on with Aunty Connie?" Bree asked.

"Nothing."

"We heard you and Granny discussing her last weekend."

"Did you." Milt scratched his head again. "I should have been following up but I've...well, I've had other things on my mind. You're all part of the family business so you should know."

"Know what?" Laura's expression was puzzled. "What's been going on? What did I miss?"

"This is to do with your Aunty Constance." Olive strode into the room. She was dressed smartly as always, today in purple jumper and beige slacks, with her usual light application of make-up and a purple clip keeping her hair neatly in place. No-one had heard her coming.

"Is she trying to steal our property?" Laura asked.

"Not steal. We just want to even things up a bit." Olive sat at the table. "Has the kettle boiled? I'd love a cup of tea." She brushed at the clean wooden surface in front of her then looked up.

For a moment no-one moved, then Kate reluctantly rose to make it. All her life she'd believed her grandmother to be a selfless, kind woman with the best interests of her family at heart – her whole family. Now Kate wondered what else had happened over the years to *even things up*, as Granny had put it.

"We have to sort this out." Milt turned to his mother, his voice firm. "And I want the girls to be part of it."

"Last week you said you wanted to wait until Natalie got back."

"I'm sure she'll approve any decision the girls and I make."

Kate put a cup of tea in front of Olive and went back to her seat. Olive lifted the lid from the sugar bowl and put a teaspoonful into her cup, stirring it slowly. "I don't like being ganged up on."

"What would you call what you and Connie are doing?"

Olive looked at her son, put her teaspoon on the saucer, clasped her hands and pursed her lips.

"We've been over this, Mum. Connie has been compensated and she'll inherit your nest egg one day. She can't keep dipping her hand in."

"She's not."

Bree leaned in, spoke softly. "We've discovered you're getting two allowances from the property. And that one of them, the bigger one that used to be for you and Pa, is going to an account in Connie's name."

Olive lowered the cup she'd been raising to her mouth. It rattled on the saucer.

"Was that your idea or Connie's?" Milt asked, his tone soft like Bree's.

Olive's face paled. Kate didn't like to see her being harassed but they had to have answers. "Take your time, Granny."

Olive gave her a weak smile then turned her gaze back to her son. "When Natalie set up the new account for me I was so busy trying to get my head around that, and deal with...deal with being on my own and moving house, I assumed the old account had been closed. A couple of months ago I was visiting Constance and I was looking for some card or other. I pulled everything out of my purse and she noticed the card for the old account. I said there'd be not much in it, that you'd opened a new account in my name." She sighed. "Constance checked."

"And you decided to help yourself," Milt said.

"I didn't, I wouldn't..." Olive's chin went up. "You obviously weren't missing it."

"That's not the point, Mum. I don't know how we overlooked it but with the volume of accounts Natalie deals with...I'm sure she would have noticed eventually."

"I don't understand why Aunty Connie is stealing from us." Laura shook her head.

"She's not stealing."

"What would you call it then, Mum?"

Olive glared at her son. "A balancing up, she called it."

"Now we're getting to the bottom of things," Milt said. "Was it your idea or Connie's to siphon the money off into her account?"

Olive glanced at Kate who reached out a hand to her.

"Connie set it up, didn't she?" Kate said.

Olive's shoulders slumped and she suddenly looked like a frail old lady. "I wanted to talk to Milton about it but Constance convinced me you wouldn't miss it and—"

Milt blew out a sharp breath.

Olive sniffed and went on. "They've been struggling with this last loan they took out for more land for the boys. She said she was using it to put food on the table."

"She can damn well pay it back," Milt said.

"She can't."

"Well, she can earn it then."

"Don't be ridiculous, Milton. You and Natalie are well off. You can afford to be generous."

"We're well off, as you put it, because we've all worked hard, Natalie and the girls as well as me. And out of those earnings we also support you."

"Constance does what she can for me."

"Perhaps she could take over your cleaning, Granny," Laura said. "Give Mum a break and pay the money back that way."

"What cleaning?" Milt said.

Olive shifted in her chair. "It was kind of you to vacuum when you called in the other day, Laura, but I think it would be too much to expect Constance to come up to do that." She looked at Milt. "Natalie offered when I moved in to the unit. She's in town regularly. I'm sure she'll help me out again when she comes back."

"Natalie's doing your cleaning?" Milt gaped at his mother.

Kate was surprised. She hadn't known about that either and, by the look on Bree's face, neither had she.

"It's just a light go-over," Olive said. "I can manage most of it myself."

"It's a bit more than that, Granny," Laura said with a hint of reproach in her voice. "Mum's been doing the vacuuming, mopping the floors and cleaning the bathroom every fortnight." She ticked the items off on her fingers.

"Poor Mum," Kate said. "She's got her work cut out with this place."

"It's been very good of her to help me," Olive said.

"Something your own daughter won't do." Milt stood up and began to pace.

"I wasn't going to bring this up but Constance reminded me the other day how much I looked after the girls when they were young."

Milt stopped pacing and glared at his mother. Kate felt a surge of nausea. She pressed her fingers to her mouth. She felt bad enough first thing in the morning but this fighting made her stomach churn harder.

"You helped with her boys too. How dare Connie play that card? This property puts a roof over your head, pays all your bills, pays you an allowance. You've been well compensated for a bit of babysitting."

He spat the last words out and they splashed across the room like lemon juice souring milk. Kate held her stomach with one hand and pressed her finger harder to her lips with the other. This was all too terrible.

"I'm sorry to be such a burden." Olive's eyes watered as she looked at each of the girls, her gaze stopping at Kate. "I didn't look after you to be compensated." Her words wobbled from her mouth, sad and almost inaudible. "I did it because I love you."

Kate swallowed the bitter taste in her mouth and wrapped her arms around her grandmother. "I know you do," she soothed. Olive's small shoulders shook inside her embrace. Kate looked imploringly at her dad, who'd stopped his pacing and now looked dismayed. Bree and Laura were both out of their chairs hovering beside Olive.

"Don't get upset, Mum. You're not a burden." He reached out, put a hand on her shoulder. "This is all my fault. I should have sorted it out, made everything clear." He shook his head. "Damn it! It is clear. Connie's inheritance was all arranged. Dad's will set everything out. After he died I focused on the girls and how to manage their future."

"I don't know what to do," Olive whispered. "Constance keeps on at me to help her."

"She's had so much already, Mum." Milt squatted down beside Olive and took her little hands in his big ones. Kate sat back, fighting her own tears.

"Connie can't keep asking for more, Mum. It's not fair to you or me or my family. Dad was clear Connie had been well and truly compensated. She's not getting any more from my hard work." He looked up at his daughters. "While you girls are home we're going to the lawyer again and get this sorted out. With any luck we can get an appointment tomorrow or Tuesday."

"What about seeding?" Bree said.

"It'll cost us a half day but it needs to be done."

"What about Mum?" Kate asked.

"She's not here and this has to be dealt with once and for all."

Laura offered tissues. Kate took one, noticing tears rolling down Laura's cheeks as well. Bree remained stony-faced. Olive took a hanky from her pocket and dabbed at her eyes. "Thank you, Milton."

"I'll make some fresh tea," Laura said.

"Thank you, dear." Olive gave a little shiver. "And, Milton, do you think you could put the door back on. There's such a draught in here."

Milt opened his mouth.

"I'll give you a hand, Dad," Bree said quickly. "Won't take us long."

Kate reached for the toast. It was cold now but she buttered it anyway, smeared on some Vegemite and took a bite. Olive reached out and put a soft hand to her cheek. "I'm glad to see you eating, dear. You only picked at last night's meal."

The toast congealed in Kate's throat.

Laura put a fresh cup of tea in front of Olive. "Here you go, Granny."

Kate struggled to her feet. "Back in a moment." She wove past her dad and Bree and shut herself in the bathroom where she took deep calming breaths, willing the toast to stay down. Granny had looked at her so knowingly Kate was sure she'd guessed.

There was a tap on the door. "Come in." Kate splashed water on her face and when she wiped herself dry it was her dad standing there, not one of her sisters as she'd expected.

"Are you all right, love?"

She nodded. Tears brimmed again. He reached out and wrapped her in his arms.

"I know I'm being a sook," she mumbled into his shoulder. "But I wish Mum was here."

"Why don't we ring her?"

"No." Kate took a deep breath, stepped back and wiped her face again. "I'm all right. I just don't want Granny to know before Mum."

Milt held her at arm's length. "You know what, I've been thinking I might go and meet her while you girls are here. Spend a few days in the sun and we can come home together."

"Really? What about seeding?"

"I won't go until it's underway and Bree can manage with a bit of help, and I want to get this money stuff sorted with the lawyer but then…" His eyes lit up as if he'd just had a wonderful idea. "I'm going to surprise your mother."

"She might have left before you get there."

His smile wavered. "I don't think so."

"So Mum might be home in a week?"

"Or so."

Kate felt that was such a long time.

There was another tap on the door. It was Laura who put her head around this time. "Granny's going."

Milt pulled the door open. Olive, Bree and Laura were in the passage, all studying them with a questioning look.

"I'll talk to you soon, Mum. We'll sort out this business with Connie."

"Diplomatically," Olive said.

"I'll do my best."

Olive glanced around the bathroom. "You know if you're all going to spend so much time in here it could do with some tidying up. A few extra hooks and some shelves wouldn't go astray, Milton."

She flicked her gaze to Kate and her eye twitched. "Bye, dear."

Milt followed his mother out and Kate lowered herself to the edge of the bath. Had Granny just winked at her?

★

Bree stood next to her dad, waving Granny off. "I'll go and let the dogs out."

"Wait a minute."

She turned back. Milt was fidgeting with his hat.

"Can we talk a moment?"

"What about?"

"I wondered if you've made a decision about heading off to be with Owen?"

She folded her arms. He'd pressed her last week for a date and she'd put him off. Owen had been asking too. She felt torn between the two of them.

Milt held up a hand. "I was hoping you could stay here a bit longer, that's all. With all that's going on, we've got a few things to sort out, and the seeding of course. And then…I might need to go…well, I could be away a few days. Could you stay, keep things going here until I get back?"

He looked so worried the resentment left her. "What sort of time are you thinking?"

"I'm not sure yet. I needed to see how you were situated first. Owen must be keen for you to join him."

Bree nodded.

"I'm sorry, Bree. Once I've sorted things you can do whatever you like. All this stuff with Connie has made me think. No-one asked us what we wanted to do when we were your age. It was assumed I would work the property and she would go to university."

Bree had never thought about her dad wanting to do something else.

"Did you want to go to university?"

"Not really. Connie had the brains for that." He studied her closely. "I don't want you to feel tied to this place, like it's a duty. If you think you need to be doing something else, you do it. You've still got time to work out your own path. I'm not going to pressure you."

Bree was surprised. "Thanks, Dad, but when I go to Marla it's only temporary. I can't imagine doing anything else but living and working here."

"Like I said, there's time to decide. And if you're serious about Owen he might want something different."

Bree frowned. She hadn't thought that far ahead. "It's early days with us yet."

"Oh, right, yes. It's just that your mother…" He grabbed his collar and tugged it away from his neck. "Never mind. So you don't have to rush off to Marla?"

"No, I can stay here till you've sorted what you need to." She took a deep breath. While he was being candid she had another question. "What were you going to say about Mum?"

A dog barked and he looked in the direction of the kennels. "Nothing. It doesn't matter."

"Is Mum okay?" Bree decided to press on while her dad was being chatty.

"Why would you ask that?"

"She left in such a hurry after she'd had those tests. You told us to give her some space. But hearing about Mrs Halbot, well, I wondered if there was something you're not telling us."

The colour drained from his face. "Hell's teeth, I'm sorry you've been worried. Your mum is physically fine." He took a breath, blew it out so that it whistled over his lips. "We had a bit of an argument. It's nothing that can't be sorted but your mum's always wanted a holiday and she decided she was going. It's partly my fault. I keep putting her off."

"Then I announced I was going away."

"We both want you to do what's in your heart but I guess... well, the timing was off."

Bree's shoulders sagged.

"Like I said, your mum wanted a break. She's having a great time in the warm. She's fine."

Fear wormed its way inside her. If her mum had left over an argument that sounded serious. "Will you two be all right?"

"Of course we will." Milt threw an arm around her shoulder, gave her a squeeze. "You know what a grumpy old bugger I can be. Your mum needed some space and I've given it to her."

"Do you think she'll come back soon? Not 'cause I want to leave but...well, I miss her. Kate and Laura do too."

"Me too, love." Milt's arm stayed around her shoulder but he stared off into the distance. "That's why I want you to stay. As soon as we get seeding underway and this bloody stuff with Connie sorted I'm going to fly over and join your mum, have a few days in the sun then bring her home."

Bree wasn't sure whether to be reassured or not. Her dad leaving the property during major work like seeding for a holiday was unheard of. Something was happening between her parents and she didn't understand what.

Twenty-Nine

Natalie took a deep breath of fresh air, captivated by two little birds hopping among the branches of the shrub in front of her cabin, at one moment invisible in the shadows and the next illuminated by the sunlight glinting through the leaves, their happy chirrups punctuating the quiet morning.

At the first hint of light she'd woken, made a coffee and come outside. She liked the early morning, as the sun's rays first peeped over the horizon. The lower temperature was cool on her skin and she enjoyed the sense of taking a deep breath, a pause before whatever filled her time.

Each day started as a clean slate but was soon filled with her regular beach trips, chatting with other campers and reading, and sometimes, when Rosie wasn't busy, she took Natalie off for little tours. Yesterday they'd gone to Cygnet Bay to the pearl farm. The days here rolled on so casually and Natalie went with them; not making plans, taking each moment as it came. There were no alarms or bells, appointments to keep or lessons to plan; no-one to feed or take care of but herself. It was complete decadence in comparison to the frantic, busy life she lived at home…and yet she felt restless.

She gripped her coffee mug in her hands, stretched her legs, closed her eyes and tilted her face to the sun trying to reclaim the sense of freedom the early-morning calm usually bestowed on her.

Her phone rang, startling her. She dumped the mug, plucked her mobile from the table and saw Milt's picture. She did a quick calculation as she jabbed *accept* and put the phone to her ear; seven-thirty here would make it nine o'clock at home. Usually he'd be outside working on a Thursday at this time.

"Milt?"

"Hello, Nat."

Her stomach lurched. "Is something wrong?"

"No."

"We usually speak at night."

"I know but I haven't heard from you since last Saturday. There are things we have to deal with. This Connie stuff has to be sorted. I'll have to change some paperwork for the farm. It'll need your signature…and there are other things…Jack—"

"I can't, Milt. I'm still not ready."

There was a pause. "I wondered how much longer you're planning on staying."

She let out a sigh of annoyance. His call had frightened her but it seemed there was no real news. "I don't know but I'm not ready to leave yet."

"So you're still up on the peninsula?"

"Yes."

"It's just that originally we thought you were going to Brisbane." Once again a pause. "You could be anywhere."

"Well, I'm not just anywhere. I'm enjoying life in this community and I'm staying for a while longer." She was sharp, deflecting him.

"Okay," he said. "I love you."

Natalie looked at her phone. He'd rung off. When was the last time he'd told her he loved her? When had she said it to him? She gripped her head and groaned.

And at that moment Rosie stepped around the corner of the cabin.

She eyed Natalie a moment before she spoke. "I came to see if you wanted to go on another fishing trip."

"That'd be great." Anything to clear her thoughts. "I'd love some more fresh fish." They'd gone to the supermarket again yesterday after their trip to the pearl farm. She'd topped up her supplies but she hadn't bought much meat.

"How about we have a cuppa first?" Rosie said.

Natalie looked at the coffee she'd made earlier, unfinished and cold in the mug. "Good idea."

She made herself a fresh cup and a tea for Rosie and brought them outside.

"You all right?" Rosie asked.

"I had a call from Milt wanting to know how much longer I was staying."

"Fair enough."

They sipped from their cups.

"I miss my girls," Natalie said.

"Maybe it's time to go home then."

Natalie looked out over the grass and the little park area she'd grown used to. "It's so peaceful here."

"I know." Rosie settled back in her chair. "But I also know you can't hide here forever. The world's still out there waiting for you to re-join it."

"Dot, who I met back in Broome, said something similar. Always leave while you're still enjoying yourself."

"What is it that's stopping you getting on a plane and going home?"

Natalie could feel Rosie's penetrating look. She kept her own gaze resolutely on the treeline and shook her head.

"This thing that you argued with your husband about, can it be sorted?"

"I don't know. It all seems so hard. We've been through tough times before but this time…Something happened early in our married life. I thought our marriage was over then but we overcame it."

"How?"

"It was terrible at first. I shifted into the spare room. Eventually, my father-in-law found out about it." Natalie smiled. "He was an insightful man, Clem. Anyway, he suggested some options and eventually Milt and I talked. We talked and we talked." Natalie dragged the words out, remembering those days when talking was all they had left. "We covered everything, what had happened, what we wanted from each other, we made a new set of life rules… we had some time alone without the girls. We only had Kate and Bree then." Natalie felt a warm shiver wriggle down her spine. "We had good sex."

She turned. Rosie was still studying her, a slight smile playing on her lips.

"So can't you do that again?"

"Maybe." She thought about her earlier stilted phone call with Milt.

"Do you want to?"

And there it was. The question she'd asked herself but not in the bright light of day. She'd lost her purpose in life and somehow her marriage had come adrift with it. Natalie lurched forward and gripped her head in her hands to stop it from exploding.

"I don't know. I don't feel as if I know anything any more and I feel so guilty."

"About Gabe?"

Natalie felt heat rise up her neck.

"I'm guessing there's not a lot to feel guilty about...yet." Rosie's eyebrows lifted.

Was there? Natalie's cheeks burned now. Gabe was often in her thoughts. She'd even imagined kissing him, wondered what it would be like to be held by him, but nothing more. It was flattering to think that another man might find her attractive. She shook her head. "He's a good man but I refuse to feel guilty about the friendship we've developed."

"Fair enough." Rosie's look was open, trusting. "Everyone needs friends."

"Perhaps I feel selfish rather than guilty."

"Why?"

"I think about what happened to your family and what you went through, and my neighbour Veronica and the battle she's facing, and I feel such a fraud. What have I got to complain about?"

"This is your life, Natalie, not mine, not your neighbour's. You have every right to question your own life and what you want from it. Don't let anyone else tell you what you should do." Rosie put her hand to her chest. "It has to come from inside you."

Natalie felt a bubble of laughter rise within her. "Faye, the other woman I met in Broome, said don't let anyone *should* you."

Rosie nodded, drained her cup, placed it back on the table and stood up. "If you need more time, you take it. You know you're welcome to stay but right now if we don't get going Charlie will be getting tetchy. He wants to come fishing with us."

"I'll get my hat." The weight of decisions to be made felt lighter on Natalie's shoulders. "Thanks for the chat. I feel like I've become one of your lost boys."

Rosie nodded. "Sometimes you have to lose yourself to find yourself."

They weren't out fishing for long. Charlie and Rosie caught a decent feed of fish in quick time and as usual Natalie had no luck. She hadn't been focused on the fishing – her mind had wandered over the short conversation she'd had with Milt and then the conversation she'd had with Rosie before they'd set off. Both had stirred feelings of guilt and uncertainty she couldn't shake.

She was relieved when they dropped her back at her cabin. Charlie had promised to bring her some fish once he'd cleaned them and Rosie had given her a perceptive look as Natalie had waved them off. Now her cabin was hot. She flicked on the air-con and wandered restlessly between the rooms. She picked up her current novel but put it down again, still not happy with the way the woman was dealing with her problems. Natalie didn't believe anyone could be so resolute as to turn their back on their family.

The wind went out of her and she flopped to the bed. Hadn't she done the very same thing? She stretched out and stared at the ceiling fan going around in lazy circles. It was old and greyed by the years.

"Certainly not sexy," she said out loud then rolled over. Now she was talking to ceiling fans. Perhaps she was really losing the plot? Dust motes swirled in the stream of bright light shining around the curtain. She watched them for a while, then her gaze drifted to the bedside chest and there, poking out from under some magazines, was the corner of the little red book.

Why had it come with her? She should leave it here in a bin when she moved on. She sat up and propped herself against the pillows, then tugged it out and held it on her lap, one thumb rubbing the soft leather of the cover. Then, steeling herself, she opened it to the second chapter. Her big bold *NO* written next to the words – *The model wife should accept her husband's friends and receive them in her home*, her own statement – *but not in his bed* – the photo of the tennis party with Vee beaming out at her. She flicked to it now and the words she'd underlined when she'd been struggling after Bree's arrival in their lives. *She should not bother her husband with too much baby talk, even though he is the father and may stand a good deal of it, she must remember there are other interests in the world.*

The birth itself had been protracted and she'd ended up with a lot of stitches; her milk had been slow to arrive and then copious when it did. Life on the property was difficult. Keeping feed and water up to stock, checking their health, was daily, full-time work for Clem and Milt. It was a long hot summer and Natalie had dragged herself around, unbidden tears falling at the drop of a hat, and feeling as if she leaked from every orifice. She was constantly tired, uncomfortable and sad, but determined she could manage, and then the final nail in her coffin.

She could see back to that terrible day like it was yesterday. There'd been a country tennis carnival in Adelaide and Natalie, concerned her husband needed a break, had encouraged him to go. Brianna was three months old. The day Milt left for the carnival Olive and Clem had also been away visiting Connie who'd just had her first baby.

Natalie remembered so well her overwhelming tiredness, and Bree wouldn't settle. By lunchtime, all out of ideas, Natalie had parked the baby in the pram in the kitchen under the fan and taken Kate with her to the bedroom. She'd set Kate up with crayons and paper, put on some music and laid on the bed. She could still hear Bree's cries so she'd put a pillow over her head and that's how Olive had found her when she returned from Connie's.

Olive had settled Bree and put her to sleep, she'd sent Kate off with Clem to check troughs, then she'd made Natalie a cup of tea and drawn a chair up beside her bed and they'd talked. Olive was the only one Natalie had told how bad she felt. Neither of them had understood that she had post-natal depression but Olive had done her best to help, saying she could manage the girls for twenty-four hours and Natalie should take a break. One thing Natalie had no trouble with was breastfeeding and she had extra breastmilk stored in the fridge. She could go to Adelaide and spend the night with Milt, just the two of them away from the property.

She'd jumped at the chance. The first half of the drive she'd felt weak with failure then she'd felt guilty with relief. Relief that someone else knew how she felt and that her baby was safe and she could have some time with her husband just for themselves.

She'd arrived unannounced at the motel just on dark and pulled in beside Milt's car. The room had been in darkness and she'd thought perhaps he was off having a meal but when she knocked a light went on. She'd heard voices, had knocked more insistently, and then Milt had opened the door in a pair of tennis shorts, looking drunk and dishevelled. The shock on his face was only outdone by the look on the woman's face behind him. Veronica Halbot was wide-eyed and red-faced. Natalie remembered lurching to the side of her car and being sick and by the time she'd straightened herself up Veronica had disappeared so that Natalie could almost believe she'd imagined what she'd seen.

It had been a dreadful, sleepless night. There were no other rooms free so she'd had to stay in Milt's. He'd slept on the floor. The old rattling air conditioner had barely lowered the temperature in the stuffy room and the next morning Natalie had driven home leaving Milt to continue with the carnival.

Her life had fallen apart. Not only was she struggling with being a mother but she believed her husband to be an adulterer. She'd moved into the children's room, telling Olive it was so Milt could sleep better and she could deal with the girls more easily. She'd been consumed by embarrassment at first, thinking people would find out, then she'd felt guilty, blamed herself for not being a better wife. Whatever the reasons for Milt's glitch she couldn't bear everyone knowing about it; her parents who hadn't liked Milt from the start, her friends, everyone in the district would know.

It had been Clem's understanding and his generous offer of support and lots of talking between her and Milt that had got them through it. Eventually she had decided her marriage was worth saving, and she'd accepted Milt's adamant claim that it had been nothing more than a fumble and a kiss. She'd decided to forgive him and stay. Ever since then they'd both worked hard to make a happy marriage and, until the arrival of Jack in her home, she thought they'd succeeded.

She looked down at the book again now. When she got home from Adelaide she'd seen herself in the mirror. There were dark shadows under her bleary eyes, her hair was lank and in need of a cut, her dress faded and sack-like. Then she'd pictured Veronica and her pretty, if surprised, face; her shining, golden hair; and how the little clothing she'd had on was lacy and seductive.

In that moment Natalie had known the words in the little book were true. She flicked back to the first chapter and read them now.

A frigid or indifferent wife could be supplanted by an ardent mistress. And for the same reason she should always be clean and not permit her person to become unattractive. I must

> impress upon her the fact that love begets love, politeness
> begets politeness, and if she does her part the husband will be
> more likely to do his part, and that much depends upon her
> own individual effort.

And there it was. The words sounded loud in the empty room even though she'd only murmured them. A chill rippled down her spine again, *Her own individual effort*. She remembered how those words had stuck with her. For a long time she'd believed the affair had been her fault, that her lack of effort had driven her husband into another woman's arms. When she'd begun to feel better and she'd decided to save her marriage, she'd been able to put it into perspective and realise she wasn't to blame but she'd kept the book. She'd filled it with positive sayings – *A perfect relationship isn't perfect, it's just that both people never give up*. She and Milt had vowed that together and it had become her favourite quote out of the many she'd written in the book. Her finger trailed over Clem's funeral card. She'd noted the sad times as well as happy family events. The photos rekindled fond memories, and then there were the extra loose leaves, recipes, household hints, flyers – she'd done it all to break the book's spell. *The Model Wife* had rarely seen the light of day over the last ten years; why was she dwelling on it again now?

Natalie rose from the bed. She knew what she had to do. If she was to move forward, in whatever form that may take, she had to face up to the past and counteract it just like she had with the book. She wasn't a hundred per cent sure what that would entail but she was certain of one thing – she had to go home.

Thirty

The grey of the last few days had lifted and although the air was still cold, the streets sparkled in the weak winter sunshine as the King family drove into town for their mid-morning meeting with the lawyer. Well, four of the King family anyway. Bree still wasn't sure if they shouldn't wait until their mum came home before they had this meeting but Milt and Kate had both been convinced it should be sorted as soon as possible.

Milt turned off the main street and pulled up in front of a grand old house with a neat garden and ivy trailing along its wide verandahs. A simple sign on the fence announced *Clarke Lawyers*.

Bree glanced at her dad. "What are we doing here?"

"Couldn't get an appointment till next week at Burrows and Burrows."

"And it's a good idea not to go to the same people Granny does," Kate said from the back seat.

"You haven't used Clarkes before." Bree gave her dad a sceptical look.

Milt sat back in his seat and looked at her. "It's time for change." Bree had the feeling he meant more than just changing the law firm where they conducted their business. "If we're making fresh plans for our future I thought it was time for a new lawyer as well."

"Fair enough," Bree said and as she followed the others into the building she felt a surge of anticipation. The only time she'd felt that way lately was with Owen. A smiling young receptionist greeted them and then Phoebe Clarke stepped into the waiting area with her hand extended. "Hello, Mr King."

"Call me Milt, please."

She smiled and shook his hand then Kate's and Laura's and finally Bree's. Her grip was warm and firm. "I haven't seen you all for years. You're living on Eyre Peninsula, aren't you, Kate, and I think you were still at school last time I saw you, Laura. You've moved away too, haven't you?"

Laura looked down at the floor. "I've come home for a while."

"Which is just as well at the moment." Milt gave her an encouraging smile.

"Would you like tea or coffee?" Phoebe turned to her receptionist. "I can recommend Kelsey's skills as a barista."

"The coffee kind of barrister, not the law kind." Kelsey grinned. "I have trouble with those words."

Phoebe chuckled too and Bree relaxed a little more at the thought of the discussions ahead.

They followed Phoebe through to a comfortably furnished office. Kelsey brought their drinks and finally they all settled around Phoebe's desk with an air of expectancy. She had a manila folder in front of her and Bree could see *King* in bold letters on the front but Phoebe didn't open it. Instead she clasped her hands on top and smiled at Milt.

"I must say, Mr King...Milt, your affairs are in far better shape than some I've seen. You've got a succession plan mapped out and although it needs a few details filled in it's a sensible start." She glanced at Bree. "It seems you're the one keen to take over the property in the future but you've been given some time to make a decision. Is that why you've come today?"

"Not exactly," Bree said.

"It's more about protecting any assets we have from my sister," Milt said, then he looked at each of his daughters. "But it might be an opportunity to talk about the future in more detail while all three of my girls are here."

"And your wife doesn't want to be included?"

"She's away," Laura and Kate said quickly in unison.

Milt clasped his hands and turned back to Phoebe. "I know my wife and I are on the same page when it comes to our succession plan but this is only a discussion. Nothing would be finalised until she has the opportunity to look it over."

Bree wondered if her sisters detected the slip of confidence in his voice that she had.

He cleared his throat. "Natalie has given us the go-ahead to sort this issue about my sister."

Phoebe didn't miss a beat. "Certainly. From reading your father's will it appears your sister has been provided for already. Can you elaborate?"

Milt began to talk and Bree felt relaxed enough now to take a sip of the coffee Kelsey had made. It was good. She continued to drink. Her sisters did the same, listening to their dad's explanation of Connie's deceit, as he called it, peppered with the odd question from Phoebe, who made notes as he spoke.

Phoebe was matter-of-fact and efficient. Less than an hour later they'd said their goodbyes and were out on the footpath again with a plan in place to make sure Connie got no more than she was entitled to and a better strategy for Bree to take on the property in the future.

Milt unlocked the vehicle.

"Have I got time to whip to the chemist before we go home?" Kate asked.

"There's something I'd like to do too if we've got a few minutes," Laura said.

"We've got to get back to the seeding." Milt frowned then his face relaxed. "You've got ten minutes."

Bree climbed into the front beside him.

"Haven't you got something you need to do?" he asked.

"No."

He nodded and picked up a council newsletter that had been between them in the console. He flicked through it but Bree could see he wasn't really reading it.

"You think Phoebe's suggestions for a succession plan are sound?" she asked.

He looked up, a frown on his face. "Yes, I thought you did too when we were discussing it inside."

"I'm happy; I just wonder if Laura and Kate might change their minds and we end up with a situation like Connie's creating."

"That's fixed now, and we'll make things very transparent so there can't be any surprises for you or your sisters."

Bree pondered that. "People can change."

"Don't let your judgement be coloured by Connie. Laura and Kate are quite clear on what they're entitled to if you take over the property. It can never be equal but I think they understand that."

"Phoebe's scenario helped."

Milt chuckled and glanced back towards the office they'd just vacated. "She's got a sound head on her shoulders."

After they'd sorted the Connie thing, Phoebe had moved on to the succession plan. She'd listed off the remuneration the girls had already received and what Milt had put aside for Laura either as a start for a house or a business. Bree had raised her eyebrows at that but Kate had simply nodded. Laura had said she'd tell Bree about it later and Phoebe had moved on. If Milt and Natalie decided to leave the property and buy a house they would use a combination of Natalie's super and farm collateral to purchase it. In the event of their deaths the house would go to Laura and Kate and any money or shares belonging to Natalie would also be theirs. Phoebe had paused then and looked at each of them sagely. "The farm would be worth much more of course but that could never be realised unless Bree sold it," she'd said.

Laura's eyes had widened at that point. "That would make her an instant millionaire," she said. "Shouldn't there be some proviso that gives Kate and me a share if she sells?"

Phoebe clasped her hands together and looked directly at Laura. "Should Bree sell at some future date, whatever she realises from that sale would be from her own work which, and I'm assuming here, you have no interest in and would not have contributed to."

Laura pursed her lips. Bree imagined dollar signs flashing before her little sister's eyes but there would only be money if Bree sold and, for the moment, anyway, she couldn't picture that in her future.

"What about the business you're considering, Laura?" Phoebe went on. "The one that will be given a start with money from your family property. I don't know what you're planning but let's say whatever it is becomes very successful." She paused and smiled. "I hope it does. Anyway, perhaps some time in the future you decide to sell this highly successful business. Will you be giving Bree and Kate a share of that?"

Laura frowned and Phoebe went on. "We have to draw a line in the sand somewhere when it comes to properties and your parents are being as fair as they can be from what I can see. You have to be prepared to accept that if Bree goes ahead and takes over the property it becomes hers in its entirety and it's not without its encumbrances. She has to continue to pay your grandmother's allowance while she's alive and pay for your parents during their lifetime. This would not be something you would be expected to do, nor Kate."

Laura had shifted in her chair. "I was just wondering," she'd squeaked and Phoebe had smiled and moved on.

Bree studied her dad now as he flicked the pages of the newsletter again.

"Thanks, Dad."

He looked up, surprised. "What for?"

"For trusting me with the place."

"It's not yours yet."

"I know."

"There's still time to change your mind."

"I know."

He scratched his chin. "Do you think you might?"

She thought about that a moment then looked him in the eye. "No."

"This trip with Owen—"

"It's only temporary. We've done a lot of talking since he's been in Marla. We think our future's here even if his business is in town."

"It's not easy running a property alone."

"I'll have to employ someone when I need help." She gave him a tentative smile. "But I hope you'll be around for a while yet."

"I didn't think you liked working with me."

"I don't mind working *with* you, it's the *for* you that's tough."

Milt gave her a sharp look. "When I'm sixty-five it's all yours." Then his gaze softened, and he looked almost contrite. "I hope we can continue to work together and even after you take over the property. We both want beneficial outcomes for the place."

She nodded.

"You understand the property, managing stock..." He swallowed. "And you have some good ideas. I'm proud of the way you work, Bree, the things you achieve...you've got a sensible head on your shoulders."

Bree was speechless a moment. "You've never said...I thought you were looking for help elsewhere."

A puzzled look crossed his face.

"You spend a lot of time with Jack."

"Hell's teeth, not you too."

"What do you mean, me too?"

He shook his head. "Nothing. Look, I'm helping Jack out because he's interested in a couple of things we do differently but you're the future of our property, not Jack."

"Thanks, Dad."

He reached for her hand, gave it a squeeze. "I know I can be a bit short when we're working together."

"You think?" She raised an eyebrow.

"I really am going to try to do better."

His look was earnest but she knew it still wouldn't be easy. "It's not a one-way street. I know I can be a bit prickly too."

"You think?" he mimicked and they both laughed.

"You two sound happy." Kate climbed into the back seat. "What's happened?"

"Nothing much,' Bree said. "Just chewing the fat."

"What's Laura been up to?" Kate said.

Bree and Milt both turned to look back as Laura clambered in beside Kate carrying a large paper bag.

"What have you been buying now?" Bree said.

"Something I've had my eye on," Laura said as she stowed the bag at her feet.

Milt started the car.

"What is it?" Kate prodded.

"Boots."

"If there was something you didn't need it was more footwear," Bree said. "Have you seen how many pairs she has, Kate?"

"They were on sale at that new place," Laura said before her sister could answer. "Dad said we should shop locally."

"Hell, Laura," Bree said.

There was silence from the back seat then a chuckle from Kate.

"What?" Bree said, turning to look at her sister.

"You and Dad are peas in a pod."

Bree turned back, bristling at the suggestion, but she caught a glimpse of her dad's face as he checked the rear-view mirror and she relaxed against her seat. He was smiling and she realised suddenly that she could do far worse in life than to be like her dad.

*

The aquamarine water of the Indian Ocean rolled onto the long wide curve of beach, edging forward then slipping away. The late-afternoon tide was low, exposing shells and small clumps of weed that wobbled and swayed with each gentle wash of water. Natalie sat in the shade of the only shelter, a rustic structure of wooden posts partly thatched with ragged palm leaves, as she had done after every swim, but today her visit was tinged with sadness. Even though she'd made up her mind to go home, she was finding it hard to leave this patch of paradise and the friends she'd made.

She shifted on her towel and adjusted her sunglasses. The heat pressed on her and the breeze caressed her skin with the blessing of cool air. At home it would be freezing but at home was the life she'd abandoned and now knew she had to return to. She'd been sorely tested, come to another crisis point in her marriage and this time Clem was not here to offer her a choice. Her girls were grown up, she had no-one depending on her, but she did have a husband, a marriage that she'd invested so much of herself in. She felt stronger now. Today she'd faced up to the fact that she could stay or she could walk away but she couldn't make that decision until she'd talked to Milt one more time. Her faith had been shaken by the obvious likeness between Milt and Jack. She needed something more tangible than a simple no to the question that had haunted her for so many years. Was Jack his son?

She dug in her bag for her water bottle and her fingers brushed the soft cover of *The Model Wife*. She'd brought it with her to the beach with the intention of holding a ritual dispersal before she went home and she'd almost forgotten. She tugged it from her bag and gripped the cover, ready to rip it off, but her fingers brushed the smooth face of a photo. Under her fingers her girls gazed back at her along with Milt's proud smile. Her hold loosened and the book fell to her lap. Looking on their trusting gazes she knew that the book, like her children, her post-natal depression, Olive, her parents, the challenges of her marriage and the many other moments documented in it, were all part of her life. She flipped the pages idly with one finger then closed it gently and stared at the faded red cover. She couldn't destroy it.

At the sound of a distant vehicle she looked up and shifted her gaze left, searching. A four-wheel drive ploughed over the sand but it was white, not the dark green vehicle she'd wished for. She berated herself. Gabe was gone. She'd been beguiled by the idea of him but thankfully that was all. It embarrassed her now to think that if he'd...she might have...

"Natalie!"

The vehicle had come to a halt further along the deserted beach and Charlie was waving to her from the driver's window.

She waved back. The other doors flew open and the happy sound of children chatting and laughing drifted on the slight breeze as they made their way to the water. Charlie trailed along behind them. He'd said he'd pick her up when he brought the kids for a swim.

Back at camp her bags were packed, even though her ride to Broome wasn't till tomorrow. One of the families had a spare seat for her to travel with them. She'd booked a room at a place in the town and flights for the following day and would arrive in Adelaide late Saturday night. She hadn't let her own family know about her plans yet. Perhaps she'd ring them from Broome, or maybe Perth or maybe she'd just surprise them. She hadn't decided yet but she was ready to go.

She ran her fingers over the soft cover of the book and gave a rueful but happy thought to her morning spent cleaning and tidying her cabin. Perhaps there were some parts of her that wouldn't change, that she didn't want to change even, but she was working on the rest.

Squeals of delight drifted up from the water. She stood and slipped off her sarong. She had time for one last swim before she began her journey home.

Thirty-One

On the King property, rain had been bucketing down again from the big dark clouds gathered overhead. The ground was too boggy and Bree had stopped seeding. She pulled her ute up near the dog pens and took a deep breath. More rain was forecast, which might mean no paddock work for a day or so. The last few days had been crazy between seeding, keeping on with the tennis court – she didn't want to let that go now her dad had started it – and visiting the lawyer the day before. It had been a relief when her dad had finally driven off to Adelaide after lunch but it had meant extra work for her. Now it was late on Friday afternoon and she was looking forward to sitting back with a beer and phoning Owen in Marla. She hoped he might have knocked off a bit earlier too.

She unleashed the two kelpies from the back and fed them a bone each from the old fridge in the shed.

"We can all put our feet up for the afternoon," she said as she shut their pens.

"Bree!"

She looked across the yard towards the house. Laura was waving at her from the front gate. Bree waved back and climbed into the ute, drove over and lowered her window.

"What's up?"

"There's no water in the house. I've been out to the pump and it's switched on but it's not working."

"Damn!"

"Can you fix it?"

"I don't know what's wrong with it."

Laura's hands went to her hips. "Well, can you check? Kate hasn't been so good today and I think she'll feel better if she has a shower and washes her hair."

Bree frowned. She understood Kate was feeling miserable about the pregnancy but she wasn't sure how much of this sickness and lying around half the day was real and how much was put on. She gave a brief thought to the beer she'd been looking forward to and sighed.

"I'll take a look."

"Thanks." Laura threw her a grateful smile and went back inside.

It was another hour before Bree could join her. The sun had all but disappeared from the sky and the outside temperature had dropped dramatically by the time she let herself inside.

The water spat and chugged in the laundry pipes and then started to flow again as she washed her hands.

Laura appeared in the doorway behind her. "You've fixed it."

"I had to replace a part. It should be okay now."

"Thanks. I don't know if Kate will have a shower after all. I've got her settled in the den in front of the TV with a hot water bottle. She's really not looking good."

Bree went to check for herself. There was a quiz show playing on the TV but Kate's eyes were shut, her chest rising and falling in a gentle rhythm. Her hair fell in lank locks around her pale face and there were dark shadows under her eyes.

Bree backed away and followed Laura into the kitchen. She closed the door softly but it popped straight open again so she used more force. Her dad had done several jobs around the house before he left but he'd had no luck fixing that door.

"What do you think?" Laura looked worried.

"She looks tired."

"She said she didn't sleep much last night."

"We probably should leave her then."

"Okay." Laura chewed her lip.

"She'll be fine once she's had some sleep." Bree started for the fridge then stopped and looked around. An enticing aroma was coming from the crockpot on the bench and there was something cooking in the oven, yet the benches were clear and there wasn't a dirty dish or a spoon in sight. "Dinner smells good." She continued on to the fridge and the beer she'd been hanging out for.

"It's vegetable hotpot." Laura followed her and took a beer for herself.

"By that you mean no meat?"

"And chocolate pudding."

Bree took a swallow, wiped her mouth with the back of her hand and looked at Laura, who was watching her closely.

"I like the sound of pudding," Bree said. "Not so sure about the idea of no meat but—"

"Kate said the smell of red meat cooking makes her feel sick."

"Okay, well, I don't care, I guess." Bree remembered the rip in the back of her shirt. She'd hooked it on barbed wire as she'd climbed through a fence. "I don't suppose you run to sewing as well, do you? I've got a hole in my—"

"No!"

Bree felt mean then. She couldn't sew and she didn't enjoy cooking. Laura had made life easier while their mum was away. Bree wasn't sure she'd let her know that. "I do appreciate you cooking for us."

"I've invited someone for dinner." Laura glanced towards the door.

"Who did you invite?"

"Paul Brown."

"Mum's principal!"

"He's a really nice guy." Laura sipped her beer. "I like him."

"When have you even seen him?"

"I met him a couple of weeks ago. We've caught up several times since."

Bree grinned, tapped the neck of her beer bottle against Laura's. "Go for it. You might as well be getting some action; Kate and I sure as hell aren't."

Laura's face went pink. "Paul's not...we're taking things slowly."

Bree lifted a hand in the air. "Okay, don't be so touchy."

"I'm not but I'm wondering, if Kate's not well, do you think I should cancel?"

The kitchen door opened and Kate stepped through, a rug draped around her hunched shoulders. Bree was pleased to see she'd brushed her hair and pulled it back into a ponytail and she'd put some colour on her lips.

"What are you cancelling?" Kate fought with the door to make it stay shut then crossed to the fire and held her hands to the heat.

"I thought if you're not feeling up to it I should tell Paul not to come."

"I'll be fine." Kate pulled her face into a smile but it didn't reach her eyes. "I'd like to meet him and you've gone to all this trouble for him." She winked at Bree. "He's a vegetarian."

"Oh. I see." She looked back at Laura. "So the vegetable hotpot is for Paul, not for Kate."

"We'll both enjoy it," Kate said. "Shall I set the table?"

"I'll do it," Bree said. "For four?"

"I guess it's a bit late to call it off now," Laura said.

By the time Bree had set the table, Kate had drawn a chair up closer to the fire and was sitting staring at it. Usually she said it was too hot and stuffy in the kitchen. Bree went to her, put a hand on her shoulder. "You all right?"

Kate pulled a smile. "The sleep helped but now I feel cold. I've got a bit of a scratchy throat."

"Maybe you're coming down with something." Laura drew a chair up beside Kate's. "It's impossible to keep this place warm. Mum and Dad should install ducted heating."

"Good luck with that," Bree said.

"Do you think Dad surprising Mum is a good idea?" Laura asked.

"Should be," Kate said. "I hope it works out."

They'd discussed their parents' odd behaviour in detail once their dad had left but they were no closer to working out what was going on. Like her sisters, Bree harboured a fear there was something wrong with their mum in spite of their dad's reassurance she was simply taking a break. When he'd said he was going to join her they became more suspicious. On top of that he wouldn't say how long he would be. Bree was anxious to join Owen but she couldn't leave until her dad came back.

She glanced at the clock. Owen would have knocked off work by now.

"If you've got everything under control here I'm going to have a shower and ring Owen," she said.

"Don't be too long; Paul will be here soon." Laura almost bounced on her chair.

Bree left them to it, one pale, sad-faced sister and the other pink-cheeked with a sparkle in her eyes.

Paul arrived at the farmhouse at five-thirty exactly. Bree was coming back from the quarters as he knocked on the door. He was clutching a bottle of bubbles and a bottle of red. "I didn't know what everyone liked to drink," he said.

Laura was beside him before Bree could shut the door. She introduced him to Kate and Bree, who thought him better look-ing than she'd remembered. He wore a thick knit navy sweater over tan chinos and his hair was perfectly groomed. He obviously used product. No wonder Laura was smitten.

Laura served up her vegetable hotpot to great acclaim from Paul and Kate, and Bree had to grudgingly agree it wasn't bad but she enjoyed the chocolate pudding with ice cream more.

"So your dad's gone to join your mum at last." Paul patted at his lips with the paper napkin. "She must be glad."

"Probably more surprised," Bree said.

His look turned quizzical.

"Mum doesn't know he's coming." Laura looked at the clock on the wall. "This time tomorrow he'll probably be there."

"No," Kate said. "He couldn't get the flights he wanted. He's spending tomorrow with his cousin in Adelaide and going to the footy. He'll fly out Sunday morning."

"He may as well be enjoying himself," Bree said. "It's too wet to get the seeder going again."

"Where is your mum exactly?" Paul asked.

"Somewhere north of Broome in an Aboriginal community," Laura said.

"The Dampier Peninsula?"

"I think so."

"I had a friend who taught up there for a while. At a place called One Arm Point. He loved it but it was fairly isolated."

"I think that's why Mum chose it," Bree said.

"Have you heard about the family fun day being organised to support the Halbots?" Paul asked.

"I heard something about it while we were in town," Bree said. "They're looking for people to do things.'

"Like what?" Laura asked.

"I think they've got pony rides and face painting covered," Paul said. "And they're trying to organise some kind of fashion parade and an auction."

"Is it to raise money?" Kate asked.

"I guess," Paul said. "There was some mention of pamper packs. And I think funds will go to the McGrath Foundation or the wig library or those places country people stay at in the city when they have their treatment. There's no end of places to send money. Evidently there are a couple of other women in the district who are having treatment too. It's meant to be as much about community support as fundraising, I think."

"Perhaps I could do hair styling or manicures," Laura said.

"When is it?" Bree asked.

"The middle weekend of the school holidays," Paul said.

"I'll be back at my place by then," Kate said.

"And I'll probably be in Marla," Bree said. "You'll have to make the King family contribution, Laura."

"And Mum and Dad," Laura said, her eyes round with worry. "They'll be home by then, surely."

"I can help you," Paul said brightly. "I've been asked to join the committee and I'm a bit out of my depth. I don't know much about nails and styles but you could cut my hair if you like."

"I think the idea at these things is to get people to pay you to shave it all off," Bree said.

Paul's eyes blinked behind his glasses and he put a protective hand to his head.

"You could be my guinea pig." Laura jiggled on her seat. "I could demonstrate cutting your hair and maybe con a few other guys into having theirs cut, with money going to the fundraiser." She gave Bree a stern look. "A lot aren't prepared to shave their head but they might have a trim or a style."

"Or don't some of them go for colour?" Kate asked.

They all looked to Laura. Her rainbow hair was loose and flowing over her shoulders tonight. It was fading but the strips of colour could still be seen.

She screwed up her nose. "I don't fancy doing that in a tent. I'll stick to nails and styling."

Bree was pleased to see Kate smile along with her, even if it was at their sister's expense.

Thirty-Two

The day was grey but dry outside and the farm kitchen cold when Kate struggled in to make herself a late-morning cup of tea. Neither of her sisters were there. Laura had brought her tea and toast in bed first thing before she'd headed off into town, evidently to have breakfast with Paul even though she'd only seen him last night, and Kate had no idea where Bree was. The house was so quiet it compounded her gloomy mood.

She sat hunched over the table, her hands gripped around the hot mug for warmth, and stared at the dark glass of the slow combustion. The fire had gone out and she didn't have the energy to get it started again. Her night had been restless – nowhere in the bed could she get comfortable for long. If she was like that now how would it be later in the pregnancy when she got bigger?

She sipped the hot tea and wondered again for the hundredth time since the doctor had told her she was pregnant how she was going to manage. She had another week before Sean would be back. Their nightly phone calls were a struggle. She'd taken to making a list of things that happened each day so that she could fill their calls with chat.

She wondered at Sarah and her wild enthusiasm at the prospect of being a mother, when Kate had no such feelings. She was filled with a heavy dread when she thought of the future with a baby. She didn't mind kids but they needed to be three or more. Babies were not her thing. It wasn't from lack of experience. Sean had several nieces and nephews and they'd even looked after a couple of them from time to time but never when they were babies.

A lock of hair fell forward. She took it in her fingers, inspected it and was appalled to realise she hadn't washed her hair in several days. She sat back and groaned just as the kitchen door opened. Bree strode in carrying some bags.

"What's the matter?" she asked.

"Nothing," Kate said. "I just know what a wreck I look."

"I'm going to fix that." Laura followed Bree into the kitchen and she also carried bags. "We're having a girls' pamper day. I've bought every type of treat." She lifted a shopping bag in the air. "There has to be something in here to tempt you."

"Do you have chips?" Kate asked.

Laura's eyes sparkled. "Three different flavours." She emptied one shopping bag onto the table.

Kate sifted through bags of chips, biscuits, chocolates and lollies, then opened a bag of chicken chips and put one in her mouth. "Yum," she said between crunches. "That's just what I felt like."

"I have healthy stuff too." Laura carried her other bag to the bench. "Strawberries, bananas, crunchy rolls and ice cream."

"I thought you said healthy," Bree said.

"Ice cream's made with milk and milk is good for mothers-to-be. They need calcium."

Bree rolled her eyes and Kate chuckled. She took another chip. "I feel better already."

"That's not all," Laura said.

Bree set her bags on the other end of the table. "Evidently I have the makeover gear."

"What makeover?"

"A hair wash and trim for a start," Laura said. "Then we'll get on to facials and nails."

Kate couldn't be bothered washing her hair but to have it done for her would be rejuvenating, she was sure of it.

"And…" Laura peered into one of the bags Bree had carried and drew out a handful of DVDs. "These are from Paul."

"I don't think I'm in the mood for crime and gore," Kate said.

"I didn't pick those. He watches chick flicks as well. Have you seen *On Chesil Beach* or *Crazy Rich Asians*?" She waved a couple of DVDs in the air.

Kate shook her head.

"There's plenty more. We're going to have the best pamper day ever."

"I don't know about nails but I wouldn't mind a hair trim," Bree said.

Laura spun around. "I forgot! There's still a bag of food in the car."

"More." Kate eyed the piles she'd produced already.

"Little pies and pasties, sausage rolls. We're having a party-food DVD night."

"Isn't it Saturday?" Kate said.

"I've cancelled Granny roast night," Laura said. "I popped in to see her while I was in town and she'd organised a card game for this afternoon so I suggested she not drive out here tonight."

"Had dad called in?" Bree asked.

"Yesterday on his way to Adelaide."

"Did she seem okay?" Kate asked.

Laura nodded. "She said he explained all the assets were in his and Mum's names now, which includes the unit in town and her car. Granny was happy enough with that but said she was still worried Dad would try to get Aunty Connie to pay back the money she'd siphoned from Granny's old account."

"We've stopped those payments," Kate said. "Dad has every right to chase Connie over it but I don't think he will, do you?" She looked at Bree who shook her head.

"He might bluster about it but as long as we've tidied up all the loopholes, I think he'll let it go for Granny's sake."

"Granny must feel as if she had to decide between her children," Kate murmured. "It's awful but I think it's best she didn't come tonight."

"I'll go to see her tomorrow," Bree said.

"So..." Laura clapped her hands. "We've got the place to ourselves and we're going to have some fun."

Bree grimaced but Kate knew she'd enjoy herself; they all would.

Later that afternoon the den fire was burning brightly and the sounds of Elton John's 'Rocket Man' blared from the old CD player in the corner. The three sisters sang along, Bree the loudest, and they all had grins on their faces as the song finished.

Bree wriggled in her chair. "Is that polish dry yet?"

Laura surveyed her sisters' feet from her position on the floor. They sat in the two recliner rockers, their legs stretched out with their feet up and bright blue separators splaying their toes. She'd painted Kate's fingernails and toenails a lovely plum pink. Bree had said no to nails but had allowed Laura to paint her toenails deep red.

"Give them a bit longer," she said.

Kate picked up the CD cover that lay in her lap. "Remember when we used to have those dress-up nights and we'd pretend to be famous singers and Mum and Dad and Granny and Pa would be our audience?"

Bree groaned. "I don't want to."

Kate waggled the CD cover at her. "You always wanted to be Elton John."

Laura laughed and picked up another cover. "What about Pink? Remember when we did our own choreography to 'Get the Party Started'?"

"Dad nearly had a fit," Kate laughed.

"And then Mum took us to the Pink concert," Bree said. "He wasn't happy about that either. You were only little, Laura."

Laura puffed out her chest. "I was ten."

"I've got the hair for it now," Kate said and ran her hand over her new short style.

"Not quite," Laura said. "But I could cut it like Pink's if you like."

Kate shook the neat bob that sat just under her chin. "This is enough of a change."

"Mum and Dad really do have an impressive music collection," Bree said. "It's a pity they hardly ever play them any more."

"It's such a pain to swap CDs." Laura waved her phone. "I could put my playlist on through my speaker."

"Let's leave it for a while," Bree said.

Laura tucked her phone back in her pocket. They'd been having such a great afternoon she didn't want to spoil it with an argument over music preferences.

"Surely these nails are dry now." Bree lifted her feet in the air.

Laura leaned in again, tested Bree's small toe and sat back. "Give them another minute. You don't want them to smudge."

Bree groaned.

"Are you hungry?" Laura looked from Bree to Kate but her question was really for Kate who hadn't eaten much but half a bag of chips and a bowl of strawberries and ice cream.

"One of those little pasties would be good," Kate said.

"You two stay here while I put the food in the oven." Laura looked pointedly at Bree. "By then your toenails should be ready." She put the bag of Paul's DVDs between them. "You can decide what we're going to watch first."

They were into the second movie when Kate felt something was wrong. Bree and Laura were laughing hysterically at the TV. They'd decided to watch *Crazy Rich Asians*. It was funny but Kate could barely manage a smile. She shifted in the recliner rocker and lowered the footrest. She'd felt a bit achy on and off yesterday but it had eased. Now she was uncomfortable with a period-like pain, had been since their dinner of party pies and pasties, and it was making her anxious.

She eased from the chair and Laura glanced her way. Both her sisters had been attentive today but Laura was watching her especially closely.

"Just going to the bathroom."

Laura nodded and turned back to the TV.

The air in the passage was freezing and Kate shuddered as it sucked the warmth from her body. She wrapped her arms around her middle and walked faster, closing the bathroom door behind her.

Five minutes later she sat on the edge of the bath, dread pulsing through her veins. The cramps had stopped again but there'd been blood. She pressed a hand to her stomach and rocked gently back and forth. She hadn't wanted to be pregnant and now it was possible she wouldn't be and she was racked with guilt and fear. She wished she'd told Sean but she couldn't ring and say she was pregnant but maybe not any more. If only her mum was home. She'd know what to do.

★

Natalie sat in a cafe at Perth airport. Her current book was open in front of her but she was making slow progress. Her flight to Adelaide had been delayed and she kept looking at her watch as if it had the power to fix whatever was holding them up. Now that she was on her way home she just wanted to be there.

Her phone rang. She plucked it from the table beside her and saw Laura's photo. She pressed the phone to her ear.

"Mum, I'm sorry but I had to call." Laura's voice was full of panic. "This will be a surprise but Kate's pregnant."

Natalie pushed the phone harder against her ear. "What?"

"Or at least she was—"

"What's happened?"

"She's had some cramps…and, well Bree and I are taking her to the hospital in town."

"That's good." Natalie paced the small area by the table with one eye on her bag and tried to picture the three of them in the car. "Is Bree driving?"

"Yes."

Natalie let out a breath. That was best. Bree was more level-headed than Laura in a crisis.

"Can I talk to Kate?"

There was a rustling sound.

"Hello, Mum?"

Natalie halted as she heard the fear in her daughter's voice. "Hello, darling, you've had a lot going on."

"I didn't know…I…it's all such a mess."

"How many weeks are you?"

"Fourteen."

Natalie would have hoped that meant she was past the miscarriage stage but babies could be lost at any time.

"Tell me what's happening now. Have you been bleeding much?"

"No. Not really. Only spotting but it gave me a fright. It's the cramping feeling that's been the worst."

"How long have you been having cramps?"

"The last few days, on and off."

Natalie paused, turned and began to pace again. "Darling, you're doing the right thing. Your body might simply need rest. The doctor will know what's happening." Natalie wasn't sure if any of that was true but she couldn't hold her daughter's hand so it was the best she could do.

"We're nearly in town now," Kate said.

"Good. Can you pass the phone back to Laura?"

There was a pause then Laura spoke. "Mum?"

"Get Bree to drive right to the emergency door and make Kate wait until you bring out a wheelchair."

"Okay." Laura's voice sounded small.

"I'm sure everything will be fine." Natalie pressed a finger to her lips. She'd used that blasted word again.

"Okay."

"Ring me back as soon as you've seen the doctor."

"Okay." Laura sniffed. "Mum, do you think you'll be home soon?"

"I'm in Perth now." Tears pricked at her eyes. "But my flight's been delayed. I might not get to Adelaide tonight but I'll do my best to get there." In the broil of thoughts she pictured Milt. "Where's your dad?"

"Oh...I forgot. He was coming to surprise you."

"Where? When?"

There were muffled voices then Laura was back. "He's still in Adelaide. We think his flight to Perth leaves in the morning."

Natalie had never imagined Milt would do such a thing. "Don't worry. I'll ring him. You take care of Kate."

"Okay."

Still clutching the phone tightly, Natalie let her arm drop to her side and said a silent prayer for her daughter. Then she selected Milt's number. It rang and went to voicemail. She ended the call and tried again.

"Natalie?" Background noise competed with his voice.

"Where are you?"

"In Adelaide. Just leaving the footy. It was a close game. North Adelaide and Norwood."

"Did you know Kate was pregnant?"

There was a pause. "Yes. She didn't want me to tell you."

Pain stabbed at Natalie's chest. Why wouldn't Kate want to tell her she was pregnant?

"What's going on?" Milt asked.

"Kate might be losing the baby..." The voice that she'd kept steady for the girls wavered now.

"How? She was fine when I left. Off-colour but fine."

Natalie curled her fingers and her nails dug into her palms. "She's had some cramping and some spotting."

"Hell."

"It doesn't mean she's losing the baby." She said it as much to reassure herself as Milt. "You should go home to be with the girls."

"I can't, Nat. Not yet anyway...I've had a few drinks."

On the departures sign above her a word began to flash beside her flight number. Cancelled. Natalie pressed her fingers to her lips and closed her eyes.

*

Laura hated hospitals at night, with their wide echoing corridors and darkened rooms, or those with a dim light on and hushed voices, staff who walked on silent feet and suddenly appeared, like the woman who'd just come out the door Kate had been taken through. Helen was her name. Laura didn't know her but Bree seemed to think she was a midwife. The only available doctor had been called to the nursing home and Laura hoped Helen knew what she was doing when she'd wheeled Kate away.

Now Laura gripped Bree's arm and they both rose to their feet as Helen approached. She was about their mum's age, wore a thick blue cardigan over her uniform and looked like she hadn't slept in a week.

"Your sister and baby are okay."

Laura let out the breath she'd been holding.

"The baby's heartbeat is strong but I've had a quick chat with Dr Strauss and she wants her to have an ultrasound."

"Can she have it here?" Bree eased her arm from Laura's grip.

"I'm afraid not. Your best bet is the Women's and Children's in Adelaide."

"Adelaide!" Bree's surprise echoed Laura's.

"It's the weekend. We don't have the staff or the equipment here."

The large clock on the wall behind Helen ticked over to midnight.

"Okay." Bree glanced at Laura then back to Helen. "How soon does she need to have it?"

"Doctor wants her to spend the night here. Can you take her tomorrow?"

"I can be here first thing."

"Excellent. I can let them know you're coming."

"Can we see her?" Laura asked.

"Of course, but don't stay long. She needs sleep and so do you if you're going to drive her in the morning." Helen's face lifted in a kind smile. Behind her a buzzer rang. She sighed and set off down the corridor and disappeared into the room where a red light glowed. The cavernous corridor fell silent. Laura shivered and reached for Bree's hand.

Bree frowned at her but continued to hold her hand. "Let's say good night to Kate."

★

Natalie had just settled in her hotel room near the airport when her phone began to ring again. She snatched it up from the bedside table, took a breath when she saw Laura's photo and pressed the green *accept* button.

"Mum, she's okay." Laura spoke before Natalie had a chance. "The baby has a strong heartbeat."

"Oh, that's good news."

"She couldn't see a doctor—"

"Why not?"

"She was already on another call-out but there was a midwife there."

"Helen?"

"Yes, Helen."

Natalie felt a small wave of reassurance. Helen Bond had years of experience and was well regarded as the local guru for all things to do with pregnant mums and babies.

"Helen rang the doctor and she wants Kate to have an ultrasound in Adelaide tomorrow to see if they can work out what's going on. Bree's going to drive her."

"Where's Kate now?"

"In the hospital. Helen said she'd keep an eye on her."

"That's good."

"Mum...Kate said before we left to tell you not to come back...it's such a long way..." Laura's voice was sounding small and uncertain again.

"I was already on my way," Natalie said firmly. "My flight was cancelled, engine trouble. But I'll be back as soon as I can tomorrow."

"It'll be great to see you." There was relief in Laura's voice. "We've missed you."

"I'll be there as soon as I can." Natalie glanced at her watch and did the calculation. It was almost one am at home. "You girls get some rest and I'll ring in the morning once I know when I'll get back to Adelaide."

"Okay, night then. Love you, Mum."

"Love you too, darling, and love to Bree."

Natalie glanced around the minimalist hotel room and gave a brief thought to the cabin that had been her home for almost two weeks. She'd enjoyed the guilty pleasure of total indulgence and time to herself and now...She picked up her phone and rang Milt.

He answered straight away.

"Bree's driving Kate to Adelaide tomorrow for an ultrasound but everything's okay for now," she said. "I've been delayed in Perth."

"I can meet them."

"I wish I was home."

"You being home wouldn't have changed anything, not about Kate and the baby anyway." He paused. "It'll be good to have you back, Nat. Let me know when you have an arrival time. I'll pick you up."

Thirty-Three

Laura shoved one hand in her coat pocket and waved with the other as Bree drove away. The sun was still a dull glow beyond the horizon and the early-morning air was freezing. Her breaths puffed out in little clouds in front of her. The cat wove between her legs. She bent down and picked him up, pressed her face to his soft warmth.

"Thank goodness you're here, Bubbles." The thought of staying alone in the big empty house behind her filled her with dread. This morning she'd suggested she drive Kate but Bree had been adamant she would. Then Laura had thought she could go too but they didn't know how long Kate would be in Adelaide and someone had to stay home to feed the animals and keep an eye on things.

Laura took Bubbles and went back inside. The house felt brooding instead of the happy place she'd grown up in. She never liked being here alone but today she was extra uneasy.

Nothing had been quite right since she'd come home. Her mum had been distant then left, there'd been the money trouble with Granny and now Kate could lose the baby and Laura was all alone.

She would have gone to town for a while to see Paul but he'd had a full day of schoolwork planned. There was always her grandmother to visit but it was way too early and she'd seen her only yesterday.

She locked the back door behind her and went into the kitchen where at least there was some warmth from the fire Bree had brought back to life before she left. Bubbles immediately jumped from her arms and settled himself on the mat in front of it. Laura took off her coat and hung it over a chair. She turned on the radio, found her favourite station, increased the volume then looked around. Everything was tidy except for the two cups and plates she and Bree had used for breakfast. She stacked them in the dishwasher then turned and leaned against the bench. What was she going to do to keep busy?

Her gaze drifted to the cookbooks on the top shelf above the desk. It had been a while since she'd done any baking other than the pudding they'd eaten when Paul had come for dinner. The supplies in the freezer were getting low and cooking would keep her busy and her mind off the empty house.

She'd just put her first batch of choc-chip biscuits in the oven when her phone rang. It was her dad checking in. Laura cleaned up – she'd learned to do that as she went, especially seeing there was no-one to help her – and had moved on to mixing a batch of little cakes. She was about to pour the mix into the patty pans when her phone rang again. This time it was Bree to say they'd arrived at the hospital in Adelaide and were waiting for Kate to be seen. The cakes were in the oven and she was considering making some slice when her phone rang next. It was Spritzi and they talked so long Laura nearly had a disaster with the cakes but she managed to get them out of the oven before they were ruined.

Talking to Spritzi had left her exhausted for a moment and made the house seem even more deserted. Laura threw herself into making slices and had two in the oven before she decided she'd done enough, just as her phone rang again. It was Bree to tell her both Kate and baby were fine but Kate had something called cervical insufficiency, which put simply meant the baby could be in danger of falling out too early. They would be staying in Adelaide overnight while the staff assessed her further and decided what to do.

Laura looked at the clock on the kitchen wall. It was only just past midday and now she had the whole afternoon, the night and possibly another day to get through before anyone came home. The time stretched out before her like a long empty road. She set the fire going in the den and made herself some lunch. Then she saw the plate of scraps she'd meant to feed the dogs. Outside the day had barely got any warmer and the sun was well hidden behind a bank of grey cloud. She fed the dogs, left their kennels open and hurried back across the yard. Inside she locked the back door again and took her lunch into the den. Bubbles followed her and made himself comfortable in front of the open fire.

"Oh, to be a cat," Laura said then flinched at the sound of her own voice loud in the room.

She chose one of the DVDs they hadn't watched yesterday, snuggled into her dad's recliner rocker and took a bite of her lonely sandwich.

*

Natalie strode up the ramp into the arrivals area at Adelaide airport and tried to gather some strength for what lay ahead. It had been almost two days since she'd left the remote community on the Dampier Peninsula and she was exhausted with lack of sleep and worry for Kate. She'd slept poorly at the motel and not at all on the flight from Perth, and with the time difference between states it was nearly midday already. Back on the beach she'd been feeling smug about her decision to return home. She'd thought she'd put the jumbled pieces of her life back together but now that she was almost home the doubts returned.

"Nat."

Milt raised a hand in a brief wave from the back of the crowd of mingling passengers and those greeting them. She wove between the people and stopped in front of him. The sounds of happy reunions drifted around them but she felt like she was made of wood.

"Welcome home," he said and wrapped an arm around her.

She had a bag in each hand and fell against his chest but there was no solace for her there. Instead it felt as if everything was unravelling all over again.

His lips brushed her cheek. "I've missed you," he said.

She pulled back. "How's Kate?"

He took one of her bags and they started walking. "She's okay."

"The baby?"

"Is okay too."

"Thank goodness."

"Bree and I spent a couple of hours with her this morning. I don't fully understand the condition she has but the doctors reckon it can be managed."

"I want to see her."

"I'll take you straight there."

Natalie found her case and Milt took it and her to the four-wheel drive. They were out of the carpark and on the road to the city before he broke the silence between them.

"You are all right, aren't you, Nat?"

The question surprised her. "What do you mean?"

"Physically. It's just that the girls were worried we…well…they thought perhaps you were hiding something to do with the tests and, to be honest, they got me a bit edgy. I thought you would tell me if there was but after you left I began to wonder too."

"I am perfectly f...well. I've done a lot of walking and swimming and I feel so much fitter. I'm tired now from the travel but I'm okay." She felt a pang of guilt. "The girls weren't too worried about me, were they?"

"They missed you." He grinned, teeth clenched. "I did my best but...well, it's you they turn to when things are bothering them. I can't believe Kate kept the baby news to herself. You didn't have any idea she could be pregnant?"

Natalie shook her head. "I thought she was a bit peaky before I left but she'd always said they weren't having kids."

"She was feeling unwell and went to the doctor." Lines creased Milt's forehead. "It was a surprise and...she hasn't told Sean about it. She says she doesn't want the baby."

Natalie's heart broke for her daughter.

Milt shook his head. "I know this has been a setback but when she first got the news, well, I don't understand how she wasn't excited."

"I can." There'd been a time, it was hard to imagine it now, when Natalie hadn't wanted children. "I know exactly how she feels."

"You do?"

"I didn't yearn for babies, Milt. I liked our lives the way they were. Babies were expected of me." She gave a brief thought to the old book then banished it. "I wish I'd known."

"Kate was adamant she wanted to wait until you came home to tell you. Only Bree and Laura know besides me."

"How are they? I've been getting the odd text but not much news."

"They're both fine."

Natalie pursed her lips. There was that code word again.

"We're going to be grandparents, Nat." He grinned and turned into the hospital carpark.

Natalie let out a sigh of relief that was a mix of concern for Kate and a niggle of excitement at the thought of being a nanna.

It was an emotional reunion in Kate's hospital room. Bree was there and Natalie couldn't help the tears that rolled down her cheeks as she hugged both her girls. Milt stayed a moment to get the latest on Kate and then left them in search of coffees.

The girls were full of questions about her holiday but Natalie wanted details from Kate.

"They've told me it's a simple procedure. They're going to put a stitch in," she said. "I'll still be able to have a normal delivery..."

Natalie gripped her daughter's hand, seeing clearly the uncertainty in her eyes.

"Are you staying in Adelaide?" Kate asked. "They're doing it tomorrow morning."

"Of course I'm staying."

"It's good to have you home, Mum." Bree moved up beside her and put an arm around her.

Natalie saw tears brimming in her eyes. A rare occurrence for Bree. Tears filled her own eyes and then Kate started sobbing. Bree and Nat leaned over the bed and hugged her.

The door opened behind them.

"Hell's teeth, what's happened now?" Milt said.

*

The credits of the last movie were rolling up the TV screen when Laura jolted awake. She'd spent most of the afternoon watching movies, though the last one had been through the backs of her eyelids, she had to admit, and now a noise had woken her. She looked around for the cat. He was no longer in front of the fire but sitting at the closed den door staring at the base of it.

"Did you knock something, Bubbles?"

He gave her a scathing look and turned back to the door.

She lowered the footrest, stood and scanned the room. Nothing appeared out of place but the fire had burned low. Perhaps a log had shifted and that had been the noise. She moved towards the door then paused and tilted her head to one side. There was a sound in the distance. She snatched up the remote, pushed mute and listened. The dogs were barking. She'd put them back in their kennels before she started the last movie knowing it would be dark by the time the movie finished. There was agitation in their barks, like when there was someone or something about.

Laura picked up her phone. There were two missed calls from Paul an hour apart. The last had been only a few minutes ago. She frowned at the screen wondering why she hadn't heard them then realised the phone was on silent. She flicked it back to full volume then let out a surprised yelp as it immediately started ringing, then followed with a loud scream as someone pounded on the window behind her.

*

Natalie looked around the large, well-appointed hotel room. She'd been so excited by her beautiful accommodation in Broome but now she couldn't care less about the luxury of her surroundings. She moved across to the window as Milt deposited their bags. The night was clear and she had a bird's-eye view of the river and the brightly lit Adelaide oval where a football game was in progress.

She studied Milt's reflection in the glass as he joined her.

"Port Adelaide are playing," he said as he gazed out of the window. "I haven't heard who's winning but it must be nearly over." He turned and picked up the television remote.

Natalie watched in the window. She crossed her arms and gripped tightly as annoyance rose up inside her. There were obstacles that needed to be faced, decisions to be made, and when at last they were truly alone Milt wanted to know the footy score. The blare of the television filled the room. He stabbed at the remote to turn it down, glanced at her then back at the television.

"It's over. Port won."

Natalie could already see ant-like figures streaming across the footbridge fifteen floors below.

The television went silent.

"This place is pretty flash, isn't it?" Milt opened a cupboard. "Should be for the cost, but everything within easy distance of the hospital was booked. Steve offered us a bed of course but they live so far out. Lucky Bree has a friend a bit closer to stay with… Are you hungry? We could go down for dinner…"

Natalie took a breath, swallowing her irritation. She dropped her arms to her side and turned, knowing he felt as awkward as she did. "We need to talk, Milt."

The expectant look on his face crumpled. He dragged his fingers through his hair. "I know. It's just that this business with Kate and the baby…"

"I was already on my way home. Kate and the baby are perfectly safe for the moment and we've got time and space."

"Fair enough, but I'm having a drink." He opened the fridge and took out a beer. "Would you like something?"

She shook her head. She wanted no more distractions. "I left because we'd hit a wall I felt we couldn't overcome. I tried to talk to you about it but…"

"I didn't listen." He slumped into an armchair, placed the beer on the table unopened and clasped his fingers together. "Can you tell me now?"

Natalie sat on the couch trying to get her thoughts in order. "It was the worry I might have cancer that set me off, made me look at my life under a microscope. Then I got the all-clear and I was determined to make the best of the soul-searching I'd done. I think I almost flew out of the consulting room. I wanted to grab you and jump up and down and laugh and dance and…" She swallowed as she remembered arriving in the waiting room.

"Instead you found me consoling Vee."

"Yes. It was selfish of me but you and I never talked about what happened…what nearly happened."

"Vee had a cancer diagnosis, you didn't."

She lifted her gaze from her hands and stared straight into Milt's eyes. She could see his confusion. "I know that, Milt. We couldn't do a happy dance in front of Vee but there were plenty of times after that…you didn't once ask me how I was, how I felt."

"Relieved? Happy? Guilty?" She frowned, tipped her head to one side. "What a release it was after the worry," he said. "I felt that way and assumed you did too. I kept thinking it would be nothing and imagined us celebrating. I'd planned to take you out to dinner and a show that night."

"You…how?"

"I researched it while you were having the tests. I kept thinking it would be positive news and I was all ready to ring and make bookings as soon as you came out but then…when I came across Vee, I was swamped with guilt when she was in the position I feared you might have been. If Bob had been with her… well, anyway, there wasn't a chance to talk about it then and life went on."

Natalie was amazed he'd felt the release and then the guilt like she had. And the fact that he'd been planning to surprise her… She stopped herself from being distracted. She needed to tell him the rest.

"I didn't want life to go on as it had been, Milt. It was a wake-up call for me and I've had plenty of thinking time since." She drew herself up straighter in the chair. "I've come to some decisions about changes I want to make to my life."

"Hell, Nat." He sat forward. "What changes? That sounds serious."

"Some of it's simple stuff, more about streamlining for me, but others, well, all of it really, rests with you."

"Me!"

"I need you to speak to me honestly about Jack."

Milt leaped to his feet but she held up a hand. "Don't brush me off. I think I can deal with it if Jack is your son but I need to know the truth…now." She blew out a breath. She'd said it and very soon she'd have her answer.

"Hell's teeth, Natalie. I've told you Jack is not my son."

"But how can you be sure?"

He rubbed his forehead, sighed and sat down again.

"I know he can't possibly be because Veronica and I…" He sucked in a breath. "We never consummated what we started that night after the tennis carnival. I told you back then nothing actually happened. We'd both drunk too much, we were both feeling lonely. I know that sounds like excuses again but I faced up to what I did at the time. The fault was mine, not yours. There was nothing between Veronica and I except some groping in the dark, a clumsy kiss and then, before you'd even arrived that night, we'd sobered up and realised how stupid we'd both been." He shook his head. "I hate that it's caused you pain all over again, Nat, but you believed me then, why won't you believe me now? There is no possible way Jack Halbot could be my son."

Natalie saw his hurt, felt her own as she remembered that terrible time.

"Natalie?" He broke through her scrambled thoughts. "You do see Jack can't be my son, don't you?"

He was asking her to believe his story all over again. She'd done it once before. If it hadn't been for the likeness she'd seen in Jack and Milt she'd still believe it. "He looks so like you."

"He looks like Bob. Don't you remember Bob's fair curly hair...back when he had hair? And we have the same colour eyes. People who didn't know Bob and I used to think we were brothers on the tennis court." Milt shook his head. "Jack's not my son, Nat. If it weren't for the fact that it would raise questions we don't want raised I'd do one of those DNA tests they talk about."

Natalie thought about the time when tennis had been such a big part of their lives. Milt had been a star player for their local club but he'd given up the game he loved so they could avoid the Halbots. He'd done it to save their marriage. When Jack was born he'd been like a question mark for Natalie, niggling inside her, but by that time her relationship with Milt was healing. She didn't want to open the wound again so she'd never raised Jack's parentage. Now she had to believe what he was telling her if she was to save her marriage all over again.

She drew in a long, slow breath and made her decision. "I believe you."

"Thank God." He lurched across the space between them and gripped her hands.

"You know if it was anything else, an illness, a financial blow, I could have talked to a girlfriend. Brenda and I shared so much but you can't even tell your best friend that your husband's had a fling with his tennis partner. Once you cross that line there'd be no keeping it a secret."

Milt nodded. "I don't know how it did stay a secret. As it turns out my parents both knew but they obviously kept it to themselves. Veronica told Bob something plausible that made it possible for us to be neighbours but never socialise again. It's amazing there's never been a hint of a murmur when usually everyone knows everyone's business in the district." He reached out his hand and took hers, gave it a gentle squeeze. "Thank you."

She looked at him, puzzled.

"It's been a huge burden I've put on you," he said. "Thank you for not telling anyone…our daughters. Thank you for staying true to me when I tested your love in the worst possible way. Thank you for trusting me like I trust you."

His gaze was steady. It bored through her but she didn't flinch away. She gave a brief thought to Gabe. Was imagining a kiss the same as actually doing it? She'd known deep down there was nothing more than friendship with Gabe but she had been tempted. A long time ago Milt had taken temptation too far but he'd paid a price for it already. She had to either forgive him and stay or walk away.

"Are we going to be okay?" he asked.

She stood and wrapped herself around him, felt the comfort of his arms around her. "Yes."

They clung to each other then Natalie felt the rumble of Milt's stomach against hers.

He pulled back. "Sorry, I haven't had much to eat today. Do you fancy continuing our discussion over dinner?"

Natalie gave the cosy furniture and the big bed another look. "Let's just order room service and stay in."

*

Back at the farm Laura was sitting at Paul's feet, her head on his knee, enjoying the reassuring feel of his hand stroking her hair. He'd heard about Kate's trip to Adelaide on the town grapevine and had tried to call Laura, knowing she hated to be out at the farm alone. When she didn't answer he'd driven out but the house was locked up and he couldn't make her hear him so he'd kept calling, knocking on the door and finally on the den window, when she heard him.

Once she'd recovered from her fright she'd made them a pot of tea and they'd settled in the warm den.

"I can stay the night if you like."

Laura sat back. "Would you?"

"As long as you've got a spare bed."

She smiled. He was so proper. It was one of the things she liked about him.

"That's something we have plenty of."

"I'll have to leave early. I need to be at school by seven-thirty."

"Seven-thirty! You've been working all weekend."

"Regardless I have to be on the grounds first thing on Monday. It's always busy. Anyway, some of my weekend was spent on the fundraiser." He reached out and lifted a strand of her hair, which was almost back to normal now. "When I mentioned you were available for haircuts etcetera there were a couple of people interested and one woman who thought you'd be just the thing for her mum. She doesn't want to leave the house and is badly in need of a makeover."

"Where does she live?"

"In town. She's lost her hair and borrowed a wig from the wig library but she's not getting on with it very well. Her daughter thought she could do with a pedicure as well but she can't talk her into visiting the salon."

"I suppose I could go to her."

"It might help drum up some awareness for the fundraiser. A couple of the committee have pulled out for various reasons and one of our sponsors too. I think we might have to cancel."

"That'd be a shame. I thought there was lots of interest."

"There was, still is, but there's not enough time to get everything happening for the date it was planned for."

"I wish Mum was here. She'd have some ideas."

"So do I. Her class misses her and Eloise and..." Paul adjusted his glasses. "I miss her."

"Do you?"

"She's an exceptional person, your mum."

"I know."

"And she's also experienced. We have a lot of young staff, me included. She's a steadying influence."

"Have you told her that?"

Paul looked thoughtful, grimaced. "Maybe not. I assumed she knew."

"Perhaps you could tell her when she gets back."

He nodded, gave her that absent-minded professor look that made her heart skip. Laura nestled her head on his lap again and he resumed stroking her hair. She could almost purr, it felt so good.

Thirty-Four

Natalie, Milt and Bree were at the hospital first thing the next morning, only to be told Kate was already in theatre. That had been a shock – the day before, Kate's procedure had been planned for closer to lunchtime. They'd been reassured it was a shuffle of the theatre list and that both Kate and the baby were well. While they waited they decided Bree would return home and they'd waved her off with Milt giving last-minute instructions. Now he paced the small space left empty by Kate's bed.

Natalie patted the extra chair the nurse had found for them. "Sit down, Milt."

"Do you suppose she's told Sean?" he said.

"I don't know."

He shook his head. "I don't understand how a mother can't want a baby. Will she change her mind, do you think?"

"I don't really know her reasons. Perhaps she'll have some counselling." Natalie shook her head, overwhelmed again by guilt that she hadn't been there when her daughter had needed her – perhaps another of the things she couldn't discard.

"You said you changed your mind once Kate was born."

"I'm not Kate so I can't speak for her." She gripped his big hand in hers. "It was different for me. I liked the no-baby lifestyle but all our friends were having babies and you were so keen to be a dad...when I found out I was pregnant it took a bit of getting used to the idea."

"I thought you lost your spark in the early days of your pregnancy because you weren't well."

"That didn't help but I worried I wouldn't be a good mother."

His other hand went over hers. "You're a wonderful mother."

"I grew into it but it wasn't easy. When they put Kate in my arms I wasn't overcome with that surge of maternal love everyone says you get. It took me a long time to get used to being a mum."

"We were both learning, Nat. I remember being too scared to hold her in case I dropped her."

"Your mum was a wonderful help back then."

Milt scowled.

"No matter what's happened between us since, I was so thankful for her in those early days. She fussed and clucked and rocked and sang, she got meals and did washing while I sat in an exhausted heap."

"We were both a bit overwhelmed."

Natalie chuckled but there was no mirth in it. "I felt like I was just getting into my stride and along came Brianna and I sunk again even lower the next time."

"You had to physically recover. Hers wasn't an easy birth."

Natalie shuddered even now at the recollection of the stitches she'd needed. She had been a mess physically and mentally after Bree's birth. "Now, when I look back, I know I was depressed but I didn't understand it then."

"And I made it worse."

Natalie tensed. "Between us we weren't much chop. I felt guilty I wasn't a good mother and then I felt I'd been such a terrible wife I'd driven you to Veronica's arms."

Milt lurched to his feet, crouched down beside her and gripped both her hands with his. "Don't you dare feel guilty, Nat. I made a stupid mistake but it was me who did it, nothing to do with you. I'm just sorry I didn't understand better what you were going through...how you felt after the babies."

"I should have told you but I didn't understand it myself and I didn't know how to talk about it. Olive understood, but her way of dealing with it was to help with the children. We never discussed it again but I knew she was watching me. I had to work hard to hide the cracks." She looked steadily into his eyes. "So I can relate to the way Kate's feeling."

The door to the room opened and Kate was wheeled in. Natalie reached for her daughter's hand while the nurses finished getting her settled.

"All went well," one said as she lifted the chart from the end of the bed. "Now it's some rest for you, young lady." She turned to Milt and Natalie. "It's not visiting hours but I hear you've travelled a long way so you can stay for a few minutes." Her gruffness was swept away by her brief smile. "I'll leave you to it."

"Mum." Kate's lip trembled.

Natalie leaned down and held her daughter close. "Just breathe," she murmured. When she felt Kate relax she sat back. "One day at a time, darling."

"They want me to stay in Adelaide for a few days once I'm out of here. I could ask one of my friends but I'm not ready to explain..."

"Don't worry about anything," Milt said. "We'll sort something out."

Kate's eyelids were heavy. Natalie patted her hand. "Sleep now. I'll be back later."

They waited until she drifted off then let themselves out.

"I can book another room at the hotel we were in," Milt said as soon as they were outside.

Natalie shivered and pulled on the coat she'd been glad to retrieve from her car. After her weeks in the west she was feeling the cold. "Let's think on it for a while. I'm not sure if we'd be better somewhere like Glenelg rather than the city. A place where we can get some fresh air, maybe walk on the beach." She looked up at the grey sky. "Even if it's freezing."

"Shall we find somewhere for coffee and a bite to eat?"

Natalie nodded.

They'd only just finished eating when both their phones rang. Natalie's call was from Laura. She filled her in on Kate, told her Bree was on her way home and that they were staying on with Kate for a while. Natalie sent Laura a cyber-hug. The brightness was back in her daughter's voice and that buoyed her own spirits.

Milt's call ended at the same time.

"That was the stock agent. I've got sheep to get ready for the sale. Bree can manage but we're seeding as well—"

"Why don't you go home, Milt? I can look after Kate. It's only a few days and then we'll be home."

"What about Sean?"

"I'll talk to her about that when I go back later."

His phone rang again.

She did some Google searches for two-bedroom apartments hoping to find a place where Kate could have some space. They were all rather pricey.

Then her phone rang too, a number she didn't know. "Well, that was unexpected," she said as she finished the call.

"What's happened now?" Milt asked.

"That was Veronica." Natalie stared at the phone in her hand. "She'd heard about Kate and wanted to know if there was anything she could do while she was in Adelaide." She looked at Milt. "She's offered us her apartment."

An hour later Veronica was letting them inside. And Natalie felt a strange sense of deja vu.

"This is very good of you, Vee," Milt said.

"It's the least I could do. You've both been so kind since my diagnosis. Jack has certainly appreciated your hospitality. And as I told Natalie, I'm going home in the morning so this place will be empty. I've got a week off from treatment so I'm making the most of it."

The woman who gave them a tentative smile was so different from the one who was in pieces the last time they saw her. The apartment seemed more welcoming too; it was fresher than it had been the last time and brighter in spite of the grey day.

Milt took Natalie's case into the spare bedroom. "Bit of a waste of time really," she said. "I haven't got much with me for cold weather but I guess I can make do till I get home."

"I've got several jackets and cardigans here," Veronica said. "We're about the same size. You're welcome to help yourself."

Milt came back and stood beside them. "Thanks again, Vee." Natalie knew he was anxious to get home now that things were sorted in Adelaide.

"I'll drive Milt over to pick up his vehicle," Natalie said. "Then I'll go back and visit Kate. I'll probably spend the afternoon at the hospital." She wished Veronica was going home today too but evidently she had an appointment first thing tomorrow before she headed off.

"I'll make us some dinner," Veronica said.

"I could buy something on my way back."

"Let me. I don't always feel like it but today's a good day and it's more interesting to cook for two."

"If you're sure." Natalie agreed and she and Milt stepped back into the cold winter's day.

★

Laura went to the back door at the sound of a vehicle. The dogs weren't barking and she was expecting Bree but it was her grand-mother's car pulling in by the back gate.

Just as Olive opened her door there was a sharp shower of rain. Laura plucked an umbrella from the rack and dashed out to meet her.

"Thank you, Laura dear," Olive said as they reached the shelter of the verandah.

"I didn't know you were coming out today."

"I've come to stay. There's a case in the car. I gather you're on your own." Olive fixed her with a sharp look. "The rumour mill is running rife in town. I thought I'd better come out and find out for myself what's going on with my own family before one more person tries to tell me."

Laura felt bad she hadn't rung Olive but Kate had been deter-mined to keep her baby a secret, at least until she'd had the chance to talk to Sean.

Another vehicle cruised across the yard and came to a stop. This time it was Bree.

"Come inside out of the cold." Laura waved to her sister over Olive's shoulder. "I'll put the kettle on."

Bree didn't stay for a cuppa, she'd bought one on the way. She stopped long enough to change her clothes and accept the sand-wich Laura made her before she dashed out to do sheep work.

Faced with her grandmother's steely look across the table alone, Laura wished her sister was still there.

"Kate's okay," she squeaked and cleared her throat.

"And the baby?"

"You know about the baby?"

"I put two and two together and got three quite some time ago."

"Kate didn't want to say anything until she'd told Sean."

"You seem to know about it, and half the town, judging by the comments I heard in the supermarket this morning."

"Oh."

Olive sat back with her cup of tea. "You'd better fill me in."

★

Natalie slipped quietly onto the seat beside Kate. Her daughter's eyes opened instantly.

"Oh, Mum, it was you earlier. I thought I'd dreamed you up. And Dad."

"He's gone home but he sends his love. How are you feeling?"

"Tired. I'm always tired."

"That should pass soon."

Kate's lip wobbled again. "I don't know what I'm going to do."

"About what, exactly?"

"The baby?"

"Termination, you mean?"

"Oh no." Kate shook her head sharply. "Sean would never forgive me."

Natalie blew out a soft breath. "You've told him?"

"Not yet but I know he'll be happy."

"But you don't feel the same?"

She shook her head. "I'm a total weirdo, I know."

"You're not weird." Natalie reached for her daughter's hand. "You're entitled to your own feelings. Not everyone wants to be a parent."

"Dad said you went through a rough patch after Bree was born?"

"Did he?"

"He was such a rock, Mum. I was too scared to talk to Sean. You weren't there."

"I'm sorry."

"Don't be." She gave a wobbly smile. "I hadn't expected Dad to be the one to help me through it but he was great."

"He loves you…and so does Sean. Don't you think he should have the same chance?"

"He won't understand."

"How do you know? He wasn't expecting to be a father. It will be a shock for him too but he's a level-headed bloke and he loves you. You'll work it out."

Kate still looked doubtful.

"When's he due back? I don't understand how he hasn't worked out something's up. You usually ring each other every day."

Kate chewed her lip. "I sent him a text yesterday morning and said I'd be out and about and I'd message when I was free to talk."

"I think that time has come, don't you?"

Kate nodded.

"Where's your phone?"

"In the drawer."

Natalie gave it to her. "You ring and I'll go and get a coffee. Is there something I can bring back for you?"

"A bag of salt-and-vinegar chips?"

Natalie smiled. "I'll see what I can find."

★

Back in the farmhouse Olive was determined to stay no matter how much Laura assured her that she and Bree could manage. She'd insisted on taking over the spare room Kate had been using. Laura gave in and retrieved Olive's case, overnight bag and a swag of groceries from the car, thankful that she'd checked the room after Paul had left. She'd tidied and put fresh sheets on the bed for him the night before and then this morning he'd left it looking as if no-one had slept in it.

"I'll leave you to settle in," she said, wondering why Olive had brought so much stuff with her for a night or two.

"Who does this belong to?"

Olive held a jacket aloft, the brown tweed one that Paul had worn yesterday, his weekend coat, not the long-lined deep blue one he wore to work.

Laura could say it was Sean's but they both knew he wouldn't wear a coat like that.

She stepped across the room and took it from Olive's grasp. "It's Paul Brown's, Mum's principal."

"I know who Paul Brown is but what's his coat doing in this bedroom?"

Laura thought of several lies, he'd left it after dinner one night, she'd put it there for safekeeping, but she was tired of telling half-truths. "He knows I don't like it here on my own. He stayed last night. Here in the spare room." She tried to keep a straight face. It was the truth but it so nearly hadn't been. His caressing of her head had led to her kissing him, which had got fairly heated, and clothes being loosened, but Paul being the gentleman he was had slowed things down and they'd gone their separate ways to bed. That hadn't stopped her dreaming about him and what it might be like to have shared her bed with him.

"I see." Olive's sharp gaze bored through her and Laura scurried from the room.

Her dad arrived home then and not long after that Bree came back. Laura put the kettle on again, made some more sandwiches and set out an assortment of the sweets she'd baked.

Over their late lunch, Milt told them about his brief trip to Adelaide and the latest about Kate, then he and Bree made a plan for the rest of the afternoon and he went to change. Bree took off again and Olive disappeared. Laura stood, hands on hips, surveying the messy kitchen. Once more she was in the role of family servant.

She scratched Bubbles under the chin, put another log on the fire and started collecting plates. Out in the passage beyond the kitchen door she heard her dad.

"You don't need to stay you know, Mum. The girls and I are fine and Natalie will be home in a few days."

"Laura's had a lot of cooking to do. I can help her at least."

Olive's softer voice could barely be heard beyond the door but Laura's shoulders lifted. "Thanks, Granny," she muttered. At least someone realised her workload.

"You should have told me she was here on her own last night," Olive went on. "I could have come out."

"We had other things on our mind."

"Did you know Paul Brown was here?" Olive's voice rose a notch. "All night."

Laura stopped collecting plates and moved closer to the door.

"Well, Laura wasn't on her own then, was she."

"Don't be smart, Milton. They were out here alone – unchaperoned."

Laura held her breath then let it out as her dad laughed. "Times have changed, Mum. They're both adults and quite capable of making their own choices."

One of them bumped the kitchen door. Laura scurried back to the table. Her dad stuck his head in. "I'm off, love. See you around six."

"Okay."

Olive bustled past him, shutting the kitchen door behind her. Laura carried the plates to the sink to hide her wide smile. "Would you like another cuppa, Granny?" she asked over her shoulder.

"Good heavens no, I'll turn into a cup of tea. I thought we could plan what we'll have for dinner tonight. Do it together."

Laura bent to open the dishwasher. "That's a great idea, thanks."

Thirty-Five

Kate lay still as the release of sleep slipped away. She'd been dreaming she was home but the stiff sheets with the crunch of the plastic underneath told her immediately she was still in hospital. She opened her eyes. The room was only dimly lit and her mum was sitting near the window reading a book in a shaft of late-afternoon sunshine. She looked up as Kate stirred.

"Hello, sleepy head."

Kate stretched. "I can't believe how much I want to sleep."

"Listen to your body." Natalie came over to the bed and brushed some hair from Kate's face. "And talk about how you feel."

Kate wriggled up in the bed. "Did you have post-natal depression, Mum?"

"It was hardly talked about in my day but I definitely had something."

"I can't imagine you being a mess. I haven't even had the baby yet and look at me. You're so strong."

Natalie smiled and shook her head. "There are people who can help these days. I had your gran. She was supportive in practical ways."

"What about Dad?"

"I didn't really tell him how I felt. I thought if I told him I wasn't coping...well, it's silly and all long ago now. We need to focus on you." Natalie placed a hand on Kate's cheek. "I know it's not always easy but you should talk to Sean about how you feel and get him to tell you what he's thinking."

There was a soft tap on the door. They both looked up and Kate's heart gave an extra thump as her husband stepped into the room.

"What are you doing here?" she squeaked. When she'd called him he'd said he'd be there the next morning.

"That's a nice welcome." He strode to the bed and wrapped her in a gentle hug. "I left the truck at your parents' place and brought your car."

Kate nestled against him, relieved and anxious at the same time.

"You made good time then," Natalie said.

"Hello, Natalie." He grinned and released Kate. "Let's just say I got here as fast as I could."

Kate watched as her mum went round the bed, hugged her husband and planted a kiss on his cheek.

"I'm glad you're here. I'll head off now."

Kate gave Natalie a pleading look. She wasn't ready to face the talk she knew she and Sean had to have. "You don't have to rush away, do you?"

"I've got a few things to do." Natalie gathered her things and pressed a kiss to Kate's forehead. "You two need some time and I'll be back tomorrow after lunch. Ring me if you want me to bring anything." She squeezed Kate's hand, her gaze piercing. "You need to talk."

Kate chewed her lip as Sean turned away to wave Natalie off.

The door closed softly behind her and he came back to the bed and took Kate's hand. "This is not where I expected to find you after two weeks away."

"It's not a place I ever imagined I'd be."

"You're okay?"

She nodded.

"And…" He glanced in the direction of her stomach. "The baby?"

"Is strong and healthy." She explained the tests and procedures she'd had and when she finally stopped he let out a sigh.

"I wish I could have been with you. I would have come back sooner if I'd known."

"You wouldn't have made it. It all happened so quickly."

He drew up the chair her mother had vacated and took both her hands in his. "So tell me what happened? It must have been a shock to head to the hospital and be told you were pregnant."

Kate chewed her lip. She recalled the firm squeeze of her mother's hand, her knowing look.

"I knew I was pregnant before that."

Sean frowned. "I don't understand."

"It wasn't much before," she said quickly. "I hadn't been feeling well and I went to see my childhood GP. I thought she was going to say I needed a tonic or something and instead she told me I was pregnant."

"And you didn't think to ring me with that news?" He looked hurt now.

"Of course I did but you were so far away and my mind was a mess. I didn't know what to do."

"Except you could tell your family but not me."

"I didn't tell them at first but Dad found me one night. I was miserable, the smell of meat cooking and…well, it all came out and then Bree and Laura knew. I swore them to secrecy though.

I was planning on telling you as soon as you got back. I just couldn't get my head around it. We weren't going to be parents, Sean. It was all such a shock."

"How do you feel about it now?"

A lump formed in Kate's throat. "When I thought I might lose the baby I was even more of a mess. I thought it was because I'd wished it away. I felt so guilty."

He kissed her softly on the lips. "I don't think wishing can end a pregnancy, Katie-Q."

"I'm sorry I didn't tell you sooner. I didn't want you so far away driving all that way worrying about me and thinking about a baby and in the end that's just what's happened."

Sean studied her a moment. She could see he was full of questions and he had every right to be.

"I'm sorry, Sean."

"Don't be sorry." He took her hands in his steady, comforting grip. "I know we didn't plan to be parents. We said no to intervention but nature has made it possible...I won't pretend I'm not excited at the news of a baby but what about you?"

"I still can't believe it and if I'm honest I'm not sure how I feel about being a mother but they've been helpful here at the hospital."

He leaned closer and locked his gaze on hers. "So apart from wishing you weren't pregnant you hadn't thought about... termination?"

Tears pricked at her eyes. "No." The guilt she felt when she thought she could lose the baby had been all-consuming. "I've talked that through with a counsellor already. She said she'd come back once you were here."

"We'll get all the help we can, Katie-Q," he murmured and wrapped her in his reassuring embrace.

Kate closed her eyes and let the tears roll down her cheeks, not with sadness but with hope that things might just work out.

★

It was dark when Natalie knocked on the apartment door.

"I'm sorry, I forgot to give you a key," Veronica said as soon as she opened it. "I should get one out now for you before I forget."

She went off to the kitchen and Natalie followed, her stomach responding to the delicious aroma wafting out to greet her.

"Here you are." Veronica held out a key.

"It really is good of you to let us stay here."

"Our pleasure. How is Kate?"

"Looking much brighter when I left. Sean was interstate when it all happened but he's there now." Natalie hoped Kate was being honest and open about her feelings with Sean. Her own experience made her worried about her daughter's mental ability to cope but at least there were doctors and counsellors who could help her if she needed.

"That's good."

Natalie glanced at the casserole she could see in the oven. "That smells inviting."

"It's lemon chicken. Something simple but just what I felt like. I hope you'll like it."

"It's one of my favourites too."

"Great." Veronica nodded for extra emphasis.

They were facing each other over the small table setting, being painfully polite.

"It'll be another ten minutes or so. Why don't you sit down?" Veronica brushed a hand over her spotless bench. "I can get you a drink. I don't have any wine but I think we've got brandy in the cupboard. I've gone off alcohol. Or there's orange juice or mineral water."

"Mineral water's fine but I can get it myself."

"That's okay, you sit down."

Natalie went back to the lounge and sat in the chair she'd last occupied over five weeks ago. She looked around the tidy room. This time it was comfortably warm. She watched Veronica through the arch as she poured the drinks. She was impeccably dressed as always, with a mustard-coloured cardigan over a white tee and blue jeans, and a leopard print scarf knotted neatly at her neck.

"Here you are." She handed Natalie a glass, sat on the couch, kicked off her shoes and tucked her feet gracefully beneath her. Her face was perfectly made up and her long blonde hair piled neatly on her head. She was undergoing treatment for cancer and looked as if she'd stepped out of a fashion magazine while Natalie felt like she'd been pulled through a prickle bush backward.

"You're looking good," Natalie said. "How do you feel?"

"Surprisingly well. I get tired but I'm not nauseous. Just off food a bit with a funny taste in my mouth. That's why, when I have a yearning for something, I try to cook it. Bit like when I was pregnant and had all those weird cravings."

Natalie nodded. She hadn't ever had cravings. They both sipped their drinks and she searched frantically for something else to talk about. How had it come to this? Sharing an apartment and a meal with the woman she'd tried to avoid for most of her married life.

"When's Kate due?" Veronica broke the silence.

"End of December."

"You might have a grandchild for Christmas." She clapped her hands. "How exciting. I don't suppose you've had a chance to shop for baby things yet?"

"No." Natalie hadn't given that a thought.

"I can't wait to have grandchildren. I don't imagine Jack will be first. He doesn't even have a girlfriend. The girls might though, once they come home from their travels..." Her face fell. "I'm sorry. I'm raving on. I might be pushing my luck expecting to see grandchildren." Tears glistened in her eyes.

Natalie's heart softened. She moved across and sat on the couch.

"Don't talk like that. You're strong."

"I try to be."

Natalie lifted an arm, hesitated then put it across Veronica's shoulders. Immediately she rested her head against Natalie.

"You've got a loving family supporting you." Natalie patted her. "You'll beat this and you'll get to enjoy grandchildren."

"Thanks." Veronica sucked in a deep breath. "I get a bit over-whelmed by it all every so often."

"One day at a time." Natalie was using the same advice she'd given Kate.

"I just need to go home for a while, see Jack and Bob, walk in my garden."

The oven timer buzzed. Veronica lifted her head then gasped and put her fingers to her lips. Natalie looked down to see what she was staring at. Several strands of golden hair lay on Natalie's black top.

"They warned me it would happen. I found some this morning on my pillow." Veronica flicked frantically at Natalie's shoulder.

"Don't worry about it."

"There's more in my brush each time I do my hair. I don't want to lose it. It's the one thing I can't face."

"Oh, Veronica. I can't imagine what you're going through but I'm sure you can do it." Natalie reached around her again and pulled her close. They sat like that a moment longer, then Veronica sniffed into a hanky and shuffled upright.

"There's lots of time to think over your life when you're having treatment." She wiped her eyes and looked at Natalie. "I never apologised to you—"

"There's no need." Natalie flapped her hands, not wanting to have this conversation.

"Yes, there is. I'm sorry, Natalie. I cringe when I think of what I did. I was young and stupid and drunk. I can't think of any other excuse for what happened. Not that anything much did happen," she added quickly, her cheeks turning pink.

"It's past history now," Natalie said, glad that she and Milt had talked things through or she didn't know how she'd manage this conversation.

"All those wasted years."

Natalie frowned.

"We're neighbours. We could've seen more of each other."

Natalie recalled the photo of their last social tennis day, the smiling faces. "We can't change the past."

"I know." Veronica flopped against the back of the couch and dabbed at her eyes again then a grin tugged at the corners of her lips. "Do you know the reason I gave Bob for not wanting to talk to you? I told him that Olive had been rude to me." She pressed her fingers to her lips. "Poor Olive."

"It's not so hard to imagine," Natalie said.

Veronica snorted. "She can be outspoken, can't she? You're a saint to have lived with her all these years. Anyway, I told Bob you defended her and said some awful things and that I was extremely hurt. He's such a softie. I felt bad lying to him but I could never tell him the real reason I wanted to avoid you all." Her eyes widened. "Not even now."

"He won't hear it from me."

"We managed to keep our distance and then over the years it became a habit. Bob and Milt gradually made contact again. Did you know?" Veronica barely paused for breath let alone an answer to her question. "Earlier this year I came home to find them having coffee on the back verandah. Jack was with them. They were talking sheep but it was quite a shock to see them together. Then I felt bad that because of me they'd been denied that friendship." Veronica's tears flowed again.

"Milt had a part to play in that too." Natalie leaned in and put an arm around Veronica. "Maybe we need to follow the men's lead. Keep the past in the past and move forward."

"You're such a good person, Natalie."

Natalie stared at the sparkling glass coffee table. Was she? Not always – she had her flaws just like everyone else – but she tried to be a good person. She'd worked out there was a difference between that and being a dogsbody and there were things she was going to change.

The strong aroma of the casserole wafted around her. She moved Veronica gently upright.

"That chicken should come out. How about I dish up the food and we eat it on our laps?" she said.

Veronica nodded.

"I don't suppose there's anything on TV?"

"We subscribe to something." Veronica blew her nose and stood up to get the remote.

"Find us something cheerful."

By the time they were settled back with their food and a comedy show on the TV, Veronica had composed herself again.

Natalie's stomach gurgled a welcome to the casserole. "This is absolutely delicious, thanks, Vee."

The other woman looked up from her plate and smiled. "That's the first time you've ever called me Vee. You've always called me Veronica, even before…well, anyway, no-one else but my mother calls me that."

Natalie smiled and tucked into more of Vee's lemon chicken.

*

Milt and Bree had gone to bed but Olive and Laura were settled in the den watching another movie from Paul's collection, *Ladies in Black* this time. Halfway through the movie Olive had asked Laura to pause it while she went to the toilet and when she came back she had a Cherry Ripe bar in each hand.

"I brought a few supplies with me. And I thought in the morning we could plan the rest of the meals for the week."

"The week!"

"I know your mother will be home but she'll want to settle back in, look after Kate. If the meals are organised that's one less thing to worry about."

"I suppose." Laura had imagined her mum would take over the cooking as soon as she returned home.

Olive passed one of the chocolates to Laura and wriggled back in her chair. "This is fun, isn't it? Just like old times."

Laura nodded, bit into the soft, rich chocolate and pressed play again. She and her grandmother had often watched TV together, especially on weekends. They were special times. Her sisters were out or away, her parents visiting friends and, not being one to watch movies, Pa would go off to bed. That's when Granny would bring out her lolly stash. There'd been a better selection on TV back then or if there wasn't, they'd hire a video and then, when she turned thirteen the family got their first DVD player. The two of them had watched so many movies together through all those changes.

Laura glanced at Granny, who was intent on the screen. She knew they'd discuss the movie once it was finished and even again over breakfast. If it was a musical, Granny would hum the tunes for a week or so after, and she'd catch Laura's eye and they'd laugh.

She reached out and squeezed Granny's hand. "Thanks for the chocolate."

Olive smiled. "You're welcome."

Thirty-Six

Two days later Natalie pulled up outside her back gate. She paused for a moment to take in the house and let out a sigh. She was glad to be home. Not all the pieces of her life were back together. She and Milt had finally cleared up the Jack issue but there were others to be worked out. And some of the pieces had fitted back in different ways, like her renewed acquaintance with Veronica. She wouldn't use the word friend just yet, but they'd made a start.

Bubbles looked up briefly from his chair as Natalie approached the back door.

"So glad to see you too," she said as he nestled back into the cushion. She couldn't blame him; it was a freezing cold day.

Her arms were loaded with bags and she cringed and held her breath as she shouldered the wooden door, but there was no bang. She hooked the door with her foot and it swung away from the wall to reveal a rubber stopper. She continued on up the passage, feeling the old house wrap around her in welcome. She placed her bags against the wall, making her first stop the bathroom.

When she came out she heard a thud from the kitchen. Someone was home. She opened the door. Milt was on his hands and knees by the desk with a tape measure stretched out beside him.

"Hello."

He sat back abruptly, bumped his head on the desk. "Hell's teeth!"

"What are you doing?" she asked as he lumbered to his feet, rubbing at his head.

"Measuring up for a new desk."

"What's wrong with the old one?"

"Not big enough, Bree says." He held his arms out. "Welcome home, Nat."

She stepped into his embrace. It had only been two days since he'd left her in Adelaide but it seemed much longer. Kate had been discharged the morning Veronica went home and they'd gone back to the apartment. Sean had spent the day in the city doing some jobs for the family business and Natalie had kept a watchful eye on her daughter, tempting her with food, keeping her amused so she'd rest. The following day she'd gone out and given them space. She'd spent nearly all day at Burnside shopping centre where she'd wandered, lunched and shopped. She'd had no idea how much stuff you could buy for babies these days and hadn't been able to resist selecting a few basic clothing items and a couple of soft toys. She hadn't shown Kate and Sean her purchases. Last night she'd cooked the two of them dinner then this morning she'd driven home.

"How's Kate?" Milt asked as they pulled apart.

"Doing well. Better since Sean arrived. They're staying one more night in Adelaide then they'll come here tomorrow before they go on home."

"Is she up to that?"

"Physically, the doctor says yes. The mental stuff, we'll have to see, but they've organised an appointment for her with someone closer to home."

Natalie pulled her sleeves lower and shut the kitchen door to block the cold air from the passage; she was still adjusting to being back in winter. She glanced around the room. Everything was neat and tidy and something was brewing in the slow cooker. Her gaze rested on a vase of gerberas in the centre of the table. She bent over them.

"What a beautiful combination of pinks."

"Laura bought them."

She smiled. "I see someone's weeded my patch." She'd noticed as she'd come in the yard.

"I did."

"Thanks." That was something he'd never done before. "Where're the girls?"

"Bree's out checking troughs and Laura's gone with Mum into town to do some shopping."

"Was Olive here?"

"She's been staying the last couple of nights, helping Laura with the cooking. They've been thick as thieves. You made good time. We didn't expect you till lunch." He crossed to the coffee machine. "Would you like a cup?"

"I'd love one." Natalie watched as he set the machine in motion. "I don't think I've seen you do that before."

"Just because you haven't seen me doesn't mean I don't know how." He brought the coffee to her. "I had one a while ago."

He rubbed his hands together and put more wood on the fire. The kitchen door popped open and he shoved it shut. "I did try to fix that while you were away."

"I see you've done the back-door stopper."

He nodded.

"And there're hooks and a shelf in the bathroom."

"Something I should have done years ago." He was inspecting the desk again.

"And what did you say you were doing there?"

"While you were away Bree and Kate did the BAS and they both complained about the cold up in the dining room. Bree thought we could make this corner of the kitchen into a proper office, get a bigger desk, move the computer. And in the summer it's cooler here with the aircon."

"Great idea." Natalie took a sip of coffee.

Milt looked back at her, hands on hips. "Do you know what they discovered while they were going through statements?" She shook her head, more interested in the fact that the girls had done the BAS. She'd be making sure Bree kept that up. There'd been talk of shifting the office years ago but nothing had come of it. Perhaps she should go away more often but she wasn't going to say that out loud. "We hadn't stopped the payments going into Mum and Dad's joint account."

Natalie sat forward. "I'm sure I did that?"

"No."

"No wonder I was having trouble making things balance. I'm sorry, Milt. I don't think I've been on top of the bookwork lately."

"I'm sorry I haven't been much help to you in that department. I'm going to improve."

She raised her eyebrows.

"This new corner office is a start and we can talk about other things I can do later, but guess who was draining that old account?"

"Not Connie?"

"Yes, Connie." He waved his hands in the air. "Mum had allowed it, of course, but Connie had wheedled it out of her playing the 'poor me, I didn't inherit the farm' card."

Natalie was instantly angry with her sister-in-law. She'd been given so much over the years. Clem had been very generous with his daughter, but then Natalie felt a little sorry for Connie. "She's never had her own separate income."

"You're not making excuses for her, Natalie."

"I guess she didn't get a choice about the property like our girls have."

Milt's eyes flashed with anger. "I didn't get a choice either. It was expected I would work the property. No-one asked me what I wanted to do. I had a duty to take it on."

"But I always thought you loved the property, the work, the lifestyle." She had questioned so much of her own life in the last few weeks without thinking her husband might be questioning his.

"It's not always been easy but it has been a good life. I just get annoyed when it's assumed I had a choice in the matter. Connie was expected to go to uni and I was expected to run the property but sometimes I wonder if I'd grown up in the town or in the city, perhaps I could have done something else."

"Like what?" It was hard to imagine her Milt as anything but a farmer.

"Fly planes." He threw his arms out, knocking some papers off the desk.

"Really?"

"No." He gave her a sideways look as he bent to pick up the papers. "But I often wondered about the life of a fireman."

She smiled. "Every little boy's dream."

"Maybe."

The reflective look on his face made her pause. Perhaps he truly had thought about it.

"You were in the Country Fire Service for years; you could go back or you could join the Emergency Service."

"I'm too old."

"Milt, you're turning sixty next birthday. That's not old. They don't knock back volunteers who've got two strong legs and a level head on their shoulders."

Milt shrugged and went back to the desk. She watched him take some more measurements and thought back to her early days on the property.

"It's funny, isn't it?" she said. "When we were first married I really wanted to become more involved in the running of the property."

He looked back at her. "But you had your teaching."

"I know and I loved it but I sometimes wonder if I'd been allowed to learn more about the stock and become more involved than cooking and paperwork and roustabout duties, perhaps I might have...learned to be more help in other ways."

"You just told me we're not old. It's not too late."

She thought about that as she sipped her coffee and he kept fiddling around the desk. When she'd left home she'd questioned her existence and part of the reason had been the knowledge that her own sixtieth birthday was only two years away. While she'd been away she'd worked out there were still plenty of things she wanted to do with her life. "I love the property but my interests have changed and I don't think we're too old to try something new."

"Which reminds me, I haven't told you about the paperwork the girls and I sorted with the lawyer last week. Everything's in our names now, yours and mine until Bree decides what she wants to do."

"I thought everything was in our names already."

"Not Mum's unit in town and several other assets. We were joint owners with her but now it's just us. We've paid for that place, for her car, and Connie's not going to get her hands on them."

"Fair enough." She could see Milt's temper rising.

"And I've made it clear to Bree that she needs to decide whether she wants to take the place on or not, before I turn sixty-five."

"We discussed that after Clem died."

"We'd started talking about a decision date but we hadn't made it definite."

"You can't push her, Milt. I think she wants to stay on the property. This thing at Marla is only temporary."

"I know." His look softened and he sat in the chair opposite her, his big hands resting on the table. "I've talked with her about it. I wanted to be clear that Bree has a choice."

Natalie suddenly understood what he was trying to say. "Because you didn't."

"Yes, but I don't want to be like my father and die with my boots on either. I want you and I to do other things, maybe move off the property to our own place while we're young enough to start again…travel."

Natalie couldn't believe what she was hearing. Her husband and the word travel.

"I've given Bree time," he said. "But there's a line in the sand and if she doesn't want to stay we'll sell the lot, buy a motorhome and go around Australia."

"Wait." Natalie glared at him. "What do you mean a motorhome?" There was no way she was moving from her big house to be confined in such a small space.

Milt chuckled. "That got your attention."

She relaxed. He'd been teasing her. Once upon a time he'd done that a lot. So much had changed in their lives in recent years.

Later in the day Natalie strolled back down the passage. She'd been up in her bedroom unpacking and had added another layer to her clothes for warmth. She paused at Laura's room and looked in. The bed wasn't made but the rest of the room had been tidied up at least. She moved on. The next door was firmly shut. Olive was resting in there. Natalie wasn't sure how long her mother-in-law planned to stay but if she was still here tomorrow night, Kate and Sean would have to sleep in Bree's spare room.

She let herself into the kitchen where Laura was on her own, chopping vegetables. Bree and Milt were both working outside.

Natalie gave her daughter a hug. "That soup we had for lunch was delicious."

"Thanks. Granny made the bone broth the day before."

"What are you doing here?"

"Preparing a stir fry."

"Can I help?"

"Sure." Laura passed her a chopping board, a knife and some carrots.

"Dad said you and Granny have been doing lots of cooking."

"The freezer's full again." Laura glanced over her shoulder and lowered her voice. "Why did Granny move into town?"

Natalie paused her chopping and thought about Olive's announcement not long after Clem's death that she'd found a unit in town. Natalie and Milt had both been taken by surprise. "She said it was something she and Pa had planned to do and she wanted to have her own place."

Laura stopped chopping too. "You and Dad didn't ask her to leave?"

"Of course not. Why would you think that? Did Olive say—"

"No. Granny hasn't mentioned it but...we've spent a bit of time together while you were away and...well, I think she's lonely."

"It was her choice to move."

Laura winced. "While you were away I cleaned for her and when I told Dad you usually did it he got cross."

"I don't know why; he knew I did it."

"I don't think he realised how much you did. Anyway, yesterday Granny and I gave the lounge and dining room here a going-over."

"That was kind of you. I hope Olive didn't overdo it though."

"She mostly sat in the chair and gave instructions but she said something while she was dusting the photos. She said if she didn't live in the unit it would be less work for you."

"I suppose she's right. I didn't mind at first but recently...I've been thinking I'd investigate some home help for her."

"I think she made a mistake," Laura said.

"A mistake?"

"Moving into town. I think she'd rather still be here at the farm with her family." Laura went back to her chopping and Natalie felt the stirrings of guilt. It had been Olive's decision to move but she'd been happy to help her, encouraged her even. Natalie had started talking about making over rooms, delighted at the prospect of being totally in charge of her own home after all those years of sharing. She remembered making a joke about not needing to form a committee to make changes any more and Olive's response. It had been swift. "That's why I'm moving. I've never had a place of my own," she'd said. It had taken Natalie aback.

She'd often hated the fact she couldn't make decisions about her own home but that had been Olive's lot as well. She'd moved into Clem's family home with her parents-in-law and they'd only moved to a retirement home a little before Milt met Natalie. Like Natalie, Olive had never had her own space.

"Mum, there's something else."

Natalie dragged her thoughts back. Laura's voice had that edge to it again.

"I've met someone. I really like him and…he's…he's someone you know."

Natalie's heart froze as she imagined Jack Halbot's smiling face, his hand on Laura's hair, but then she remembered he wasn't Milt's son so…

"It's Paul Brown."

"Oh." The breath she'd been holding rushed out.

"Mum, I know you don't like him."

"It's not that I don't like him."

"What then?"

"It's nothing. I'm glad you've met someone."

"He thinks you're great."

"Does he?"

"He's raved about what a fantastic teacher you are and how you're willing to share your experience with the new teachers and watch out for them."

"Did he?" That was a big surprise. "Well, that's kind of him. He has nice manners and he's…he's a…"

"A nice young man." Laura giggled and hugged her. "I'm so glad you're home, Mum. And you look so well." Laura pulled back. "Bree and Kate and I were worried. We thought perhaps there was something wrong and you weren't telling us."

"Nothing wrong that a holiday didn't fix." Natalie picked up her knife again. There were things between her and Milt that she could never talk to her girls about.

Olive came in then. "Anyone for a cuppa?"

Laura flicked the kettle on. "Sure, Granny."

A few minutes later the three of them were around the table with their cups.

"Milt said you were staying at the Halbots' apartment," Olive said. "How is Veronica?"

Natalie took in Olive's sharp look and the formal tone she'd taken when she mentioned Veronica. Milt had said his mother knew about the night he and Vee had been together and yet she'd never let on to Natalie.

"She seems to be holding up well," Natalie said.

"Treatment improves all the time."

"She's trying to stay positive. She was looking forward to coming home." Natalie thought about the evening they'd spent together. After they'd eaten Veronica had talked about how much she missed her garden and Natalie had talked about how much she longed for a garden, and she'd been invited for a visit to the Halbots' property. "She'll be here until next week. I thought I'd call in and see her."

"Really?" Olive's tone was censorial.

"She has a beautiful garden. I'd like to see it properly. Get some ideas. It's a shame we haven't kept in touch. We both thought we should change that."

Olive remained silently stony-faced.

"Are you planning on doing some gardening?" Laura asked.

"I'm thinking about it."

"Gardens are a lot of work." Olive sniffed. "You won't have time."

"Veronica's is all planned out. She has certain jobs for each time of the year and she has watering systems in place. You know she can even set them going from her phone?"

"Modern technology, Mum." Laura smirked.

She turned to her mother-in-law. It was time to offer an olive branch, she thought, and smiled at her pun. "I'd like your advice, Olive."

"I don't know anything about gardens."

"We could do some planning, get some help, learn together. The front garden would look pretty with a border of roses, don't you think?"

Olive's sharp gaze softened. "Clem would have liked that."

"We could go the day after tomorrow, once Sean and Kate have left," Natalie said. "And, Laura, I'd like you to come too."

"To look at gardens?" Laura groaned.

"I thought you might be able to give Veronica some advice. Her hair's starting to fall out and it's upset her more than anything else."

Laura tapped her lips. "I styled a few ladies while they were having cancer treatment when I was still at the salon and Paul's got me lined up to do a home visit for another lady."

"I'm sure Veronica would be pleased to have you visit her."

Bree strode in at that point. "Well, it's all right for some. Dad and I have been working."

Natalie smiled at her middle daughter. Bree was working like a trojan doing as much as she could before she left for Marla on Friday. "Would you like a coffee, Bree? And some of Laura's chocolate cake."

Bree's stance softened. "Thanks. I was hoping someone could come out with me and help shift some sheep."

"I will," Laura said.

"No." Natalie got up to make the coffee. "You're preparing dinner. I'll go. I have to get my hand in again for when Bree's in Marla."

"And I am still capable of driving a ute and opening a gate," Olive said. "We can all pitch in while you're away, Bree."

Natalie put Bree's coffee on the table.

"How's the fundraiser coming along, Laura?" Bree asked. "Dad and I were trying to work out what would be best for a donation."

"What fundraiser?" Natalie asked.

"It's a community thing going towards breast cancer," Bree said.

"Paul says it might not happen." Laura looked glum.

"Why ever not?" Olive asked.

"A few people have dropped out and I think it needs someone to take charge. Paul hasn't got the time and he doesn't know so many people."

Natalie smiled. "Has anyone asked Nancy?"

Thirty-Seven

Crowds streamed through the oval gates as soon as they were opened. People were rugged up with coats and boots against the cold July day but, after watching the weather report anxiously all week, the sky was almost clear of clouds making for a perfect winter's day. The district had rallied once Nancy had taken the helm and the oval was well covered with stalls and activities of all descriptions, and they were confident the fundraiser would go well.

From their position behind their cake stall, set up at a vantage point near the entrance, Natalie and Olive took in the festive sight before them. They smiled then winced as Nancy's voice blared from the loudspeaker.

"Welcome, everyone, to the district Cancer Council fundraiser. Our stalls are open for business so please open your wallets and purses and dig deep." There was a crackle and a squeal then Nancy was back. "And Mr Brown would like all participants for the bike-a-thon to meet at the southern end of the oval immediately. More information will be broadcast as it comes to hand. Enjoy the day." There was a final loud thud, a scratching sound and then music began to play.

Natalie just had time to give Veronica a thumbs-up at her plant stall next door before a crowd of people gathered in front of the cake stall. Immediately the combined baking efforts of Natalie, Laura and Olive were being snapped up.

Surprisingly, Fran from the bakery was one of the first to buy some cakes. "I love the names you've thought up," she said as she picked up a tray of Laura's Luscious Lamingtons and another of Milton's Mouth-watering Melting Moments.

"It was Laura's idea," Natalie said as she took Fran's money. "She thought it made everything sound much more tempting."

"Anything you make is tempting, Nat," Fran said. "Perhaps I'll have to get Joe to rename some of our buns at the bakery."

"Your pies all have exotic names, why not your buns?"

"What about Fran's Fancy Finger Buns?" Olive pitched in.

Fran chuckled and moved on and the next person stepped up.

Nancy was back at the loudspeaker letting everyone know the hair shaving and cutting was about to begin in the central marquee. Laura had offered to do the cutting, one of the girls from a local salon was doing the head shaves and the volunteers from the wig library had brought some wigs along for people to try. Some had chosen to have their hair dyed bright pink before the event and were helping gee up the crowd.

Olive took out some more cakes from the boxes of extras they'd brought. "I think Laura went a bit over the side when she named these," she said as she set two cakes down in a space on the table. "I didn't even make them. Everyone knows orange cake is your speciality."

Natalie grinned at the names Laura had stuck on. "I think Olive's Out of this World Orange Cake is perfect. It's your recipe I always use. And anyway, Milt certainly didn't make the melting moments."

"Laura's worked hard for today," Olive said. "I know everyone has but she's gone the extra distance."

"She certainly has." Natalie took in the pretty checked bunting strung along the front of their table that Laura had insisted would add some style to their cake stall and had roped Natalie into sewing together the previous night. "She's got an eye for detail."

Paul strode past with a folder in his hand and gave them a brief wave.

"That young man's come into his own as well," Olive said. "I used to think he was a bit wet behind the eyes but he's very thoughtful and well organised."

"Yes he is." Natalie smiled, both at Olive's funny way with words and at the recollection of the conversation she'd had with Milt not long after she'd returned home. He'd taken her aside and gravely warned her to be prepared for some news. After all they'd been through she'd wondered what on earth he'd been going to tell her. He'd sat her down and warned her to be aware that Laura and Paul were an item, his way of telling her they were a couple in the full sense of the word. She'd smiled quietly to herself over that.

It was late in the afternoon and Natalie and Olive were packing up their sold-out stall when Olive paused and gave Natalie a close look. "I haven't had a chance to ask how your holiday was," she said.

"It feels a distant memory now but I really enjoyed it, thanks, Olive."

"You do look refreshed."

"I feel it." Natalie thought now might be an opportune moment to talk to Olive about the cleaning. "I thought now that I'm trying to organise my time a little better that perhaps we could see about getting you some home help."

"That's a good idea and Laura and I are already on to it." Olive whipped the cloth off the table and began to fold it.

"You and Laura?"

"Yes. She's been such a help while you were away. She popped in one day with some information about home help and someone's been to visit me already to see what might be available."

"That's great." Natalie stacked the empty cake containers into a large cardboard box. That had been a conversation she hadn't been looking forward to.

"You know I never want to be a burden to you and Milton," Olive said.

Natalie opened her mouth but Olive cut her off. "I should never have let you do my cleaning. You do so much, Natalie, for everyone, but I enjoyed our little catch-ups even if you only came because you had to clean for me."

"Oh, Olive." A surge of guilt swept through Natalie and then she dismissed it. She looked Olive in the eye. "You know when you first moved I was happy for you and for me. We both had our own space at last, but we've lived together for so long and...well, I missed you."

Olive humphed. "Missed my interfering."

Natalie shook her head. "We've had our moments. I know you didn't like me teaching but—"

"It wasn't that I didn't like you teaching." Olive's expression had a guilty edge. She lowered her voice. "I got to have the place to myself when you were at work. It was more that I worried for you."

"Worried for me?"

"After everything that happened back when the girls were babies."

Natalie blanched and looked around but there was no-one nearby to hear them. Most people were headed to the other side of the oval where the final event for the day was taking place, the monster auction.

"I mean your difficulties coping," Olive said quickly and jerked her head in the direction of Vee's plant stall. "Not the other." She pursed her lips.

"I don't understand."

"Do you remember that book I gave you? *The Model Wife*."

Another pang of guilt surged through Natalie. She nodded.

"It was rather old-fashioned, of course, and there's no way you'd follow all that it said, but there were elements of truth, especially for a farmer's wife. A farm is a huge business and a farmer doesn't just need a wife, he needs a person who can help him with that business, and before you say you do that, of course you do, but when you first wanted to go back to teaching I was concerned it would be too much. You'd had some tough years and I knew how hard it would be for you to juggle everything. I never worked beyond the property but there were days when I'd be out in the paddock or up in the shed as long as Clem and then I'd have to cook a meal, keep that huge house clean, see to children. I knew your...mental health wasn't strong after the children and I worried that you would push yourself too hard."

Natalie let out the breath she'd been holding. "It was the teaching that kept me sane."

"I think I understand that now. I've had a few chats with Laura and Paul. They really are so well suited and Paul is very impressed with you."

"Really?" She still found it hard to believe.

"Anyway, it seems you're well respected and I won't say another word about you going out to teach."

Natalie wasn't sure whether to feel pleased or annoyed about that. Olive's sentiments were a little late considering Natalie was thinking of retiring.

Nancy's voice blared from the loudspeaker again, asking everyone to gather outside the clubrooms where the auction was about to begin.

"Nancy's been a champion keeping this together today," Olive said. "We're done here now, we should head over."

Natalie followed after Olive, pondering all that she'd said. She'd never imagined Olive's reason for not wanting her to work was because she was trying to look out for Natalie. They passed the second-hand book stall, all the unsold books packed in boxes.

"You know, you should have brought that old book to the sale," Olive said. "Someone might have had a giggle over it."

Natalie pressed her lips together and walked with her mother-in-law to join what seemed like the greater part of their local community gathered for the final session of the fundraiser.

"Hi!"

Laura gasped as Paul stuck his head out of the committee tent and beckoned her in.

"What's up?" She glanced around – there was no-one else in the tent. "I was just on my way to pack up my gear."

"I've only seen you in passing all day."

"You were busy. The bike-a-thon was more like a marathon. Some of those kids wouldn't give up."

"I was impressed, especially with a couple of boys whose behaviour hasn't been the best. They threw their hearts and souls into it and raised a lot of money between them."

"This is a supportive community."

"I know. When I first moved here I didn't know how I was going to stick a three-year appointment but now…it feels a bit like home. Especially since I met you."

He gripped both her arms and gently drew her forward.

Laura glanced around again. "I thought you were keeping us a secret."

"There's no-one here."

Before he even pressed his lips to hers a tingle went through her from head to toe. She melded her body against his. His hands slid around her back and pressed her tightly against him.

"Are you in there, Mr Brown?"

They jumped apart but Nancy had already stepped into the tent. "Well, I never," she said.

Paul brushed at the front of his jumper and Laura swept some hair back from her face.

"I was just wondering if there were any more announcements to be made before we packed up the sound system." Nancy took a step back. "But I can see you're busy."

Paul cleared his throat. "I don't know of anything else that needs to be said. It will be dark if they don't start packing up soon."

"Right you are." Nancy looked from Paul to Laura and then smiled a knowing smile. "I'll be off then. Leave you to it." She backed out of the tent.

Paul's face was a picture of surprise. Laura couldn't stop the giggle that erupted from her mouth. She took his hand and brushed a kiss across his lips. "I hope you'll cope with everyone knowing about us," she said. "Because it won't be long and the whole district will have been informed."

The startled look left his face and he shrugged. "It's no big deal."

Laura grinned. He leaned in and kissed her and then they both broke away, laughing.

★

It was dark before Natalie and Milt arrived home. Laura and Olive had both stayed in town so it was just the two of them. Milt stirred the fire in the kitchen back to life but they'd been gone all day and it would take a while to put some heat back into the room. Natalie kept her coat on while she heated some soup.

"I'm not very hungry after all the food I ate today but I could make you something else," she said.

Milt closed the door of the pot belly and stood up. "Soup will be fine, thanks, Nat. We're both too tired to do anything more."

"There's some fresh sourdough to go with it." Once upon a time he would have insisted on more than soup and bread for an evening meal. "You and Trevor did a fantastic job of the auction."

Milt set the table then sat. "Trevor's a competent auctioneer. I was only his runner and don't I know it." He gave a groan and arched his back.

"You donated several items and got others on board and it was a perfect end to the day. The bean counters were still tallying when I took our stall takings over but it looks like the final total will be well over ten thousand dollars raised."

"A great effort." He buttered a slice of bread and took a bite. "This is good. Where did it come from?"

"Mel who married the youngest Rolland son had a stall today. She's making other breads and rolls as well, all from home and running an impressive little business, from what I hear."

"It was encouraging to see so many young ones from around the district involved today. Makes you feel positive about the future when you see their collective brains trust."

"And their fresh ideas. Laura had a chat with Mel about running her business."

"I'm glad Laura's thinking seriously about running her own mobile salon. There'd be a lot of people who'd book her up."

Natalie recalled the first visit she'd made to Veronica's and the professional way Laura had conducted herself. Veronica's smile when she'd looked in the mirror had been heart-warming. "A shorter style makes the hair you have look fuller," Laura had said. "And other ladies who've had much longer hair have told me it prepares them better for going bald." Laura had also suggested she go with Veronica to the wig library so she could start looking at what might suit her.

Natalie poured the soup into bowls and took them to the table. "Laura's got a lot of talent."

"I know. She was lacking in some self-belief. I had a few chats with her while you were away."

Milt had supported all three girls in her absence. Natalie hoped he'd continue to be more open with them.

"She'll have a few starters," Natalie said. "It was a smart idea to give away some beauty vouchers."

"A lot of the stalls look like they sold out."

"There wasn't a crumb left from our stall and Vee only had a few plants left."

"Would they be the two boxfuls in the back of the four-wheel drive?"

Natalie grinned. "It's for a good cause and Vee did such a good job organising her green thumb friends, and I think she even got a couple of nurseries near Adelaide to donate plants as well."

"How's Vee getting on, do you think?"

"Okay. Not looking forward to going back for treatment. She misses home and her garden. It really is beautiful, Milt."

"I know."

She looked down at her soup. Of course he did. She wondered again how often he'd been over there then pushed the thought away. What did it matter?

"What are you planning to do with the last week of school holidays?"

"Help you, put the house back together, make a start on the garden."

"Mum's taken with the idea. I never thought she would be."

"Vee's garden was inspiring," she said. "I see you've done more work on the tennis court."

"It's nearly all levelled out and we've started fixing the fence."

"Milt—"

"I know you don't want us to ever have a court again but it was my way of building a bridge with Bree. Something we could do together that wasn't work."

Natalie was surprised he'd thought that through and come up with the idea but glad he had.

"That was a worthy reason to do it, Milt, but I was going to say I have another. I'd like to incorporate it into my garden plan, use it as a boundary, build a gazebo."

"Hell's teeth!"

"We could have tennis parties again."

"You've certainly changed your tune."

"I used to love having people over and the tennis court was the focus."

He raised his eyebrows at that.

"You know why we stopped the competition tennis. It would have meant seeing the Halbots. I wasn't much of a player but I loved the social aspect. It used to be fun when we went to other people's places or they came to us for social tennis days."

Milt's spoon clattered to the bowl. "Hell, Nat, I'm so sorry."

It was a big statement covering so much.

"I'm sorry, too."

"What for?"

"For running away, leaving you with everything."

"I should have been paying more attention to what you were saying. I was so wrapped up in work…Oh hell." He lurched forward again and looked her directly in the eye. "I appreciate everything you do for me, for Mum, everything. You do know that, don't you?"

She nodded.

"I don't want you to go off like that again, not without me."

Natalie took his big hand in hers. "I'm sorry everyone was worried but I needed the break and I'm glad I did it but…next time I go away I want it to be the two of us. A holiday we can enjoy together."

"That's good." He smiled a rather smug smile. "You see I was hoping we might go away next weekend, before school starts."

This time it was Natalie's spoon that returned with a clunk to the bowl. "Go where?"

"Melbourne. I couldn't get a refund on my Broome tickets but I can convert to a different flight."

"But…" Natalie couldn't believe what Milt was suggesting. "But Bree's away, who will—"

"It's only for two nights. Laura will be home and Paul and Mum both offered to stay and help keep an eye on things."

"You've already worked it out?"

"There was a show Laura thought we might see and I wondered if you'd be up for seats at the footy? It's at the MCG. It will be our wedding anniversary but if you'd rather stay home I can use the credit another time."

"No!"

Milt smirked.

"No," she said more softly this time. With all that had gone on she'd been the one to forget their anniversary was close but Milt had remembered and that meant so much to her. "I'd love to go to Melbourne with you this weekend." If she'd had the energy she would've dragged him to his feet and danced with him round the kitchen but given that they were both very tired she simply leaned in and kissed him instead.

Thirty-Eight

Six months later

Natalie scrutinised her dining table and liked what she saw. The special dinner plates, the crystal glasses, Olive's silver cutlery; it had all been set out with the napkins, the crackers and the sparkling decorations. All ready for Christmas dinner even though Christmas had been two days ago. That day it had just been Natalie, Milt and Olive for dinner; today there'd be fourteen, fifteen if she counted her new granddaughter. She'd made little Olivia Rose a place card and sat it between Kate and Sean's.

Their baby had been born three days before Christmas in Adelaide. Her name had been a nod to Olive and to Sean's grandmother, Rosalie. Olive had been thrilled. Kate had slowly come to terms with the change in her life plan – there'd been lots of long phone calls in the months prior to the birth and Natalie had visited as soon as the baby was born, of course. Given Kate's anxiety about parenting they'd kept her in hospital for a few extra days for which Natalie was grateful. If only she'd had the support her daughter was getting, her baby days might have been less traumatic.

Next to Laura's she adjusted Paul's place card, never imagining he'd be sitting at her Christmas dinner table. She smiled as she thought of Laura and Paul. The stiff young principal had loosened up and Laura had blossomed. They were so sweet together.

And then there were Bree and Owen's names. They'd travelled back from Marla a week ago, visited Kate and the baby and had Christmas with Owen's family in Adelaide. They'd arrived home last night and were out with Milt now looking at the new tennis court. Owen would go back to Marla for a month or so in the new year but then he'd be back for good. He and Bree were busy planning how they were going to manage her work on the property and his taking over the garage in town.

Natalie had placed Olive's name next to her mother's. Althea and Ray were arriving today for a few days and they were bringing Lina and the twins with them. Marcus and the staff were looking after the shop in Victor and Bron and Karl were having a short holiday. Natalie was so pleased for them.

She cast another look around the table. They wouldn't dine in here till tonight. Lunch would be eaten under the side verandah next to her garden, which was beginning to take shape even though the plants still had a lot of growing to do. Veronica had helped her with the planning and once her treatment had finished and she was feeling stronger she'd helped Natalie do some planting. She'd lost her hair but it was already growing back and it was quite wavy. "I used to have curls when I was younger," she'd said, "but I hated them then."

"Mum! Kate and Sean are here." Laura's voice was full of excitement.

Natalie gave her dining room one last glance and went out to join her family.

The conversation after lunch was punctuated by the thuds of tennis balls and the laughter of the players. Laura and Lina had teamed up against Paul and Owen, and the twins were being ball boys. The rest of the family were spread out in the scattered shade. The day was getting warmer but there was a bit of a breeze. Natalie had said they'd go inside if it got too hot but everyone seemed happy. Olive and Althea had hardly stopped talking since they sat down and Ray was dozing in his chair. Bree was nursing Olivia and Sean and Kate were looking on with the tired, spaced-out gaze of new parents.

"You know, Natalie, I've just remembered that book again." Olive leaned forward in her chair. "You should pass it on to Kate now."

"What book, Granny?" Kate asked.

"You know the one, Natalie," Olive persisted. "*The Model Wife* it was called." She looked back at Kate. "It's a family heirloom. It was Pa's mother's. She passed it on to me and I gave it to your mother. It will give you a laugh and perhaps it should stay in the family."

Natalie shifted in her chair. "I don't know exactly where it is at the moment." It wasn't really a lie. She couldn't remember which drawer she'd shoved it in this time but its journey stopped with her. There was no way she was going to pass it on to the next generation. "Anyone for more sweets?" she asked, which raised a collective moan.

"Relax, Nat," Milt said. "They can help themselves."

And After Anomaly Natalie did just that. She sat back, her fingers playing with the smooth pearl at her neck.

"That's so pretty, Mum," Kate said. "I can't believe Dad gave you jewellery."

"I gave her a ring once."

"Thirty-five years ago," Kate said and Bree groaned.

Natalie smiled. He had given her the odd piece of jewellery over the years but the pearl had been a lovely surprise. Evidently he'd ordered it online with Laura's help from a place in Broome.

"Pity I didn't actually get to Broome," he said.

"Oh no, how many times have we heard that lately?" Bree sat forward and passed Olivia to Sean. The baby had given a few small cries and Sean seemed to be the one who could settle her.

"You'll just have to go, Dad," Kate said. "But together this time."

"I would but we've got this cruise your mum's booked."

Natalie raised an eyebrow at him. It had been his idea. He'd just finished reading a book on Papua New Guinea by an Australian zoologist and when he saw a cruise advertised that went there he'd suggested it and she'd jumped at the chance.

"And if we like it there'll be more cruises," she said.

Paul came back at that moment, patting the moisture from his neck, his hair still neatly in place despite his exertion on the court. The tennis had gone into recess.

"In school holidays, I hope," he said.

"Of course." She still hadn't got used to having her boss as a potential son-in-law.

"What was Broome like, Natalie?" her mother asked. "Your father and I thought we might go somewhere warmer next winter."

"It's definitely warmer," Natalie said. She told them a bit about the things she'd managed to see in her short time in the northwest.

Then her mum had asked Bree about Marla and the conversation drifted in another direction.

Natalie's thoughts went to the small community with its beautiful beach. That's where her fondest memories of her Kimberley adventure had been made. There'd been a Christmas card from Rosie. One of her lost boys was going to move back with his family. He was a chef and the community had received a grant to do up the old mission house into a cafe. They were hopeful it would mean some extra employment opportunities and extend their tourist offerings. Charlie was keen to learn to cook and had applied for some training so that he could eventually come back and help with the cafe.

Natalie truly hoped they'd go back one day and see it all.

"Your turn, Nanna." Sean held the baby out to her.

"Gosh, she looks pink," Natalie said. "Perhaps we should go inside now."

Everyone helped, taking armloads back to the house. Milt walked beside her, lugging a pile of folding chairs and gazing down at his granddaughter. She'd seen a different side to him when he was with Olivia. He'd always been capable with their girls when they were babies but he was besotted when it came to his granddaughter.

So was she. Natalie recalled her holiday and Rosie asking her what she wanted in her life. A grandchild had been one thing. And she'd wanted some meaning for her life. The garden had helped with that. It had given her a new focus, as it had Olive who had taken to living some of the week with them and some at her unit in town.

Natalie had also decided to keep teaching, at least for another two years. Paul had convinced her to accept a more formal mentoring role with new teachers and she was keen to give it a go.

She and Brenda had caught up in the previous school holidays. They'd had a weekend in Sydney and had decided they'd make a trip away together an annual event. Who knew, she mused, one day they might be a Dot and Faye touring partnership. And there was the travel with Milt, something they were both looking forward to.

They reached the back gate and he rested his pile of chairs against the fence.

"Your turn," she said and handed over their precious granddaughter.

His face lit up as he took the baby in his arms. Natalie wrapped an arm around his waist and hugged him close.

Milt's big, kind smile was one she knew so well and said without words that he loved her. She smiled back at this man who she'd known for so long, her husband who had feet of clay but had rebuilt his life on firmer footing and become her rock. She knew he would be there for her through thick and thin and yet she'd turned away from him, travelled halfway across the country to find answers that were here, within her family, her home.

She leaned in and kissed him, a gentle but loving kiss and her heart gave an extra thud. They still had a spark together and maybe Rosie had been right, Natalie had simply had to lose herself to find her way home.

Author's Note

When I began to write *The Model Wife* I had the strong feeling that something lurked in Natalie's mind, an influence that she tried to ignore but came to realise had, at various times in her life, controlled her thoughts and actions. As I wrote the story this 'thing' manifested itself as an old book from almost a century before, full of advice for women.

Once I realised it was a book I tried to imagine what kind of advice would have been written on its pages for women in the early nineteen hundreds and I came up with a series of chapter headings. These headings were topics Natalie grappled with at various stages of the manuscript and were declarations such as

A Husband is Master. The model wife loves her husband truly, does not highlight his faults and provides for his every desire.

or

Family before all else. The model wife spends her time taking care of her family and putting them before her own needs.

485

I did some more research and eventually came up with my own little book to embed within this book. I called it *The Model Wife* and gave it this introduction:

The Model Wife by Mrs Gladys Norman, London, 1928

In my role as a surgeon's wife I have managed a busy household, raised three children and maintained a healthy happy marriage. I feel it my bounden duty to offer the benefit of my wisdom and experience here in the pages of this book.

Mrs Gladys Norman, bless her heart, is a figment of my imagination, as is the book I created, but I tried to capture the tone and content of the original sources. Many of them sounded laughable and even cringeworthy to me living in the current day but of course they were based on the way lives of women were viewed at the time. All I can say is thank goodness times have changed... although scarily, even today some of those pervasive ideas linger.

Acknowledgements

In 2016 I travelled to Western Australia and up to the Dampier Peninsula in the north-west. It was a day trip during which I visited several local communities, swam and walked on the beautiful beaches, and explored the local heritage. In particular I enjoyed Cape Leveque and Lombadina, home of the Bard people – and it was there I had a brief meeting with a wonderful woman called Pip, who shone with love for her community and, I discovered, was also a keen reader. That ever-so-short visit had an impact on me and last year I returned for a longer stay. I met up with Pip again and over a cuppa she was kind enough to chat with me about life in her community. When I needed someone to read the manuscript she was excited to help so a big thank you, Pip, for sharing your love of your country and your love of reading with me.

This book touches on breast cancer and I wanted to make sure I'd tackled the topic in a way that appreciated what so many go through, both the person and their families. Besides the experiences of several women close to my heart I also contacted friend and McGrath Breast Care Nurse Ros, who also read an early draft and gave feedback.

So many anecdotes of life on a farming property helped feed this story. I would like to thank several women who chatted to me about life on their patch, in particular Joy, Meredith and Jackie, who took time out from their busy lives for extended conversations and some jolly good laughs. Resilience would have to be the middle name for people living on the land.

Thanks to Rob for help with describing life with Year Three. It's a while since I've been there. And thank you to Selina, my talented hairdresser, who let me pick her brains about hair colours and how they work.

While all of these wonderful women mentioned above helped with aspects of the story, I often wriggled things about, so any mistakes, although unintentional, are mine.

Just as I finished the early drafts of this book my dear big sister, Vivonne, lost her battle with cancer. Sisters share a special bond and, being the oldest, Viv was sometimes mother, sometimes mentor, my sounding block and always in my corner. She was the poet of our family – we agreed a long time ago that talent missed me – but thankfully she's passed it on to her daughter, Nerrilee. Through Viv's cancer experience she constantly lobbied for better services for regional patients. I know that some of her efforts have helped others and I also know how grateful she was for the support she did receive. On Viv's behalf I'd like to thank all of you working to improve the lives and wellbeing of cancer patients, especially those in regional areas where distance can be an extra obstacle. You do make a difference.

Also a nod to my sister for Giraffe Soup, which gets a mention in this book. It's really just pumpkin soup with a few extra vegetables but years ago Viv was making a batch for her grandies and when one turned up his nose she told him it was Elephant Soup, which he ate quite happily. It became a family joke and evolved to

Giraffe Soup at our place because we thought the flecks of colour from the other veg against the orange of the pumpkin was more giraffe-like. It's these special memories that enrich the tapestry of family life.

The team at Harlequin Books/HarperCollins Australia who support me and each new story are amazing and I am so grateful to the many who had a hand in bringing this story to publication. In particular to my publisher, Jo Mackay, and my editor, Annabel Blay – thank you for always stretching the boundaries of what I can achieve. Thanks also to proofreader Annabel Adair and to the fabulous design team headed up by Mark Campbell – I'm always in awe of your work. And to Darren Kelly, Adam van Rooijen, Natika Palka, Sarana Behan, Johanna Baker and the rest of the gang – thank you for all you do to get my books out into the world.

Writers know writers and I'm forever grateful to the many writing buddies I've met from all parts of Australia who understand the intricacies and the fallibilities of a writer's life. It's so good to be able to share experiences and ideas. Whether it's a brief catch up at a conference, a hello via social media, a phone call, an email or time talking over a meal, it means a lot – thank you.

Once again my love and thanks to my family and dear friends for their unyielding support. My husband Daryl holds the fort at home, helps with research and reads early versions, and my children, their partners and my grandchildren are always in my corner doing so much. I love you all to bits. This book is dedicated to my talented daughter-in-law Alex, for the many ways she supports me and, in particular, her event organisation and social media help are much appreciated. I am so very lucky.

Readers, booksellers, librarians and everyone else in book land, thank you for championing my books, for loving them and coming back for more. Rest assured another is on the way.

Turn over for a sneak peek.

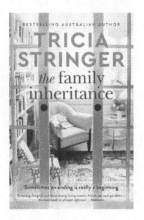

the family inheritance

by

TRICIA STRINGER

OUT NOW

one

Felicity Lewis paused a minute to take it all in.

It was a balmy night in Adelaide; the temperature had dropped just enough after a hot March day for perfect outdoor entertaining. At number seventeen Herbert Street, West Beach, two streets back from the ocean, a party was in progress. Behind Felicity the carefully selected mood music resonated from the curved teak speaker, enough to be heard but not so loud people couldn't hear themselves speak. It had been a birthday gift from Ian and Greta, not a total surprise, not any kind of surprise. She'd dropped several hints, which included leaving shop brochures lying around opened to pages with the desired gift circled.

The speaker sat on the polished shelf below their wall-mounted television in the big open-plan family room that stretched almost the full width of the back of the house. The glass doors to the deck were all thrown open. Around her milled friends and family enjoying the food she'd cooked and the drinks she'd selected.

Light spilled across the freshly oiled deck and out onto the back lawn where strands of festoon lights, hung in precise loops across the garden, added their glow to the glorious spectacle of a million stars twinkling overhead. It was a perfect autumn evening.

An arm slipped around her waist. "Everything looks fabulous, Mum."

"As do you." Felicity beamed at her daughter.

"I've taken lots of photos of the guests." Greta lifted her phone and leaned her head against Felicity's. "Selfie."

Felicity blinked at the flash. "I haven't had a chance to tell you how good you look in that outfit." She adjusted the soft bow pulling Greta's drapey pants in.

Greta batted her hand away and readjusted the bow. "I don't know that cream is a good colour for me."

"It's perfect against your tan."

"I was thinking more that I'm likely to spill something down it." She glanced around. "Where's Suzie? I haven't seen her yet."

"I told you Paul took her to America for her birthday."

"No you didn't." Greta frowned.

"They'll be gone for two months."

"How will you manage not seeing her for that long?"

"Technology."

"Dad should have taken you away, instead of you doing all this work."

"I've enjoyed it—"

"Oh look, there're the Gilberts. Thank goodness there's someone more my age. I'll get a photo of them too." Greta dashed away.

Once more Felicity stood alone. She'd organised this special night to the last detail, a combined celebration for her fiftieth birthday and the completion of the renovations. She'd been planning, styling, cooking for weeks. The only downside was her best friend Suzie couldn't be there.

Suzie and Paul had only been gone for two weeks and were having the best time. Felicity had already seen the photos of their Caribbean cruise and now they were driving themselves up the coast to New York. Suzie had rung this morning via WhatsApp to sing her happy birthday all the way from Jacksonville, Florida. Her brilliant smile and animated words had filled the room. Felicity had sat for a long time after the call had ended trying to swallow her glum mood and lack of enthusiasm for a party without her best friend. Suzie had provided all the energy for both of them during the call.

"Happy birthday, Felicity." Humphrey from next door drew her into a bear hug and planted one of his sloppy kisses on her cheek.

She adjusted her new glasses firmly back in place as his wife Melody also wrapped her in a hug.

"Perfect night for a party," Melody said.

"Thanks for coming. What would you like to drink?" Felicity waved over one of the young uni students Greta had organised to act as waiters for the night.

"Feliciteee, I love what you've done with the house." Pam, her social tennis friend, air kissed her cheeks. "I haven't seen it since you did this back extension, and the deck is fabulous. I can picture us having a few post tennis sessions here." Pam clutched a glass of champagne and as her arm swept out in a dramatic arc it connected with a man just stepping up onto the deck.

"Oh, I'm so sorry." She dabbed at his wet sleeve.

"No problem."

"Pam, I don't think you've met Tony," Felicity said. "He's been overseeing the renovations."

"Has he now?" Pam looked him up and down. "Well, there's a secret you've been keeping to yourself."

"Nice to meet you, Pam." Tony smiled, and offered his hand.

Pam's return look was vampish.

"Let me get you another drink," he said.

The bar was an old table Felicity had scrubbed to create a rustic look, adorned with ice buckets and glasses and one large bowl of flowers in soft pinks and mauves. She'd canned Greta's suggestion of balloons but had allowed the banner, which looped across the sheer curtain she'd hung on the wall behind. In cursive letters cut from sparkly gold it said 'Cheers to fifty years'.

Tony set off towards it. Pam stared after him.

"Did you knock into him on purpose?" Felicity said.

"Moi?"

"He's married." Felicity didn't actually know what Tony's marital status was but he was too nice a man to get tangled up with Pam. Every one of her relationships since her last divorce had ended in drama.

"Really? No ring on his finger."

"You've checked already? He's too young for you."

"Past the age of consent."

"Hi Felicity, Pam." More hugs all round, this time from Tansie, another of their tennis group, and her husband Charles.

"This is Tony," Pam said as he came back with several glasses of sparkling gripped between his two large hands. "He's responsible for Felicity's fabulous renovation."

Tony shrugged. "Felicity was the driving force, I just made sure the structural stuff was legit."

"You're very modest, Tony," Felicity said.

Tansie and Charles were planning a new bathroom and when Felicity could see Tony was safely in a discussion with Charles she edged away.

At the other end of the deck her own husband, Ian, was deep in conversation with their across-the-road neighbours, Sal and Les. Like Ian, they were bike riders. They rode regularly, along with several others from their neighbourhood. Not Felicity, of course. She didn't own a bike and never wanted to. Getting hot and sweaty in lycra had never been her thing. Nor Ian's until they'd moved here. Two years older than her, the approach of his fiftieth birthday had seen him turn into some kind of fitness freak. Not that Felicity minded. She was a homebody and the renovations had kept her busy, first in the planning, then in the construction and the refurbishing. Her workout was her weekly social tennis match and that was more about the company than the exercise.

After they'd moved they'd started taking regular walks to the beach but hadn't gone together in ages. These days Ian power walked everywhere on his own or with his walking group, training for more arduous treks, while she'd been filling her time with colour charts and fabric swatches. Ian had been involved in the renovations when they were deciding on the structural changes to the house but after that he'd been happy to let her make decisions about the finishing touches.

This party was a birthday celebration but also the official end to the whole house renovation, a project that had consumed her since the moment they'd made the decision to buy the fixer-upper more than five years ago. She'd given up her job as practice manager at a doctor's office when they'd moved. Now she'd have to find something else to fill her time. It wasn't until she'd been dressing for the party that she'd realised she had no idea what that would be.

"Have you seen our parents yet?"

Felicity gave her sister a quick look then shook her head. Tall and lanky like their father, June was wearing a grass-green all-in-one jumpsuit. It reminded Felicity of a praying mantis. For two sisters born less than a year apart they were chalk and cheese.

"Not like them to be late," June said.

"Dad's hard to get moving these days."

"We did offer to collect them."

"I'm sure they'll be here soon," Felicity said. It was possible her father had pulled another of his tantrums and they wouldn't turn up at all but she kept that to herself. He could do no wrong in June's eyes but there had been so many times over the years when he'd spoiled celebrations or social occasions.

Her wedding day had been mortifying. Most dads were proud and happy on their daughter's wedding day but not her father. Felicity had caused a ruckus by daring to find a husband before June. Not that June minded but their father did. She was always first in his eyes and Felicity had stolen her position this time.

On the day of the wedding he'd been grumpy, oozing disapproval of the goings-on, as he'd called it, as Felicity and her bridesmaids, were getting ready. Just before they'd been due to leave for the church he'd gone out for a walk – to clear his head, he'd declared. They hadn't been bothered until the photographer was tapping his toes waiting to take the standard father–daughter photos. June had been the one to track him down and drag him home to walk his daughter down the aisle. Their mother had been upset and so had Felicity. They'd arrived fifteen minutes late to the church and for the rest of the day her father had told anyone who'd listen it was because Felicity had been disorganised with her preparations and the household had been carrying on like a bunch of chooks.

"Perhaps I should ring Mum." June cut into her thoughts.

"Let's leave it for a while. They'll turn up."

Hazel Gifford was a saint to have put up with her husband all these years and if her father was in one of his moods Felicity would rather he didn't come.

"Oh, isn't that your old neighbour talking to Derek?" June waved in the direction of her husband and another man, both towering over the crowd. "The one that lived down the road and sold up and bought a caravan."

"Yes."

"Such a lovely couple. Can't see her, what were their names, but then she's so short, isn't she." June set off towards the new arrivals without waiting for an answer.

Instead of following her Felicity stepped down off the deck, fanning her face with her hand. The air was slightly cooler out from under the verandah and she relished it. Hormone replacement tablets ensured the hot flushes of menopause didn't affect her too terribly but just at that moment she felt as if her internal thermostat was ready to boil over. She moved further away and took the path to a corner of the yard that wasn't lit. From her vantage point she had time to let her body cool down, to take a breath and observe. She'd been on her feet since she got out of bed this morning and she needed a few minutes to regroup.

She enjoyed creating special dinners for friends, loved parties and entertaining, but she was far better at the preparation, the cooking and the serving than the conversation. If it wasn't for Ian insisting they go out for dinner, see an exhibition, travel, she'd simply stay home in her comfy clothes and slippers.

It had been more her idea to move than his but he'd gone along with it, liking their proximity to the beach and the walking and bike trails. His income was a good one and even though they'd extended their small mortgage to do the renovations they were comfortable these days. Felicity had been careful to stick to the budget they'd allocated and they hadn't overcapitalised.

She took in the sleek lines of the back of the house, the glass, the deck and the party now in full swing. Someone had turned up the music and the voices carried loudly on the still night. All their neighbours were here so the noise shouldn't bother anyone. They'd been lucky with the people in their small street. Ian had made it his business to get to know them all as soon as they'd moved in and they'd proved to be a friendly lot. She was glad they could all come. Even a few who'd moved away were here.

"What's the birthday girl doing out here on her own?" Ian came towards her, a glass of champagne in each hand. He offered her one, brushed a kiss across her forehead and tapped his glass against hers. "Happy birthday, Lissie." She smiled, took a sip and watched as he did the same.

"Thanks," she said. Ian rarely drank these days so she was pleased by the sentiment and that it was just the two of them.

"I should make a speech soon and you should cut the cake before our friends drink too much more of this champagne."

"One more minute," she said. Butterflies flapped inside her at the thought of being the centre of attention and she took another sip.

"You wanted this party." Ian's words were accusatory and yet his tone gentle.

"I love parties, just not being the main event."

"Remember my fiftieth? I wanted us to go away but you insisted on a big party instead."

"Hiking the Inca trail to Machu Picchu wouldn't have been a holiday."

"But it was what I wanted."

She looked away from the yearning in his eyes back to the party. "We've been so lucky," she said.

His yes was barely more than a whisper.

"I worry one day it's all going to come crashing down."

He took a sip of his drink before he responded. "That's a morbid thought on your birthday."

"We've had a trouble-free life."

"Not always." This time his reply was quick and sharp then he drew in a long breath and let it out again, slowly. "Remember when we first married. We had nothing."

"Everyone started that way. We lived on love." She smiled at him but he was looking at the crowd.

"You were laid up with that broken ankle and we nearly lost the house."

"That was so long ago it's hard to imagine now." They'd not had income insurance in those days – a combination of thinking they were bulletproof and not being able to afford it. She'd asked her father for a loan. He'd refused. Ian came from a big family with not much money to go round but his parents had lent them a bit to get them by. They'd paid them back of course, but it had been a terrible struggle.

"Then the babies we lost." Ian was still staring at the crowd. He was usually a cup-half-full kind of guy. This melancholic side of him was rare.

"I wish I hadn't said anything now." She sipped some champagne then tried a light laugh but the liquid caught in her throat and the laugh came out as a series of clucks.

"There were three little ones we never got to know," he said.

She gripped the stem of her glass. She knew how many babies they'd lost as well as he did. It wasn't something she was ever likely to forget but there was no point bringing it up now. "You really are going down the sad old memory lane. The miscarriages were tough but we've got our beautiful Greta."

"She's a wonderful young woman," he said.

Happy to banish any further maudlin thoughts, Felicity tapped her glass to his. "I'll drink to that."

"We should go back to our guests, get the formalities over then you can relax." He started to walk away, his look distracted. She'd hardly seen him these last few days. She'd been so caught up in party preparations, and now that she thought about it they'd not said more than two words to each other for...she couldn't think how long. Weeks?

"Ian?"

He stopped, turned back. The frown he'd worn changed to a smile but she could tell it was forced. He reached out a hand. "Come on, Lissie. This is your night. Time to face the music and have your friends sing 'Happy Birthday'."

"Mum?" Greta came towards them across the lawn, the brightly lit house glowing behind her. "What are you doing out here? I've been looking everywhere for you." She held her mobile phone towards Felicity. "It's Nan. She sounds upset."

Damn Dad, Felicity thought as she pressed the warm phone to her ear. He's kicked up a fuss and decided not to come. "Hello, Mum."

"Felicity, I tried June's phone."

"She never has it on her."

"Then I tried yours."

"Mum, take a breath. Why aren't you here? Is everything all right?" She hated asking that question knowing everything wouldn't be all right. Not that she really cared but for her mum's sake...

"It's your father."

Felicity pursed her lips. Of course it was her father. "What's he up to this time?" She raised her shoulders and gave a slight shake of her head at Greta and Ian who were both standing by.

"Is June there?" Hazel's voice had an edginess to it. Felicity hoped she wasn't going to have one of her dizzy attacks.

"Not right beside me but she and Derek are here."

Ian began to tap his foot.

"I'll call you back, Mum, we're about to cut the cake."

"Oh, I've ruined your lovely party."

"No, you haven't. I'll bring you some cake and leftovers tomorrow." Damn her dad for his moods. For the zillionth time in her life she wondered how her mother put up with him. Tomorrow there'd be the aftermath of the party to clean up and Felicity would be tired but now she'd be stuck in the car for nearly two hours going to and from her parents when they could have come tonight.

"You'll have to be strong for June," Hazel said.

Ian was tapping his watch now and pointing back to the party.

"Mum, I have to go – can you tell me tomo—"

"Felicity, brace yourself." There was a sharp intake of breath. "Your father's dead."

Other books by

TRICIA STRINGER

FICTION
HQ

talk about it

Let's talk about books.

Join the conversation:

 facebook.com/harlequinaustralia

 @harlequinaus

 @harlequinaus

harpercollins.com.au/hq

If you love reading and want to know about our
authors and titles, then let's talk about it.